Them Girls

Eva Verde

**SIMON &
SCHUSTER**

London · New York · Amsterdam/Antwerp · Sydney/Melbourne · Toronto · New Delhi

First published in Great Britain by Simon & Schuster UK Ltd, 2026

Copyright © Eva Verde, 2026

The right of Eva Verde to be identified as author of this work has been asserted in accordance with the Copyright, Designs and Patents Act, 1988.

1 3 5 7 9 10 8 6 4 2

Simon & Schuster UK Ltd
1st Floor
222 Gray's Inn Road
London WC1X 8HB

For more than 100 years, Simon & Schuster has championed authors and the stories they create. By respecting the copyright of an author's intellectual property, you enable Simon & Schuster and the author to continue publishing exceptional books for years to come. We thank you for supporting the author's copyright by purchasing an authorised edition of this book.
No amount of this book may be reproduced or stored in any format, nor may it be uploaded to any website, database, language-learning model, or other repository, retrieval, or artificial intelligence system without express permission. All rights reserved. Enquiries may be directed to Simon & Schuster, 222 Gray's Inn Road, London WC1X 8HB or RightsMailbox@simonandschuster.co.uk

Simon & Schuster Australia, Sydney
Simon & Schuster India, New Delhi

www.simonandschuster.co.uk
www.simonandschuster.com.au
www.simonandschuster.co.in

The authorised representative in the EEA is Simon & Schuster Netherlands BV, Herculesplein 96, 3584 AA Utrecht, Netherlands. info@simonandschuster.nl

Simon & Schuster strongly believes in freedom of expression and stands against censorship in all its forms. For more information, visit BooksBelong.com

A CIP catalogue record for this book is available from the British Library

Paperback ISBN: 978-1-3985-3667-8
eBook ISBN: 978-1-3985-3665-4
Audio ISBN: 978-1-3985-3666-1

This book is a work of fiction.
Names, characters, places and incidents are either a product of the author's imagination or are used fictitiously. Any resemblance to actual people living or dead, events or locales is entirely coincidental.

Typeset in Palatino by M Rules
Printed and Bound in the UK using 100% Renewable Electricity
at CPI Group (UK) Ltd

for my girls
Zoe, Joanie and Eliza

★

"Once you know who you are, you don't have to worry anymore."
Nikki Giovanni

One

GOLDIE

The Glamorous Life

Another letter lands on Goldie's doormat. A slim, quality envelope, embossed with the iconic logo; a snake, curled around the initial 'V' of Vine Recordings. It pushes into her privacy, bringing the past far too close for comfort. Making her world suddenly feel fragile.

A true snake in post form, showing up as an old can of worms.

Goldie snatches it up off the flagstone floor and stuffs it into the drawer of the heirloom dresser, where two other identical letters live in the darkness, just as her mother's debt management reminders and CCJs had all those many years ago, best forgotten, too.

Out of sight, out of mind.

It's a little after 5 p.m. when Ben lets himself into the Coach House. Dressed to impress, he finds Goldie upstairs at her dressing table, making her own finishing touches.

With a small cough first, he enters the bedroom.

'Car's here at six twenty,' Ben says, admiring Goldie with the same reverence as ever, as if he can't quite believe she's fully real, let alone his. 'You're perfect.' Popping first to the kitchen for glasses, Ben opens the champagne he arrived with, setting her flute on a slice of amethyst working as a coaster, before perching on the bed just behind her that he's never once slept in. 'And what about me?'

Without turning, Goldie watches him through the mirror as she puts on her earrings, the scene like something off the TV; the glamorous lives of a decadent husband and wife. Diamonds and luscious lashes, tuxedos and ties askew, begging to be straightened.

'Quite the part,' she says, because it's true. And even Goldie would admit that to anybody viewing them from the outside, their moment would seem like an entirely regular picture of married life.

Tonight, in a rather traditional fashion, too, husband and wife will be stepping out to dazzle for yet another of Ben's company events – something to do with a new business initiative. Fundraising – where rather than anything truly charitable occurring, the wealth's simply regurgitated around the right circles. It's a sad fact that the more time Goldie's spent in Ben's circles, the more she knows it's true; feeling manufactured, false, in a way that has so little to do with her hair and lashes and facial fillers. That's mere preservation.

Goldie means fake; like the money-cold people who'll be there tonight. Outwardly winning. Yet soulless.

'Is your father coming?' Goldie asks.

'Sadly. Thinks showing up adds some sort of kudos. Forgets his status doesn't quite hold the same appeal these days. But enough of all that.' Ben bops the end of Goldie's nose with his finger. 'You look wonderful. Let's drink this fizz, shall we? Tell me all you've been up to.'

Goldie knows she could say anything and he wouldn't hear it. Understands how this is only a role. A cosplay marriage. The most peculiar of arrangements. He is polite, kind, very, very generous.

And entirely absent.

Ben's secret life with his real love, Therese Fry – a family nemesis, their beef going back generations; think Montagues and Capulets – must always be denied. Which is easy to do when he's happily married to goddess Goldie. All smoke and mirrors.

Soap opera bollocks with an upper-class twist.

Tonight's charity gala is a case in point. Goldie and Ben will pretend to be together for the benefit of his parents, Baron and Baroness Bickham, and the glimmering hope of the inheritance they've forever held over Ben's head. Dangling their riches like carrots, along with their caveats over claiming it. Why is a long story, and though neither of them is remotely dead yet, it's more about control – and, of course, the games. The kind only those with generational wealth are allowed to play.

A loveless marriage of immense convenience is the truth of Goldie's situation. Yet she gets to keep her crown. Living like a perfect house cat.

At the dressing table she sits in front of, Hollywood

theatrical, bulbs framing the length of glass, Goldie talks of the things Ben wants to hear; how she's filling her time with her charity work, salon appointments and lunches, naturally cheerleading him at every opportunity. Thinks of all the stuff she holds back.

Unwinding her hair from the Velcro rollers is second nature. But as Goldie secures her honey gold waves with a clip to finish making up her face, it oddly feels a task too many.

Inertia. Little to do with her hair or even the make-up, but more from keeping up this front. Of her life.

Of all this empty luxury.

Guests gather in the foyer of a grand building a stone's throw from London Bridge; the effort and importance of tonight obvious from the way Ben's forehead began to drip on arrival, as if the Merc had become a sauna. Visual proof of how the family business – something hotel-related or foody, Goldie can never quite remember which – is everything to him.

But Goldie's ignorance over the intricacies of the Bickham empire isn't entirely down to her own disinterest. The enormously wealthy rarely tell you where their old money comes from. It is a secret club, thriving on evasion to keep their circle tight. Anybody new might disturb the truth, and then it'd be a frightful battle to paper over the cracks.

It's been fifteen years, and Goldie's still not part of the clique.

Deep in the throng of Ben's people, the weight of his hand against her arm brings her back into focus; his gentle cue for her to sparkle socially.

'More fizz? A bottle?' someone suggests, red-faced and caddish, and the idea is met with much encouragement. These are new faces to Goldie, yet cardboard copies of the same old, nonetheless. 'Glorious venue, Benedict. Must've been a bugger getting permission – how did you get around that?' they ask, without manners or filter.

He's Benedict here, yet to Goldie, black cabbies and the common masses, he is Ben. 'I agree with you on the venue front.' Ben laughs off the question. 'My Goldie's always been glorious, too, haven't you darling? Seriously, I couldn't pull this off without her.'

As if in response, a woman just to the left of them, dressed in the dreariest Chanel suit, shudders rudely through her nostrils, with a sideways sneer towards Goldie.

It doesn't offend, and it's nothing new. Goldie's forever been the oddity; the one with the fault, flaw, lack of ... down to her brownness/commonness/body shape/hella awesome style – take your pick – yet all Goldie can see, all she's ever seen, is that parties like this, where everybody is born into money, protected by affluent friends in elaborate places, where the entitled slip so greasily and easily together, all feel rather similar to a crowded stable full of horses – which the rich admire by default, yet Goldie also finds pointless, even sad.

Life's so easy, it's left them characterless. Generic. A glossy braying stable of empty noise.

The best thing Goldie ever did was create her own music. Dancing to the beat of her own tuneskis, instead of measuring herself by other people's standards, has proved infinitely better for the soul; looking after herself because it matters – not to impress, but rather to maintain all she was born blessed with.

But the odds are strong that regardless of any age she's lucky enough to reach, Goldie will likely be a hot grown woman all her life.

And so petty insults glide off her like hot honey, too.

'Why don't you tell them who your father is?' Ben suggests, wiggling his big brows at Goldie like it's a party piece. 'You'll never guess ...' Letting it linger, he vanishes.

They stare. And stare.

Is this really where her entertainment career ended up?

Somebody starts humming. And it's all so painful Goldie's face gives it away.

'You're never Amos Fliss's daughter?' they ask. Against her better self, Goldie nods.

Now she has value, they become instantly warmer.

'What was he like? Crikey, I remember the news when he died. Twenty-seven ...'

'Made him a legend, though – I mean, wouldn't you rather be a legend ...'

Goldie thinks that if her dad knew the twats still listening to his music all these decades later, he'd never have penned a tune at all.

'And ... and didn't you do some "*pop*" once upon a time as well?' A man leans into Goldie's space, like he's analysing some post-modernist abstract. 'They do say music runs in the family.'

'Poor thing,' adds the woman in the depressing Chanel

suit, also far warmer now. 'How old were you when it happened?'

'Five.' Goldie clears her throat. Cross she's even answered. 'I was five. My sister Valeria was four. And if you think for a second that I'll open my wrists for your amusement, well ...' Only just stopping herself, Goldie gets up, her body straining against the seams of her dress. Knows they are looking as they've always looked at her – full of the same appalled fascination – as she goes in search of Ben.

'Everything's aesthetics.' Ben's voice comes from beyond a closed door just ahead of Goldie, behind which is tonight's green room and temporary office in a quieter part of the building. 'You can have eyes made of worms, but if you've hip-as-fuck vegan-made sunglasses hiding them, who gives a shittle?'

How can a made-up word deflate her so? Goldie can't find nor invent her own word to describe it – only that Ben in this mode makes her despair. Pricked by the truth she's chosen mostly to ignore.

How Goldie's guilty by association.

Shittle. *Really?*

'The rest we can kick up the road. But for now, just get that chav's signature if it's the last thing you do.' Ben opens the door just in time to see his father turn into the corridor. 'Fuck. When will he just fucking die?' he adds under his breath as Goldie backs into a shadowy corner, holding her own.

Tony passes without noticing her, bypassing Trevor, Ben's lickspittle PA and lackey, too, focused with a one-track dour determination, his eyes set on his son. 'Impressive,' he says, turning without any proper greeting into the office. Slamming the door, his voice booms through it anyway. 'And all totally unnecessary. Who's paying for this?'

'The minnows here tonight selling me their start-ups.' Ben snorts as Goldie's teeth start to grind in discomfort. 'Why do you always take me for a fucking idiot?'

She should go back to the party. Before she hears something she shouldn't. So shielded from everything these days, even eavesdropping feels like a misstep. Yet something keeps her there. Learning the truth of Ben is a basic right – plus she's watched *The Handmaid's Tale* on Hulu. Goldie's not in Gilead.

She has freedom full stop. If she wants it hard enough.

Does she?

'How very typical. Spending money before it's yours.' They fall quieter, into mumbles of speech Goldie can't quite make out. Until, 'you know, you can't expect to be carried forever—'

'Carried? It's been ME half killing myself, bringing this broken old ark up to date!' Ben pauses. 'And ... while I'm still trying—'

Tony gives a loud cough. 'No.'

'Just a bridging loan. Fifty k. Dad, please.' Ben exhales with a sigh so enormous it feels as if he's right next to Goldie. 'I ... I admit I'm waiting for a few last-minute signatures, but an early injection of funds, just to take advantage of PR from tonight. By next quarter, everything will have balanced – but we need this fresh blood, Dad.' He pauses. 'We can't ignore that. And these flimsy little start-ups are perfect to see us out the other side of this lean spell; we buy them cheap, absorb their good characteristics, swallow them whole.'

'I suppose at least you're not drinking your inheritance away like your sister.' Tony sighs. 'Expect a bank transfer in the morning.'

When the door opens, it's as if Goldie's just come looking for them.

'What gorgeous timing. Escort me back to the facade, angel.' Tony offers Goldie his arm. 'And let's have a gin.'

'Thank you, Dad.' But Ben doesn't sound much like he means it, and as Goldie links arms with Tony, she finds she's relieved to be at his side instead of her husband's.

'You deserve a double gin, at least,' Tony tells her, charm perhaps the sole similarity between father and son. 'For putting up with him for far longer than his mother and I ever had to. And people think boarding schools are bad things . . . ' His eyes twinkle, forever the flirt but never a threat. 'Graham Egelston!' Tony shouts across the room, on spotting his friend, forgetting Goldie's eardrums are mere inches from his mouth. 'Come! Have a gin with us!'

'You go,' Goldie says. 'I've a few bits to check on before things begin.'

Before Tony protests, Graham fills her place and Goldie moves seamlessly out of the picture, unable to return to the overcrowded foyer, or absorb any more of the energy.

What has she overheard? She can't make sense of it, other than the overriding feeling that tonight is a sham.

But what's so new about that?

Suddenly, Goldie's extraordinarily tired. Knows it's quitting time on this charade, as leaving Ben occurs to her unthinkingly. Landing like fact. A decision made.

It's been years since an Archers and lemonade seemed a good idea, yet it feels a sudden necessity, as if Goldie's reaching back, perhaps remembering the girl she'd been before all this, taking her hand, pulling her close again. Quite why, she doesn't know.

But no joy. The bartender ignores her, would rather ingratiate himself with the needs of a group of noisy men making complicated orders, and impatient, Goldie heads into the main ballroom, yet to fill with guests. Thirty candlelit tables, set for so many courses Goldie feels sick, doesn't think she can do it, like her battery of tolerance has at last expired.

Circling the main table, she finds her name card between Ben and Tony's. Quickly, she swaps them around, putting Tony in the middle.

And it is then when the idea comes.

She takes her new seat before it gets too busy. Wonders if Ben and Tony will enjoy the company of Jeannette Jenkins, the person Goldie's covertly swapped places with for a corner table at the very back of the ballroom, hidden, draughty and near the kitchen.

Instant realness. And relief.

'Hello,' says the only other person at Goldie's new table. Wincing into his glass and without looking up, he pushes a bottle of red in Goldie's direction. 'Please, have some terrible wine.'

'Thanks.' Giving him a sideways look, Goldie pours and sips. God, it is disgusting. Chateau Neuf's been reserved for the front tables, already breathing in crystal carafes. Hierarchical gradients of importance at play, even at a new business fundraiser. 'To be honest, I'd been craving an Archers and lemonade, but the dick behind the bar was being – well, a dick,' Goldie says absently. Her table companion's face lifts as he looks at her properly for the first time. 'Sorry.'

'Oh, please, don't be.' With purpose, he stands. 'I'll be back in a bit.'

Fifteen minutes pass. People trickle into the ballroom, taking their seats as Goldie picks at a bread roll, wondering if the food will also be served according to status. Quality inequality. It really is a very tacky trick.

Goldie's table companion returns. 'Popped to that offie near the tube.' With a flourish, he takes out four slim cans of Archers and lemonade. 'Very well stocked. And look what else . . .' He slides two black straws from his shirt pocket and Goldie claps her hands in delight. 'Cheers.'

'This is so kind. Thank you.' Touched, Goldie sips through her straw, discovering the drink is everything she wants it still to be; cloying, synthetic, sugary peach loveliness. 'I'm Goldie.'

'Goldie Fliss-Burden aka Goldilocs – consider me starstruck.'

Studying her drink through her lashes, she's uncharacteristically awkward.

'This really was "the" drink for a while, wasn't it?' He carries on. 'That and Bacardi Breezers. Smirnoff Ice. Remember Hooch? Hermit as I am these days, I bloody loved going out; drinks turning all ultraviolet from the lights, cigarette burns on the dancefloor . . .' He smiles in a warm true way which reaches his eyes and sends prickles of familiarity through Goldie as she can't help but remember, picturing nights like that. Though she was usually cordoned off in clubs, VIPing behind a velvet rope, momentarily special, before realizing she was mostly decoration.

How little has changed since.

'This chutney's a bit ...' He grimaces. 'And I'm not going near that pâté. D'you think we'll have to eat everybody else's?' Only four other guests have taken their seats, the table for twelve feeling a bit big. 'So, how many of these have you had to suffer?'

Goldie tries working him out. With his curly mullet and accent as Essex and obvious as her own, it's hard to place him here, yet she knows he can't be staff. Staff sounds so ... Goldie checks herself. How did she become this person, and why should it matter if he does work here or not? He is talking too much, but that might just be his way, instead of him being on the chat-up. And why must she presume that's what every man is doing when they speak to her?

'I've lost count,' Goldie says truthfully. 'You?'

'Only do them under extreme duress. Like tonight.'

'So, what do you do?'

'What do you think I do?' He sits up straight, putting his shoulders back as Goldie gives him the once-over; noting how long he is, how his moustache is as dark as his eyes, and how he's thought that wearing a shirt – admittedly a very nice shirt – with the darkest of tracksuit bottoms is a look ... Then Goldie notices. Couldn't give two shits about what he does for a living.

'I had them trainers!' Forgetting her indoor voice, Goldie presses her fingers to her lips, but she needn't worry. No one gives one when you're a nobody in the corner. Adjusting the tablecloth, she gets a better look at his Air Jordans. 'God, they're perfect. New?'

'They're 8 Retros – originals. Brilliant shop in Wellsend sources them in.' He slips out his phone, his fingers long and lean, like he should do something creative with hands like that, as he shows her the screen. 'There are some nice new shops popping up round there these days – unique, you know. I can send you a link if you want?'

'Wellsend's not far from where we grew up,' Goldie says. 'Me and my sister, Valeria.' Valeria. She should call her. Meant to send her some dates so they could celebrate Goldie's birthday – months ago. The same chronic guilt that's forever lined Goldie's stomach tugs its achy thread. Much as she loves her.

And she does.

'I know you, don't I?' Recognition lands in Goldie's brain, the past perhaps bringing him back into her thoughts. Of school. 'Wolfie.'

'Wondered if you'd twig,' he says. 'Though to be fair I didn't have the 'tache then. You, of course, are far more recognizable.'

'My gran says when someone tells you it's a small world, point them to Essex.' Goldie's not thought of Wolfie for years. 'It was a sports scholarship, wasn't it? Why you left?'

'Till an injury – completely non-football related. Just messing about on holiday. My mum was livid.' He grins, like it's typical. 'Hadn't even done a full term. So, I changed schools again – to one of the language ones, for kids with foreign parents.'

'I remember your language skills. You rapping the German alphabet.'

'Must've been what, twelve or thirteen, then.' Wolfie claps his hands. 'And you remember.' He beams, like it's the biggest compliment on earth, and so does Goldie.

Who for once truly means it.

The seabass salad is accompanied by a cellist. Then there's boeuf en croute. Forecast speeches. An assiette of desserts. Cheeseboards, ports and shorts. It goes on and on as the space between them closes in step with the years, Goldie and Wolfie bridging the gap of almost three decades, talking club culture, rave culture (more Wolfie's thing than hers) reminiscing over long-dead celebrities (Prince destroying them both), how quickly everyone forgot about the brilliance of Ceefax, how *Eldorado* never should've got cancelled. How they can't remember the noughties with any true clarity, likely because it was so fucking bland. And then the truly shit years.

'Woolworths closing.'

'An absolute flipping tragedy,' Goldie laments, a little tipsier than she'd usually allow herself to get, just as Ben takes to the stage with his father. 'You know, all this took eight weeks to put together.' She rolls her eyes. 'Planned to an inch of numb. Yet . . .' As Ben begins talking, becoming the focus, Goldie leans away.

'Yet what?'

'I'm wondering how you fit here,' Goldie whispers, 'when you're not one of them?'

'Well, that's easy, innit? I'm flogging him my business.'

Wolfie nods towards Ben. 'I bought a house, a sea view property if you please – bit off more than I could chew if I'm totally honest.' With his eyes back on Goldie, he drops his voice. 'Now, I'm not gonna lie, he does seem a bit of a prick, but needs must.' He shrugs as she concentrates, piecing this new info together. 'You're looking great, by the way. Really great.' Goldie has the flicker of a memory of them sharing a textbook in science. Always nice – and a little bit detached. Can't remember his scholarship skills for the life of her. 'Hard working out how you fit, too.'

'Once again, I thank you all for coming, and for your continued support of our company.' Ben rounds off his speech. 'We are at heart a family enterprise. An honourable mention to my father for his continued patronage and vision,' he says, as skimming as he dares. 'And, of course, my wife, for her continued support of me.' Ben searches the crowd and spotting Goldie at last, lifts his glass towards her. 'Who I think deserves her own round of applause.'

With his brows thoroughly raised, Wolfie claps for Goldie along with the rest of the room. And where usually she'd play along, stand, graciously blow Ben a kiss, Goldie can't move. As a contaminating realization closes in.

'So this is where you got to!' As the rest of the room begins to disperse back into the foyer, Ben makes his way over, high colour and damp all over again. 'Just in time for the photo. How wonderful you've met,' he says, too much through his teeth for Goldie's liking as he catches her eye. 'Now, darling, slip that coat off.' He fusses, adjusting the straps of her dress, which feels vastly over-performative, before turning his attentions on Wolfie. 'And you. Man of the hour, and no plus-one?'

'No,' says Wolfie. 'Just me.'

'Wonderful, wonderful! Though not a lone wolf for much longer. Not now you're one of us.' Goldie aches inwardly as Ben pushes her coat into the arms of an aimless waiter, barking orders and briefly breaking his own charm spell, as she and Wolfie try not to look at each other. Because they know.

Just as Goldie knows, that when she overheard Ben demanding some chav's signature earlier, he was probably talking about Wolfie.

Two

VEE

The World Don't Owe You Nothing

Vee's a walking ball of anxiety, but she makes herself go. It has not been easy, throwing herself back into the world, knowing the only way to break the mindset of existing as a habitual twosome is to get a life of her own. The process starts with truth. That's what all the self-help divorce podcasts keep telling her, anyway. Fundamental truth. What makes Vee happy? What's always made her happiest?

Writing.

So here she is.

'Here' is Write Pub, a writing class and community Vee's obsessed over from a distance, too socially awkward to join – until tonight. The class is held monthly, in a beautifully anonymous pub not far from the publishing house Vee's been freelancing for, but there are nationwide groups, and even little splinter factions. With everybody scribbling up and down the country, no wonder it's so bloody hard to get published.

Nerves aside, Vee's glad the class is in a pub. Of course, the informality appeals, but places of learning, particularly schools, still do funny things to her, the unresolvedness of how her once favourite place became an actual living hell. This, coming here, perhaps one day sharing her own work, would be a brave move for anyone, but especially for Vee – even she will give herself that. With a double gin and slimline, she approaches a group who look how writers might look and seem to know what they're doing. 'To revising and resubmitting.' Two ladies in baggy jumpers clink glasses of red wine.

'And whatever kills us first – though it's progress in the right direction, at least.' On noticing Vee, one of them adds, 'war stories', giving off vibes of jaded exhaustion. 'You new?'

'I am.'

'Performing?' The woman nods to the makeshift stage.

'Oh no. Purely spectating.'

'Well, should you want to, but getting up there's not your thing, the forum's a good place for feedback.'

With a polite 'thank you', Vee excuses herself, though she's nowhere really to go. She pops to the loo instead.

When Vee had left the office earlier, wearing her hair up instead of down as usual, her neck and shoulders wrapped in an enormous scarf she'd all but retracted into, some other attendees who she'd met through the day invited her out for drinks. Glad she had an excuse at the ready, they'd all collectively oohed when Vee told them where she was going.

'Writing? Sounds a bit ...' Violet, the receptionist – and

organizer of the networking event – had pulled a face which Vee couldn't interpret, yet knew was rude. 'No offence.'

Wondering why on earth Violet even worked in publishing, Vee had remembered that Violet was there thanks to her uncle, influential and head of the marketing department, who thought it would jazz up her CV. Vee feels, profoundly, for the less privileged, dying for a spot in a bookish environment, remembering with a shudder the big maroon record of achievement she'd haul around interviews, filled with certificates and other minor achievements like first aid from when she'd worked in a local supermarket, hopeful her additional efforts might open doors a little more. Interviews which went nowhere, though she'd paid for her travel, spending hours on applications, and even more hours of nervous apprehension, all to be met with silence.

But no matter now. Vee is respected. Industry people know her for her attention to detail, so much so that she works mostly freelance; researching and copyediting for the big publishing houses – but a true documentarian first. Often, when a celebrity is involved in a big scandal, or some national treasure dies, it's likely Vee's research that's had a hand in unearthing the footage on the news and telly which follows, sometimes almost as if she's pre-empted it. Her sleuthing skills are instinctive; bio docs, snippets of interviews, clippings of collected wrongdoings that get swept under famous carpets and become nothing for years, Vee collects like gold dust. And dust does collect. As her research takes its truthful shape, Vee would be the first to admit how the unmasking of a certain ego gives her a hit of power – though she's merely a conduit, exacting payback on behalf of all the poor exploited bastards in the world. Herself included.

Despite her month in a mental health hospital which led to Vee being homeschooled, she achieved eight GCSEs. An E in maths, but mentally well or not, Vee passing maths was never going to happen. A levels, then a London uni; an English Literature degree. And lost in the chaos of the best and busiest city, Vee found the invisibility she craved.

In all the years since of quietly achieving, ticking the boxes of a successful adult life, Vee can't pretend she hasn't been tempted to root good and deep on social media, to uncover the cunts she went to school with who witnessed her pain and did nothing. It's proved far better, though, sticking to the premise of staying in her own lane, winning in every possible way, so that when the time comes, when she eventually bumps into some teen-witch now mumsy and soft with a face like a collapsed sofa in say, Sainsbury's, Vee will be ready.

To be, just for once, the one on the front foot, has forever meant everything. Becoming someone who created – despite the hurt of all those years – to anybody looking in, an enviable life.

Even if it isn't quite true.

But she mustn't waste these writing meets by retreating into backwards thinking. Telling herself to focus, she tunes back in.

Vee's entry G & T vanishes along with all the small talk, as a woman in a stripy dress and amazing boots stands on tiptoes to address the crowd. 'Share Aloud' kicks the whole thing off, live pieces based around monthly themes, and as these ordinary people – *writers, just like she is* – take up the mic to read their words, it gives Vee courage.

After some middling performances, rounded off by a poem so powerful Vee found herself blinking away instant emotion, the open mic rounds off into the next phase; those who've asked for their work to be critiqued, and the audience begins fracturing into groups, leaving her hovering at the bar. How typically Vee, to find herself a spare part on the outskirts of the activity; classic, and exactly how she'd write herself, if this were Vee's storyline.

A man, standing a couple of feet away from her, exchanging pleasantries with the bar person, notices her people-watching. He nods towards the tables, at everybody's focus. 'Amazing how serious it gets.'

'The power of critique,' Vee replies, so naturally you'd never believe she was allergic to small talk and all she wants is another gin. To be left to observe the room. Because it is intense. And it is fascinating. 'Are you not joining in?'

'Not had anything new to share for a bit.' He shrugs. 'Life can get in the way, can't it?'

'Of creativity?' Vee thinks of the years she's spent scribbling away in secret. Deeming it worthless. 'Absolutely.' Feels herself give a little. 'I'm Valeria –Vee.'

'Ru,' he says, with a smile as warm as the colours he is made from. Dark eyes and red-brown hair. He's halfway down a pint of golden ale. 'Nice to meet you, Vee.' He stops to exchange farewells and hug the ladies from earlier in the quality knitwear goodbye.

'One of the made-its, and still he can't keep away from us,' says the one who spoke to Vee earlier. 'Mr Faber, if you please.' She squeezes Ru fondly as his shoulders turn inwards, reminding Vee of herself when put in the spotlight. 'Not that he'd dream of shouting about it.'

'Luckily I've you to do that.' Ru clears his throat, clearly flattered. 'And you to thank. Seriously,' he says, mostly to Vee, 'Judith must've read my book about sixteen times. A very patient and—'

'Overcritical pain in the arse, is what he wants to say,' Judith interrupts good-naturedly. 'And he is far too modest, but proof it can happen – though we do have quite a good success rate here,' she adds with a proud wine-stained smile. 'So much hope in a happy ending, isn't there? And so the rest of us cling on.' Taking Vee by surprise, she hugs her, too. 'Lovely to meet you. And remember, there's always the forum.'

It's the energy here, the whole vibe which comes from a common passion.

Vee, without a doubt, will be back.

'Sorry,' Ru says, 'I can't remember what we were saying.'

'How it's like a compulsion,' Vee prompts him, her curiosity piqued. 'To write. And I agree.' Whenever she struggles and words become a necessary act, Vee does, completely, understand. 'Don't you find it painful, though, to write – and then share – the stuff that truly matters to you?'

Offering up your soul.

To be judged. God forbid.

'But if we don't write about the things that matter, is there really any purpose to writing at all?' He makes a good point. 'Honesty brings connection. Which is a good thing – and a problem. Brilliant that I have a book coming out...' Ru bares his teeth like the anxious emoji. 'But bloody exposing, too. I'm absolutely dreading people reading it.' He drains his pint. 'Because—'

'Because then they'll know your truth.' The moment feels like an epiphany. 'Would you like another drink?' Vee keeps her good posture, along with the rising feeling that for once in her life, she's exactly where she's supposed to be. Having the kind of conversation she should've been having all her life. But couldn't.

'I'll have another pint, thank you.' Ru's cheeks grow ever so slightly pink. 'If, if you ever want me to read over anything – not that I'm an expert...'

Heart banging, Vee makes a groundbreaking choice. 'Perhaps I could show you this, then?' Before deciding against it, she slips her phone from her coat pocket, opening her notes. 'I wrote it on the train this morning. Not looked at it since, so this is me being totally brave.' In nervous distraction, Vee orders new drinks as Ru picks up her phone and starts to read.

It is the longest ninety-odd seconds in human history, while Vee tries not to stare at his face in the same way people avert their eyes when you enter your pin number. Only for longer. Has she been holding her breath? Did he smile then? Why on earth has she shown her words to this auburn fucking stranger?

Because it matters.

CLARITY DAY
by Vee Hughes

The day before her period came, she named 'clarity day'; a day she'd doubt the world and hate her husband. During the rest of her monthly cycle, his flaws and irritating habits would be masked by the good hormones, but then, when it was obvious and imminent, and there was no longer the need for any chemistry or closeness between them, she couldn't stand him.

He would pick up on it, try harder. Call her a 'mean little rock of a woman at times'.

And he got her about right.

Then the blood would come, and as her hormones flat-lined, the two of them also returned to normal.

Getting along. Being nice.

But what if clarity day was the absolute truth and the rest, all that nice, merely blubber? Gentle lies, masking a lifetime.

What then?

These are my thoughts, my feelings, Vee reminds herself. Which is hard when they feel so very much like betrayal. It's not like she used any names. But anyone with half a brain—

'You've got something … I don't know …' Ru pauses, thinking. 'The detachment. In battle with a whole different spirit just beneath the surface,' he says, wildly and writerly, revealing Vee in a way she rather likes. 'It's good.'

Giving herself away completely, Vee beams at him, astronomically flattered.

'You really remind me of someone,' Ru says, glancing into his pint before looking up at her in a way she surely must be reading wrong.

'How do I do it?' Vee asks him. 'How do I write a proper book?'

'You've just got to get on with it,' he says matter-of-factly, as if there's no other way around it. 'Judith would say it's about protecting the time to write. Which isn't easy, with a real life to live, too. I write mostly in the holidays, which is likely why I'm empty-handed tonight. Never seem to be very productive in term times.'

'You're a teacher?'

'I am. Think I wanted to be a teacher for as long as I wanted to be a writer,' he says. 'Secondary school. Very good prep for the bad reviews – teenagers can ruin you with their savagery.'

Ain't that the truth?

Perhaps not all small talk is evil, Vee thinks as they part ways outside the pub. With an entirely respectable micro-hug, Ru kisses her goodbye.

Just on the cheek, but it's all in the linger.

On the journey home, Vee's quietly astonished, a smile – another real one – glued to her face, unable to process someone finally praising her work, and just as unable to process the idea of potential sexual chemistry. It's not even ten p.m. yet.

Perhaps this slow unravelling of her usual uptightness, the pretence of being perfect, is officially wearing thin.

Which would be such progress.

When Vee's train slows into the tiny station nearest home,

and she follows the shoulders of other commuters to the line of taxis and cars where partners wait to collect the other halves of themselves, Vee wonders if any of them are living as she currently is, in a loose sort of 'almost' of the married life before. Ease minus the intimacy, as she and Jamie make their gentle steps towards official separation without the jump-from-a-plane anxiety of being untethered in this, frankly, let's face it, pretty shitty world.

Starting Again.

Can she do it? Thinking back on her night, the excited bloom of feeling Vee's carried all the way home from Write Pub makes her a little more certain that she can.

Jamie's kind face smiles as she climbs into the passenger seat, just as she always has whenever it's dark.

Vee doesn't mention the pub, nor the writing. Instead, she eats a late supper of cheese on toast with the telly on in the background, scrolling on her phone throughout the ten o'clock news and it's not long before Jamie's making tea and drawing the curtains, while Vee lets out Onion for her last wee of the night. The same jobs as always, only now that it's bedtime they'll retire to different quarters; Jamie turning left on the upstairs landing, as Vee turns right. And, as time – four months and ten days, for accuracy – has proven, where Vee expects to feel some sort of loss or perhaps a sadness from their decoupling, especially after so long wed, she instead feels calm.

Forty-four, and getting divorced. An excellent career but a terrifying mortgage that even two decent wages struggled to afford, because of inflation, interest rates – the cost-of-living crisis being so flipping expensive – and because they both fell for the Great British Property Myth, believing that owning a bricks-and-mortar solid piece of England was the key to a good solid future. Because that's what you do, don't you, as an adult? Work, save, invest. Secure a nest. Think Monopoly. Buy property.

Don't you?

Vee's new bedroom's not as big as the old main, which sits central and empty on the landing, overlooking Clementine Park; fate, they'd thought at first, imagining a dog and counting their luckies at having such a gorgeous green space on their own front doorstep. All three bedrooms are large, light, full of character. Every inch of the house perfect. Vee's taste. So it is no hardship waiting for this forever home to bounce back from its negative equity, no hardship to share with a good man Vee still trusts more than anyone.

But never enough to ever share her writing.

At her desk beneath the window that overlooks the back garden, gently illuminated by star-shaped solar lights, Vee opens her laptop, letting it come to life while she updates her diary; a resolution this year, to get back into the habit. It has always been through books, or with a pen that Vee thrives. Making up stories in the dark, like she's still doing. Slowly moving towards the light.

Astonishing. How her feelings are so much clearer on paper.

★

Three

GOLDIE

Miss-Understood

Apparently, Wolfie's company – Starling-Meyer – manufactures kitchen equipment on an industrial scale, his factory in Basildon supplying restaurants and caterers throughout the south-east. Built from scratch eight years ago, and though Ben tells Goldie all the intricacies on the journey home, she takes very little in. Can't do much more than think how awkwardly telling it was to be caught with Ben sucking up in one breath and punching down the next.

And Wolfie's face, when it dawned on him that Ben was her husband.

Wolfie hadn't mentioned his man-of-the-hour status, both having played themselves insignificant. But not completely. Instead, there'd been an openness between them in a space usually denied. Because nothing quite slaps like the class divide.

Just as nothing brings you home like commonality.

Dropping the mask, if only briefly, had created a lightness

which felt nourishing. Necessary. Good reasons why she should've suggested they keep in touch – because what even were the odds of him being there, Wolfgang Meyer of 8B who could've been there all night and she would've been none the wiser – if she hadn't swapped tables.

'Are you even listening?'

'I am.' Goldie's quick to reassure Ben. 'Of course I am.' His current peculiar funk reveals a side she rarely encounters. It's taking proper effort to reread him.

Goldie looks out of the car window, low-lit streetlamps flattering the quiet high street so upmarket it's not been allowed to modernize. Quaintly stuck in time, but for the almond croissants in the artisan bakery, which cost the sheer fucking earth. The pub on the corner of the forest is bright and lively still, and Goldie thinks for a moment that she might've clocked Jamie, Valeria's husband, with a woman too tall and fair to be her sister, leaving the beer garden hand in hand to cross the road.

In a flash they're gone. Unsure if it even was Jamie, she's left with the chills. 'Are you all right?' Goldie tries again. 'Everything seemed to go brilliantly tonight. Yet you're different.'

'If I'm different, it's only down to you being distant.' In the back of the cab, sitting opposite Goldie, he crosses then uncrosses his legs. 'Is it him?' Ben asks, avoiding her eyes.

'Wolfie?'

'Stupid name,' he spits, making Goldie smile despite herself. 'There, see, your face has gone all soft. Very cozy and ... overfamiliar.'

'Familiar, perhaps. We went to school together. I'd not seen him since we were about twelve, that's all. You've nothing to worry about.'

'Who says I'm worried?' But again Ben won't look at her. 'Business is business is all I'm saying. So we'll have him round for dinner, corner him that way.' For... what was it Ben said earlier? Ah yes; to 'swallow him whole' – oh, the disease of association. 'That sleazy, salt of the earth pizzazz he's got about him is exactly what we're crying out for.'

Pizzazz? Jeez Louise.

'Sleazy's a bit much.'

Ben clicks his tongue. 'You know what I mean. Down to earth. Ethnically ambiguous – like you, too.' Only Ben could make it sound as if being born brown-skinned with fuck-all was a quirky life choice.

'Dinner feels a bit much as well.' Goldie ignores everything else, because there's simply too much to unpack. She's tired. And she has never been bloody sleazy in her life. Sexy, yes. Deliciousness personified – that, too.

And there had been nothing remotely sleazy about Wolfie either. No innuendo, just good company and excellent manners – a very different creation from Ben's usual party guests. 'You don't live here Ben, you can't expect...'

But he can when he chooses to. The Coach House is part of the Bickham family estate, and what else is Goldie really but a house pet?

Bare thigh shines through the slit of her velveteen, olive green-coloured dress; Ben's hand feeling alien, suddenly there, just above her knee, drifting upwards, which she catches and removes without feeling remotely violated.

They both know how this goes.

'Therese will be expecting you home, I'm sure ...'

'Therese.' Ben tuts as the car slows to a stop outside the Coach House. 'At least, I suppose, I've someone who truly loves me.' He shifts as if done, signalling for the driver to open Goldie's door.

'Ben.' Spoilt, stubborn twat. 'Let's not have him over for dinner.'

'All you need to do is set a table and order some food in. Just be your usual fabulous self.' He pushes, his entitlement blurring all boundaries. 'Unless, of course, you're too old for this game.'

Without a goodbye, Goldie's soon alone on her enormous driveway.

In her true heart, Goldie could've done without getting married at all. But with her own self-earned security long gone, Ben solved financial famine. She's not the first to have done this, and people get by doing a lot worse.

Getting by.

But not fully living.

Television's always a tonic. Kicking off her heels and pouring a large Scotch, Goldie considers watching a *Power* series, just for the serotonin of seeing Mary J. Blige in more killer outfits, but there on the TV's homepage is Goldie herself. Clicking on iPlayer, the screen fills with an old episode of *Top of The Pops*.

She's wearing high-waist leggings – in gold, of course. A black sequinned corset with an oversized shirt and trainers not dissimilar to those Wolfie had been wearing earlier. Extensions in her already long hair. The roundest baby face. And bum. Turning the volume up, and probably for the first time ever, 'Free Me, Be Me', Goldie's debut single, fills the enormous downstairs of the Coach House, the sound of her own voice as shocking to her own ears as to all the ghostly Bickhams of the past, those who'd once considered here their home, too.

Again comes the feeling that she's not really living, as she takes her own breath away. Transfixed, Scotch in one hand, remote in the other, Goldie reads the scrolling info accompanying her performance.

> Goldie Fliss-Burden aka Goldilocs, was the first solo female signed to Vine Recordings following the scandal of Rocki Ramirez, in 1993. Between 1995 and 1996 Goldilocs scored three top ten singles, one MOBO award and two Brits nominations.

'*I rise, like I was born to, I was made for, what I prayed for . . .*'

> Though unconfirmed, it is rumoured that Goldie Fliss-Burden is the illegitimate lovechild of musician Amos Fliss, known to the world as Master-Fly, believed to be one of the most successful posthumous artists of all time.

It proved a genius PR move; Goldie reclaiming the Fliss surname catapulted her into the public's interest, but once her debut hit the airwaves, the name had already done all it needed to. Not only was her song catchy, but the disco influence made for a great look; Donna Summer, Eurodance, and the Kids from 'Fame' in a blender – with a dash of Essex girl perspicacity. Everything that was authentically her.

> Signed at only sixteen years old, Goldiloc's breakthrough onto the global dance scene was the brainchild of PR manager, now director of Vine Recordings, Grant Love, also credited for the successes of Knights of Temptation, EastSide Extras, Domaine and the now infamous Ill Lothario, currently awaiting trial for six reported accusations of assault and exploitation.

It is the sight of his name, not Ill Lothario's, but Grant Love's, that has Goldie turning the television off just as the show comes to an end anyway, with the other musicians and presenter gathering on Goldie's stage to say goodbye to everyone watching at home, her joy from meeting her childhood icons uncontainable. The screen goes black, taking her with it.

It's hard not feeling sad. Harder still not to wonder if that was really her.

How in the name of shitting shittle is she here living this life now?

Four

VEE

System Addict

It's Wednesday night. Vee preps the beginnings of a prawn linguine, and even though it's only her in the kitchen with her audiobook, she resists in every way the self-help she bloody knows would do her the world of good, addressing all the negatives she's hoarded internally over the decades within those hidden soft-spot places Brene Brown talks so much about. But words like *vulnerability, shame,* or the truly awful *self-awareness,* give Vee the proper terrors, her gut instinct to close herself off like a house made of shutters. Why disturb the truth of what really lurks within?

'*I recognized my own shame web when my husband and I divorced . . .*' The audiobook begins with another story that sets off pangs of similarity through Vee's barriers, peeling her like an onion, giving her eyes the same sting.

There's a lot of packing and unpacking during a divorce, in the mental sense, as well as the other. A lot of revisiting and reflection. Their ending hadn't come as a shock to either Jamie or Vee; they'd simply ground to a halt. Going through the motions, both knowing, deep down, that life was far too short for games of that kind. It has not, so far, been cruel. Neither have had their heart broken, their world destroyed. Yet they are both a little tender. Vee wonders if it would've been any different if they'd lived apart from the moment the decision to separate was made, instead of being here, in the 'almost' space.

With a tea towel over her shoulder, like she's now some integral part of a frenetic commercial kitchen, Vee twists the ignition, placing the pan over the heat before adding a swirl of oil. Waiting for the sizzle, she tastes her wine as a warmth grows in her tummy. She's healthy. Safe. There's food to eat. And because she's only half listening to Brene, she swaps Audible for a Spotify shuffle.

Vee's mood and hips move with Solange into the better. She's doing all right.

It's important to recognize the feeling. And own it.

From her dog bed in the kitchen corner, Onion snaps alert. Registering the noise of the front door opening, she barges towards Jamie as he appears with an, 'All right girls?'

'Yep.' Chucking the prawns into her bubbling sauce, Vee gives him a quick smile over her shoulder. 'Good day?'

'Yep.' Jamie fusses Onion, sending dog hair shedding. 'Going for a piss.'

Vee thinks – which she admits she probably does too much – that living separately with Jamie in this house is not entirely dissimilar to when they'd very much been a couple.

Better, in some ways.

It is weird to admit that at last. How since their split, these past few months have been filled with more politeness and compromise than there had ever seemed to be in the together years. And even with her head far too full of yes, frankly rather negative thoughts, Vee's felt herself slowly coming back, returning to her standalone self without Jamie as her measure, and without playing off his autonomy like a subsidiary character, rarely thinking of her own wants – if much of their togetherness was ever truly based on her wants.

Once, Jamie fancied Vee like mad; had to woo and win her round, because serious relationships hadn't featured in her plans. She'd been temping at his parents' small indie press; they'd been teachers before becoming publishers of well-respected medical journals. Not the feast of fiction Vee yearned for.

That she's still yearning for.

The lure of the writing forum feels like incredibly niche porn. Secret and hers, all night long.

All the same, Vee offers, 'This'll be five minutes if you want some?'

'Thanks, but I'm not hanging about.' Jamie keeps his eyes on hers. 'I have a date.'

'Ah.' Though undoubtedly new, strange territory, it doesn't hurt in the slightest.

He actually blushes. 'Any plans yourself?'

Should she tell him? What can it hurt now? 'Writing, actually. I joined a group.'

Even his expression ... Vee wishes she could stuff her

revelation back in her face. 'I thought after the last time, you ... might've put all that to bed.' Knowing he's touched a nerve, Jamie adds, 'Putting yourself through such upset again.'

Rejections are part of the process. Vee gets this, even though it's destroyed her every time it's happened, the sad despair of a 'not for us,' bottoming out in the pit of her gut. But then the hunger; her hurt from a 'no' fully fermented into an annihilating I'll-show-you-next-time. Failing better and all that jazz. Precisely the reason Write Club's necessary, because her dream won't die and it's time for a new way in. Vee's singular objective is to be published. And she will prove Jamie wrong.

One day.

'Don't think I'm being unkind,' Jamie says, rubbing his nose. 'I just don't want you to waste your time hoping for something that might never happen.'

Like the baby they wasted their time hoping for, which never happened?

They are silent. Both thinking it.

Had Vee truly wanted a baby? Was Jamie keener, being from a nice family, naturally thinking he'd follow suit? Telling his parents about their divorce had been one of the most difficult parts of their separation – not so much Jamie, but all the stabilizing comforts which surround him.

It is good for Vee to admit these things.

Is Vee sorry? Sorry the IVF was too expensive and the wait too late? Sorry that she turned forty and thought you know what, fuck it, there's more to life, more to my life than this constant pursuit to bring another into the world, something which in her heart of hearts felt daunting and never quite what she wanted anyway.

Christ. She would only ever admit that in her head. To herself. But it is acknowledgement, regardless. Perhaps Brene's working after all.

When Jamie shouts goodbye, Vee's already upstairs. Pretends she can't hear him as she swaps clothes for her dressing gown, breathing free when his footsteps fade out, home expanding in tandem with her lungs. Away from small, constricting, somewhere she's outgrowing, like during lockdown, the impossible return to rigid waistbands after the joy of months in joggers.

Away from Jamie.

When Vee distils everything baby-related down to its finest measure, the truth before anything else is that she's never, ever wanted to be a mother. And Vee knows now, more than ever before, that she never will.

There is another calling. The writing's come full circle, re-emerging just when she can devote time to it. Because the fulfilment Vee gets when she sits at her desk and loses herself is unparalleled. Her mind quiet at last from her own noise, while her imagination's at work translating all she's ever absorbed and experienced into stories.

The compulsion. Vee's purpose.

Five

GOLDIE

What's Love Got To Do With It?

'He's your son!' Goldie snaps, having seen far too much of Ben lately. This morning, it's coffee to talk over the Wolfie dinner plans she can ignore no longer.

'But he likes you more. I'm not supposed to have a son, remember?' he adds pointedly, lest Goldie forget. 'And I am not cancelling tonight.' With his laptop bag and coat draped over his arm, Ben heads for the door. 'By the way, I'll need you for Sunday brunch as usual, and next Thursday evening – low-key, City drinks. I'll fill you in properly later.' Give him a top hat, rewind their scenario sixty years, and he'd fit the part still. The smart and respectable breadwinner. So obviously wearing the trousers. 'Toodle-oo.'

Ugh.

Ben and Goldie met, rather romantically, one starry evening at Liverpool St station taxi rank; Ben insistent that she took the only cab, which led to them sharing, both heading east, home in the same direction. Chaste, and eternally chivalrous, he invited her for drinks, then dinners, Ben presuming Goldie to be in her early twenties when she'd already waved goodbye to thirty – and it wasn't his business anyway. But he did so like to talk in numbers.

Benedict Bickham. A six and a half out of ten, which made him try; work out, trial a hair regrowth treatment, and drive a ridiculously sleek car Goldie promptly named KITT and he didn't have a clue what she was talking about. How could he have missed out on *Knight Rider*, the TV show about the talking car and David bloody Hasselhoff? Goldie wondered if they even had TVs in boarding school.

A lot of their early communication was hit and miss. Ben himself was only just forty when they met, yet he still marked time and era-defining moments by what government was in power, even when discussing events which had happened before he'd been born. For instance, 1966 wasn't defined by the World Cup, but rather by an unfortunate landslide Labour win. The TV shows Goldie and Valeria grew up practically glued to, Ben had no clue about. *Byker Grove, The Krypton Factor, Why Don't You? Brookside*. He'd chuckle as if Goldie had made it all up yet would often say how he liked listening to her, charmed by her Essexy-cockney twitter. Goldie found his complete ignorance of pop culture endearing; it was as if he'd hatched in 1945, such was his vocabulary. He knew of her father's music, enough to be impressed, yet nothing of Goldie's own brief success, which felt cleansing in a way she couldn't explain. Reserved, loaded and with perfect good manners ... Ben's list of refreshing attributes seemed never-ending. He didn't try and sleep with her. And he never got drunk on their dates.

Until his birthday. It was the first time Goldie had met Ben's friends, and had been, in hindsight, a foreshadowing of the life to come. Shark-like, cold and powerful people, unrufflable, and verging on robotic. They talked in surnames and titles, achievements used as commodity. Conversations felt like battlefields. And their disdain for those less fortunate shocked her; politicians, surgeons, solicitors, a judge – a lord, who despite the grand title, looked like a bogey. Said, while he'd stared at Goldie's chest, how money had always got him everywhere. He'd then slid his hand between her bum cheeks, like a credit card slicing through a machine for payment, and so Goldie had grabbed his arm and held it up and asked the room if anybody knew the slimeball it belonged to. Ben had been outraged, terrifically apologetic, and though Goldie assured him she could handle herself, he declared he didn't want her to have to. Tipsy, pink-cheeked, his lips flushed, fuller than usual, he somehow looked more alive.

'I know. I'm going to marry you.'

Goldie didn't say yes. It wasn't a question anyway, though regardless, plans began to happen.

It felt nice and neat; becoming the wife of a director, looked after for the first time in her whole life. Their sole moment of sexual intimacy had been on their wedding night. Missionary, cuddles. Not what you'd imagine. Ben, believing the stereotype of the look of her, found he'd had far saucier times with Therese, and for Goldie it was a relief. A marriage of convenient companionship felt just the sort of relationship she could really commit to – because wasn't love, especially romantic love, life's greatest ruin anyway? Goldie got to keep her heart safe and protected, and Ben stayed Benedict – secretly devoted to Therese. The years passed, routine setting in by nature, and Ben's been far from the world's worst husband. Never anything premeditated in their arrangement, which works.

Worked.

The pretending's tiring, getting wheeled out more and more, and unignorable, the way Ben glides around weaving his spells, so oily and contaminating now they've lost all their magic. Fleecing the ordinary. Begging his father for money. Goldie can't unhear what went on in that makeshift office.

Sickening to think he's out to skint Wolfie, too.

'Was that my loving father leaving without a goodbye?' Yawning, Rufus scratches his chest hair, heading for the fridge. 'Can I make you breakfast?'

Send Rufus on his way? As if.

'What are we having?' Goldie's hopeful he'll help her cook later, too. Her kitchen skills are basic – and that's generous. Rufus, Valeria too, are much better cooks ... There she is again, popping up in her head. On the other side of this headfuckery, Goldie will shake off her sisterly guilt and call her.

'Poached eggs?'

'Perf.' Much as she loves Rufus, Goldie's glad she didn't have to birth him. Glad he was just there, toilet trained and able to wash himself. 'Do you think you might be able to help me out tonight too? It's your dad's thing. All systems on show.'

'Who's it for?'

'Wolfie Meyer. Very nice, probs won't want any fuss.'

'Sorry, G, I have plans. Not to sound like I'm using you, but it's partly the reason I'm crashing here.'

'This is tragic. What can I do? Not a takeaway, it'll make me look ...'

'Thought you didn't worry about stuff like that?' Rufus says as Goldie clips him around the ear. Goldie, who without truly realizing has been warmer, easier company for Rufus than Ben's forced fatherliness, so stuck and stiff, forever talking to his son as if someone were listening. And a terrific shame how Ben's missed out on properly knowing him, now fully grown, with all his books and lesson plans and flying working visits. Goldie's proud.

Ben and Goldie were only a year married, when he found out about his secret son, already thirteen years old, the revelation surprising then reigniting his liaisons with Therese after years of resistance, away from the eyes of their families. After that, Rufus arrived at the Coach House every other Friday; always the same car with the same driver, and always with flowers for Goldie – a gesture which chimed with her realization that weekends with Rufus meant weekends of just the two of them, while his parents got their rocks off in total privacy. The car would then return on Sunday evening to collect him. 'Thanks so much for having me,' Rufus would say, ever polite, looking only ever at Goldie as he said it.

At first Goldie had been irritated by the flowers. Until the chauffeur made a point of telling her how Rufus would make him stop at the petrol station before they came here, spending his own pocket money to buy them. The same flowers every week. Six yellow, or sometimes orange, roses.

Only once was Therese in the car, too. Goldie had been waiting outside the house for Rufus, as had become their routine, but on spotting Therese had invited her in for tea – their sense of competition so astonishingly absent, for curiosity more than anything else. Goldie remembers how she'd said something flip, like how she wouldn't bite, which led to the weirdness.

Of Therese hugging Goldie. 'He's so very, very fond of you.' A tall yet bird-framed woman, in cropped jeans and a Breton top, healthily bare-faced with shortish hair as if she'd stepped out of a Boden catalogue, flying into her arms. 'Thank you for being kind to him.' Refusing tea and squeezing Rufus goodbye, she'd slipped back into the car, and from that day Goldie had never seen her since.

There have always been duos of women at opposite ends of the food chain, yet tied, nonetheless. Both useful, and both women strangely grateful for each other. It is better that Goldie keeps an independent household and Therese gets the sexy parts. Like a mistress in reverse. All part of a hushed posh scandal.

Feuding families, though; so medieval-sounding Goldie's never quite understood why anyone would really give a shit these days. But an obvious break in the chains of cold linkage and enemy lineage has been Goldie's influence on Rufus. A warm undercurrent of all that's ordinary. And normal. He has a sense of humour for one thing, and Goldie's sure that's because of her.

'Couldn't you do something heat-uppable? That way you can order in and decant into the Le Creuset. Job done,' Rufus suggests, Goldie's love of delivery drivers on mopeds no secret.

'I can do that. From the Greek place under the viaduct. Moussaka with a green salad, followed by ...' Goldie clicks her fingers. 'Baklava. I won't do a starter.'

'Casual but classy. Is it just him?'

'Yeah,' Goldie says. 'Just him.'

Ben's in standstill traffic, fifteen miles away, already fifteen minutes late.

'Lovely house,' Wolfie says politely when Rufus opens the door. 'Suits them.'

Goldie's tried adding her own taste to the Coach House, which isn't really taste but more statements of oversized, garish coloured impracticalities, like the chaise longue in the shape of a stiletto, upholstered in neon velvet cheetah print. The standing lamp with the body of a bronze Marilyn Monroe, fuchsia shade and pea-green tassels. Assault pieces.

'I don't think Dad's spent more than a month here in his whole life,' Rufus says absently, searching for his headphones and running late.

'He doesn't live here?' Wolfie's surprised.

'Welcome to the house of make-believe.' Putting his headphones around his neck, he shakes Wolfie's hand. 'It was good to meet you,' Rufus says, and as Goldie comes round the corner with drinks, he pecks her on the cheek. 'See you soon, G. Thanks for putting up with me.'

It feels a little too silent when he closes the door. And no point in pretending she hadn't heard their conversation. 'He's—'

'You and Ben,' Wolfie says. 'Don't live together?'

'We're not together.' Goldie tells the truth, admitting the lie. 'Not in any emotional sense.' Is that hope on his face, or horror? 'We're friends, living entirely separate lives, until somebody visits, or we go to things like the other night.'

'Why?'

'It's a long old story.' One Goldie's not prepared to share, especially not in defence of herself. She has nothing to prove or explain, yet in front of Wolfie the whole lot of it reads somehow shittier. 'I don't want you to have to know it.'

'But I'd like to know you. Again.' Weird how his words disarm her, removing her from this and putting her back to the person she'd been.

Before.

All those deeply entrenched lines in the sand, which seemed to come all at once. Her mid-teens packed with landmark moments, shaping Goldie into the adult of now. Mum leaving. Her expulsion from school. The revelations of Valeria being bullied, then sectioned. Testing times which make you grow regardless of whether you're equipped to cope. Or was it the fame, Goldie's brief pop stardom which truly marked the goodbye to the kid Wolfie once knew?

Or, was it—

Goldie knows the true reason. Same as why those letters from Vine Recordings remain unopened. Why she keeps to herself as much as she can.

Why this gilded cage exists in the first place.

'I . . .' She clears her throat. 'I don't know how we got here.' Goldie's heart rocks in her chest. Can't stop herself. 'Please don't sell—'

'Apologies!' Ben rushes in, a tad sweaty for being simply stuck in traffic.

This must really matter, yet Goldie can't see how an ordered-in supper's supposed to help anything.

'I can't claim I made it,' Goldie says a little later as they eat in the kitchen – like old friends do, according to Ben. One small mercy is that it's an excellent moussaka. 'I just have good mates on mopeds.'

'So, tell me about yourself.' Leaning on one arm, Ben studies Wolfie with fascination, having put much time into researching his business, yet finding little about him personally. Ben doesn't mind admitting it. 'Your business presence is spot on. But LinkedIn and Google've told me nothing of your background. My missus tells me you went to school together?'

The use of missus feels off-key, alerting Goldie to Ben's already questionable behaviour this evening. How he's taken three bites tops of the meal he insisted on (his total loss though), setting his phone to silent because the vibrations were out of control. So many calls. Each sending a tiny tremor ticking in the corner of his eye.

'Yes. For the first couple of years of secondary.' Wolfie scrunches his face up. 'If I remember correctly, I sat on the same table as Goldie in science. Then we moved near the sea – we being me, my mum and sister. And here I am.' He shrugs his shoulders and stops talking, like he knows this routine, comfortable with what he's prepared to give away, and Goldie admires his boundaries. Admires pretty much the whole lot of him, if she's honest.

'And Wolfgang.' Reclining his chair, Ben makes himself larger. 'It's quite a name.'

'Down to the German in my gene pool. Jamaican and Irish makes up the rest of me.'

'And Essex,' Goldie reminds him, which makes Wolfie smile, his lips framed with that moustache which just somehow rocks him up the hotness stakes.

Hotness stakes? Oh God ...

'So, married? Kiddies?' Ben presses, as Goldie rolls her eyes. 'It's only a question,' he says good-naturedly, but it leaves a sour note, adding to the weird, forced nonsense.

'I met your son, briefly, on my way in.'

'He ... he was just on his way out, too – running late,' Goldie smooths, avoiding Ben's face, knowing she'll be in trouble later.

Putting together his knife and fork, Wolfie's sudden distance has Goldie again casting herself as terrible in his imagination, caught on the strange worry that he thinks she's some sort of gaudy concubine, a person who would compromise her whole soul for comfort. Not that this dinner atmosphere is remotely comfortable.

It's because Wolfie's like her. From an ordinary background, meaning not from much, meaning you can't kid a kidder – especially when they're holding up a mirror.

Same as Ben and his cronies know their world inside out, so do they.

Neither Goldie nor Wolfie truly fit here. Ben's inherited empire has nothing in common with Wolfie's manufacturing business, all from scratch and off his own back, which is another very attractive quality.

'You'll have to excuse me – I must make the quickest call.' With his eye on the clock, Ben sweeps his phone off the table. 'International business hours. No downtime for the wicked.' Doing a Goldie, he rolls his eyes, too, before leaving the front door open a crack, his footsteps crunching back and forth across the gravel frontage as he makes his call. A clever method to cancel out his conversation.

But Goldie's had a stomachful of eavesdropping.

'Thank you for dinner ...' Wolfie stands, straightening his perfect leisurewear, the dark blue Fila tracksuit truly smart, better than smart because he's unique and can carry it. '... and your hospitality.' He dips his head in Goldie's direction. 'But I best be off. Early start.'

Boundaries. She wouldn't dream of trying to change his mind.

'D'you mind if I tell you something first, though?' Wolfie asks, hands in his pockets. 'It's something I was thinking, just crossing the road the other day. This car had stopped to let me and, I don't know, maybe eight or nine other people cross the road, speakers blasting, do you remember "Respectable"?'

Mel and Kim? Of course she bloody remembers. With a nod, Goldie smiles down at her feet, thinks of herself bossing Valeria through dance routines in their front room.

'So you know how it is then; my head's instantly bopping, I'm even walking in time to it; big, big smile on my face, and then I look around. I don't know what I was even looking for, but not one person reacted. Everyone blank, like sad robots. Which made me think, like, is anyone really living? And it hit me. How I'm on my own. Totally alone.' He watches her. 'Weird innit? Just a couple of hours round a table, and I thought, I want to tell Goldie that.'

Oh God.

'Wolfie. Please don't part with your business. None of . . .' Listening for Ben's crunchy little footsteps, Goldie lowers her voice. 'None of this is genuine.'

'Apart from you.' He heads for the front door himself. 'And I appreciate your honesty.' Wolfie glances back at her over his shoulder, with a parting look Goldie doesn't know quite what to do with, the energy between them undeniable. 'You're too good for this game you know.'

A game of what? Surely a game implies fun. Then it dawns on Goldie completely. She's merely a component. A toy. Her, Wolfie, Therese, Trevor the lickspittle, are all part of it; but it's not their game that's in play.

And as for being too good. It's easy to forget her own worth, such is the internal discomfort these days. All of which comes from being linked to Benedict Bickham.

Yet Goldie knew this moment would come – not the catching feelings part, which, for the record, she must rise above – but the saying goodbye to all of this. To the Coach House, to Ben – and quitting while they're ahead. Because forty-five is forty-five.

'You let him just leave?' Ben's become a Ribena blackcurrant in a Savile Row suit.

'How should I have kept him here then? Please tell me?'

'From my third-wheel perspective,' he says rather sneeringly, 'I do have some thoughts – and don't think you're going anywhere, because I'm not finished!' Ben barks her back into sitting. Raking his hands through his hair, he huffs, 'I can't stress how important it is that I ... Jesus Christ, for the life of me, I can't take another crying woman today.' Groaning, he sinks to his haunches, picking up a napkin from dinner which Goldie refuses to take. 'I knew it. Felt you on the turn ever since you met him.' Ben tilts her face, so she has no choice but to look at him. 'Have you forgotten Goldie, darling, all we've been through?' Very gently, he dabs her eyes. 'Everything I've done for you?'

Later, when Ben's on another call and yet to leave, Goldie tidies the kitchen. It takes seconds to load the dishwasher, wiping down the enormous oak slab of table, the tiny corner of it set for three. On the chair by the door waits Ben's bag and coat, looking imposterish. A folder called 'The Home Project' pokes out from his pile of belongings. A business card clipped to the corner; Starling-Meyer Catering Supplies and Distribution. His name, Wolfgang Meyer, underlined in fountain pen.

Goldie slips the card into her bra, skim-reading the folder. There is the picture from the new business event the other night, the group one, Wolfie and Goldie stuck on the end, throwing the whole picture out of symmetry. Her first genuine smile for ages.

Wolfie. What a strange re-entry, she thinks; running her thumb over his image.

Some pages at the back of Ben's folder have been marked up in red pen – notes in the margins of biased recruiting practices, persistent failure to address diversity targets and another picture, of the entirely white board of directors at Bickham Co. A woman – though still a Bickham – is the only female. There are three other potential new business associates alongside Wolfie, another note scribbled at the top of the page: *to pursue this gay/race/gender hat-trick.* Underlined AND with exclamation marks.

Looking at the picture of the fundraiser again, Goldie's mortified when she spots the new associates with ease, three poor souls who look as if they might tick Ben's diversity boxes centralized most uncomfortably in the front row. Wolfie, being late to the photo opportunity, was clearly spared from the same treatment. What a grotesque, disingenuous little game. And further proof of how Ben may be a man of material, but not a man of substance. Simply a controller of all the things that rock his world. Coming first. Preserving his own exceptionalism – even at the expense of others.

His world has eclipsed Goldie. The years masquerading in his spotlight, bloody hard work. The times he coached her before events, always with the same reminder to 'never mention the boy', dear Rufus, Ben's world compartmentalized – forever cold.

Back in their early days, when Goldie had googled whether boarding schools had TVs, though lots of problematic, paedo-related answers appeared in the search results, she had been left none the wiser. Decided she couldn't give a shit anyway.

Couldn't give a shit being the overall feeling she has about Ben now.

By the time she's oiled her face and got ready for bed, it's eleven forty-five, but that doesn't put her off. Knows if she doesn't text now, while her mind is set, she won't.

> **I'd like to know you, too.**
> **Again.**
> **G x**

Six

JULIA

Race Against Reality

'So much easier when separations are amicable.' Jamie sips his beer. 'I thank my lucky stars. Truly.' His speech has become the standard on each date, as though he must first go over the circumstances of how he's found himself here, sexually involved with her, while his almost-ex remains in residence at home.

Which, to date, has been the only red flag.

Yet because of every insubstantial, short-term fling Julia's ever had, equating to three decades of idiots, it's a red flag she's prepared to overlook.

'A straight, competent adult male who gets on with his ex.' Julia doesn't overdo it, just gives him the benefit of her best angles, tilting her face with a slightly open-mouthed pout. 'You're a unicorn.'

The Forest Inn is the venue for their third date. Sharing plates and genuine delight from being together again. Easy convo, though nothing earth-shatteringly intellectual. No worries on the lust front; date one took good care of that. Then came date two, laden with the hope of a repeat date one performance. And the shock that their heat returned so easily.

'I'm every man,' Jamie says. 'Totally average.'

He's not even being modest. So transparently nice that Julia feels herself tense, the urge to keep him escalating.

She pushes those thoughts away.

Jamie's talking, almost to himself, which he's probably used to. Employing the life skill of many a long-term lover, Julia tries it herself; giving a little laugh as she touches his arm, pretending to listen as if she's right there with him, that makes him stop mid-sentence and gaze at her.

'What?'

'I don't know,' he says softly. 'This all seems ... a bit too easy, doesn't it? Both of us. No baggage.' He puts a hand over hers, still resting on his arm. 'All the possibilities.'

Jamie Hughes. A forty-eight-year-old solvent professional in the early stages of divorce. A conveyancer – whatever they do. Quite the dish. Exceptionally keen, as if he'd been celibate for fifteen years instead of happily married – and such a straight player Julia hasn't the foggiest how to play him.

A very basic online presence, without any obvious deviances or secrets.

And a very clear desire to have a family.

When he'd said those words so openly on their first date, Julia had found herself a little less distant, replacing her usual aloofness so often employed, especially in early dating. Men are peculiar creatures, most expecting women to be almost psychic as to the type of relationship they're after. It is all a dance. Few do conversation, and others simply can't, but most, she's found, can always talk about themselves. So transparent, rarely durable.

But then Jamie. Just in time.

When she'd moved back into her childhood home only yesterday – and only temporarily – Julia's father had the front to suggest that Julia's problematic romantic history might be likely down to Julia herself, which was hilarious coming from him, the king of dysfunction and a serial cheater – usually with somebody half his age. But she couldn't bite back because aspirational living costs a fucking bomb.

Help and handouts are needed right now, her old bedroom too, but such a comedown from the apartment in Hammersmith. Overspending; £106k in debt. And proof how fast things can fray financially, even for a sassy metropolitan professional.

'All I know is that you make me very happy. And I'm so glad we're on the same page.' It's getting late. She could rely on her usual charisma. Or she could take the initiative. 'I best go,' Julia says reluctantly. 'Don't want to miss my last train and have my parents worrying like I'm sixteen again.'

'I bet they're thrilled to have you back. Must've been hard for your dad, looking after your mum for so long on his own,' Jamie says considerately.

Not a lie exactly. Mother's always been ill. Another thing to thank her father for.

'It's not forever. I'm happy to support them. Though I bloody miss my flat.' Leaning in for a kiss, she waits, just long enough to rouse his interest, before breaking away. 'Especially in moments like this ...'

'We ...' Jamie blows out. 'I suppose there's always mine?'

'Could we? But what about ...' Julia lets it drift, making sure to sound like she cares.

Later, in the darkness of the house, Jamie shows Julia to the living room. Closing the door, like he's relieved. 'Welcome to my crib,' he says as she looks around. 'Drink?'

'After.'

'After ...' Jamie trails off, transfixed, as Julia steps out of her knickers.

Won. So easily. Julia's hips brush against Jamie's groin. Such an instant, teenage reaction; gorgeously ego-boosting, as he leads her upstairs.

And such a gorgeous house, too.

Seven

GOLDIE

Doin' The Do

Dozing in the bath, drifting dangerously in and out of the bubbles, Goldie's sleepless night catches up with her as the hurt from last night's discovery looms on.

It's a lonely, isolating decision, yet it feels cleaner pretending she never knew the true mechanics behind Ben's 'Home Project'. Because reducing ordinary people to commodity raises another uncomfortable question, of how she herself might've been beneficial in Ben's schemes all this time. A notion which gives her the creeps. Goldie sinks beneath the bubbles, enjoying the feelings of weightlessness, the disassociation from being not only a trophy wife, but a token trophy wife.

Fuck Ben's world, truly.

Resurfacing to the sound of the door, Goldie reaches for her phone, watching, charmed, as with his hands in his pockets, Wolfie peers into the unflattering spherical camera of the doorbell as if to check it's working. With her hair in a big white towel, wearing a floor-length robe to match, Goldie opens the door to him – but only after she's moisturized.

'Sorry to just appear. I wouldn't normally, it's ... Well, after your message last night ...' Wolfie looks at her. 'I just wanted to ask what it is that you're waiting for? When you know.' His brows twist towards each other, such a gentle, kind expression that Goldie wants to cry. 'That it's time. To go.'

'I am thinking of going away.' It's as much of a surprise to Goldie when she hears herself saying it; what till now has been little more than a loose fancy of an idea. 'A few weeks in the French house to gather my thoughts – and my strength. Then back to do it. To leave him.'

Wolfie takes Goldie's hand. 'That's good you've got yourself a plan then. Because when you get back, it would make my life to take you out.' Wolfie makes sure to meet her eyes, his gorgeous smile topped by his gorgeous moustache. 'Like, with romantic intention. If ... if that might be something you wanted.'

Oh God. In floods everything Goldie remembers from old – a warning reminder too, against opening her heart. No good has ever come from an oh-God feeling, and she's certain it never will.

And yet.

With the offer of breakfast, Wolfie accepts. Goldie closes the front door behind them, giving herself a quick once-over in the mirror hanging above the drawerful of letters she's learnt to compartmentalize and distance from, just as she will with her life with Ben. Past and gone. Surely, what's most important is right now. Releasing her hair from its towel, Goldie likes the way it settles damply across her shoulders, the overall unfussiness of her natural self. All that's true. Which matches how she's suddenly feeling.

Wolfie's assembling teas when Goldie moves next to him, closer than they've ever been. Such a fluky decision, swapping to his table at the fundraiser. And maybe all the better for it. Leaning her head against his arm, Goldie wonders how to begin. It's not as if she's a novice. It's just been a long time since she considered intimacy. Sex must mean something. Clearly, so must Wolfie.

And it's time she drew her own line in the sand and broke the spell of the Coach House and Ben's hold for good. 'So,' she says to be clear. 'You're saying you fancy me?'

'I am very much saying that. Yes.'

On her tiptoes, Goldie reaches to kiss Wolfie's cheek, delighting in the smile it brings to his face as she turns his chin gently towards her, encouraging his mouth on hers as she leans into the warmth of his body, surprisingly solid.

Desire roars through Goldie like a forgotten memory, their unhurried kisses bringing the feeling clear to the surface as Wolfie slips his fingers into the knot of her dressing gown belt, easing it undone, all the guardedness of yesterday absent as he looks upon her with wonder, dipping his head, licking along her slit before devouring Goldie like he's feasting. There's a fuzzy disconnect between life and sensation that brings tears to her eyes as something gives within her; how his name right now spectacularly suits him.

She feels perfect in his hands. Moreish, and delicious, his

lovely mouth climbing her body as Wolfie leans her against the tabletop, Goldie hooking her thumbs beneath his waistband, giving him the slow eyes as she kisses him again, taking his top off, discovering a vision; enormous, intricate tattoos landscaping his arms, entire back, and across shoulders built for gripping as he pushes himself inside her for a few frantic seconds of out-of-the-ordinary bliss, everything juicy and beautiful – which proves almost too much as he pulls out fast.

'Oh my days,' Wolfie says, exhaling to collect himself as he takes Goldie in properly, in all her open dressing-gowned nakedness. 'Best I be careful.'

'Best you not.'

On the dining table, so massively immovable it barely budges beneath their efforts, immersed in the sex that's made the world quiet and – for once – honest, Goldie senses herself becoming part of Wolfie, a feeling so delicious and terrifying it reminds her of everything she's known before. When lust becomes lovemaking, more than just flesh. And the giving feels like danger.

Which is careless.

It takes her a while to recover. On the tip of Goldie's tongue to overshare how this sort of pleasure has always felt like bargaining chips, made from power games and exchanges; behaviour so fundamentally manipulative and planted so early in her head that it means she can't admit even to herself how being with Wolfie is by far the most truly connected experience she's ever had.

But neither lust nor love makes the world go round. And

Wolfie, no matter how seemingly wonderful, is still a man, with the very same potential to hurt her. Hurt Goldie doesn't think she could suffer again.

France. It lands again in her brain like a lightning bolt.

As Wolfie moves to stroke her face, Goldie flinches away, turning her back on him. Pulling her dressing gown back tight around her, she makes her decision. 'This was a mistake. You should go.'

'You can't be serious? I never thought I—' Confused, he gets up, pulling on his joggers. 'Sorry, but didn't ... didn't you feel that?' But Goldie doesn't turn around, not even when he's leaving, slamming the front door on her silence.

Done. The truest act of severance all round. Ben. Wolfie. Equally out of her system. Goldie needs to build a nest elsewhere; prove she can do it on her own. Men, as they always have, only complicate life. Better looking after herself. By any means possible. Survival is survival.

In a text, Goldie tells Ben that she's planning a trip to Antibes and she'll be back in a couple of weeks. It's not as if she's never taken herself off before. And it's not long before he texts a reply saying bon voyage. With a giant red meaningless love heart.

And then she does something even more spontaneous than breaking all her years of celibacy. Rather than texting, she rings.

Valeria.

★

Eight

Vee

When The Game Is Played On You

There are voices downstairs. Jamie's, in happy conversation, as it dawns on Vee. The new girl is here. Girl sounds a bit weird. Yet the voice is girlish, horrifyingly familiar ...

Covertly, from the upstairs landing, Vee watches them say their goodbyes; heads together, smiling sleepily at one another, coupled and soft. Gazing up at Jamie for a moment, the woman reveals her face properly, showing sharp, tiny fanged teeth, pointed like a descendant of Dracula, straight from hell itself.

But it can't be her.

Vee's heart stops all the same as she just about keeps on breathing; the moment she's forever imagined arriving like a thunderclap, sobering and sudden, as all her inner birds, sent circling in nervous flight, settle to witness the wicked reality playing out at the foot of her stairs.

Outwardly composed, yoga and hypervigilance keeping

her spine straight – the only thing still holding her together – Vee studies the woman with her arms around Jamie.

Julia.

Jamie's new girlfriend is Julia Fensby.

Thirty years anticipating coming face to face with her.

Thirty years. And Vee, braless, with morning breath, in a sleep bonnet.

Jamie and Julia part with terrible reluctance as Onion pads up to them, nuzzling her head in the nook behind Jamie's knee as Julia moves to fuss her. But knowing things, as dogs do, Onion snaps. Not quite a bite, more of a gnashing together of her own teeth. A flick of her golden head. Overt disapproval.

As Julia plays hurt.

'Onion!' Jamie says, brows raised. 'That's not like you, girl.' But it's not surprising in the slightest. Onion's reaction is confirmation.

As, for a fragment of a second, Julia's eyes flash upwards, meeting Vee's.

The second Julia's gone, Vee rings an emergency locksmith, paid for straight from the joint saver. Soon, everything – even the wedding albums from the back of the sideboard – is in her bedroom. Every piece of personal shit, from old school certificates to the utility bills, has a new home in what's become a sorry excuse of an overstuffed room, full of shit that doesn't really matter yet suddenly does. Incredibly.

Emerging from the shower, Jamie spots the locksmith working cheerily outside Vee's bedroom door.

'D'you think we should talk?' he asks, following her into the kitchen. Opening the fridge, Vee finds her punnet of strawberries now almost empty, pictures Julia in her head, nibbling on them with her small sharp teeth.

'Let's have lunch,' Jamie says. 'Clear the air. Thinking about it, I should have asked you before I, I . . .' He screws up his face. 'But look, what's the point of any awkwardness? It was bound to happen eventually.' Would his words sound any less atrociously smug to anybody else's ears? Vee fights to hold herself together. Totally together.

'Julia Fensby, right?' Vee checks first. 'We went to school together.' And Jamie's indifference is so obvious Vee just can't stop the emotion, her roaring feelings avalanching, building up behind the door she's forever had her back against. But Vee must not cry. 'She bullied me, relentlessly, for years. Ask her.'

Jamie's bemused. 'I can't just come out and ask, did you bully my ex-wife?'

'Why not?'

'Well, you've never once mentioned being bullied before,' he says, shaking his head as though Vee must've got it wrong. 'And you're forty-four for God's sake. Not twelve.'

'I was twelve when the bullying started.'

Jamie doesn't speak. Nor does he look at her.

'I lost my hair because of her. The fear she put in me.' Which led to a stammer, only disappearing once the pressure of facing Julia on the daily was behind her. The joy she'd found from turning Vee so inside out that even her words would emerge jumbled, which kept her quiet and then silent. 'I was her punch-down device.'

Briefly, Jamie's chastened. 'Vee ... people change.'
'Do they really?'
'We did.' His expression cries out for a good slap.
But of course, Vee resists.

Later, though in no less a state of shock, Vee's finger seeks out the little camera icon on her home screen, about to do what she can't believe she's not done yet but knows won't do her any good.

She's right.

Julia Fensby could be the poster child for social media, her Instagram just the right mix of perfection and PC predictable realness – the prerequisite little black square for #blacklivesmatter for example – which is laughable, especially to Vee.

How quickly people forget. Distancing themselves from the people they were. Even if Vee didn't know what a monstrosity Julia was, she's certain her spidey senses would've sniffed out her online fakery in seconds.

But clearly her followers can't. Her posts are liked in their hundreds, bookmarked, the comments sections brimming with saccharine enthusiasm for everything she shares. Consistent daily posts of an incredible life. Vee's social media is sporadic – at best; pictures of mostly food or of Onion and rarely a picture of herself, though she has a small secure presence, people who feel like friends, who, should she ever meet them in the flesh, it'd probably work out fine with.

Like Ru from Write Pub and his follow request, which appears before her very eyes. She blinks, swiping it away, an intrusion too many.

There will be no work today. Vee declares herself sick. Officially sick. Has she ever been so ill?

And how can someone who works in fucking risk insurance have 42.5k followers?

Picture after picture of Julia. Skiing, selfie-posing, bridesmaid-ing, yoga-ing, cocktail making, fucking... fucking sailing!

A very smug post of Jamie with his arm around her, dated three weeks ago; Julia a living, breathing smirk of a person, with the caption 'In my sights'. Which does just what a knife would. And though Jamie's not Vee's anymore, it must be noted, underlined, written in giant fuck-off capitals, that this is not heartbreak. Nor is it jealousy – absolutely not.

It's just that it's Julia.

Vee rereads her profile.

> **Julia Fensby:** Corporate rebel – Gemini – not *that* sort of cat person – founding member and wellness coach of 'The Me You Want to Be'.

Clicking the link to Julia's page, Vee rubs her eyes like an astonished cartoon. What unbelievable, utter shit. Life coaching packages, holistic healing sessions for corporate awaydays, wellness affiliations with big brand names. A #BeKind ambassador.

Imagine.

As fast as the rage swept in, it retreats. Leaving Vee with the small, sad feeling that she might as well have spent her whole existence screaming into a vacuum. It's been exhausting to be so frustrated, unable to fix – despite her hard-earned achievements – whatever is in her that's never enough. And Julia's lifetime of easy eternal approval only proves it.

Vee, top to toe, house included, feels contaminated, her life no longer personal nor fully hers as she begins studying her possessions that Julia must've surely examined, too, now that she's been in her space, judging, inspecting, taking the measure of.

Everything looks as it should. Vee's timeless good quality decor proves she's got her shit down to everybody, too, especially those – Julia Fensby included – who thought all this was beyond her. Vee yearns as basely and plainly as she always has, to eclipse them all, to shine so successfully it'll cause their eyeballs permanent damage; the imprint of her brilliance burnt on their retinas for eternity.

Yet is it not deeply childish to be so fixated on proving her worth to people who don't matter?

Vee can't answer. Any of it.

It's the personal items, like Vee's books, which bring the waves of true overexposure. You can judge an awful lot from somebody's bookshelves. And just because Vee's most telling reads are upstairs in her bedroom, that doesn't mean Julia's nosing couldn't possibly extend there in the future ... Vee knows to her core that given the chance, Julia wouldn't be able to resist. And because of that, despite the new locks and all her privacy precautions, home, in every wholesome context from Vee's impeccable taste to the fact that everything within these walls represents the only form of true stability she's ever known, crumbles.

Unexpectedly.

As Vee's life has forever been so.

The clear-the-air lunch takes place in a bar that's just opened nearby, a bit too trendy for either Vee or Jamie ordinarily, yet here he is displayed as if Vee never even knew him, wearing a red shirt that's a bit too tight, drinking an Aperol spritz instead of his usual draught ale – though he does seem a bit embarrassed by the fact, which slightly boosts her. A hint of discomfort in others is always wildly soothing.

And makes her feel a little more put together. Ice globes have worked a treat on her skin. Vee does not look remotely shocked, broken, caught out or surprised. It is also a fucking fabulous hair day, her almost black corkscrew curls hiding her shoulders like a big protective aura.

Though Vee needn't be too guarded, it's only bloody Jamie.

Inevitable that it's him out dating first, riding the wave of hot middle-age so many men do; coming across all wise and capable, their years rewarding them with an entirely socially acceptable air of maturity and experience.

'I'm so glad Jamie reached out to you,' Julia says, appearing from thin air with a light hand on Vee's shoulder, touching her hair as Vee longs to respond as Onion had when she'd snapped earlier.

Instead, everything slowly warps; from Jamie's bashful expression to his words, seeming distant as he says something like 'so we could all clear the air'– so clichéd that it provokes something ruinous in the back of Vee's eyes. Unimaginable emotion.

Because all she can do is remember.

Julia seems not quite fully real; her face expressionless, unlived in as she smiles only with her mouth, the rest of her as cold and unreachable as she'd been at fourteen.

Which very suddenly feels like yesterday.

All the films Vee's adored – and for good reason, too – the revenge tale of I'll chop your knob off, steal your job, your throne, your poor mother's bones, all in the name of payback ... all the films that she's watched with relish, enjoying every tense reckoning, have hinged on the hope that justice is served, imagining her own similarly cinematic moment, from the camera angles to what she'd be wearing, down to her own queen-like expression, as if Julia's impact on her had been microscopic.

But the moment's unexpected, and Vee forgets her lines. Smiles at Julia.

A complete betrayal of self.

Instinct has Vee reaching into her curls, pulling them longer, over the shoulder her schoolbag once sat on and got yanked at with such repetition it branded her like a burn, never able to heal before Julia would do it again.

Never getting the chance to recover. Same as Vee's inner hurt.

'It had to be one of us, didn't it?' Jamie repeats the line from when he'd first mentioned being out dating again. Back when Vee couldn't give one shit. 'Inevitable.'

Surely this wasn't his idea? Vee can't even try hiding her disgust. Jamie may be morphing into a whole other person before her very eyes, but from the way he can't quite look at her, she knows, absolutely, it was.

How dare he facilitate this?

Ordering a tonic water and a Greek salad, Vee feels a bit sick. Sweaty and disorientated, too, as Jamie clears his throat. 'Don't worry,' he says, 'Jules has filled me in on ...' With a smile he looks to Julia, now sat on his left.

'How I wasn't very kind to you back in the day.' Julia finishes for him, glancing self-deprecatingly at Vee. 'You know, you're partly the reason I do what I do.'

Her wellness bullshit. Wellness Vee's arse. Julia slips her hand into Jamie's and Vee stares at it without staring at it, all respect for him gone. All those years married, and he's completely disbelieved her. Yet he's swallowing Julia's untruths as gospel in the first five minutes of their relationship. Which reads like cruelty.

And would make them the perfect match.

Back in the day, Vee adored going to Brownies. The most normal night of the week, Granny Saunders picking her up from school, treating Vee to a Wimpy tea after. A slice of normality; Brownies, dinner and the insistence she had a bath, which always felt good and comforting, before Vee would have the best night's sleep. True rest, without listening out for Goldie's breathing, because what could be more terrible than being left alone in the world without her? Brownies were good girls, neat girls, organized and kind girls. Friendly, helpful, practical ... all the things Vee knew in her heart would make her a perfect grown-up. How she'd longed to fast-forward her childhood, frustrated by being small and so very useless.

It was at Brownies where Vee first met Julia. And when

secondary school started, being bright and streamed into the same lessons meant they formed a friendship; Vee a brief member of Julia's small adoring crew, girls who followed her everywhere, called Lucy and Laura. Girls as plain as their names Goldie would say, while Vee longed to be like them, with their mousy manageable hair, textbook parents, and TV-perfect lives.

An after-school invite to Julia's house ended when Julia's dad dropped Vee home in a car so plush and silent she'd been nervous to breathe in it, and as she'd sat in the back next to Julia, wondering why she'd been chosen by this perfect, popular girl.

Julia pinched her.

It comes to her clearly as if it's happening now. The flare of hurt which shrieked through Vee's body as Julia twisted her flesh. And how, though Vee yelped plenty on the inside, no sound came from her as Julia watched on, bemused by her non-reaction.

How they'd regarded each other then – Vee with confusion, and ... Even sitting across from her now, Vee still doesn't know, doesn't understand the expression on Julia's face. The empty look which came to trouble Vee most because it made her doubt Julia's humanity, her moral boundaries. Exactly the cold detachedness which made Vee scared in the first place, sat in the back of that car that day.

What makes bullies bully? What had been the spark, the reason which made Julia hate her so? Because there was never any true reason for Julia to pick on Vee.

Other than the fact that she could.

Had Vee reacted, as she'd have been right to, then perhaps the four years which followed might've been very different. Instead, a pattern formed of one girl's power and cruelty over another who'd never once been equipped with either of those traits. A prolonged act of hurting, without anything ever pricking Julia's conscience.

'So,' Julia says, as if the past is dealt with and they are completely okay with one another, 'what have you been doing with your life? Jamie mentioned publishing, you always were a bookworm.' She flicks her hair in the exact same manner of old, the sheet of gloss blonde cut bluntly, perfectly, as if it gets trimmed every day. From the way she wears a camel-toned lightweight rollneck with a gold bangle cuffed around its sleeve, to the simple polished nails and the flawless, lineless face, everything about Julia is effortless.

But nobody, not even Goldie, is truly this put-together.

It is not the first time the thought's occurred to Vee, how Julia might be a robot person, which would explain her absence of empathy and incapacity for kindness. The irony that she was once a bloody Brownie.

As Julia talks about women supporting women, frankly the biggest load of cacapoop Vee's ever heard, she feels the truth in Julia just as she always could; her coldness, nothing like the inner glow of spiritual awakening she's apparently discovered. And what a slippery gaslighter, how she's managed to use Vee's shock to paint a different story.

'Vee and I worked together on the school paper. The teachers adored her. Always so diligent, you know,' Julia tells Jamie, dropping snippets of the Vee he never knew, which he gobbles up in a way which keeps Vee quietly whitewashed, her thoughts punctuated with memories, vivid and painful. Concentrating on her knife and fork, Vee chews her feta cubes in mechanical motions, crushing them first with her tongue, unable to swallow as everything rushes back, a life flashing before her eyes.

All her bullying best bits.

Vee would bet her life that Julia wouldn't try reminiscing about the time she burnt her one chemistry lesson. How, when she'd flung flecks of liquid from a test tube at Vee's back, Vee had been too shy to disturb the test conditions. How it wasn't until the teacher asked about the burning smell and noticed Vee's silent tears that she'd bundled her into a side room where all the Bunsens were kept, asking if this was deliberate. Yet she kept silent, as Julia knew she would. The same acid burn exists now as a small change in skin texture, just across Vee's right shoulder blade. Nothing that anybody else would likely notice, except her, wearing it to this day as a reminder.

How had Vee sat there and let it happen? Her own burning flesh, and unable to utter a 'please, Miss'. She could show Jamie the scars. Reveal the truth of it. Yet the fact that she should ever need proof of her sufferings provokes the worst sort of hurt. An immovable feeling Vee doesn't think she will ever be able to get past. Along with gargantuan disappointment.

But is anybody ever who we think they are?

'Jamie was telling me about your little book.' Julia smiles cuntishly.

She must mean the anthology Vee was selected for a few years back. Which made her heart soar but never moved writing mountains. Jamie's parents had been as pleased for her as if she was their own child, which made for the most precious of feelings.

'There's a copy at home.' Swept up, Jamie forgets himself. 'My mum and dad were so proud.'

His mum and dad. Not him.

'Ah, how sweet,' Julia says, rather as if she's praising a child. 'And so good you never gave up with all that,' she adds, as though she'd been there through the lot, making note of all Vee's failures and rejections.

It takes the earth for Vee to remind herself that she can choose to respond to Julia.

Or not. All the same, it's as though Julia has the supernatural skill to see right into Vee, exposing for ridicule all that Vee tries to shield. *'Little book.'* So clever how she does it, both then and now, the tiny flip things she says which have forever left Vee unable to explain why they hurt as deeply as they do. Julia's lifelong ability to keep Vee silent, because way back then, whenever Vee tried to speak, the more stop-start her words would become, leaving her pausing for breath, to rephrase. Which was when Julia, all wide-eyed and confused, would say to Vee, 'S-s-s-sorry, I d-d-don't understand g-g-gobbledy-wog.'

Vee's first direct racism.

Remembering makes Vee's chest grow fluttery, her heartbeat irregular and somehow higher in her body than usual. So many inner confusions; impossible to trust anybody at all – which might explain Vee's chronic lack of girly mates. Because true friendship would mean her guard coming down.

The closest Vee ever came to having a real bestie was the godsend of a human she'd shared a flat with through her twenties; a houseproud, chain-smoking *EastEnders* addict, as sworn off men as she was, and who cooked and remembered her period because his mother had excruciatingly painful cycles too. But the best part was that he was kind, having been bullied himself, keeping them both in check with his high savagery and fierce protective streak. Their years together were the best of Vee's life – until he fell in love and forgot her. Back to the games of landlord robbery.

Maybe Jamie had simply been a way of breaking free from renting tiny rooms in smelly houses; the threat of men somehow more transparent than sharing with wicked girls.

Look at him now, though. Lost to the wickedest of them all. But telling him so will only leave Vee seeming jealous, and if there's one thing left which is worse than this lunch, it's that.

Dates, into nights staying over, to now meeting Vee are very real steps towards a proper relationship – and then there's the intimacy.

Her hands have been all over him. And he's been inside her.

In Julia.

The vortex fanny of evil.

A few nibbles of her falafel and off Julia flits to the loos, leaving Vee and Jamie alone once more. He gazes out of the window as if in deep interest with the goings on beyond, and though Vee's got half a salad left, she can't sit on it a second longer.

'Did Julia know I was your wife ...?'

Jamie chuckles. 'I wasn't exactly talking about you on our dates.' He shakes his head, amused, as if Vee was, as if she might always have been the last thing on his mind. 'Honestly, Vee.' He grins across the table.

Silly Vee. Honestly.

Jamie and Julia. They even sound like a match made in mainstream heaven. But was it really a chance meeting? The probability of Julia keeping their plot line active since adolescence seems impossible. Or does it?

Regardless, they're back in play. Only in this new round, Jamie, like some crucial chess piece, has been claimed by the dark side, and though he's no longer Vee's anyway, it still very much sits like game over.

In Julia's favour.

Same as always.

★

Nine

Goldie

Ex-Factor

Rufus always knocks before using his key. A polite forewarning, though usually he'd text as well to say he was popping in. Maybe he did, but Goldie hasn't wanted to look at her phone all afternoon.

When Wolfie left with a bang earlier, Goldie had returned to her same bath water, letting the hot tap run and work its magic, wondering if anyone would truly care if she sank beneath the surface forever. Drowning in opulence would be an apt end, typical, and though she's not remotely Whitney-famous, people might give her a mention in the same sad topic of bathtub finales of troubled stars gone too soon.

Star. Hard to fathom she ever was one. Overshadowed by impossible love. How, ambition aside, all she could ever think about was him. Grant Love. The origin story Goldie's no intention of ever fucking revisiting. Which was enough to make her get out of the bath, slip back into her white fluffy robe – only with underwear this time – and choose the telly instead.

But he's back in her head all the same. Taking up so much space, he eclipsed Wolfie; the glimpse of something new and good. Goldie, tainted as always by the emotional baggage she can't ever rid herself of.

It's a murky admittance, yet all the same Goldie thinks she might still love Grant. Somewhere strange and never to be said aloud. Her pledge, ever since him, has been to protect her heart. Lucky she was ever able to rescue the massacre he'd made of it in the first place. Her devastation when they were over, while his life carried on as if she'd never fully featured in any significant part of it.

Despite herself, Goldie wonders if he's thought of her since. Whether he remembers then. Remembers them.

He must. Goldie is briefly bereft.

His rejection had been more devastating than the industry's, and the loss of the fame and the money, put together. Worse even than her own mother's. The rage Goldie endured from the woman supposed to love and protect her, because Grant had been Mum's boyfriend first.

And of course, betrayal's betrayal.

But is it?

Goldie's foetal on the stiletto shoe chaise longue, watching but not watching *A Place In The Sun,* when Rufus comes into the lounge.

'You sick?' he asks, concerned.

'Not sick. Just sad.'

'You're never sad.' Opening her arms, Rufus holds her tight until she lets go. 'What's the matter?'

'Real life, I think,' Goldie says with a sniff. 'Feeling a bit raw, a bit hurt – my own doing of course.'

'Nothing to do with my dad, I hope?'

Not in the way Rufus imagines. Amazing how they are even related; thoughtful Rufus with his natural bloody empathy for others. What's perhaps even stranger is how he's now a man. It's hard shifting perspective, keeping up with time, with who people become once they are grown.

But none of us are ever truly known. It is not only Goldie.

'Yes and no. I don't say that to be confusing. But I do think the time's come for us to go our separate ways.' Goldie watches his blink-and-you'd-miss-it reaction, as Rufus stands up straight. 'You can't really be surprised.'

'Ah, it's not that. Rather just how you've always been here.' Even his sigh sounds hurt. 'It would've been so much better if I'd found out that you were my dad,' he says, making Goldie laugh as he always has.

'Shall we have some toast?' Ruffling his hair, off Goldie pads to the kitchen, taking four slices of Hovis granary from the freezer and popping them into the toaster, doing all she can not to look at the table, surprised it hasn't burst into flames.

'Maybe this will be a good thing all round,' she says. 'Time for your dad to be with your mum properly. I'm serious. He practically lives there, anyway. And Tony, surely—'

'Tony the grandfather I'm yet to meet? No offence, G, but I'm almost thirty and still Dad's dirty secret.'

'You are not that,' Goldie says fiercely. 'He's—'

'A pointless, greedy prick, with no real clue who I am.'

Opening the peanut butter, she sets out plates. He's not wrong.

'Well then snap. But you know what?' Goldie's fury returns the second she thinks of Ben luring in the less fortunate to save his reputation. 'I reckon that's probably a good thing for the both of us.'

Goldie bowing out of the triangle truly could benefit Ben, who'd be free then to fully embrace the life he wants, with the woman he's always loved. It could all be so simple, but for money, the dangled inheritance of three and a half million pounds. Double that, if his sister Camille drinks herself into an early grave. So much money in the pockets of Tony Bickham, ex-MP in their safe seat and generational wealth. If Ben can just cling on denying his own heart.

Denial of a different sort was exactly why Ben had so appealed to Goldie in the first place. There was never the 'oh God' feeling of losing control, of losing her heart; never the worry of that with him being so straight and sensible. Old money meant security. Forever. Peace of mind against all she'd earned then lost, working harder than anyone she'd ever known. Ben helped Goldie re-evaluate her punishing existence – which by then was really for nothing. Struggle wasn't the only way. She could be admired instead.

And almost loved.

Peanut butter saltiness stings Goldie's mouth, making her flinch and remember, before she turns her back on the dining table altogether. Sex has stirred something in Goldie. A muddled feeling, murky and forgotten.

'Why now, though?' asks Rufus. 'Has it anything to do with Mr Mustachio, the dinner guest?' Mr Mustachio. Wolfie's left quite the impression. On all of them. Thrilled to be right, he claps his hands together. 'Could read the chemistry a mile off.'

'Could you?' Goldie can't help herself. Replaying Wolfie's face, his touch, his love.

Not love.

'The look on him when I said you and Dad were make-believe. It was like, like ...' Rufus pauses. 'Hope.'

Goldie puts her face in her hands as Rufus beams. How terribly she'd behaved towards Wolfie earlier. Undeserved and unfair, her emotions taken out on the wrong people, as usual. She will have to put that right, and quickly.

'You totally deserve it. To be happy.'

'Bless you, child. So much. In moments like this I wish I was your dad, too.'

Goldie will miss this. Kisses his head as she gives him his toast. But the end of Ben doesn't have to mean the end of everything associated with him. She and Rufus will just have to adjust to catching up and eating toast in a different kitchen.

'I'm going away – to the France house for a bit. Before I tell him.' Goldie pauses. 'Isn't it strange, I don't know how he'll react. And I did want to put you in the picture first. Haven't you always said I sleep my life away, like a cat? I even tried ringing my sister, to see if she might want to come with me.'

'And what'll you do when you come back?'

'Stay at my Gran's for a bit. She's hardly there, so I'll either modernize, or move on.' Goldie can't lie, she is thoroughly terrified at the prospect. 'To what or where, though ...'

'But you'll keep in touch, won't you?' There, just for a moment, is the little boy made of manners, full of hope himself. Who has always deserved far, far more love and happiness, too.

'Always,' Goldie replies instinctively, before she spots the pile of post on the kitchen island next to him, her stomach dropping just from the quality of the envelope sat on top of the rest. 'What's all that?'

'Picked it up when I came in.' He slides it across the worktop, confirming Goldie's hunch, his hand on her shoulder feeling ominously symbolic. 'Looking like you've seen a ghost, there, G.' As if simply thinking about Grant has caused more mail to rise from the dead.

'There's no stamp. No ...' With an enormous sense of unravelling, she turns the envelope over, ready to cry until she remembers Rufus, his covert curiosity reminding Goldie of Valeria, which annoys the shit out of her.

And so she gently gets rid of him.

Once alone, Goldie adds the letter to the rest from Vine Recordings in the dresser drawer. And as she worries for the billionth time about what they contain, knowing all the same how she can't hide forever, her most terrifying thought is whether they came direct from Grant Love himself; A & R superstar, now man at the almost top. Second in charge, and MD of Vine Recordings.

Quiet in her big house, Goldie's imagination takes over, as clear in her head as if it's playing out now – the first time she saw him, that late night Mum brought him home. Whatever Grant stirred in Goldie, just from sitting there on the sofa watching some old stand-up, was the moment she turned from being a kid into ... not grown-up, but something else. A duality within which she only right then became aware of. How everything about him, from his physicality to his energy, made Goldie hot; her blood noisy, thumping beneath her skin – though he'd barely looked at her.

And right so.

Smiles and smooth elegance, from his fingers to his feline, beautiful eyes; from the moment Grant held her in their gaze, Goldie never recovered.

Still hasn't.

But it's 2025, for God's sake, not 1995.

1995. The electricity that made for such power in his favour, Goldie would do anything he wanted. To her detriment, mostly. And for far, far too long. Goldie wonders if he's changed. What time does to a man who back in the day, flew ageless. An impeccable, successful grown-up who could have whatever he wanted. And did.

It could be as easy as a Google search or downloading Instagram and typing in his name. But the thought makes Goldie even more queasy; in both her stomach and her tender heart. Why provoke the hurt? The damage of then became part of her forever, so why on earth risk more?

Yet Goldie must also remember that Wolfie isn't Grant. She checks herself, regrets forgetting that very much. He's not a billion years older and a billion times more powerful. He's not got a partner, nor a penthouse full of kids.

And neither is Goldie's mum his long-term side chick.

Goldie covers her face with her hands. It's becoming a habit. Everything messy and painful and closing in. And though she'd longed to ask Rufus what the man who delivered the letter looked like; she was far, far too terrified of his answer.

The very possible reality of Grant Love on her doorstep.

Back in her life.

At a little before lunchtime the following day, Goldie sits in an empty corner of the high street Costa nearest her gran's house, feeling like she's wearing everything that should belong on the inside – crucial organs included – out. Vulnerability. But talking in person is better than phones. Wolfie said that himself.

He's seven minutes late.

Goldie watches the women at the table nearest her, noting how they look around, dropping their voices conspiratorially, a questioning recognition on their faces that Goldie's seen a billion times before, when the truth is if she belted out one bar they'd realize that she wasn't a mother from the school, a fleeting face from the past or an ex-colleague, but a pop star.

Without the trimmings, obviously.

The second he steps through the door, Wolfie's eyes meet hers. Hands in his pockets, he raises his shoulders in greeting, like a proper geezer. Made from graft and little else. In his leather coat, turned up at the collar, he makes his way over.

Wolfie Meyer. After years of fakery, a proper connection again. Human to human.

That slipped effortlessly into so much more.

Goldie sips her tea, remembering his armfuls of Archers and lemonades, the very thought of it now tinged with all she remembers when drinking it as a girl; a weariness, heavy in her chest, that she can't quite account for, as if the fun's done.

Yet Wolfie is here – and surely that's a good sign.

'I'm so sorry. About yesterday,' Goldie begins. 'It's been so long since . . . and I . . . reacted so immaturely.' She stops, tries collecting herself, can't sit still now he's in front of her. Back where they both come from.

'Let me get some water.' Returning with two tall glasses, and before he's sat down, Goldie speaks again, without knowing if they are the right or wrong words.

'You remember what it was like for most people living around here? I don't know about you, but we never had much growing up.'

'Us as well. Strange even being here again. I've not had much reason to, since we left.' He looks out onto the high street, considerably sanitized since his own stint, before giving her a little nod. 'Go on.'

'Getting signed meant money,' Goldie says. 'I never had any delusions that I was the next Mariah or Ms Lauryn, but I was good. And hand on heart, I truly believed that my talent was the reason I got my contract. Honestly, it was the most incredible thing, to look after myself. Treat my sister, you know? I even paid off my gran's mortgage.' Falling quiet, Goldie glances across the street to that very house, where she and Vee had lived throughout their teens. Ensuring the security of home was one of the best things Goldie ever did.

'But in all that time, what I never saw was how they – the record company – were exploiting me, too. Even down to how I got my initial foot through the door.' She takes a deep breath. 'Because of Grant.'

From her bag, Goldie retrieves her letters from Vine Recordings and places them on the table.

'He was my manager. On-off boyfriend.' Chief exploiter. 'Stuff that as a grown woman I should totally have worked out by now – and these arriving hasn't exactly helped. I'm scared to open them,' Goldie admits. 'It's a time I'd rather forget, which is sad, when those years were also the most brilliant, too. And then there was me wanting to leave Ben but at the same time being scared to. But . . . I suppose this is where everything stems from.'

Looking at the letters, Wolfie notes the dates, the earliest from January 2023. Over two bloody years ago.

Goldie's always suspected that people only love her because they have to. Valeria, because she's her sister. Rufus, because she was nicer than Ben. And Ben himself? Aside from the masquerade, Ben's only ever loved the fact that none of his circle could believe that he'd pulled her. Ben arrived on Goldie's scene at the stage many a woman goes through; the pre-prescribed panic of turning thirty, the ultimate societal failure of being left of the shelf, Goldie neither old enough nor wise enough to yet see through it.

Another influence had been Valeria, suddenly so happy in her pairing with Jamie. Ben had seemed the ideal solution. To protect her neck. Choosing safe at last. People have married for a lot of worse reasons. Plus, the Waitrose deliveries and trips to the salon, the fact she's never even seen her credit card bill, avoiding all the daily admin that's always made her mind scramble round the edges. How simple it was, settling into the role of Lady Muck, a perfect avoidance from the humiliation of being too bloody young and too bloody willing to make her dreams come true by any means possible.

'So, there's been all this going on in my head. And then ... you. Everything I felt ... that I'm feeling, well ... it's confused me.' Filled with sad premonition, Goldie wants to cry. 'I've been on my own for such a long time that I think, I think ... I'd just got used to it. Same as when I lost my creative value. Nothing synthetic ever truly stands.'

'You weren't synthetic. Bloody hell, you were energy. And incredible,' Wolfie says, as Goldie's chin wobbles with emotion. 'Are incredible.' He sighs. 'Isn't it strange, in all our reminiscing, we've not truly talked. There's so much I wanted to ask you.'

Wanted to ask.

'Well, go on then,' she prompts him. 'Anything you like.'

'Goldie, aka, Goldilocs, aka "Golden Born". "Free Me, Be Me".' Wolfie says after a moment, acknowledging the titles of her songs. 'Three massive hits. Then nothing.' Here comes the question every motherfucker wants to know. 'What have you been doing with your talent all these years?'

Does anybody ever ask Kate Bush what she's doing? Or Enya, sitting up in her castle with her cats?

It's another long story Goldie's not keen on having to tell.

But that's not how getting to know somebody works.

'Look, my gran's is bang opposite.' Seizing the moment,

Goldie nods across the street to the house on the corner. 'I hate coffee. And coffee shops. And well ... I think things might make a bit more sense if I show you.'

Outside, the damp day has Wolfie's mullet curling ferociously at the nape of his neck, Goldie watching with affection as his hair slowly shrinks just as hers does. Crossing through the usual traffic, she lets them into the three-storey end of terrace, just on the turning of Saunders Road. Though the area's significantly nicer than when they'd lived here, even back then it hadn't been terrible. Just a bit run-down and neglected, same as most overspills.

Gran's house is just the same. Stuck in 1993. Primary colours and *Changing Rooms/Home Front* DIY home decoration projects. Black iron candleholders against brilliant yellow walls, blue curtains and Aztec print cushions. And temporary storage.

'Christ,' Wolfie says the moment he clocks the boxes which have overtaken the living room. 'What is all this?'

'All this' is mostly skincare, cosmetics and hair products, most functional living space lost for some time behind the deliveries of styling equipment, replacements and refills. Goldie's worked it out, and her stash should last about two years, because products have shelf lives just as she does. Future-proofing herself beyond that is what the £16k under Gran's mattress is for.

It's an exposing move, but Goldie wants to show him. Wolfie follows Goldie upstairs.

'You see?' Flipping the mattress down, she neatens the covers, thinks they smell a bit stale as they leave a funny film on her fingers. The room too long unlived in. 'This was all preparation.'

'You don't have to prove anything. Especially not to me.' Goldie senses how he's thought better of it yet can't stop himself from stroking her face. 'It's good you've covered your back, but it wasn't what I meant.' He looks sad. Staggeringly handsome. 'It's just . . . you being you in that Jane Austen pad in the middle of Epping Forest, twiddling your thumbs for God knows how long.' Wolfie searches her eyes. 'Well surely you must've been more than Ben's . . .'

Cheerleader, chaperone, fake wife, hot wife, trophy wife.
Lonely wife.

Telling Wolfie the truth means he'll be the only person to know. About Goldie's sole link, other than Valeria, beyond the Bickham bubble. Because in a separate, secret savings account, is another £37k. Enough to live here ordinarily for the next couple of years.

When Goldie's contract ended and the music died, there was only one colleague at Vine who she kept in contact with. Mr Maybe; a kind, married, entirely non-threatening bear of a man, completely committed to his craft. An acclaimed producer, who in the aftermath of Goldie getting dropped, kept their communication open enough so that in time – because it was only going to be a matter of time, Goldie never not musically fascinated – when she got creating again, there'd be an outlet already established. And so, in complete secret, for years Mr Maybe has syphoned Goldie's musicality through him; baselines, verses.

But not singing. Never her voice.

The stream of income is independent money. And though it's taken forever to accrue, while Mr Maybe coins it in claiming the lion's share, everything in his name, it is still earned, hers, and to date, untouched ... £37k.

What would it be like though, to see her name once again on the credits of an album, to be involved, acknowledged in lyrics, arrangement – even production, though Goldie's technical skills have stayed basic, completely limited to the cutting-edge tech of around 1995, the 'space-deck' as she called it, when Grant would put in his hours at the recording studio, and Goldie was first in the background, long before she was in the booth. Self-taught through watching him, the flicks of switches, the way the controls were instruments in themselves, an art, as she scribbled and scribbled a double album that then condensed into three songs – and isn't this all exactly why she'd rather not think about it? Why she'd rather hide the sorry story away in a drawer in a comfort zone?

For decades.

God. There was so much more to come from her. More than the textbook template they tried pushing her into, because the people at the top preferred a cardboard repetition of what had worked before. Cookie-cutter success.

Money, money, easy money.

Left to her own vision, her own creativity, who knows where she could be now.

'Still. It's nice to know my influence is out there, even if I'm not,' Goldie explains, feeling as if she's delivered a speech. 'Whenever I catch a lyric, or a rhyme that came from me,

I feel like a mother might feel.' A good mother, anyway. 'Proud how something I've created is out thriving in the world.'

The truth, though selfish – better than the altruism and even better than the money – has been the tiniest fraction of a view where Goldie's dream might've lived on, had she stayed a part of the world she loved, working properly on the inside of the industry. What-ifs and Mr Maybe, her pet name for him, because he gave her that small view, maintaining her musical longevity without anyone even knowing she's still part of the business.

Which is quite the achievement. And even sounds quite bold, said aloud.

So, now Wolfie knows.

'The night of that new business fundraiser ...' Goldie may as well tell him the lot. '... I'd switched table seats, had overheard some things; final, unignorable things. I don't believe in fate. But I do believe it's important to stay awake to what gets put in front of you. What might be ...' Stopping, she closes her eyes, knows in her heart where this is heading. Rejection. The same devastation repackaged as her fault. 'I'm too much, aren't I?'

'I don't think you could ever be too much.' Wolfie's eyes are full of feeling. 'I appreciate ... thank you, for explaining. And though I get it, the truth is I've not been in a good place myself ... for a very long time. Your life is complicated. And me, well ... I don't think my heart could take any more than it has already.'

Wolfie means she is complicated. Tainted by the ex-factor.

By the history he doesn't want to know about. The mess which belongs only to her.

'We carry a lot, don't we?' What foolish notion had she been hoping for? That he might ...

What – swoop in? Become the next saviour? The blast from the past to reset all the damage? Sitting upright, Goldie remembers herself. She is not her mother. She does not need a man to save her. 'Which is completely the same for me, too. I'm not ready. I might not ever be. I'd just rather there wasn't any bad feeling. Because I really like you.'

Adored what happened between them. The way he'd looked at her.

How he's looking at her now.

'Don't be a stranger, Goldie Fliss-Burden.' Kissing her cheek like it's been his great honour, Wolfie walks away, another person now carrying a piece of her around with them, which feels the most unfair loss.

Yet as soon as the front door closes, it opens again.

Returning an entirely different piece of Goldie with it.

Ten

VEE

1980

Before Julia re-emerges from the lavs, Vee vanishes, hopping on the first bus that swoops into the lane in front of her, wanting to put as much distance between herself and the smuggos as she can.

Simmering in a seat halfway up the bus, Vee holds her elbows in a vice-grip.

What's all the fantasizing been for? Imagining encountering Julia again, Vee on the front foot, with the nice home, dream career – and let's not forget how well she's kept herself, in the same size jeans today that she was wearing at twenty-five years old. How it went without saying that in every one of these fantasy encounters with the vicious past, Vee would find Julia now to be totally miserable. Totally ugly. And totally lonely, too, living a shit life because she was a total shit of a person.

Rather than looping the town and coming back on itself through the new-build estate, the bus moves towards the main road, picking up speed as it takes the slip road, heading in the direction of where they used to live, as Vee sits passive, letting the bus deliver her back to where she came from, which would only take thirty minutes in the car but well over an hour this way ...

What else has she got to do? Isn't she sick anyway? Giving herself over to the journey, Vee stares out of the window, and before overthinking gets the better of her, feels herself slowing down, the repetitive rumble of the engine moving soothingly through her body as she closes her eyes.

It must be a rare thing for a bus route of such meaning to exist in such a perfectly straight line, connecting them along the way as if they'd been placed strategically apart, from Vee's, direct to Goldie's Barbie Coach House – still living considerably closer to Saunders Road – and how the bus passes by there, too, practically stopping outside, before it carries on to the very beginning. The first home.

Even with her eyes closed, Vee pictures it all; their small low-rise flats above a parade of shops, a short walk from the train station, the supermarket, the Wimpy and Percy Ingle's bakery. Remembering the brick buildings, all dirty, everything dirty in the eighties, ingrained old brick filth. She'd hoped to go to the good school, even passed her eleven-plus, but it was too much effort for Mum who instead enrolled her in the sprawling comprehensive Goldie already attended, in the catchment nearer to Gran's.

Leaving primary school had been like having her heart ripped out, especially when they began staying with Gran for longer and longer spells. It seems very dramatic, the absolute grief Vee felt for even the most basic geography, the familiar order of shops, and how the landscape, her forever blueprint, was taken from her.

Vee opens her eyes, knowing exactly where she is. Decides to get off.

Rupert Street. Otherwise known as Memory Lane.

Here is Rupert Street Primary School, where Vee had been head narrator in four plays and though she never had a best friend, she was never lonely at playtimes.

Vee pictures herself getting collected from this very spot, just outside the school gates, always the last one waiting; so well-behaved the teacher once said how she didn't know she'd got her – adding, most pointedly, that neither did her mother. Looking along the street, Vee feels again the tug on her wrist from Mum pulling her in the direction of home, claiming Vee's teacher would likely never have a boyfriend making her late, especially with an arse like hers. *'Mark my words, Valeria, no one wants a fat girl.'* Parents of the 1980s, supremely unaware of the life-long dysfunction from their words.

For a week of voluntary work experience, Vee had returned to Rupert Street Primary, the nearby school her easiest option, which would look good on her CV. Imagine, worrying about your curriculum vitae at fourteen bloody years of age? But it hadn't been easy at all. The never-ending 'why?' questions, and the never-ending yards of snot, every child too tactile, with their unwashed hands, all wanting to speak first. Vee remembered the same irritation from when she was small herself; how she was not like the other children, who seemed aimless and highly strung, full of misplaced energy, while Vee was already observing, imagining, or disappearing into the book corner.

Longing to be grown.

The school bell makes Vee jump in recognition. A fire alarm – Vee suddenly uncomfortable about standing there, staring through the fence as kids spill into the playground, being barked at not to run, and how this is only a practice. A boy who's disregarded all the rules is front of the line, ignoring the 'leave your belongings and exit in an orderly fashion', clutching everything he owns. Pity the person who tries separating this lad from his snacks and colouring pens. He turns, catches Vee smiling, and is exactly the prompt she needs to carry on walking. Towards the first home.

The two-storey flat above the old chippy has had a glow up, and so has the chippy below, now a Chicken Cottage. The Londis is still a Londis, but the laundrette has been repurposed into a vape bar. Their old bamboo blinds are a thing of the past, too, and the flat has new UPVC windows. A new front door with a brass cat's backside and tail for a knocker. Upmarket for the up-and-coming, never quite London sprawl. Same old grayscale pebbledash, though. What can be done to jazz up pebbledash, other than perhaps a blue plaque? If not for Dad's brief stay here, then for Goldie.

Amos Fliss's presence in Vee and Goldie's lives had been fleeting; his name never on the bills or registered at the local doctor's surgery, and so despite her better judgement, Miri, their mother, hadn't put his name on their birth certificates either. It made sense to do things solo, especially when trying to claim housing benefit; all dad's touring, trying to get noticed, meant he was with them very rarely, anyway. All Mum truly had as proof of their relationship was a handful of photographs. And two daughters who looked just like him.

Mum would spend hours in her wicker armchair by the window, ever hopeful of something, anything, to distract her away from the daughters she thought would anchor Amos to her forever, but never did. Where the armchair came from Vee never knew, but it was high-backed, like a giant fan. And her favourite topic, aside from herself, was Amos. She'd talk of how they met, the whirlwind romance; her the budding actor (groupie) and him a budding legend of the musical sort. But Miri wasn't Mrs Fliss, wife of Amos Fliss aka Master-Fly the Great. She was just his baby mother. An on and off option. And while she played wifey, pining away till he returned from gigs and months on the road, she suspected he was with other women, playing similar roles with them, too.

Of all Mum's rose-tinted stories, the tale Vee hated most was the one that was all true. A story Goldie would cover her ears for, about the shock plane crash, the tinpot danger of a jet which fell from the sky, that no one knew about nor noticed until Master-Fly's absence at the concert he was the opening act for. Gone, just as people had started to sit up and take notice of him as a serious talent, forecast as the next iconic thing; a Gil Scott-Heron 'Black Bowie' type, though a poet first and foremost. Critics, unable to define him, fell into lumping him in with the white male artist who was also unique and unpigeonholeable.

Master-Fly barely got a glimpse of his potential success,

though he'd put in the hard work, his debut album, the collection of loose songs now considered so intrinsic to the times, a Black American trying to break through in London, returning to the States for the opportunity of a lifetime, and never setting foot on stage.

Weird to think someone so astonishingly famous is her own flesh and blood.

Weirder being related to two famous people.

Goldie's arrival on 25th December was family folklore – described as a gift from God. And just as baby Jesus had been gifted gold, so it seemed had Amos Fliss and Miri Burden. Wiping her bloody newborn head clean revealed springy golden hair, declared by Dad as a sign that she was special.

So special, that Goldie was barely three days old when he went back to gigging, and Mum was left livid and abandoned. But on the road was no place for a baby. And a baby had been what Mum wanted.

He was back just a few weeks later. Mum less angry by that time, and glad to see him, Dad cross because Gran was looking after Goldie over at Saunders Road, and he'd missed her. But things must've worked out, because during that little welcome home spell they made Vee.

Arriving perilously premature on 1st September, like autumnal doom, like the Sunday dread of a looming Monday, and with none of the show of showing up on Christmas Day.

How very Vee.

Without knowing quite why, Vee takes out her phone, snapping a picture of their facelifted flat, zooming out to capture the parade of shops before she swaps to film a thirty-odd second burst of footage, which takes in nothing special apart from the tree Vee walks into. She presses her palm against the bark, questions if she's ever touched it before. Never noticing the tree until now, whether it had always been there, growing alongside her, but never leaving.

This early part of Vee's history has always felt as if she's watching the story of her life on TV, without participating in any of it. Memories, apart from the stark and shocking standout ones like Dad dying, don't evoke any true emotion, which is probably a good thing, psychologically self-taught trickery to feel so detached, especially from her parents, who were only ever adults suiting only and always themselves.

It's a terrifying lottery, hit and miss, the sort of parents we're dealt.

Here is the secondary school. Vee finds her fingers again twisting into her hair. It had been in her first few months here, when it dawned on her how thoroughly alone she was. Goldie was that bit older, naturally cooler, and Vee was the lost soul, her neat little reputation of 'year-six-good-girl' null and voided, replaced with the growing unease of not knowing who she was or how to fit. She'd watched Julia's besotted little group from a distance, and despite herself, despite the pinch, longed for her friendship. So beautiful, and charismatic, too; how Julia spoke with such assuredness, as though she'd never been corrected, nor talked over. Never told she was a drain, a mistake, a noose.

A burden.

What enormous contrast there was between Vee's absent parents and those like Julia's, bestowing cars as birthday gifts or the reward for passing exams. No scrimping and saving and begging for lessons. Just everything ahead lined up in easy reach.

Whereas Vee ... From day one, struggling. To be seen, loved, listened to. Yet resentful now at forty-four, how she'd held herself for so long responsible for her own shortcomings, when it was the world, and poverty and her parents, while her peers, especially the wealthy ones, were never the equals she imagined, but profiteers of a system forever in their favour. Gliding off to uni because it was simply the presumption that they would, not the first person in their family to go, to break the mould, to become entrapped in the web of trying to fit there too, another bizarrity on the social hierarchy of learning how to navigate herself, Vee caught in the intersectional crosshairs by so many labels it made her queasy. Knowing the correct masks to wear and the right heads to swap. The chronic exhaustion which comes from pretending. Too much time trying to prove herself, yet every time she did, something else crucial splintered within, slipping away, approval mattering more than her soul. And just when Vee had started making good progress, beginning to extract herself from it, the biggest nemesis mindfuck of mindfucks turns up to kick the shit out of all her mature logic.

It is not 'Vee behaviour' when she checks first for witnesses, before gobbing most neatly at the Davis Hobbs Academy school sign, watching with satisfaction as her spit hits the O of Hobbs, which would never have happened if anybody was watching.

Vee keeps walking. Everywhere looks so small. And much,

much cleaner, like round here in general. Tidier roads, and tidier looking people populating them, weaving through the pavements, busied in their own worlds.

As the road in front of her widens off, Vee thinks about the time she'd spotted Gran aimlessly wandering the aisles of that very Asda just across there near the industrial estate, realizing, as she watched Gran's trolley wheels veering towards the shelves, her mouth slightly open and her thoughts elsewhere, how she was just another helpless human – which might've marked the moment Vee's world came caving in. Terrified that if she was ever going to survive, then it was all on her, and made for the constant hypervigilance, and the overriding desire not just to succeed . . .

But for true stability.

Wasn't stability why Vee resisted her creative streak for so bloody long anyway? Could never imagine herself drifting with the same flighty misdirection as her sister. Vee craving order, plans, achievements. A ladder to climb.

Here is the library. Entering, Vee drifts unthinkingly to the kids' section, and as the smell of old pages warms her bones, knows this is where her heart lives. Sitting on a tiny plastic chair, she takes out her phone, typing industriously an outpouring of words that reaches the capacity of her notes section, so Vee copies and pastes into an email, sending it back to herself, immediately empowered, which is better than actively putting herself back in the bullied box. Choosing the category of victim.

No more.

*

Buying herself a massive hot chocolate, Vee looks through the window of a travel agent's as she waits for the return bus home: Florida, seven nights, £1,299; Greece, self-catering, four nights, £599, thinking who uses travel agents these days, but also how the deals make her prickle with temptation, just from the thought of beach cocktails, blistering heat and a place where no one knows her – anything to get away from Jamie. And Julia.

Vee doesn't feel remotely ready to go home. The thought of their smuggery turning her stomach. You think you know someone ... Dropping out of the queue, Vee walks with determination up the street, knowing suddenly the perfect place to give her some space.

Even before Vee's got her keys out, she hears voices inside Gran's. There's a light on, too. Backing around to the side of the house, Vee listens to more noises coming from somewhere downstairs. Burglars. Squatters?

Squatters or burglars, who speak to each other most gently. Like a couple might.

Suddenly Vee's not so alarmed anymore.

Goldie's here, too – only she's with a man. Making out his silhouette through the frosted glass, Vee hears, 'Don't be a stranger, Goldie Fliss-Burden'.

His voice is unfamiliar. Nothing like the deep drone of Benedict, Goldie's husband. Whoever this is sounds a bit like them – or rather how Vee sounds when she's unselfconscious and ordinary. A bit common.

It's gone quiet again. Are they kissing? And bloody déjà vu

too, because how many times has Vee stood eavesdropping on Goldie and some ...

She's having an affair. No doubt about it. Which is just typical.

Vee watches the man leave, forensically taking note. Super tall. A leather jacket turned up at the collar, in a buttery brown that has her thinking of 1970s New York disco. Trendy – how on earth have mullets made a comeback, moustaches ditto; and yet. Vee must admit he wears it all very well.

Letting herself in, Vee makes Goldie jump, with the repeating thought of disco as she takes in Goldie's *Charlie's Angels* inspired blow-out blow-dry, the animal print catsuit and enormous raincoat in an expensive shade of vanilla beige. High-tops and leg warmers. Nothing changes. Though she is a bit heavier in the face. Astronomically beautiful – and then more so when she beams at Vee, surprised to see her, too, back round Gran's.

But Goldie's smiling face falls into concern as she takes in Vee, her eyes, as they always have, giving her heart away. And it's like they're going backwards, the years rewinding; Vee ever overemotional, and Goldie the reluctant nurturer.

It all feels a bit too much.

'Tea?' Goldie offers.

'There won't be any milk.'

'Maybe some long-life?' She even sounds shifty. Has she been using Gran's as a sin bin? How long for? As Goldie puts the kettle on, Vee sits, choosing her old place around the table for four. Stretching her legs out, she rests her feet on the chair opposite, the seat which even way back then was never, ever in use.

'Don't sugar it, G. I've not taken sugar for thirty years, at least.'

'Well today you look like you need it.' For a moment, Goldie's face is a flash of their people; Mum, Gran, the maiden aunts. Arms-length care.

'Yeah?' Steam fills Vee's nose from the mug put in front of her. 'You're not wrong.' Goldie's bloody rubbish at covering her tracks, has clearly been here; there's a half-opened pack of dark chocolate digestives, and an empty smoothie bottle – wheatgerm and bio something that Vee can't quite read from this distance. Next to a small pint of red top, with about an inch left. 'So, who was lanky legs?'

'Lanky legs.' Goldie smiles, sitting in her old seat as well instead of choosing Gran's or never-here Mum's. Vee wonders if she gets the strange feeling too. The past and all its shadows closing in, as she reaches for Vee. 'I've been thinking about you, Valeria. Tried ringing the other day—' She stops talking. Watches Vee pull her own hands out of reach. 'I know what you're thinking. Wolfie's a friend. And I'm far too tired for romantic nonsenses.'

'Wolfie?' Despite the upset of her day, Vee lets out a single howl into the ceiling.

'Bloody hell. Stop, would you?' But Goldie's not truly cross. 'Look at us, back in the nest. All we need now is for Gran to appear and cook us her three-way potatoes.' A staple of their childhoods – whatever frozen convenience was lurking in the chest freezer; a couple of croquettes, a quarter bag of French fries, six sad smiley faces trapped in an icy corner, desperate for defrosting. All incinerated together in the oven till their bottoms turned black, then covered in tomato sauce. 'Have you heard from her?'

'A postcard. About three weeks ago.'

'Same.' Gran; the woman who turned making up for lost time into a life choice. Six years ago, she won big on the scratch cards; 35k a year for life. Now she simply cruises, has been round the world twice, and when she gets to her last dregs of winnings, she returns to Saunders Road and falls into her old ways to make ends meet – till the cheque from Camelot comes in again. She deserves it. Getting dressed up every night, making friends. Life's so much better when you ain't looking for love.

And when you stop giving a fuck. Will that ever happen for Vee?

'Please don't cry.' Goldie stands, and giving in, Vee falls limp into her arms. Without hesitation she holds her close, as Vee clings back. 'Is it Onion?' Goldie's own voice wavers now. 'Jamie?'

Vee's yet to tell Goldie how she's getting divorced. Can't think of anyone, other than Jamie's parents and – oddly – her dentist who she has told. No confidante. Just her professional world, a dog and an ex-husband, who thus far has been an excellent friend. But if Julia sticks around. Is permanent . . .

Spilling seems overburdening, though Goldie's far too astute to fall for any outright bluffing, especially where she's concerned. Pulling away to blow her nose, Vee stands, wandering into the living room. Putting on the big light, she's confronted by towers of boxes, mostly from Amazon.

'Temporary storage,' Goldie says, as if she's been practising in the mirror.

'Why d'you need extra storage when you've got a house the size of a castle?' Vee asks, full-on suspicious as to what Goldie's up to. But who really knows anything about anyone? 'And who is this Wolfie?'

Goldie's quiet for a bit. 'I told you. He's an old friend,' she says. 'Very nice. Very normal.'

'Not your usual type, then.'

'What is my usual type?' Goldie bites, surprising Vee. And though it's on the tip of her tongue to describe say Grant Love, with all the facial perfection of Ashley Walters, something stops her. 'You just can't help nosing. And you know nothing, Valeria.'

'Well, that's always been your choice,' Vee says, all clipped and cutting, wishing she hadn't. 'Nothing changes, does it? Not truly. You're still gorgeous. I'm still weird...'

'You know, for as long as I can remember I've wanted to shake you. Bring down that wall of yours,' Goldie says, as if they'd had the same conversation that very morning. The wall Vee's constructed around herself so carefully, so that no one can ever know her.

Except Goldie. Goldie knows Vee. Better than anyone.

Goldie and Valeria Burden – or Vee, as became easier (for who?). The Burden sisters, in name and nature, or 'them girls,' always lumped together, duplicated, despite their myriad differences, never not talked about as anything other than a problem, or an unwanted responsibility. The moment Goldie turned sixteen she was gone, with a new charmed life ready to step right into. And hurt as it had, Vee understood.

'I'm concerned. That's all,' Goldie tries.

'I'm concerned, too. Poor Benedict.'

'Poor Benedict? You know nothing, Valeria,' Goldie repeats. 'And you've always been far too judgy.'

'Where are you going?' Vee asks, suddenly lost, as Goldie stands, doing up her coat. 'Can, can I stay with you?'

'Course you can. If you tell me why.'

Her reply makes Vee think of Gran. 'If you can keep out of bother, and not come a-pestering me,' she mimics, a little bit too well, 'we'll be good.'

'Girls need their space. Even the old ones,' Goldie adds, because she knows what comes next. 'Would've been nice, though, wouldn't it, to feel wanted on occasion? Even now I feel like I've outstayed my welcome here.' She sighs. 'I'll ring a cab.'

'Let me go and grab some stuff.'

Goldie's baffled. 'What could you possibly want from here?'

Instead of answering, Vee heads upstairs, confronted with her younger self once more. The back bedroom she once shared with Goldie smells damply familiar, with the same window condensation that Gran tried to control, rolling old towels into fat sausages she laid lengthways along the window ledges to absorb. Double aspect. That's how Vee once wrote about this room, when she'd describe it in all her many, many notebooks full of stories.

Three years of sleeping three feet from each other, in this room with its sloping ceiling, their beds twinned and parallel, tucked in the eaves, the built-in cupboard as deceptively enormous as it used to be as she pushes aside old coats and winter storage, unearthing The Dress. Still here, Vee thinks in amazement, on the discovery of the wedding gown that Gran's clearly never stopped storing for the owner who never had the room for it. As a smaller girl, long before she lived here properly, Vee would hide in here, sitting for hours in the itchy lace, making up stories about the lady she'd never met who wore the dress on a day which meant so much, only for it to end up in somebody else's wardrobe. Vee had never wanted to try the dress on, hated when Goldie did, being Madonna 'Like A Virgin' mad, of course, writhing on Gran's bed with a side ponytail of mad overbrushed blonde fluff, an image making Vee cringe now she's an adult, but was an insight into the future if you think about it; Goldie's early pop star practice, whereas Vee ...

With shaking hands, Vee pulls at a plastic box, brittle and milky-white with age, full of old birthday cards and Mum memorabilia that she shoves aside without a second thought, because here they are, notebook after notebook, her big blue A4 diaries. And the scrapbooks. Six meticulously kept albums of Goldie's public movements, from when she'd been a public figure. A pop star. Her first interviews for *Select* and *Smash Hits* magazine – a follow up piece to her debut single; everyone who knew her stunned silent by the girl least likely. But she'd made it.

Pride blooms in Vee, the same as it always has, remembering the time when Goldie had been literally everywhere; from magazine covers and London Underground ads, to the enormous front windows of every HMV, Virgin Megastore and Tower Records around the country. And Malaysia. According to Vee's newsfeed, which unsettlingly knows all the things she purposefully keeps internalized, Goldie's hit songs are now timeless classics.

Vee's momentarily mesmerized, until Goldie's baby-faced photos begin putting strange pangs in her chest. The sideways glances off camera, as if in sexy contemplation, in a way which now feels awkward. A bit like Britney chewing fluffy pens in her school uniform does. The same way so much does, in hindsight.

Clapping the scrapbook shut, the whole stack of them gets shoved aside, too. Vee must not be distracted. Is here to recover her own records, to prove ... what exactly? That everything she's carried all these years is real. That Vee's not imagined ...

She finds what she's looking for; the smooth fake leather cover, and imprint of old biro she traces with a finger. Vee's dents, by Vee's hand. All these filled pages, and written variations of herself. Penning imagined futures, ones where she'd fit in the world perfectly, and never feel the wrong shape, or lacking, or an inconvenience ever again.

That was the plan. She'd been so close.

But Vee's 1995 page-a-day diary holds little more than empty sentence after empty sentence. Pretending on the page, even to her most private self. Vee scans it through, hopeful of a glimpse of something honest, skipping forward, knowing almost to the day where she'll find life at its very worst, realizing she's holding her breath. Has she misremembered? Doubted her own core memories, almost as if she's gaslit herself? How apt and incredible for Vee to have discovered yet another method to self-punish.

But then. A sentence at the end of 19 November's entry. Like a real person has picked up the pen at last.

I don't know who I'm trying to kid.

Vee must've been upstairs for such a long time that Goldie comes to find her. 'I'm overheating in this coat. Taxi will be five minutes. Can we go, please?'

With one great heft Vee picks up her box, one side of it splitting, but not enough to be serious.

Goldie nods at the diaries. 'Are you binning them at last? Don't bloody recycle them, God knows what's in them.' She looks worried, making Vee again think of Grant Love and all she doesn't know about her sister.

Vee never got caught in boy hype, nor had crushes – other than on Keanu, which was and still is understandable. Being swept off her feet always felt too reckless. Far too unplanned and unpredictable. So unlike Goldie, who'd been barely a teenager and already surrounded by male specimens, her sexuality second nature.

Which, by the look of her, is going nowhere. So voluptuous and beautiful. The light in her that never falters in its brilliance. Setting the box on her old bed, Vee hugs her again.

There's a sad nostalgia about Goldie as she looks around. 'Weird innit? Both of us here. Can't remember the last time we were.'

But she can.

And Vee remembers, too. 'You were on telly the other night.'

'Was I?' Goldie sounds surprised.

'*Top of the Pops 2*,' Vee says. 'With East 17.'

Beaming from the memory, she turns to look out of the window.

Only a few nights back, Goldie's first song had jumped Vee and Onion awake, after they'd fallen asleep on the sofa together. Immediately, Vee had cranked the volume up, holding Onion's front paws for a sofa dance, thinking the whole time how it felt five minutes yet forever ago since then.

'It'll be on iPlayer ...' Vee watches her sister, noting the sudden strangeness. 'You know, it's a shame you don't do social media. You've got fan accounts, G.'

'Shut up,' she replies crossly.

'You're telling me you've never googled yourself?' But Goldie's face tells Vee that it's true. How, in 2025? Even Onion's probably googled herself. 'Why not?'

'I don't know. Don't think I can bear it. What people say these days. It's not a kind world.'

'Amazing.' Vee shakes her head. 'How you've just presumed it would be negative.' Though how dare she judge when she's the same? Because at least for Vee there's not yards of footage and a digital footprint the size of a small country to contend with.

No – instead Vee's got a current-day human reminder. Who's now fucking her ex-husband. Her world turned on its head. An upside-down disruption that's no less mind-blowing than it was this morning.

At random, Vee clicks on the account of a man walking through a London park, live streaming himself in absolute raptures after watching *Top of the Pops* 2 the other evening, all from seeing his nineties icon again, how much he loved her songs, particularly her first hit, 'Free Me, Be Me' which came out when he came out and his life had been full of anxiety. He says he'd love to tell Goldie Fliss-Burden how she still means the absolute world.

Goldie kisses the man on the screen, before giving the phone back to Vee. And with a little sigh she says, 'Cab's here.'

Turning off lights, they make their way downstairs.

It's getting late. There's work in the morning, but again Vee doesn't think she'll be able to function. Can barely remember what her job entails, as though everything that was once second nature simply isn't any longer. Getting into the taxi, Vee's sole thought is Julia. How without her diaries it would be impossible for anyone to have even a sliver of comprehension of how plain fucking cruel today's been. The humiliation. The utterly colossal feeling of ... shame. There it is again. The word coats her, just like her old surname had.

And here we are now. Square one in all the ways.

Almost.

This time, when Goldie reaches for Vee's hand, she lets her.

'Jamie and me. We've separated.'

'Really?' Goldie sounds far less surprised than Vee anticipates. 'Us too. Well, not officially, but ...' Goldie squeezes her tighter, and like the holy miracle she is, says, 'I don't suppose you fancy a holiday?'

Eleven

VEE

Independent Women

It is just past 9 a.m. when Goldie returns from the loo on board LeShuttle. 'I need air. That toilet's pure evil.'

'I told you – use the pouches,' Vee says, cleaning her glasses on her jumper.

'I can't openly urinate in the seat I'm travelling in. And certainly not while sitting next to you.' Goldie scrunches her face as she climbs back into Vee's car, sniffing her heels. 'Neat piss,' she confirms, accepting one of Vee's antibacterial wipes.

Vee is still the perfect Brownie. Has packed for every eventuality, leaving home pristine, effortlessly organizing their road trip despite life's current dramas. No, she hasn't moved out, but you'd struggle to find any sign of her there. If Goldie and Vee were Thelma and Louise – which makes Vee smile her first proper smile in ages – then she would obviously be Louise. Goldie's top to toe Thelma, all made-up, packing everything just in case, and leaving the place a tip. Lucky, having a cleaner.

Jamie had thought Vee ridiculous; irritated by the sudden holiday, the lock on her bedroom door. *'I thought we were trying to save? How's that going to look when we're trying to sell it?'*

But he should've thought of all that before bringing home a demon.

On her regular holidays, Vee would've packed the books which she'd been saving specifically for the break. Two books that she needed time for, and one set in the place she'd be travelling to. Should she get through them, she'd then start on her Kindle. This holiday, though, Vee's got her own shit to read, her own notebooks and journals to delve through. And door locks or no door locks, leaving them at the house was unthinkable, especially with Julia likely sleeping over in her absence. Using her hand soap. Sleeping in the sheets she's fucking washed.

Vee makes a mental acknowledgement of how just then she'd thought of the house as the House, instead of Home, and though it doesn't provoke any nostalgic or sorry feelings, it's surely another sign of things changing.

Maybe Julia reappearing has done her a favour.

Vee blinks, as if adjusting to her driving glasses, the idea of Julia perversely proving pivotal again, an intrusive thought too many.

As Vee drives off LeShuttle into Calais, with a fleeting chase of regret that she's in a black VW Golf and not a blue Ford Thunderbird convertible, she's also immensely glad for this holiday.

So classy. Antibes, and a pit stop midpoint, that Vee's booked an Airbnb for. One street away from an excellent restaurant where Vee's already studied the menu. Because this is the stuff she adores. And it has been so nice to put it all into practice, directing her energies at something more positive.

With no one thinking for a second how it's really running away.

There was little convincing needed to get her to come – even though Vee resisted saying yes immediately, because Vee, being Vee, never does like to give herself away straight away. Besides, it felt good having it sold to her, like Goldie really wanted her there.

'Aren't you freelance these days,' she'd said. 'Don't you work remotely?'

Vee does.

'I'd have to drive,' Vee had tested. 'If I do come.'

Because she won't fly anywhere. It's embarrassing, but true. Vee had been a braver creature in her twenties, because there was so much mesmerizing world to see, but shrank through the years into purely European travel, using ferries, trains and cars – all entirely possible, even with a golden retriever. All those holidays where the dog had been a baby substitute – for Jamie at least, which was what Vee imagined other people thought too, should they be studying them. Yet Vee was always just happy to have a lovely dog and a lovely husband.

A really fucking lovely life.

Goldie had been the same about planes, which could've cut her career even shorter if she hadn't been hypnotized to overcome it. Vee does an involuntary inward eyeroll. She would never let anyone hypnotize her – would like to see them try; Vee's smart-arse inner conversation reminding her that she's well on the way back to her normal self. Better acerbic thoughts than the hunted look that was settling in around her eyes. Sunny southern France is timely.

Easy. It took less than ten minutes to book her and G on LeShuttle.

'Bonjour le France!' Vee cheers, giving thanks to her satnav and reliable car, and will be driving for the whole journey because Goldie never learnt to – and is now sucking orange Wotsit dust from her fingers at just gone nine in the morning.

'Bonjour la France! Whoop whoop!'

'Use that.' Clocking Goldie using the car door pocket as her personal bin, Vee nods to a bag she's designated for rubbish.

'Are you going to be like this all journey?'

'Are you?' Ninety seconds or so into French freedom, and already bickering like they're kids again, Vee remembering well Goldie's side of the bedroom, the false eyelashes on their last legs stuck to the side of her chest of drawers for desperate measures. Plates once containing stacks of toast, stacked under her bed. It was a miracle how someone could live in such filth, where there were probably new cures for illnesses in her tea dregs and biscuit sludges, moulding in mugs like polluted sea beds. Damp towels, dirty cotton wool pads and cotton buds left mere inches from their ever-overflowing bin. Yet Goldie could've worn a pair of week-old knickers on her head and still had all the boys desperate to become her boyfriend.

And men. Who should've known better.

She glances across at Goldie, her face unreadable in her enormous Fendi shades, Vee's curiosity of then still clearly on her mind.

Which is good, too. How there are thoughts beyond Julia occupying her. And with that, Vee's already certain that this time around, healing from Julia will be far easier than the first time she ruined her life.

Ruined is a bit dramatic. Funny how the problem seems to shrink in tandem with the further she drives away from it. But this is not running away. No.

This is fucking self-care.

Twelve

GOLDIE

Down That Road

Entering France, the endless motorway, intermittent downpours over the green which flanks it and the flat heaviness of sky depresses Goldie to her bones.

'First that toilet from hell, and now ...' Goldie groans, forgetting for a moment she's annoyed with Valeria. 'It looks just like bloody England.'

'Well, we're not really that far away, are we?' Valeria glances at her, which Goldie's noticed she keeps doing, as if searching her for clues. It's irritating. 'You've got a house in France, but you've never driven to France?'

'Oh, I see. This is the game now; I tick the box and pay my carbon emissions. And I bloody recycle. And besides – it's not my house, is it?' Goldie folds her arms. Valeria's know-it-all vibes are really starting to grate. 'I'm having a nap.'

*

She wakes to Valeria nudging her leg. 'Paris,' she says, nodding through the windscreen for Goldie to look.

Recognizable in the distance is the Eiffel Tower, the sky brighter now as the sun slowly cooks away the earlier downpour. 'Wow. What a picture.'

'I've tried so many times to take pictures. None are ever great.'

'Better like this, probably. More truthful.' Goldie looks and looks until they begin descending into another ridiculously long tunnel, Valeria back on her Mrs Uptight trip as she snips at Goldie to 'do your window up, quick!'.

Glancing to the creamy car ceiling for strength, Goldie does as she's told.

'I can't believe you've never been on LeShuttle.' Valeria chuckles, clearly not as bothered as she sounded. 'Or driven to France.'

'Well, I can't fucking drive, can I? Twat.'

'Names now. Nice.'

'It's all I've got till you pull that stick out of your arse.' Goldie bites her lip, preventing a smile, loving and hating her sister. She looks at the satnav. 'Four hours?'

'To our rest-stop. It's a bit of detour, that Jamie thought looked "dull as arseholes" ...' Valeria hesitates. 'It's a place called Montmorillon; the "City of Writing" ... fancied going for that reason – obviously.' Exhaling, Valeria pulls her shoulders back, sitting taller. 'Anyway, I never have, and I'd like to. From the look of Google Maps, we've got a whole river to swim in at the end of our Airbnb's garden.'

'Nature swimming?'

'Wild swimming,' Valeria corrects. 'I've always wanted to try that, too.'

'With insects and amoebas in a turd soup? No. Thank. You.'

'No turds in the Gartempe. We've left England behind us, remember?'

Readjusting to each other eases with every passing hour, killing time with their favourite games, like how many *EastEnders* characters they can remember since the programme's inception; the list far longer now than the last time they played it – which had been Vee's fortieth, when Goldie had surprised her with a trip to Montauk, New York. Four days that started stiff from years of minimal contact, before turning magic. But then Covid rolled in, and lockdown, and life in general, and they'd returned to their separate spheres; the odd text here and there.

It is a shame they've let their distance be, for no real reason other than laziness; the assumption of the other always being there. Because Goldie's not sure what she'd do without Valeria. Doesn't think she'd have a heart left at all.

Longing for a Burger King, Goldie's chances are scuppered again and again as Vee pushes on down the motorway, telling her there are no appropriate exits, which Goldie can't argue with because how would she know, being unable to drive?

Goldie has been driven through France before, though. Plenty of times on tour buses, for the early gigs, travelling from the off in absolute luxury alongside the featured act, who were usually male artists, and never minded her tagging along.

But Grant minded. Rarely was Goldie ever on her own on the road. Usually on her back, in the nook she called her pod, not quite a bedroom, but enough of a personal space for them to be together. Never seeing any of the places she was travelling to, and certainly never the Eiffel Tower.

In two years, she'd visited every continent, Vine Recordings opening worlds, yet she rarely experienced any of it. Because if she wasn't performing, promoting, or on a tour bus, then she'd be behind cool shades in nice hotels. Kept for Grant. A similar cycle with Ben and his social events, only without the physicality. All those places and she could've been anywhere.

Had her eyes longed to see other things? Had she missed out? Had anyone asked, Goldie would've said absolutely not. Such a besotted creature. Travelling the only time Grant Love ever truly felt hers. And incredible; after so many years of trying not to, he is so easily conjured. So influential in her thoughts.

Though a little less raw and recent than thinking about Wolfie.

'What are you thinking about?' Valeria asks, noticing Goldie's hand on her chest, never flipping missing a trick; should've been in MI5 or something.

'How hard some people can work and end up with nothing to show for it.' Which is not quite what Goldie's thinking, yet an offering of truth, nonetheless. 'Fifteen years with Ben.' Goldie can't stop herself. 'I don't even know how we got here.'

Valeria's silent.

Fifteen years and leaving, potentially skinting her again. Only not so young this time.

But fuck that train of thought. One thing Goldie will never be is a woman obsessed with numbers. Will not cow to the digits like the women who went before; Gran sobbing in C&A because she couldn't do up the dress she'd had her eye on; refusing the mere suggestion of a larger size. Bony Gran fretting over her weighing scales, convinced it was those numbers stopping her from living her best life, keeping slim to please the men, trapped beneath the cloche of their gaze – and likely why Goldie's loved the Lycra and the bodycon for so long. Goldie's happy with her hefty hips, has always adored how they look and feel when she puts her hands on them. She isn't old, anyway. Doesn't feel it, certainly doesn't look it. And besides, negative self-talk is like casting a wicked spell. On yourself. Sabotage – and for what? To end up like Nan?

Or worse, Mum. Wherever the hell she is these days, Goldie's certain she's unchanged. Her obsession with ageing. Of becoming invisible. Which ate her away so much, that her worst fear became truth.

But being a loveless, embittered bastard will do that to you.

For a moment, Goldie thinks of her father, faded by memory into what seems as if she's viewing an old photograph of them sat together on their fake leather sofa, him with his guitar on one leg, and Goldie balanced on the other. Having pushed Goldie's hair from her eyes, he's looking at her as if she's the only person in his world. Held special. Complete love. Grief left behind a lonely pain, which grew into longing; a desire to be seen without fighting for it. She'd been so young, yet no matter – he's still the only parent that Goldie truly misses.

Dad.

Goldie was ten when Mum had the visit from two suited men carrying briefcases, presuming them to be fancy bailiffs, and nothing too unusual in that. But what was unusual came when the men left, and Mum told them they were never to talk of their father again.

To anybody.

After that, there were no more visits from men in suits. Not even the regular debt collectors bothered them. The final reminders also stopped, and for a time Vee and Goldie could have chicken and chips from the takeaway downstairs whenever they fancied. Mum got a new three-piece suite from one of her catalogues, paying for it outright. They all had branded new trainers, and they all, even Gran, spent a fortnight in a guest house in Bournemouth. And though they talked about Dad plenty to each other, neither Goldie nor Vee ever mentioned their father in front of Mum or Gran again.

'Do you think about Dad much?' Goldie asks.

'How do you mean – miss him? I barely, barely remember him.'

'It's sad, innit? Strange. How it became like he didn't even belong to us.'

Where the hell is this coming from?

If it's fucking avoidance, Goldie reckons she'd rather be thinking of Wolfie.

Thirteen

VEE

Back And Forth

After the world's worst motorway services sandwich, swallowed with water like a tablet just to fill her tummy, Vee wishes she'd stopped at the first Burger King she'd spotted instead of pushing on with the journey; fired up – until she was flagging.

Goldie had one thing to do. Bring the sandwiches, which were confiscated at border control because they contained meat. And she has the front to be making the faces now.

'The worst. Evil toilets. Evil weather. Now evil tuna sandwiches.'

'Honestly. It's like you're five.'

'Good.'

Even her fucking responses. Vee watches her, sat cross-legged on a carrier bag on the closest grassy spot to the car, holding her triangle of sandwich with both hands like she's in primary school. Goldie's mouth opens, showing its mashed-up contents to Vee.

'You're disgusting,' Vee says as Goldie opens her mouth wider.

'Don't keep staring at me then.'

'I'm worried about you.'

'You're worried? No offence, but I'm not the one carting half my childhood across two countries.'

'I'm going to stretch my legs.' Vee stands abruptly, doesn't bite – though it's sorely tempting. 'We've another hour or so to go.'

Soon they are back on the road, tired now, and conversationally barren, as Vee drives through fields of endless sunflowers, reaching as far as her vision allows, their heads dipped, petals offering a fringed, shaggy protection from the sun.

The sense of peace here is undeniable. Tranquillity. The rural openness, and then the river, which tells Vee they're close, her heart lifting as the satnav enters its final ten minutes of the journey. The tall sandy-coloured buildings, quaintly picturesque and uber French have their doors and shutters closed, which makes Vee fear for their chances of dinner. She'd totally forgotten about Monday closing. Ticks herself off inwardly.

But it is the most gorgeous place.

And so is their cottage. Vee opens the shutters to their temporary outdoors, as the suntrap of a courtyard cocoons her in its warmth, and Goldie carries the rest of the bags in. Montmorillon may seem quiet and safe enough to leave their stuff in the car, but you can't grow up on the fringes of East London and not stay suspicious. Going through life thinking everyone's a potential criminal is standard.

From the garden Vee looks out on the river, its banks lined with trees of voluminous green foliage, as a man throws sticks into the water, his black Labradors launching themselves in with a noisy splash, to retrieve them.

'Missing Onion?' Goldie appears beside her, as from nowhere Vee begins to cry, thinking of Onion's face. 'It's been the longest flipping day,' she says kindly, rubbing Vee's arm. 'Tell you what, you have a shower, and I'll go on the hunt for supplies. There's got to be a newsagent open, at least.' Goldie winks. 'Just like the old days.'

Left on her own, Vee watches the dogs at play, thinking of Onion – called Onion because from the moment Vee laid eyes on her she couldn't stop crying. Had always wanted a dog, a family pet. For Vee, Onion's arrival, her two-tone tubby yellowness and big brown eyes, felt finally as if life couldn't get any better. This was it. All she'd ever wanted.

And if she could've played those first few years on a loop forever . . .

But then came the baby chat, which soon became the only chat, invading every aspect of every fucking thing. From what they ate, to when they had sex, to what they watched on the telly – *One Born Every Minute*, Jamie's eyes misting up as Vee's wandered the room in avoidance from the emotional chaos on screen. The sheer danger involved. Did she want to go through that, truly? Giving birth, her life forever dominated by a little person she wasn't entirely sold on?

Just for Jamie.

And perhaps her feelings might've changed the moment the bloody little bundle of joy was placed in her arms.

But maybe not.

By the time Goldie's back with kebabs and Cokes, Vee's scrolling through cute pics of Onion, with a glass of the complimentary bottle of red wine she's found, along with a bowl of fruit, a blessing considering the nutritional content of their dinner.

Sitting across from Vee, Goldie swipes the chilli sauce from her chin before licking the back of her hand, while Vee picks out the fatty bits, making a rejected pile in the corner of the polystyrene container, far from the cultural experience she'd drawn out so impressively in her head, imagining them both down some charmingly narrow side street, eating regional cuisine in the dusk of early evening.

'Kebab shop does Magnums, Cornettos. And they're open till ten. We could get one, go for a walk along the river? Looks like a landscape. Almost imaginary.' Goldie says the most beautiful things sometimes. Makes Vee regret her horrid little criticisms. Her smug perpetual quest for self-improvement.

Why must everything become an exercise to prove her good taste?

'Beautiful,' Goldie says, looking more at peace than she has all day. 'I bloody hate sleeping on an empty stomach. Wine will help too.' Making sure Vee notices how she puts her rubbish in the bin, she adds, 'Let's go for a walk before it gets too dark.'

There's a chill in the air which requires a cardigan, as Vee and Goldie walk the clean empty roads, coming first across a creepy cinema, stuck in time by the films it's showing, too, and then the town square, which bursts with flowers and charm, though everything's closed and quiet, apart from a queue forming at a hole in the wall, which at first Vee thinks is a cash machine, but is actually a pizza dispensary and Goldie declares as 'Genius'.

It's a half-asleep place, gentle, and taking in the view from the bridge, the first thing that comes to mind is when Vee would play The Sims, selecting a plot of land far on the outskirts of a town, growing her own veg so she didn't have to visit it, and having a pet so she didn't have to communicate socially in any other way. She'd just get her cooking skills up and make money writing books on her laptop in a tiny home full of plants and sunlight.

This place looks very much like it.

How Vee's problems have shrunk, existing now in some distant limbo, is incredible. Yet she just can't help the nagging guilt. Over Onion, having to use her all-singing, all-dancing orthopaedic dog bed instead of Vee's human bed for the next three weeks.

Perhaps girls do stick together. Onion sleeping on the furniture – but mostly on Vee's bed, was one of the first changes to come about since the split. A deeper quality of sleep than she'd had for years, just from Onion's round barrel shape leaning against her; solid, secure. Onion can't tell Vee that she loves her, though Vee knows her devotion is unquestionable. And very reciprocated.

What was she thinking, leaving?

'I was worried Jamie might've been right with his "dull as arseholes" description, but could there ever be a place more up your street? Look at all the bookshops.' Everywhere and everything has an association with writing. From a typewriter museum to a library phone box, which she makes Vee pose in for a photo. 'How is everything French always so classy looking?' Goldie says, when it's her turn for a picture, each pose more theatrical than the last, God love her. She stops, suddenly busying herself in her own little flip-style mobile – making Vee question again how the fuck she's existed all these years without a smartphone. 'Rufus,' Goldie explains. 'Checking I'm here safe.'

Vee wonders who she might send a message to, confirming her arrival.

Onion, obviously, has no phone skills. So there's no one. No one at all.

How she's not accountable to anybody puts a giddy lightness in Vee's tummy as she takes out her own phone, selecting the best scenic shot of this beautiful place, and posts it on Instagram.

Vee knows it's mostly bullshit, a new religion to follow, casting choice moments in their best light for the ongoing soap opera of your digital life. A forever main character, trimmed of all the behind-the-scenes flab. Enhanced. Sugar-coated. What you're longing for life to really be.

Yet in Vee's case, right now, Instagram tells the truth.

Fourteen

GOLDIE

Paradise

After a morning trip to the boulangerie for road snacks and bonus croissants, it's back in the car, Goldie relieved by how much better equipped they are food-wise for the rest of the journey – so much so they ignore all fast-food service stations. After lengths of baguettes – jambon-beurre for both – moreish little flatbreads dotted with olives and red onion, a family bag of Lays ready salted crisps and bucketloads of mineral water, it is almost 6 p.m. when they arrive at the gates of Villa Fleurie.

'You are fucking kidding me,' Valeria says, both hands in her hair and looking ready to cry. 'Please, please tell me you're joking.'

'Shh and let me think – if you keep going on I'll never remember how to unlock it.'

'Can't you text Benedict, ask him for the code?'

'Honestly.' Breaking into a cheeky grin, Goldie pushes into

a keypad the series of digits she clearly hasn't forgotten. With a click and a buzz, the gates slowly open. 'I just don't know what you take me for.'

Valeria drags her suitcase across the crazy paving that surrounds the enormous pool, full, clean and enticing. Twinkly lights and the sound of crickets welcome them as Goldie closes the gates behind her, the entire plot walled and secure. Towering conifers border a two-storey villa of smooth white stucco, terracotta steps curling around its side, the wrought-iron bannisters smothered in wisteria, looking all lush and grapevine gorgeous.

'Jeez,' Valeria whistles.'Why don't you just live here?'

Inside, the walls are white, too; large, full of abstract art. A modern white gloss kitchen on the ground floor and a very modern-looking bedroom, with an en suite and double doors onto the pool area. 'Your quarters, milady,' Goldie says as Valeria eyes up the four-poster almost hungrily. 'Have a shower, a good kip.' She smiles. 'There's the best pizza on the corner, literally thirty seconds away. Glass of rosé, and a Reine. What do you think?'

'I think I could weep with delight,' Valeria says, as if all her tiredness has rushed in at once. She has been a dedicated driver, her concentration enviable. But now she looks too crumpled, with the same lost look as yesterday when she'd cried in the courtyard.

She's only tired, Goldie tells herself.

Hugs her stiff, strangely emotional sister close all the same.

Funny how both would describe their relationship as good; the sisterly bond and the love unquestionable. Yet, at the same time, be so removed from each other, from the past, that it seems almost improper to disturb it.

For Valeria, the Antibes effect, of sun and lots of sleep, has been remarkable. Goldie warms herself that at least one of them is undergoing some form of repair.

Though it must be said; there are far worse places to heal from heartache.

The weather's tropical in comparison with Essex, somewhere fast becoming beautifully insignificant, even for Goldie in moments like this, lying beneath her favourite palm tree in a giant cartwheel sunhat so large it shades her shoulders. She's never been one to cook herself, will catch the sun whether she tries to or not. She's already feeling healthier than she has for months, now she's not living at the mercy of British weather.

Entering their third week together, a pattern of behaviour's emerged; of Valeria and Goldie eating together yet spending portions of the daytime apart – this surely the longest they've spent one-on-one since sharing a bedroom and at times strangely intense. Goldie likes how they've gelled back together, remembering their old ways, their flow, from a hand movement to a micro-frown. And a mutual understanding – how they both need their space. So when Valeria's been working, exploring or lost in her old box of books, Goldie's been on the beach, watching all the beautiful people, the massive families who set up tables and eat and swim till it's dark, and the sprightly sorts volleyballing for some reason Goldie just can't fathom.

But she does so love to swim. Both in the sea and the pool Goldie dips in and out of all day long, busying herself also with finding tasty-looking restaurants for them to try, neatly compartmentalizing all that's at home, because if she just lives mindfully, appreciating here in this minute, everything's okay.

The only contact from home has been Ben with some upcoming dates to put in her diary – which Goldie's not yet responded to – and the cleaner, asking where the shed key was.

Nothing from Wolfie. But why would there be?

She tries not think of him. Tries also to stop her thoughts returning to Vine and, inevitably, Grant. That last hand-delivered letter.

For more unapologetic deflection, Goldie opens the new notebook Valeria's given her – notebooks as gifts, now. In swirly, girly script, she writes 'Part Two – G's Future Plans' on the first page.

- ❏ Tell Ben and begin divorce – no more stalling!
- ❏ Cost out a new kitchen at Gran's (or at least a new oven and fridge)
- ❏ And a new shower (similar to current one in en suite)
- ❏ Find out how to tackle damp – probs a new boiler and heating £££!

Money. So unfortunately vital for everything. For years, Gran said to get rid of Saunders Road. The house an unnecessary responsibility, a target sitting empty. Cash in while the area was having its glow up. Yet selling was the one thing Goldie always resisted, which came from her gut, and probably from knowing how one day, she'd need it.

Saunders Road is a sanctuary but only a temporary solution; to live there forever feels regressive, and just a little bit depressing. But still it gives Goldie options – moving on could be done simply by renting it out, because it is silly to let it sit there empty when it could generate enough money for Goldie to live elsewhere. In time.

Goldie watches the water. Little movement. No rush.

On a sunbed a couple of feet away, strategically set up with her own parasol, Valeria's absorbed in her phone.

'What you doing—' But before Goldie even finishes her sentence, Valeria's frowning.

'I'm on Amazon.'

'What for?'

Valeria clicks her teeth. Putting her phone away, she slides her sunnies down, just enough for Goldie to see that she has her attention. 'Cancelling my subscribe and save orders. And the opticians. Thought I'd stay another week.'

Valeria – all pre-booked online food shops, Amazon subscriptions, life ordered within an inch of itself; every six weeks a haircut, the next dentist appointment booked straight off the back of the one she's just attended.

'I'm flattered,' Goldie says. And she is.

As the Med's thawed her, Valeria's forever mask has melted a little, too, the world at last beginning to get a glimpse of the truth behind it; her slow realization that she's not as hideous as she believed.

Of course she's not.

Watching her yesterday, drifting up the road on market day in her orange sundress, wicker basket draped over her arm, unaware of the admiring looks towards the happy lady in bright colours doing a bit of shopping, Goldie had taken a picture on Valeria's mobile she'd been looking after on the beach. It's something she keeps doing, Goldie's own face able to unlock Valeria's screen – smartphones are a dangerous madness – snapping Valeria on the unaware, thinking it's nice, capturing moments of her sister in this way, so that when she's home she can look back, and she can see.

That she can be happy. And free.

Fifteen

JULIA

Nasty Girl

But for the MacBook and other gadgetry on the desk which once doubled as a dressing table – her reflection always a potent distraction when trying to study – Julia's childhood bedroom is the same as when she left for uni in 1998. Warwick. A First.

A collage of achievement remains, pinned above a long, pine chest of drawers. Rosettes from horse-riding competitions, along with photos of Julia and the winning pony she never much liked. More pictures; of the sixth form leavers' ball with Lucy and Laura, who she never really liked much either. Another of her and Terry Sant, who everyone fancied but who worshipped Julia, snapped at the same event. All the over-the-top glamour Mother had loved every second of.

Mother. Who can't even take in today's Ocado delivery. Claiming another of her heads. But silver linings all the same, because with Mother in bed and Dad 'away on business', Julia can almost pretend she has the weekend to herself.

Dad. Who retired six years ago. Does he think they're fucking stupid?

For the past week or so, Julia's been working from home. Couldn't be fucked to spin for her followers how making a working packed lunch is a kooky, healthy, environmentally friendly life choice. Not when she can't stop her current latest recurring thought, which is more a living nightmare – how if she keeps only making the minimum payments on her debts, then it's a certainty she'll be dead before she even clears the interest.

But debt isn't all that's on Julia's mind.

Seeing Vee again all these years later had that old feeling returning to Julia like a hunting scent – and briefly had been just as delicious. Valeria Burden at the top of her own staircase; the saddo on the sidelines same as before. Watching the gorgeous grown-ups.

It had been swift work on Julia's part to touch upon their problematic past – which was how she described her relationship with Vee to Jamie. He'd believed her easily, being an easy-going guy, but also because he only need go online for proof that she's a good person. Who on earth would disbelieve a wellness ambassador?

Vee's Instagram, which seems to be her only social media account, true to type, is set to private. What does surprise Julia, though, is how her fat bitch of a sister has even less of an online presence. Julia had imagined her as the typical *TOWIE* attention whore, but there's not a trace, except how apparently she's now some rich dullard's trophy wife.

Which, even Julia must admit, sounds fucking lovely.

For a moment she thinks of texting Jamie. Though he's not mentioned it since, their lunch with Vee certainly left its hangover, a strangeness Julia can't directly locate yet knows is there. As if she's been branded with a question mark.

It's better to play busy. The Cumbrian wellness retreat she'd bloody paid to professionally advertise only amounted to two bookings, and so Julia had to cancel. There'll be no return deposit, but she digresses. Better for Jamie to keep believing she's a super-hot catch with a life of her own than be tainted by the lingering fart of his ex. Who clearly can't fucking move on, Jamie mentioning himself how she'd even tried warning him off Julia.

Jealousy is so ugly.

On impulse, for the umpteenth time, Julia pulls up LinkedIn on her laptop. Types Valeria Hughes into the search box. A heavy-fingered click on her profile picture, of Vee looking about thirty at the 2023 London Film Festival. 'Documentarian' Valeria Hughes. Who'd have thought it? Though Julia can't say she's given Vee a second thought since the day the ambulance took her away from school.

Julia had been the first to notice, how when the mock exam finished, Vee hadn't moved. Just sat there at her desk in the hall, until Julia lit the frenzy and everyone made it their life's work to snap Vee out of the statue of a person she'd become; her head down, hands clasped in her lap, as they slapped rulers on her desk, making donkey hee-haw noises that had the invigilator racing back in.

As her eyes rise from the screen and Vee's profile to study herself in the mirror, Julia gives a slow smile in remembrance.

Maybe it had something to do with it being their final mock exam, maths, the dragging Friday before the weekend. The pent-up energy of teens under pressure, which whipped them all up as one, like a scene from Salem, until the invigilator broke the circle that had formed around Vee, still unmoved, only now with a puddle of wee beneath her chair.

Which was the moment Julia knew she'd officially broken her.

Such clever damage limitation; admitting the lot to Jamie, offering, of course, a gentler, more noughties mean-girl version of events than the Stephen King's Carrie White reality.

'No Mrs Fensby today?' The old boy delivering from Ocado looks almost disappointed.

'One of her heads,' Julia explains sweetly, lifting the first of the bags in. 'I hope I'll do.'

'It's just that it's my last shift, you see.'

Julia knows. His thank you card is behind the carriage clock on the mantel. 'Pastures new?'

'You could say that. I'm retiring.' But because Julia makes no further conversation, he reels off the substitutions, busying himself by stacking the empty crates. 'Well then. Do send your mum my regards.' He hesitates, almost a little sadly. 'She's a very nice lady.'

'Enjoy those pastures.' Julia closes the door on him, legging it up the stairs two at a time before bursting into her mother's room that's all hushed, pastel chintz, right down to the peach frilly satin valance and sheets which match the peach frilly satin eye mask she's wearing. Her hair fans across the pillow, pale grey because of the closed curtains, making her look like one of those skeletons where the hair seems determined to stay a part of things.

'Shop's all in, Mum.' The way Mother jumps, her disorientated moment of panic, is just as gratifying as it's always been. One absolute perk of living back at home. 'Sorry. Did I wake you?'

Is she properly ill? Nobody's ever clearly told Julia. Mother's many, many periods of sickness stretch back to her first memories. All Julia knows is that these days Mother's so fricking feeble, Dad's habits no longer need to be so hidden.

Weakness is so fucking annoying.

'The shop?' Mother emerges slowly through her sleep fog. 'Thank you, dear. Was it Wilf who delivered?' Without removing the eye mask, she turns in the direction of Julia's voice. 'Did you remember to give him the card?'

'Of course.' Julia turns to go. 'Oh yeah, and he said to say that you were a very lovely lady.' Mother smiles wide, her head all mask and teeth as Julia closes the bedroom door with the promise of running up with a cuppa in a bit. Goes straight for the card behind the clock.

Stepping into the garden to vape, Julia opens the card. Pockets the fifty-pound note that flutters out from it. And as her puffs plume into the sky, reads Mother's shaky, spidery handwriting – which is also very fricking feeble, with a very raised brow indeed.

Dearest Wilf,
With love and best for a long, happy retirement.
Friday food shops will never be the same!
Your friend, Patricia x
(My telephone number is below should you like to keep in touch)

The weekend is long and stifling, and so is tree-lined suburbia. The quietness of their big 1930s house, the carpeted silence and slow-ticking clocks.

And Mother. When Julia's thought all this time how it was just Dad who was the slut.

Sixteen

Vee

Emotions

Things are changing. Vee's desire for Jamie to know the truth about Julia less palpable by the hour. His decisions are his alone, nothing to do with Vee – though she can establish some boundaries, certainly doesn't have to spend another moment witnessing them together. How sure Vee had once been that she and Jamie could never become strangers, yet the prospect of Julia in his future permanently has put to bed any hopeful notions of them ever remaining friends.

On her sunlounger, making sure Goldie can't see her phone, Vee scrolls through Julia's Instagram.

Nothing stirs the creative cogs like fresh pain.

Vee can't resist. Is surely a masochist.

'What you doing—' Goldie asks from under her sunhat.

'I'm on Amazon,' Vee replies.

'What for?'

Vee puts her phone away, slides her sunnies down.

'Cancelling my subscribe and save orders. And the opticians. Thought I'd stay another week.'

There's something in the way Goldie says that she's flattered which brings Vee's head and heart in sync. An overwhelming urge to purge the weirdness she's been carrying since Julia rocked back up.

'Jamie's got a new girlfriend.'

'Already?' Goldie reads Vee's body language like it's her Marvel superpower. 'You know who it is?' Whipping off her sunglasses in a flash of rage, she claps her hands. 'Was he seeing her before?'

'No, no, it's a recent thing; a couple of months tops.' How had Vee not thought of the possibility that Jamie might've been seeing Julia for longer? Perhaps even while they were still together – however loose their togetherness had become. It seems impossible to imagine, though; completely un Jamie-like. Usually so straightforward, someone who until recently had listened to her.

Respected her.

'Do you remember Julia Fensby?'

Goldie clearly doesn't have to search far back in her memory, though she shakes her head all the same, like she can't believe it. 'You're not serious.'

'When am I ever not serious?' Vee asks, so seriously that Goldie starts to laugh. 'It's not funny!'

'It's not. It's unbelievably unfunny. Have you been sitting on this since that night at Gran's, looking like you'd seen a—' Goldie claps her hands again, attracting looks from the nearby beachgoers. 'Julia Fensby was the ghost. Fucking hell,

Valeria.' She stops talking, her shock all the validation Vee's needed.

'And Jamie's so happy.'

'But surely he—' Goldie stops, exasperated. 'You've never told him, have you?'

'I never thought I'd have to. I wasn't exactly anticipating this.'

Yet somewhere deep down, Vee was. Treating each day as rehearsal for the inevitable, all her sparkling ducks in a row, for the moment she came face to face, and won.

'But she's . . .' Goldie shudders.

'I know.'

'And they're definitely . . .' Goldie shudders again.

'Unquestionably. She's been at the house.' It's been a month since that night, yet it's just as impossible to believe it's true. 'We've even had lunch.'

'Pure reality TV fuckery. Is she still awful?'

'Still perfect.'

'Only if you're into basic,' Goldie says, getting a small smile as Vee reopens her phone, displaying Julia's social media. 'Just as I thought,' she concludes from Vee's doomscrolling. 'Same shit fringe and no tits.'

Vee's smile widens, despite herself. 'She's reinvented herself apparently, has some sort of life coaching side hustle going on.' New event details have been posted in the last hour of a wellness retreat she's hosting in Cumbria. A long weekend of hiking, holistic healing and Julia.

There she is; a thirty-second shiny little skit to sell her snake oil – 1,723 likes.

How Vee had once longed for the cutesy voice and smooth blonde hair; Julia the embodiment of every doll she'd ever played with. If perfect came in boxes. In girl form. It hurts, far more than Vee would like to admit, how well-matched Julia and Jamie are. Both tall, lean, fair, like gorgeous mannequins. Like they should be paid to sit in the front windows of fancy restaurants. A kick in the gut reminder of how very dull Vee knows she is by comparison. Like the picking of a scab, Vee recollects one school photograph day, when she'd overheard Julia saying how potato-like Vee's face became when she smiled – how her fringe didn't help, when it was Julia's haircut she'd been trying to replicate.

Emulate.

Avoiding the showers after PE, because her hair dried so awkwardly Julia named her 'pubic head', which spread through the school, and stuck.

Vee also remembers Gran's hurt when she saw the unsmiling photograph proof, hoping to send the picture to Vee's mother, as if a potato face and a tragic fringe might at last be the things that made her come home and love them.

'So now what – bite your tongue and let her get her feet even further under your table?' Goldie rolls her eyes before putting her sunglasses back on. 'You need an exit strategy.'

'We're thousands of pounds in negative equity. If we'd sold when we applied for the divorce, we'd be down almost eighty grand, which neither of us can afford to kiss off. Plus, till now anyway, it's been fine living together ...' More than fine.

'I say leave them to it,' Goldie states, as if that's something

Vee's not already thought of. 'Unless ... unless, of course, you still love him.'

'Of course I don't. But that doesn't mean I don't care about him, because I do. She's ... she's just ...'

'I know.' Goldie reaches to squeeze Vee's knee. 'I know.'

'Look. Look at her.' And who exactly are the muppets filming all these reels of Julia, especially the ones of her on gym equipment, encouraged along by ridiculously trendy-looking trainers? 'She's the worst person. And she doesn't deserve any sort of happiness. Especially with someone as decent as Jamie.'

Screwing her eyes shut, Goldie says it anyway. 'Maybe he's not that great either.'

'What do you mean?'

'Well, you are getting divorced. Perhaps it's time to own that decision.' Her words prickle through Vee, who never finds it easy to be told what to do. 'You could always move in with me at Gran's. And Onion, of course. We could eat three-way potatoes in front of *EastEnders* and tell each other how incredible we are, every bloody evening.' Goldie squeezes Vee harder, almost as if she's convincing herself. 'Because we are.'

'I'm reading, still processing those diaries,' Vee says sadly. 'Sometimes, sometimes I wish I could reach into the girl me and ...' She trails off, the tears not far away. 'Lift her away from all of it. Give her a fucking cuddle at the very least.'

How sad that each year, on almost every page Vee writes about reinventing herself, listing the things she needed to change to suit the people around her. It feels an injustice against her very soul; cruel how she measured herself by the standards of people who had such little regard for her anyway.

In rushes the awful feeling of saying too much. This is all too horribly exposing.

'Well, I can do that for the grown version right now.' Holding her before she packs up and flees the beach, Vee's caught both loving and loathing how Goldie knows her so intrinsically. 'I'm sorry.' Goldie's voice is small. 'I'm sorry I wasn't always there.'

'You're my sister, not my—' Patting Goldie's back, Vee draws the moment to an end. Needs more than a hug from a sibling on a guilt trip. 'I'll see you later.'

'Julia was a disturbed little girl who thought it should all be hers.' Goldie's right. Some people are just born horrible. 'All she's doing now is humping your cast-offs. I wouldn't exactly call that winning, would you?'

Vee heads to her usual café, chosen because it's the dead spit of the IKEA canvas print that hangs in Gran's kitchen at home; a café culture scene of outdoor brick and bougainvillea, trailed around the entrance awning, with a little blue bistro table set for two.

Her happy place works well to restore her inner peace, as over black decaf and two croissants, delicious and warm, needing no further butter, Vee reads her words once more, those raging pages written in her childhood library on the day of Julia's return. Such fearless emotion, as if she'd opened an artery across the page. Wonders, as she presses send, uploading it to the writing group's forum and ignoring the wounds of those rejections of the past, if this will be the piece which changes that.

And if it's not, well, she won't be at next week's meeting anyway. She'll be here, in this beautiful busy place, full of people who not only don't know Vee, but who don't give a shit about her either.

It is liberating.

Vee looks up, out across the road and directly at the sea, that's such a shimmering dazzling blue she shields her eyes, bringing her focus back to her more immediate surroundings; the same surly server, equipped with the aloof inner confidence Vee wishes she could pull off, too. The same blackboard of specials being placed outside and updated by the chef with blue and yellow chalks in the colours of the region. In his usual place at his usual table sits a man enjoying what Vee presumes is his leisurely after-work beer in the late sun before heading home. And though they don't talk, over the past week or so, he and Vee have started giving each other a little nod in acknowledgement, on their arrivals or departures from the café.

Vee's also noticed that whenever she looks up from what she's doing, rather like in this moment now, the man is often watching her. Which she doesn't mind.

Because he's totally fit.

Seventeen

GOLDIE

Control

Goldie thinks tonight's the night they should go out somewhere special. Though treating Valeria's the priority, a bit of dressing up is way overdue; time to get a bit pissed, because they've been so reserved. So caught in their own heads, which likely explains why they've not fallen out.

Regardless, it's unbelievable how Valeria's managed to keep this Julia shit to herself. Goldie knows it will have consumed her, cringing when she thinks of the disinterested advice she'd tried dishing out back in the day, never taking Valeria's problems seriously until the time she'd been styling her hair and found it coming away in handfuls. Overprocessed from straightening irons, home relaxing kits, plus the stresses which came from being permanently petrified. How headbands became the necessity, clever ways of arranging Valeria's sad last bits of length into a bun, before she lost her eyelashes, too – which became just another thing for Julia to crucify her over.

Marking the moment Goldie stopped the lame advice and took Valeria seriously.

How Valeria, now grown, has managed to sit at a table with Julia and break bread is truly baffling to Goldie. A girl hell-bent on breaking her, making Valeria ashamed of her every component; from who she was, to how she looked to where she came from – impossible also to forget the certain slant her bullying took.

Finding out what really happened to Valeria on her geography field trip tipped Goldie into a rage she'd never known. A kicking donkey breaking Valeria's arm had seemed such a random rural incident – and not at all the truth of Julia grabbing her hand and forcing it towards the donkey's cock, the poor sod sensing fear and kicking out, which had snapped her bone neatly, and led to the annihilating rumour of how Valeria couldn't even wank off a farm animal.

Spread by only one person.

Julia, who'd once been her friend; gaining Valeria's trust before slipping beneath her skin. To eat her alive. Literally.

As she marches back to the villa, munching on the heel of her baguette, Goldie sees as vividly as then, the bloody, perfect circle of teeth marks above Valeria's right shoulder blade. Four long years with Julia as her torturer, because slight, fair girls are often mislabelled as good. Adept at slipping out of trouble, while bringing out your very worst.

Whereas for the Goldies of the world, anger must always require much provocation; because the default reaction to overemotional women, especially bigger women, browner women is to either dismiss or destroy them.

React, either way, and you're done for. And ain't that the truth.

But how could anyone not react to such suffering? In an uncontainable rage, Goldie had beaten the sheer living shit out of Julia. Unable to stop herself – though worth noting how Goldie never once used her own teeth as a weapon. Just her fists and her feet, imagining for the whole fight – which, of course, Goldie won – that she was fighting her mother. Hating Miri Burden to the core for saddling her with all that came from the gut instinct to love and defend her baby sister. Every nurturing instinct rendered terrifying ever since.

It has never been fair. How fast Goldie was packaged into being grown.

Feeling her bag vibrate against her thigh, Goldie's heart leaps to her throat. An overreaction. And only Ben.

'Bonjour!' he says. 'I'm just with Trevor, going over a few things. Wanted to remind you that the shooting weekend for Ma and Pa is on the thirtieth.' When Goldie doesn't reply, he carries on. 'Not that I'm rushing you back.'

'I'll let you know.' Goldie leaves it there, resists filling their silence. The Julia rage making her less amenable.

Which she must admit is empowering.

'Are you all right for money?' Ben asks next, sounding almost as if he's testing her. Because if he hasn't noticed by now, then Trevor most certainly will have; how not a single transaction's been made from their account in the past three weeks. Goldie's spending has come from the separate pot, her earnt money, with Mr Maybe's word that as long as she keeps delivering, it'll keep coming, the whole lot feeling like a major independent step.

'Of course, just had a silly amount of Euros.' Goldie hears him adjusting, both his body and breathing noisy, irritating, even at this distance. 'Is everything okay?' Tempting as it is to add money-wise, she resists.

'Why wouldn't it be?'

'Well ... you rang me, Ben.' Again. No urge to make him comfortable.

'I did,' he agrees, letting it hang. 'I did. It's a, er, done deal with your old school pal, if you're wondering what came of all that.' Changing gears, Ben sounds like he's smiling. 'Went a bit over my original offer, but it all turned out favourably in the end. Sole control. The factory, contracts, staff – all mine as of Monday,' he adds, so smugly that Goldie hangs up.

Headphones, Côtes de Provence rosé – and how very sensible Goldie thought to line her stomach by baguette snacking on the way home. She rests her eyes in the sunshine, thinking everything's shit and how Valeria's right; why doesn't she just live here? Poolside forever. But Goldie needs to be on hand, to be useful.

Why would Wolfie – despite her warning – still sell Ben his business?

He did say he was skint. Something about a building project he couldn't fund? Goldie struggles to remember the detail. Can't judge. Only need think of buying Saunders Road; another form of bad money for a good thing. She could ask Wolfie herself. He did say – verbatim, because Goldie's played the moment on a loop in the background of her thoughts ever since – don't be a stranger. But it might be just what people say in moments like that.

What if he meant it, though?

Goldie's glad for the interruption when Valeria buzzes to be let in. Padding across the patio, she opens the gates, pushing a glass of wine into her sister's hands.

'Bit early.' Valeria's lips are on the glass before she's even finished her sentence.

'Early for who? Now, dinner plans. Shall we glam the fuck up? I think we need it.'

'Ah, I've got dinner.' Valeria nods at the bag on her shoulder. 'Went a bit mad at the market. Cheeses and tapenade.' Spotting the baguette missing at least nine inches, she adds disapprovingly, 'You remembered the bread then?'

Thinking of the Valeria on the beach earlier, it's hard believing they're even the same person. But Goldie knows which one is real. Won't push for her night out because of it.

They're in cheese heaven when the literal heavens open. Valeria and Goldie race from outside into the kitchen, first depositing the food, then grabbing the outdoor cushions, slipping on the tiles all the way, puddles of rainwater already forming on the inside of the house, as, soaked through, they work as a pair to pull the windows and shutters closed.

'Absolutely no hardship staying in,' Goldie says a little later, thoroughly enjoying their dinner picnic in the living room, her hair having dried massive and matted, which doesn't seem to matter either. 'I'm proper j'adoring these picky bits.' Popping another handful of olives in her mouth, she offers up a high five but is left hanging by a distracted Valeria.

'Baffling, G.' As she splits the last of an exceptional red between their glasses, she looks no less astonished than she'd been on her first visit to Villa Fleurie's wine cellar, through a hatch in the kitchen floor to the cool brick tunnel lined with bottles. 'A drink for every occasion.'

'Except for going to the park to get off your tits.' Goldie smiles. 'Not that you've ever been the type for that sort of behaviour.' Watching her sister cosy down into the cushions, she adds, 'You should be proud of yourself, you know.' Valeria lifts her head to view Goldie, giving herself serious double chins in the process. 'What? Don't you think so?'

'I did. Well, I was starting to.' Valeria sighs. Clicking her tongue, she sits upright, digging her phone from her dressing gown pocket. 'But, like, it's hard not to compare yourself when she's so ...'

'Show me again.' Together they dissect Julia's socials. Looking for signs of who she really is. At least this time around, Goldie can say with conviction that she's solid from the start.

And she's here.

'So AI coded,' Valeria says, a bit later. 'Performatively personal, but nothing personal-personal.'

'I'm just looking for signs of her secret racism – and her handsy father.' Goldie hands the phone back to Valeria, done. 'Bollocks to them. Aren't you tired of worrying about other people, anyway? With the brain you have.'

'What do you mean the brain I have?'

'Your creativity. Clouded by all your overthinking. Pulling yourself apart. Then, as if that's not enough, you go and add an even bigger black cloud of other people's judgement on top.'

'But you can't stop yourself from wondering what other people think—'

Goldie's having none of it. 'You can't get in other people's heads. Why would you even want to? Fucking creepy.'

Goldie sounds basic, but she's right. Knows firsthand how 'they', the homogenous people, like to keep others in little boxes they must never outgrow for their own cowardly purposes. Which makes them feel better about their own mediocre existences. To be the person brave enough to be different, to dream, to try, takes a lot of front. The people who once laughed at Goldie's confident claim that she'd one day be a singer. What would they have gained if their sneering won? Every single teacher had tried it at one point.

Even Mum.

'Well,' Valeria says. 'I told you, didn't I; about the writing club?'

'You did.' It is a relief that Valeria has her writing, a place to channel her emotions and energy. Same as Goldie when she was on stage. Performing offered her a clearness of thought. Like touching heaven. 'I always loved your writing, and I bloody hate reading.' Goldie watches how Valeria delights from the praise, rather as a child would – not that children polish off entire bottles of red wine.

'Jamie said to me once, "you should write for pleasure, not publication" which I took as his way of saying I should put my dreams to bed. Weird, how something so flip can keep you doubting yourself. He probably can't even remember saying it.'

'There you go then, see? So why listen in the first place.'

Flip words. Same as Wolfie's 'don't be a stranger' last refrain. He probably can't remember saying it either. But God, how the thought of him lingers. Likely the wine, loosening Goldie's determination not to fantasize, nor wonder upon how some kid from back in the day grew into a man like that.

'You've gone red,' says Valeria. 'Perv. Bet you're thinking about Lion-o.'

'Wolfie.' Goldie doesn't even try denying it. 'Men, eh?'

'Remember when Ben went on *Secret Millionaire*?' Valeria's a proper provocateur-ing motherfucker sometimes. She grins like she knows it, won't ever let Goldie forget how she was made to call, at Ben's insistence, to tell Valeria he was on the show and when it was airing, finding much humour in the awkward as he'd coached and encouraged Goldie along, while talking to Valeria as if they were in-laws who'd really put the time in.

For years, benevolent Ben and his *Secret Millionaire* story was regaled at every opportunity. Useful, and so very telling; how the measure of money is often misused as a barometer of good character.

For further torment, Valeria brims with mischief as she moves closer to Goldie so they can both view her phone, having found a YouTube clip from the show, of Ben in a fawn puffer-style gilet he can hardly move in, listening most sympathetically to some old girl who's got her back to him, her hands in a sink full of bubbles, washing up as she talks him through her woes. 'Well, that's not fair, is it?' he offers, while at the same time the camera catches him taking in the squalour of this woman's existence, his nose crinkling in revulsion as if he just can't stop it.

'Allergic to poor.' Goldie shakes her head.

'But not to you,' Valeria jokes, because she doesn't know. 'Can I ask why? Why you're leaving him now?' Breaking off some grapes, she returns to her armchair. 'With Jamie and me, it's not even about the baby stuff anymore. I just don't feel anything – especially not romantically. The thing is, I like it being just me. More than I ever thought I would . . .' Valeria smiles, gorgeous and natural, like there's sunbeams within. 'I'm serious.'

Goldie's glad she caught the moment, even if Valeria's furious. 'You of all people should know how intrusive it is to have cameras shoved in your face,' she barks, leaving Goldie stung, a little cracked open. 'Leave it out.'

'You're right.' Goldie pours herself another wine. 'I won't do it again.'

'Talking of family . . .' Valeria returns to topic. 'Don't ever forget the trauma left by our own parents. A missing mum, who was never in action in the first place. A dad we could never talk about. Is it really any wonder why we never saw motherhood as the natural order of things?' Valeria reaches for her glass. 'If I'm honest, there's always been a part of Jamie, some wholesome, faraway hopeful thing that I could never connect with.'

And so we pretend.

'Is that how you feel,' Valeria probes, 'with Ben? I know there's—'

'I don't feel anything for Ben. I don't feel much of anything anymore. Except tired.' Alcohol, as usual, works as a truth serum for Goldie. 'I'm tired of my life being signposted by people, usually men, with more power than me.' Popping a square of Milka chocolate in her mouth, Goldie means it. 'Like I said. You and me. We should be proud of ourselves.' Fuck outward judgement. Life, however strangely put together, has got them here; in one piece, in good health, and in one of the most beautiful places on earth. Growing a little wild, Goldie heads for the kitchen, coming back with a bottle of vintage Cognac and two dainty little glasses. From a smart-looking box, she helps herself to a cigar, too, as Valeria rubs her hands together encouragingly. Uncorking with a satisfying noise, Goldie sips from the bottle before pouring.

'All the trying to crush us. Silence us.' Handing Valeria a drink, she looks her in the eye. 'It gets done a lot, doesn't it? To girls. Like it's their right.'

'Men like Grant Love.' Valeria states fact, just as Goldie feels her own words coming.

Knowing once she's said them, there'll be no going back.

Eighteen

VEE

Ladies First

Vee finds Goldie touching up her toenails, everything about her round and voluptuous as she struggles to reach her feet. How fast the pair of them turned so deeply brown, no longer matching the foundation they packed. Vee's not keen to replace it, finding far more pleasure in her bare face than she ever has before, her brows no longer so dominant, finding a lighter arch also lifts her. She not only looks but feels lighter, too; the warmer weather becomes, the less she seems drawn to the comfort meals on the near perfect menus of pizzas and pastas and thermidors and steaks, choosing instead tricolour salads, moules marinière, and fish Provençals.

'You almost ready?' Most evenings, they visit the gelateria. The rule is that neither of them must ever have the same flavour ice cream twice.

'Shall we break the habit, have a drink instead of an

ice cream?' Screwing the top on her polish, Goldie sits up. 'There's somewhere I've always liked the look of.'

Vee agrees, still amazed how she woke without a hangover after the Cognac revelations the other night. Though she doubts if she'll ever look at a Camembert in quite the same way again.

Revelations. From a place of hungry curiosity, Vee had bloody well hoped for more. But the Wolfie feelings have left Goldie's emotions raw, like she's existing without an extra layer, which feels an odd swap just as Vee's feeling freer. Because it was a real relief; spilling all the Jamie-Julia fuckerations at last – which Goldie completely understood. Further proof Vee has a right to own her hurt, the emotional baggage of all Julia inflicted.

Though she doesn't have to keep on carrying it. Vee's learning.

Goldie, same as always, is all heart. Vee got an old love story, dressed up as a new one, told as usual with the same critical component missing. Something massive which sits right in the centre, in plain sight.

'All the trying to crush us. Silence us . . . It gets done a lot, doesn't it? To girls. Like it's their right.'

That sentence, so loaded, yet so fucking opaque, has rung through Vee's head ever since. And though she had tried leading the conversation that way, any mention of Vine had Goldie clamming up, with just the same look as when they'd touched upon it at Gran's house. Now almost a month ago.

So much can happen in a month.

Only last week, Vine Recordings released a statement

confirming their assistance with the escalating Ill Lothario case – which Vee had felt in her bones was only the beginning. The accusations against the music titan are multiplying – unsurprising these days, how being a ridiculously successful, notorious bully often goes hand in hand with being a sex pest. According to some, Vine's co-operation is more of an attempt to avoid investigations over their own misconduct, particularly during the late Eighties to mid Nineties.

Which had the documentarist in Vee reaching for her notebook.

For the past two days, Vee's writing has taken a big back seat in favour of a Vine Recordings bunny hole. She's barely scraped the surface, yet already the scum's rising – as it always does when you're rotten to the core, no matter how immaculately you present.

Sat at the pinnacle of Vine Recordings is Alec Champion. The next in line is his offshoot protégé, Grant Love. And Grant Love's pet project? The superstar in Vine's crown and now notorious Ill Lothario. And despite Goldie and however she might somehow be connected, what's emerged is the outline of a documentary, a potential exposé about the deep corruption right at the very core of the music industry.

Vee's already drafting a proposal, trying to find a—

'Here we are!'

Goldie leads them towards a thriving box-shaped bar in the old town near the battlements, playing music so loud it physically rattles Vee's organs. She's about to say so but stops herself, seeing how happy Goldie is, her eyes shining, all high-colour luminous and glossy that on Vee would look plain sweaty. 'What a proper tune. Wish I knew the name of it,' Goldie says, turning to order their drinks. 'What you having?'

'Double rum. All the ice.'

Fuck it, she's on holiday. She's overcoming trauma. Acknowledges yes, that's exactly what it was. Vee had a breakdown at sixteen years old. Declared a danger to herself. Which wasn't fully true. She was simply endangered.

As Goldie calls her a drink slag while she orders the same for herself, Vee opens her Shazam app. Setting it to work, she shows Goldie the result, her sister's wonderment matching that of the first person to witness electricity. 'Witchcraft.'

'Loyle Carner...' Vee drifts off.

Because it's him. The man from the café. Now on the opposite side of the bar.

He raises a hand in acknowledgement.

'Who's that?' Goldie doesn't miss a trick.

'Oh, just some man who sometimes...' Every time. '... is at my little café. The one I work in.' Shuffling in her chair, Vee clears her throat.

'Chill,' Goldie instructs. 'Just sit back like the delicious bitch you are and let him—' Goldie's shiny face beams naughtily as he indeed begins to make his way towards them. 'Think I'll excuse myself, pop to the loo.'

'Hello again,' the man says to Vee, out of context now he's away from their café, here with three other people sitting at a window table just outside, who Vee imagines are his friends, as they make a poor job of pretending not to be watching them.

'Hi.' Vee sips her rum. 'You look different here.'

'Is that good or bad?' He tilts his head, putting his big brown eyes to use, just as Onion would as he closes the gap between them. Taking Goldie's bar stool, his thigh presses against hers. 'I'm hoping you say good.'

'Are you flirting with me?' Vee asks, so directly it makes him laugh. 'Why?'

'Truth? When you're working at the café – gorgeous.' He waggles his hands with a grimace, hoping Vee won't get the wrong impression, which makes her smile as he gestures to his friends who vouch he's not a weirdo by waving and giving them the thumbs up. 'So thoughtful and faraway.' He smiles again as Vee makes her assessment; indeterminate age – though likely in his late forties, smart professional, no ring nor telltale ring tan line, friends who look both non-threatening and quite good fun.

No red flags. Just oodles of green lights, from his lashes, that she'd pay for, to the way his shirt cuffs dig into his thick biceps. No tats. Just smooth, luscious sun-kissed skin, eyes lively and bright. He looks fun.

Vee does not expect him to tell her how beautifully lost she looks when she's reading and working her way through her couple of croissants. A woman happy in her own skin, which leaves Vee inwardly baffled. Against the bar noise and buoyancy of mood, he leans towards her. 'Would you like to dance?' Running a finger down her forearm, he swirls his thumb over her wrist and into the nook of Vee's palm as he takes her hand.

As Vee's about to accept, Goldie comes back.

Gone is her glossy sheen of moments ago; Goldie looks just as she had when suffering the LeShuttle toilets. 'I feel terrible,' she announces. 'Think I should go home.'

Vee only just manages to catch her mouth from falling open in disappointment. 'I'll come with you.'

'Don't be silly. Have some fun.' Giving her a hug, Goldie says into Vee's ear, 'I know we're grown, but text that you're safe please.'

'Were you sick?' Concerned, Vee flinches all the same as she catches Goldie's hair kicking off a bit, damp from acidic smelling yack.

'Likely those prawns – I thought they didn't taste right. Serves me right for cooking for myself. Or maybe it's the other night catching up with me. Anyway, text me.' Goldie gives her a wink, before making her own summarizations, her eyes working across Vee's suitor like the Terminator.

'I'll look after your sister. I promise,' the man says as Goldie nods, and with a warning look that emanates serious Tony Soprano vibes, she exits the bar and her untouched drink, leaving them to it.

Vee concentrates hard to hold her glass steady. Her insides feeling like a bottle of fizz that's been shaken hard and slowly opened. 'So ... shall we?' he asks, and as Vee leaves her bar stool, notices he's taller than she thought; far bigger all over really.

'Valeria,' Vee says.

'Marcos,' he replies.

Leading her towards the dance floor, Vee's pleased to find she's her usual competent coordinated self, and as he takes her hand, reeling her in towards him, their bodies graze together in the most fantastic of ways.

The few outdoor tables get pulled inside. With less room to dance, Marcos and Vee keep close and to the beat, an awareness of how the other moves remarkably in sync for two people who've never fully met before. It is exciting, more so when there's a blast of eye contact, an acknowledgement of what's happening, what Vee might be prepared to let happen, as surprising for her as the moment itself.

Vee thinks he could tell her all the things. His age, full name, star sign and job description, the town he grew up in and where he's from – which is Spain, Vee thinks, going on his accent. He could talk about his loves, pets, pastimes and ailments ... his favourite film, hot beverage ...

But why. Seriously, why?

Desire rocks through Vee. Down through the chest and the guts as they kiss, feeling more vital, more human. Becoming herself. And is this not part of it? Her choice to act in desire. To reciprocate lust as an unattached human.

Here's another thrilling, fresh thing to throw her arms around. And with his body firm against hers, Vee thinks she's finally living.

All the forty-somethings, already past it in their bland houses; place the new family portrait over their old family picture and it would be a perfect replica. Why keep every generation the same suburban scene and call it a life? It is boring, predictable, safe, and it makes Vee want to scream. Exactly why she's resisted, because babies would make her just another loop in the tired old cycle, and she'd so wanted to give herself a good life.

So Christ, when's she going to start doing that, precisely?
Marcos the opportunity. Vee the opportunist.
'I'm enchanted.' His lips brush against her ear.
And Vee thinks,
Good.

★

Nineteen

GOLDIE

Disrespectful

Every holiday Goldie's ever had she's been ill this way. Nervous guts. Exhaustion. And vomiting now, which makes her promise a more respectful approach to looking after her mind, body and spirit. There's only so many Cognacs and Nutella crepes a girl can consume, after all.

Yet the ten-minute stroll back to the villa does her the world of good. The air is cooler in the evening, and beautifully ambient. After peppermint tea and some of Valeria's fruit salad, Goldie feels almost back to normal.

From the poolside, Goldie spots that Valeria's left the desk lamp on in her room, two moths prattling around in the brightness, which makes her check her phone. Nothing. But it is only 11.15 p.m. A quick shower and Goldie's starving again, helping herself to a whopping great slice of tarte Tatin and a can of Sprite.

Goldie's phone rumbles beside her.

Valeria Mob: Safe, totes OK. Not pissed.
56% phone battery.
He's called Marcos and I'm at 9 Av. Paul
Arène.
See you tomoz 😚😚

Good for Valeria.

And though Goldie knows she won't sleep until Valeria's home safe, this is yet more gorgeous evidence of her sister's emergence from her shell. She's even posted some of those pictures Goldie's been snapping of her on the off chance, to a flurry of likes which must surely feel like applause, though Goldie's still confused by people's responses to moments not usually shared. She'll never not be baffled by the wild interest in other people's gardens, breakfasts and children, relieved she stayed away from it all, unwilling from the start to lose her life – and her jawline – by looking downwards into a little electronic box sucking on her soul. But she must give slightly, acknowledge and not be quite such a dinosaur, because Valeria does seem to get so much from it, finding such joy in the comments that Goldie can't dispute, she's very, very glad to see.

And now Marcos. At 9 Av. Paul Arène.

Of course it's going to make Goldie think of Wolfie. All that exciting early chemistry, starting from nowhere yet taking over everything.

It's been a month. Yet again, Goldie asks herself the question that she'll never know the answer to; whether Wolfie would've rejected her anyway, even if she hadn't pushed him away first.

Because, what if?

What if they'd lain there, in that blissful afterglow, and allowed their bond to keep on turning them into something?

Too vulnerable. The fear too real. The only thing she's held on to, other than the don't be a stranger line, which Goldie fully understood, was when Wolfie said how his heart couldn't take it.

Hurt.

But can her heart take this? The thought of more neverending loneliness awaiting her return when the holiday is over. Looking into the sky, Goldie feels tiny, like she's the only one on the planet. Far too sad for a place as perfect as here.

Before going to bed, Goldie unpegs their swimsuits, now dry. Turning out Valeria's lamp and chucking her beach bits on the bed, she disturbs the laptop, which brings the screen to life with a Word document, open for editing.

Bad Adults
by Valeria Fliss-Burden

It's their true name – and it's how Valeria's used her full name, because it's fucking beautiful and Goldie's always thought so, that makes her sit, clearing a space on the bed, and begin to read, reminding herself that it's her book group stuff and not a diary. Goldie's only ever overstepped like that once before, which had been, absolutely, an invasion of Valeria's privacy. But better to break her trust than to lose her sister completely.

And not that Goldie ever told her.

Making herself comfortable, Goldie lifts the notebook she's sat on from under her bum, glancing over it briefly before—
Goldie can't believe her eyes.

Rage Against the Music Machine

A 60-minute evidence-based exposé [potential case study/oral testimony] on the corruption and abuse of power within music heavyweight Vine Recordings.

By Valeria Fliss-Burden

Goldie skim-reads through the accumulation of notes, scribbles and mind maps, some phrases sounding sick-makingly familiar to the things she's shared with Valeria, not only on the night of the loose tongues and the Cognacs, but throughout the entire fucking holiday. Even random things, like notes on a concert Goldie mentioned she'd attended, because Nas had been playing in the supermarket where they were shopping the other day. How Goldie had said just in passing, that he'd been so polite.

Soul Jam, Brooklyn – June 1995[G and GL together in NYC]

Flying first class, following Goldie's first practice studio session. A little treat to discuss her career and get her mixing in the right circles. As Grant's plus-one.

Notes on Vine's artists, past and present; the scandals attached to them, a whole page on Ill Lothario – which doesn't surprise Goldie in the slightest.

What does surprise, is the mind map with her own name

sitting central. Events attached to dates she'd all but forgotten about. Suggestions supposed to be leads of thought but feel like labels.

Contracts???/Exploitation of a Minor/ Adultification/Silencing/Royalties

Grant Love (Pre G) –	Rachel Lynton (ex-wife)
Grant Love (1994) –	Lacey Fletcher (fiancée now wife)
	Mum/Miri (girlfriend 1)
	Goldie (girlfriend 2)
Links/research to –	Rocki Ramirez (Vine singer – 1988–1992)
	Simone Jefferson (Actor 1992–)
	Dionne Rice (Vine singer 1997–)
	Adene Wallace (1998–)

Goldie's sliced to the bone. A certain energy for the subject which makes her think Valeria might be the same as the rest of them after all. Unable to see past the look of her. Just another in a long line of tits and arse.

As if the shell is all she can be.

Clicking through Valeria's other open tabs, Goldie's dismayed to find another document. A far neater version of the notebook proposal, and a running list of potential homes for it – *Dispatches*, *Panorama*, Netflix, *Channel 4 News*.

In less than an hour Goldie's packed Valeria's car up, denying her of another second in Villa Fleurie. The laptop Goldie leaves till the very end, as she stands now at the foot of the four-poster bed. Giving Valeria the best bedroom. Biting her tongue over so many of her tightly wound little bullshits. Given her far too much, if she's honest.

And what has Goldie ever got back from Valeria? Beneath her many, many masks?

Do you wish to permanently delete this document? asks Microsoft Word, with a warning sound. Hell yes, Goldie does.

That'll teach her sister. The piggybacking, parasitic bitch.

Twenty

JAMIE

If You Ever

Waking next to a sleeping Julia, Jamie reaches for his phone for a bit of blurry-eyed scrolling, rather than disturbing anyone by getting up. Not that Onion would know anyway, still stubbornly refusing to sleep in the bedroom, opting for her basket in the kitchen.

Opening his Instagram, the first post on his feed is Vee's.

It's not the usual identikit snapshot pose; Vee's face arranged in its standard trusted smile. These are real pictures, captured by someone who properly loves her – a shift occurring in Jamie that's almost physical.

Until he remembers. That it is only Goldie she's holidaying with.

The post contains a carousel of three pictures, all of Vee. One of her in an orange dress he's never seen before, which skims her thighs, the hem hitched a little up on one side, caused by the basket she's holding as she shops in an outdoor market. She's laughing, caught in banter with the lady stall owner. Entirely unaware, and gorgeous.

The next is a shot of Vee emerging from the sea, at a distance but very clearly her, wearing a bikini in an animal print which clings to her hips in a way that makes his mouth moist and his thoughts wander, as he looks at Vee's body as if he's never seen that before either. Her hair's in a topknot, her hand out as if she's telling Goldie not to take the picture, which again gives the photograph an unguarded, natural honesty.

A couple of complimentary comments follow, mostly from people Jamie's never heard of; bookish people, likely some of the new writing friends at her little club. Someone called Sumaira has replied: 'Salma Hayek eat your heart out.'

There's a row of flame emojis from someone called Ru02. With more odd discomfort, Jamie clicks on his profile. Ru02: Teacher. Writer. Observer. A pinned image of a book deal announcement, the rest author quotes and pictures of books and nature. Unable to find a photo and making sure first that his phone is on mute, Jamie plays a recording, a tagged clip that someone's filmed in a pub, of him being egged into giving a reading to the audience. The camera pans out to film the people listening, everybody very much engaged – including Vee, because there she is suddenly, the sight of her in the crowd making him gasp, as blink and you'd miss it, she's gone. Jamie replays the clip.

And replays it.

'That's seven times now. You can't even hear what he's

saying.' Shoving off the covers with a huff, Julia gets up. 'Or was it not him you were interested in?' she asks, stretching showily, and naked.

Jamie clears his throat as Julia folds her arms, giving him the pouty look, an obvious sexuality about it. A look used an awful lot whenever she's either got the hump or hasn't got her own way.

'Well?'

Putting down his phone, Jamie doesn't respond. It's not taken long to remember the pre-Vee dating rules; the excess of compliments, while pretending other women are invisible. Julia's continual need to be told she's the fairest of them all is not something Jamie imagines he'll be able to put up with for very long.

'What?' he asks at last, sounding short, exasperated – even to his own ears. 'What do you want?'

'What do you mean what do I want?' Furiously, she stares at him before stalking off to the bathroom, her long lean loveliness undeniable.

Vee was never like this. Not long and lean, nor hungry for attention. But always lovely. Probably batted off every compliment he ever tried giving her.

And then he'd stopped trying.

Picking up his phone, and backing out of the Ru02 account, Jamie finds himself again on Vee's page, an emptiness making itself right at home in his chest as he watches one of her reels, featuring a harbour, some battlements, the Fort Carré, the Picasso museum, and a crêpe the size of someone's head, then skims her posts, all of them scenic snaps, impossibly impersonal. The hashtags #breakfast #brainfood #amwriting alongside a picture of a notebook arranged all prettily on a café table with some croissants – and again a comment from this fucking book-boy imposter:

> **Ru02:** Love to see it. Still picturing those fireworks 📚💥

What a prick. What a total, utter ...

It feels like it's only ever when seeing Vee through someone else's eyes that Jamie's ever glimpsed the truth of her. Had he ever properly known her? He'd have said yes, unthinkingly – until those revelations a few weeks back, at odds ever since with his reaction, the mounting discomfort from how dismissive he'd been when she'd tried explaining, when he could sense her hurt, which from the moment they met, Jamie swore he'd never provoke. Knowing has altered him. Why did she never tell him she was bullied?

And why the hell had he shut her down, so unwilling to know it?

Hearing Julia in the hall, Jamie switches off his phone and closes his eyes, like he might be dropping back off, and as she slips back between the sheets, finds his forlorn genitalia suddenly taken in hand.

Jamie's not exactly keen, but a bit of yanking action, and it's mere seconds before he's loving it. How male, mainstream and midlife to be so ruled by his penis and God, isn't it a funny time for men fast approaching fifty? A little bit purposeless, with nothing truly to worry about. No wife. No kids. Better losing himself in a hand job than contemplating the second half of a very ordinary life, its lonely finish on the very distant horizon.

'Jules.' Good as it feels, Jamie lifts her hand away. 'Please.'

Julia huffs, as though they've done nothing but bicker for years.

He chooses his words carefully. 'Back in the day, when you said how you weren't very kind to Vee—'

Interrupting him, Julia rolls her eyes. 'This again. Really?' Now that he's noticed the inflection of her voice at the end of every question, like she's in an American teen drama, Jamie can't unhear it.

'Why, though; why weren't you kind?'

'Oh, for God's sake, I don't know.' She throws her hands up. 'I was a teenage girl.' With a little smile, she reaches again for his cock. 'Some people are easy to play with.'

He pushes her hand away. 'But that's cruel.'

'No, hun, it's life; survival of the fittest. I mean, look at us.'

But Jamie doesn't think he wants to be in the fit mean gang, especially not at forty-eight.

'Though your taste sure is . . . broad.'

'Ah.' Jamie reacts a little awkwardly. 'Types never work. It's the person – what's on the inside that really—' But Julia interrupts him with a retching noise.

'Come on, it was my killer selfies you looked at first though, wasn't it, long before you read my dating profile. I'm just being honest.' Out comes the pout again, the little girl confused shrug.

And isn't it funny what you begin to notice?

It's been almost three months. Yet not the first time he's

considered whether his and Julia's pairing has all been more of a testing of the water experiment of life on the outside without his wife, now clearly living her own life. Very happily.

When Jamie's mother had told him how there'd be men queuing up to take his place it had barely registered. He hadn't seen, or rather had forgotten, who Vee was.

Is. This incredible woman, who'd once been his wife.

Should've been his world.

And he'd slept right through it.

Twenty-One

Vee

Back To Life

Huge transformations are at work, a rewiring of all Vee's stuck bits, because in the here and now, this ordinary present that Vee's currently thriving in is exactly where she wants to be.

For once not so hungry for the next thing.

Vee's been waiting, longing for the moment she'd wake up and be a proper adult. But it never happened. Suddenly she's grateful, looking back and laughing; because what were all the plans for, the box ticking, overachieving, breaking into a million pieces just so her reflection was apt for some distant beholder instead of herself?

Physical connection wasn't something Vee felt she'd been missing out on. Though even when she and Jamie were lovers, it was always the same, a whole house, and sex kept neatly in bed. Their relationship had been so neat. So good. So unnecessarily wholesome. Who'd have given a shit if they'd left the washing up and had a quick go on the stairs, or the sofa, or up against the hallway walls.

All the places she's now rather familiar with ...

Vee looks at Marcos sleeping beside her, just as fucking delectable at daybreak, and thinks back to the rare handful of times in her life when a spontaneous new partner had arrived on the scene. By now, Vee would likely be making them tea, maybe not stretching to breakfast, but certainly drawing her brows on and brushing her teeth.

But Vee doesn't want to do those things.

Slipping into her dress, she's smiling as she quietly collects her bag and phone from his bedroom floor, her shoes a-dangling by their straps as she picks them up too, tiptoeing silently to the front door. Closing it behind her, she blows him and the house a kiss goodbye.

The sun's beginning to rise as Vee heads for the beach, straight towards the sea. Gorgeous soft waves lap around her calves, then thighs, till the tepid bath of the Med envelops her completely. Carried by the gentle tide in just her underwear, she lolls onto her back, watching the light across the water grow then take over completely; at peace – yes, at peace with it all. 'Thank you,' Vee says to the horizon, which remains steady. And bright.

Living with all these tight conflicting little rules Vee made up in her head. Somehow always lacking, never good enough. Too long carrying it all, she thinks, as something heavy unclunks itself from the buried place she's spent her life chained to, conservative, joyless, controlled by other people's opinions.

Never stopping to sit in her achievements. To be comfortable with them. To accept them as hers. Claim them. Hold them. Love them. To declare, this is great, actually. And to grow, laterally, into all that she is, giving thanks for her own fine self.

And finally cherish it.

Back on the sand, hidden beneath her dress, Vee checks her phone. It's 5.59 a.m. Switching on her mobile data, she jumps as several notifications appear with a rumbling alert.

Sumaira's is the first message on the writing forum.

> **Sumaira:** WOW!!!
>
> **Urdan:** This piece is outstanding. Felt every word, Vee.
>
> **Kathluvsbooks:** This would work brilliantly as spoken word. Thank you for sharing.

Vee clutches her phone to her chest, as the realization falls in.

> **Judith:** Great bones, Vee. Do see me for critique and a chat when you're back.
>
> **Jon:** Reads like the opening of a novel to me.

Vee doesn't think she could write a whole book about herself. Unsure if she'd want to invest serious hours dredging her own upset, then making it read pretty. Besides, Vee's almost got a finished proposal of the Vine Recordings documentary – which brings Goldie back into her thoughts. She should shift her arse, get back to the villa. A shower would be magic.

As would a debrief. Vee imagines Goldie's reaction as she fills her in on last night – not the lustful deets, just the fact that she can't stop smiling and could sleep for a month, all the info she'd need to give away. Dropping in at the boulangerie for almond croissants, Vee impulsively buys two huge slices of tarte tropézienne, the brioche sponge and inch depth of creamy centre suddenly a very good idea. And just when Vee thinks she couldn't get much happier, she remembers the glowing critique from the writers' group.

It's almost a shame she won't be in attendance next week.

Could she/would she be brave enough to stand on that stage and read a two-minute section like they'd talked Ru into doing? Scary no doubt, but somewhere, deep down, Vee wonders if it might also be rather exciting.

Approaching the villa, Vee double-takes at the sight of her car, loaded most haphazardly with all her belongings.

Buzzing through on the keypad. Vee buzzes and buzzes and—

'HOLD ON!' Goldie barks venomously through the intercom, not waiting for a response before hanging up on Vee.

'Have you changed the code? I couldn't get in,' Vee asks, the look on Goldie's face making her stomach drop as she emerges through the electronic gates, holding Vee's laptop, which in seconds lands in pieces around her feet. 'Goldie, what the—'

'I read everything.' Goldie's face is hard, entirely unforgiving. 'Exploitation? Look in the fucking mirror.'

It takes Vee a moment to realize she's not talking about the forum piece, but the documentary proposal. Closing in, Goldie stares Vee down, trembling and as worse for wear as last night. 'You want to thank your lucky stars I'm sick, or I'd be smashing you to pieces, too.'

'I don't know what you think you've read ...'

'What I think I've read?' Goldie tuts. 'What would you know about life, anyway? So wrapped up in your own head you've almost let it pass you by. Whereas adultified, exploited me ...'

'I never said—'

'You did! But you know what, I don't need to explain myself to you. And I don't need to look at you either. So go home, Valeria. Your holiday's over.' With a flick of her cerise kaftan, Goldie turns, heading back towards the house.

'It's ... only what I pieced together.' Vee swallows. 'But I swear, G, I truly never meant to hurt you. It's only an early draft, so much will change ...'

'Before what?' Goldie interrupts, horrified. 'Please don't tell me you've shown it to anyone.'

'I haven't. I promise.' Vee sighs. 'And I'm sorry. I am so, so sorry. I just thought it could work for you, like it's started working for me, to confront things ... facing your own story. What with Vine in the news, too ...'

'I don't want to hear it!' Goldie puts her hands over her ears, just as a child would. 'It's done; all of it. I don't want to spend the rest of my life turning over the past. That's how people get stuck.' It hurts how suddenly frightened Goldie looks, as if she's inhabited by ghosts and all she can usually keep a lid on. 'I never want any of it mentioned again.'

'Okay,' Vee agrees. Cross with herself when she adds, 'I promise. But if you've been, I don't know, controlled in some way ...' What really are the right words? 'Masks and facades, they only hold for so long.'

'Standing there with your car full of books. Keeping order and routine and living within the lines. Pretending to be all the things you're not.' Goldie stares her down. 'Is that not masking as well?'

'Is that not what we've both been doing, then?' Vee claps back. 'Please, Goldie, nothing I wrote was meant to hurt you. But it wasn't yours to read either.'

'Well, no one can read it now anyway.' Goldie gestures to the laptop, before declaring triumphantly. 'Because I deleted it.' As she opens the driver's door, Vee meekly climbs inside, her legs weak again, only now with disbelief as Goldie chucks the keys and the broken computer into her lap. 'So fuck this holiday, fuck the car journey home and fuck all our fake re-bonding. You've just been collecting choice bits for your shitty little project, anyways ...'

But before Vee can listen to anymore, she does as Goldie asks. And fucks off.

Twenty-Two

VEE

Right Back Where We Started From

If the journey down to Antibes had felt an eternity ...

All that praise for her writing eclipsed by the fact that she's totally broken Goldie's heart.

Vee's never seen her sister so upset. Not since ...

The second she'd driven a safe enough distance away from Goldie's fury, Vee had stopped, and in a panic had checked her phone, heading straight to the cloud. In less than ten seconds the deleted proposal had been restored from the recycle bin and back to the safety of Vee's OneDrive, as she wished if only everything could be as easily put right.

Best push on. Get as many miles north as possible, not as easy paying for the *péage* in a British car on the toll roads by herself. Doesn't want the radio; Goldie's endless shuffling of stations something that had desperately irritated Vee but now she desperately misses, prompts her to turn into the first Burger King services she comes across to stuff her face.

Too tired to drive safely any further, Vee flops in an Ibis hotel on the outskirts of Mâcon, and cries beneath the shower. Unable to sleep, nor shut her mind off, at 4.30 a.m. she checks out for the final stretch home, a glimmer of good fortune from rediscovering the bag of yesterday's breakfast pastries; squashed, dry, but passable.

Enough to power her on.

Maybe if Vee had stayed, tried again once Goldie had cooled off ... It was how she'd react when she was younger, flying off at something and then five minutes later be your bestie again. Vee knows this, just as she knows herself.

And she could've tried harder.

Should've.

Even now, sad and sorry as she emerges from that neverending tunnel to the view of the Eiffel Tower, Vee still has pangs to turn around. Fuck the returning hunger and tired jittery strangeness and go back to her sister and tell her that she loves her. How it could never be possible to love anyone else as much as she loves her.

But because she is Vee, easily offended, sulky and grudge-holding, she resists.

The decision is taken from her hands when a voice message pings through from Jamie.

'Don't want to worry you, but Onion's really not well.'

In seconds, Vee's ringing him back. He answers straight away. 'How really not well?'

Jamie sighs. 'The vet's keeping her in.'

'Oh.' Vee's voice is small. Lost and terrified.

'Hey,' Jamie says gently. 'I'm here, remember. I'll let you know what's happening the moment I—'

'But . . . but what happened?'

'We . . .' Jamie pauses. 'Found her having a seizure in the kitchen.'

'A seizure?' Vee bursts into tears. 'Oh God, Jamie!'

Home couldn't feel any further away as Vee remembers, berating herself, as only she could, about how she's not yet booked her return on LeShuttle.

Once she's got past the delays in Calais waiting to board, Vee's return home is quick. The house doesn't smell like hers. Nor does it feel welcoming. Not without Onion.

Nothing but a pile of bricks Vee can't wait to be rid of.

Crying at the sight of Onion's bed, and again at the sight of her toys built in a pile outside Vee's locked bedroom, she tries calling Jamie again, but it goes straight to voicemail. Deciding to visit the vet herself, and just as she's pulling back on her trainers, there's a message from Jamie.

> **JAMIE:** Discharged 🙏 Picking our girl up now.

More fricking tears.

With nothing in the fridge, cursing the freezer for containing all the things she wouldn't have touched in France, Vee settles for quick tea and toast and a shower that feels near perfect. On hearing Jamie's return seconds later,

Onion's face peeks around the bathroom door, not looking remotely poorly as she dances around a damp, deliriously happy Vee.

'Likely something she ate,' says Jamie, as happy and relieved as Vee is, as they both fuss Onion, Vee pressing her face into her fur. To think she'd been worried about Onion having the hump with her for going away. Nothing like a trip to the vet's to put life in real perspective.

'I've been so worried, girl.' Wrapped in her dressing gown, hair dripping from the shower, Vee climbs into Onion's bed, cuddling into her body, and she swears that Onion is smiling. Inhaling all her old doggy smells, and holding them inside her, Vee feels herself at last beginning to settle.

'She's okay.' Jamie hesitates. 'For now. She's getting on, Vee. They said.' He blows out in one sad long huff. 'We should prepare ourselves.'

Because she's been happy and well enough, Vee hadn't truly accepted Onion's dementia, though they've known for some time. Her legs are weak, too, and her bowels unreliable, sometimes having accidents in the house, which makes Vee cross and heartbroken all at once, because its undeniable when she looks at her girl, so very, very tired, that they don't have long left together.

It is the most heartbreaking thing.

As they lie spooning in the dog bed, Onion puts her fluffy paw on top of Vee's hand. Neither of them is ready to say goodbye.

Vee knows that when she leaves this house, it won't be with Onion.

It's unquestionable, how this is equally heartbreaking for Jamie, too. Onion the bond, another sign that their life together is ending. All these signs of closure.

Them. And now the dog.

'How was the holiday?'

'Brilliant, and then not so. We fell out.'

Jamie grins. 'It was a long time to be together. More tea?'

'I'll do it.' Kissing the top of Onion's head, Vee gets up, pulling her dressing gown tight around her she heads for the kettle. 'How have things been here – apart from the obvious.' Vee nods back at her.

'Unremarkable.'

'Good.' Vee turns with a smile, finds Jamie looking at her softly. Strangely. 'Sorry, did I say that out loud?'

'I wasn't thinking before.' Jamie screws his face up. 'I didn't mean to disbelieve you ... I don't really know what I was thinking,' he admits, growing a bit pink. 'Because lately – briefly – I ... I can see, how perhaps Julia could be ...'

Perfectly placed are the adjectives balanced on Vee's tongue, ready to be rocket launched. But she doesn't; will not bite over Julia ever again.

'She won't be coming to the house now that you're back. So you never have to worry about, you know, crossing paths.'

Now that Vee's back. Because she's noted already the hints of Julia around the house, for example the tiny cashmere cardi over the arm of the sofa. A change of shoes in the hall. The half bar of Green & Black's in the fridge.

Bathroom towels that Vee would now like to burn.

'You look . . .' Jamie can't seem to stop looking at her. 'Well. Really well.'

'Thanks,' Vee replies distractedly, thinking of the Green & Black's in the fridge. Neither she nor Jamie like dark chocolate.

Dark chocolate causes dog seizures.

But hasn't Vee's imagination caused enough damage?

Could Julia do something so atrociously cruel? Vee knows so, just as she knows that Jamie wouldn't believe anybody remotely capable of it. Home for an hour and back to square one. As the thought occurs, why not fuck all this shit off and move to Saunders Road?

It's suddenly the most appealing option. Sod her dotage here, if it gets Onion away from Julia, too. In her head Vee begins planning, thinks of ordering some moving boxes—

But then it dawns. There's no way Goldie's going to want to houseshare now.

With no other way of Vee leaving, it feels like a suffocation.

And it's as if Jamie can see it. 'Look, next week I'm off on holiday, too. Felt a bit envious of you on your travels, if I'm honest. Tuscany,' he adds, as if he hasn't quite decided if he's happy about it. 'So you and Onion. Quality girl time.'

'Space time.'

'Yeah.' Jamie sighs. 'Space time.'

Staying put with Netflix and the power shower it'll have to be. While keeping a firm hold of the acknowledgement that things need to push on here. Vee's mental to-do list grows: a deep clean of the whole house, plus a few fresh valuations from the local estate agents. Vee and Jamie swore they'd do it quarterly. It's overdue.

'I'm sorry, Vee.'

'Sorry for what?'

'That we didn't make it.' Leaving her and Onion alone in the kitchen, Jamie heads out, to where Vee doesn't know. Down their front steps, his shoulders dipped, Jamie puts a hand on top of his car, taking a moment when he reaches it. Usually so happy. So surface level predictable, that you forget about his depth.

How ferociously loveable characteristics do exist.

Twenty-Three

VEE

WAP

Usually, it's Vee with the form for pulling the cold act.

Usually. She's been home for over a week without any word from Goldie.

Vee wonders if she'll ever forgive her; space right now being the only answer, unsure if Goldie's still in Antibes or back at the Coach House. All Vee does know is that Goldie's not at Saunders Road, because she's checked, the empty house a repeat reminder of the unswallowable stone of a feeling Vee can't get rid of. After rediscovering their sisterly sync swing of things, only for it then to be so abruptly severed, has given their holiday an unreal quality, even more so now that Vee's home.

In creeps the same old feeling, as if Vee doesn't really know her sister at all.

Goldie was right. Vee couldn't help gobbling up the bread-crumbs of everything she'd shared, a habit she can't break even now she's back, tirelessly trawling though old articles, media archives, anything really for a glimpse behind the curtain. To discover the truth of what happened between Grant Love, Vine Recordings and Goldie's brilliant yet extraordinarily brief career.

But Vee's not a complete vulture; understands, now she's put herself in Goldie's shoes, how it doesn't read well. Because how would Vee feel, to have someone speak on her behalf, uprooting experiences she'd rather leave in her past? She doesn't exactly need to dig deep to get it.

Truth, though? Even in the throes of their fall-out, even when Vee felt like the absolute pits of a person, she'd also been thinking what a powerful scene this unexpected conflict between such central characters would make on paper. Goldie was spot on. Vee had spent the holiday gleaning all she could.

Vee's never been called a parasite before. How deeply unflattering. Maybe her worst insult yet.

Maybe not though.

Though the weirdness remains, their fight feels remarkably distant – in much the same way as taking off to France had felt in the first place. Goldie's grown, and Vee has her own life to sort, she really does. Starting with her own permanent space. Perhaps all that's required for true happiness is to up sticks and move to the moon. Peaceful and unpopulated. Pretty fucking perfect. And if going to France has taught Vee anything – beyond keeping her laptop password protected – it's that with the job she's got, the freedom to live wherever she chooses is limitless. She's driven across two countries;

less afraid every day of life and language barriers; the worry of being a lone woman traveller gone.

Beautiful as Montmorillon was, rural France had felt a bit too isolated to be an option; Vee needs more. A little action distraction.

Maybe Spain's the answer. Perhaps elsewhere. Or even the ultimate dream, of one day being able to afford London. Not the cusp of Essex part that she's from, but a proper city central location – the brutalist Barbican, or along the buzz of the Southbank. All the culture Vee can consume, where she might truly belong.

Vee's been making a list. A new loo seat in the cloakroom. Repaint the front window ledges and plant up the window boxes. Hire a carpet cleaner. Book the estate agent valuations. Better busy, avoiding the proverbial yet problematic elephant that's currently occupying the house; nothing to do with Onion's declining health or even Goldie – but rather Jamie's strange apology. Which read like regret.

Gut regret.

For what, though? What part is Jamie so truly sorry for?

Here at the house, every evening he's been out, Vee's rejoiced. The uninterrupted quiet feeling so much like treasure. How lucky it is to find such unparalleled pleasure from her own company. And okay, no real writing's going on – more journaling and Vine-related research with Onion back stuck to her side, but it's precious.

Vee's not sorry to admit how her thoughts rarely feature Jamie, even less so in a regretful sense – which perhaps is the problem; him so unaccustomed to being irrelevant. Unconsidered.

More truth? If it hadn't been for the night with Marcos, how irresistibly wanted he'd made her feel, Vee mightn't have joined the dots regarding Jamie's sudden over-attentiveness, how he'd looked like someone had pressed pause on him only this morning, his mouth slightly ajar from watching her unload the dishwasher in her least flattering nightshirt. Or the likes he'd given her holiday pictures, only for him to retract them a few hours later – overthinking never a Jamie trait.

A role-reversal then.

It is boosting, regardless; in a sort of one-up way against Julia, which shows she hasn't won, hasn't totally swallowed Vee's life – and isn't it time Vee started letting that sink in, too?

Once upon a time, Vee would've done anything for Jamie, even had a baby, even put herself through that. For him. But things shift. Like Vee's latest acknowledgement to herself; how she'd felt their disconnection long before they'd even properly separated, so far removed from the habits of having dinner when Jamie was hungry or waiting to finish their latest favourite TV series at a time which conveniently suited him or even waiting to climax until he was in the mood. Every tiny circumstance, where she'd unthinkingly put him first.

It's been a revelation to be back on her own terms. As an adult. Sans man.

Vee can do whatever the fuck she wants.

So here she is, cleaning the house instead of going to tonight's writing meet. Sorting the cupboard under the stairs, making space for the moving boxes she's ordered. Better to lose herself in organizing the house than lose herself in old going nowhere thoughts.

Even when she gets a text which disturbs her playlist of mostly Kelis, she keeps on task. It's an hour before she reads it.

> **Writing Ru:** Wondered if you're going tonight? Remember, there's no pressure to get up on that stage x

Before her eyes, another message arrives from him, an invitation to his book launch. Vee knows from her own work how they go down; drinks and mingling and happy accidents of perhaps chatting to an agent, or a publisher. Not that she'd dream of pitching her wares at somebody else's party, which would be a bit like wearing a ball gown to somebody else's wedding. But it's positive circles. And besides, Vee would love to witness Ru celebrating his dream come true.

> **Vee:** Thank you. Count me in x

Ru replies with a polite thumbs up, which could mark the end of their back and forth, but as Vee looks at the cupboard, at the chaos of a job she's now wishing she never started, a surge of frustration rises inside of her, which feels exactly as if she's wasting time.

Is it ambition? If so, Vee needs to be far more disciplined. Bollocks then.

*

Vee's showered, gussied up and is out of the front door in under an hour. Off the train and ignoring a magpie, she walks across three drain covers and without hesitation enters the pub.

'Vee!' Ru breaks into a smile when she nudges his arm, having found him in what seems to be his usual spot at the bar. Both of them taken aback, Vee thinks, by how pleased they are to see each other. Hairy, handsome and clever clearly the traits Vee's attracted to; Ru's a fresher-faced Marcos – apart from his eyes, which despite Ru being younger, have so much more going on in them, depth; an 'old soul,' Gran would say. 'Glad you made it.'

'You sold it so well. Though there's no way I'm reading aloud.'

'Fair enough.' Smiling, he says it like he means it. 'Judith's going to be thrilled you're here. Volunteered straight away to critique your piece one to one – believe me, whatever she tells you will be worth its weight in—' He frowns, before adding quickly, 'If that's what you want, of course. It took me a lot longer than you to post on the forum. Anyway,' Ru puts his hands up in surrender, an easiness about him that again reminds Vee of Marcos. 'Me personally, well, I'm just glad you're here.'

And while Vee's on her roll, sticking two fingers up at caution, ignoring all the usual petty obstacles, she says, 'So am I.' Which only makes Ru smile wider.

As Vee takes a seat for the read aloud, she's elevated all over again by how the emotional Julia head-spill of a piece lives on in the heads of these people usually so hard to impress. They say kind, encouraging things, and those who don't, catch her eye and smile, like they know. Like they know her, and she doesn't have to explain anymore who she is.

Vee can just be. A feeling she's so unaccustomed to it creates another settling within her. A calmness. From validation, as a person.

As a writer.

Truth connects. And people like authenticity. It's all she needed on the writing front, Vee understands now. So wrapped up in her own head, she only just catches the end of Judith's offer of a drink and a word, having sought her out at the end of the readings.

'Terrific stuff, Vee.' Judith looks as proud as if she wrote Vee's piece herself. 'You took the barriers down and my word. Such raw and energetic prose.' As she blows out through her wine-stained lips, Vee longs to hug her.

'Thank you.'

'And is there more?' God, she looks really hopeful.

'Not much. Scenes and snippets. Nothing substantial.'

'Make writing your first priority,' she says most seriously. 'It's the first piece of advice I gave him.' Judith nods across the pub to Ru, in his own pairing with his back to them. 'And it applies doubly to women.' Keeping her eyes on him, Vee studies Ru, too. 'And if things are headed where I think they're headed, don't let him read it. He'll be chronically biased.'

As if he's felt them watching, Ru turns in their direction. Can't take his eyes off Vee either.

And Judith's made her point.

*

Later on, Ru and Vee have a drink at the bar, just as they had before. What a different night that had been. One she could easily now paint over and rewrite, as if all that followed never happened.

But then, Vee wouldn't be here mentally. Because isn't it worth noting how she is so much clearer in her own head, thanks to the stacks of injustices that she's ironed out since Julia's reappearance. Oddly, if it hadn't been for Julia, Vee wouldn't even have gone to France – and even though they fell out, Vee enjoyed every moment she got to spend with Goldie. Nor would she have written the piece that turned all the heads in this East End pub full of amateur critics. And she'd certainly never have discovered the raptures which came from going home with Marcos.

Vee thinks she's glad to be here, in her current far healthier mindset.

A bottle of Pinot blush disappears easily between them, without a thought of missed trains or next day headaches. From his confident on-the-level interest in her writing to his interest simply in her, Ru makes both things clear. And as they lean into each other's space, a different sort of compulsion fills Vee, no longer built from the urge to purge words. More from the need to satisfy her sudden craving for human touch. For connection. Because all at once Vee's starving for it. Since Marcos and beyond fussing Onion, Vee's had no physical contact with anyone. Not even a handshake.

And though Vee's unsure if it's lust or loneliness on her part, she's sure all it would take is a nudge.

'Well,' she says, 'home and tea, I think.' Drawing her arms into her sleeves, Vee pulls on her cardigan, just catching his crestfallen look. Puts it another way. 'You'd be welcome.'

'Now?' Ru grabs his jacket from the back of his chair. 'Sure.'

Outside the pub, Vee and Ru find themselves in the very same spot where they'd said goodbye before. Only this time, there are no shy farewells.

Amazing how easily the sparks can fly when there's no pressure on the outcome. Just the same as with Marcos; their evening together which had felt like a shedding of skin, Vee finally done with closing herself off from her own desires. Her own wants.

What does Vee want now?

Damp from kissing a man who writes, Vee decides she would, absolutely, go to bed with Ru. Go to bed. Why so puritan in her thoughts, when it all amounts to the same? Allowing this fucking scrumptious man to blow her socks off is a new, very different achievement to reach for. And going from the way he kisses, one Vee's certain could be very simply met.

Vee invites Ru home because she can, because she wants to, and it's her own free will after so long to be making these decisions. And also because Vee loves how her writing continues to pique his interest. What an extraordinary aphrodisiac it is, how he's beguiled by her words. So far, apart from what he read aloud, Vee's avoided Ru's writing on purpose. Wanting to save herself.

For the book. Obviously.

'Because of Julia?' Ru asks, gesturing wide-eyed at the bare shelving and storage boxes as he fusses Onion, like an amalgamation of art and life, Vee's trauma served on a plate disguised as fiction.

Handing him a glass of excellent red, Vee nods as Ru sucks in through his teeth.

How far can Vee push it, to really condemn people; to show the world who they are and not flinch from it? And can they bite back? Even when they've already bitten.

Amazing how he knows what's gone on – understands, because Vee wrote a story about it. Writing, that was always such a guilty secret. Keeping herself so neatly hidden. Presenting a non-person. As it crosses her mind how it has not been all Jamie's fault.

But even as she'd penned her truth, Vee had only written what she'd been prepared to give away, and while she'll likely never be the type to share every detail of what she's thinking and feeling, Vee really doesn't mind revealing her body.

These encounters are not only about the sex. It is the decision making, Vee's choices. No deep examining of how the moment might look on the outside, but simply going with her own feelings. At last.

Finally. Letting. Go.

Vee matches Ru's desire, believes it from the way he tastes her, consumes her, electrifies every nerve ending, which doesn't make Vee feel emotionally attached, more thrillingly connected. Her heart is not involved in this. Just her brain making the right decisions for once, because this, Ru, is exactly what's needed.

Fun.
Scenes straight out of a book she'd choose to read.

Twenty-Four

JAMIE

Never Can Say Goodbye

On his way to Southend Airport, Jamie thinks better of it, and at the very next roundabout indicates off towards home. Palms sweaty. Not ill, but not himself either. In half an hour, back in front of his own house, Jamie finds himself at another mental crossroads, as he considers whether to tell Julia it's over before he tells Vee.

That he loves her. How he wants to spend the rest of his life righting the most foolish decision he ever made.

And Julia can go to Tuscany anyway, where she'll soon realize that their fun didn't mean fun forever. The holiday's only added to the pervading sense of feeling cornered. Jamie's finding that the more Julia's tried to steer their relationship with the plans she seems to pluck from nowhere, the more self-revealing she becomes, her controlling streak the complete antithesis to his dynamic, amazing, non-problematic ex-wife, out living her best life without him.

Jamie hops up the front steps two at a time, glancing through the dining room window, absent of nets which is yet more evidence of Vee's current housework trip, as if she's trying to remove all traces of them. Even a crack team of forensics would be hard pushed to find a single telltale sign of them ever being a happily married couple at all – leaving Jamie feeling as if he's in water he can't stand up in.

Helpless. And completely fucking unsure of himself.

The man Jamie spots through the reflection of the hallway mirror does nothing to help those feelings. But Vee would've mentioned having a guest over. Surely would've told him if there was somebody ...

But Jamie's meant to be on his holidays.

The potential of an empty house doesn't only work in his favour.

Sighing, he rubs his lips, unsure what to do. Fearing he might set off the doorbell, Jamie hurries around to the side of the house, stopping before he passes another window, which looks into the lounge. Where, in the other end of the room, clear as, is Vee.

In the lamplight, both starkers, Vee's straddling that bear of a man. With his hands in her hair, lost in the nook of her throat as he kisses her, the man turns Vee onto the sofa, lifting her hips, those fucking lush hips towards his mouth, and makes an absolute pig of himself.

And, as if further annihilation was possible, it then dawns on Jamie who the man is.

Book-boy. The schoolteacher. From Instagram.

It's him, without doubt; and why not? Jamie and Vee

merely, barely, share a roof these days. How vital it had seemed; to have sex with a brand-new person. Never thought what it would be like when Vee did the same. And now look.

Why is it such a shock, how Vee's flourishing without him? Because it does seem like the second Jamie stepped out of the picture, her world burst into life. As if she couldn't wait to shake him off.

Which sounds like blame.

Or had Jamie been the one holding her back, keeping her bound by all the baby making that stopped them from living in the present, seeing one another as lovers, instead of permanent fixtures and potential parents?

They were always so chaste. Neat. Never abandoned, nor fully lost in moments like Vee's now. Certainly not since they married. Companionably a natural match, but things hadn't drifted as natural matches often do, into babies that bond you into meaning – which was precisely their difficulty. When sex became purpose instead of pleasure.

'Back to the nest,' Jamie would say, as if in preparation, from pretty much the moment they moved in. As if everything about their newly married life centred on this one baby-making objective. Yet sometimes he could feel Vee's detachedness, her hesitancy to give herself physically, which fleetingly would make him wonder whether she wanted a family with him in the first place. And had he truly outright ever asked her what it might've been that she truly wanted instead?

So hung up on the family dream, Jamie forgot they were people, too.

The passion through the window, staged like a smouldering 1980s coffee advert, is another little death inside. Not at all Jamie's business, yet a new low as, voyeuring and gobsmacked, he shuffles away, with a cock far harder than he's ever known it.

Twenty-Five

VEE

Wildfires

It is Ru who makes tea for Vee the next morning.

He's got work, a class of Year 12s to teach, plus five missed calls from his father – which he finds amusing. 'I didn't think he had my number.'

Though Ru says it in jest, and despite him being, undoubtedly, an independent, deliciously experienced adult, Vee gets the smallest glimpse of another side to him, a vulnerability which chimes in her gut – and an insight into exactly what makes him pick up the pen. Vee's realizing all writers have their reasons.

And writing does help to make sense of the unresolvable. All those endless inner torments which need so much turning over, incredibly vain really. The chronic fascination with self and feeling. An obsession like no other.

But also, a form of healing. Perhaps a book is exactly what she needs to do. Stop sifting through Goldie's world – no matter how fascinating – and focus on her own story. Thinking of Judith's encouragement for more, the lovely swell in Vee's body returns. From praise. *Raw and energetic prose* ... Snuggling into her sheets, Vee couldn't stop smiling if she tried.

'Can I call you later?' Ru lifts her leg from the bed, kissing her ankle goodbye, which sends a feeling so excruciatingly delicious through Vee's vag that she whimpers, giving him his answer.

Vee hadn't expected, considering his youth, for him to be so fucking ...

Capable.

The moment Ru leaves, Onion fills his place, her warm body working like a sedative, as Vee thinks briefly of the cupboard downstairs, the unsorted shit that's still filling the hallway, before she sleeps.

Twenty-Six

GRANT

Ain't No Playa

Grant knows Goldie's been out of the country. Wishes he could make it so that she'd stay there, and they could all carry on living their lives as they have these past few decades; through the hottest of recollections.

But with so much regret.

The warnings from the top couldn't be clearer; should Goldie speak, then it's game over – especially for Grant. And is exactly why he's had to be so fucking accommodating, as everybody from the police to a proper private inquiry loom on the horizon, chomping to pick every paper trail shred of Vine activity to the bone.

In his car, Grant checks his watch, then the house on his right, waiting for the door to open. Lets his mind imagine the scene inside; Lacey likely on breakfast duty by now. Remembers back in the long ago, before this millionaire mansion lifestyle, when she'd let him sleep in, keeping their kids quiet all those nights he'd work so late, trying to make Vine something.

And also the nights when work wasn't work at all.

There has been nothing personally damning so far; Goldie and Grant remaining a poorly kept industry secret being key to his survival. Because this is #MeToo part two. Unquestionably. Another attack on those stubborn stains who survived before. And who do, truly, fucking deserve what's coming to them. Because covering for Ill Lothario as part of your job description, the many traumatizing morning-after scenes and clean-up jobs on tour buses and hotel rooms, wasn't exactly easy work.

And neither was it forgettable.

Naive, or perhaps egotistic, to hope that somehow Ill Lothario might've swerved his own moment in the eye of the storm. Grant his A & R man and producer. Too involved to make like he never had a clue, so it's time to double down on the damage limitation. And there's only one person who can truly save his skin when those accusations turn on him.

Christ, he'd even tried hand-delivering a letter to that big pile of bricks she's living in. The next Baroness Bickham by marriage apparently, which is a union Grant can't fathom, and not the Goldie he once knew, though he's glad she's secure all the same.

At least Grant can say he's been there for his kids. Not that either of Miri's girls had been physically mistreated, but they were unloved. Which made them reliant on each other, especially the little one. All big-eyed and curious; lost in a book. Always quiet. Goldie her translator. Her scaffold.

Doing all what the mother should've been handling. The girl deserved a break.

Girl.

It'll never not be a madness to Grant how a basic calendar date can dictate such an entire moral shift. Because how can it possibly make sense that having his wicked way with fifteen-year-old Goldie at five to midnight before her birthday could've landed him in prison, yet at five past the hour on her sweet sixteenth and he'd have been clapped on the back.

It remains an uncomfortable fact; how Grant couldn't get Goldie out of his head, anyway. The dilemma of resistance. Against all the reasons – excuses – to ignore her age.

Then that evening, when she'd been going out, putting in her hoops and slipping into her puffa, those matte red lips he couldn't take his eyes off, and Grant asked what time she'd be home.

'You ain't my dad,' she'd said. So cocky. *'Which is probably a good thing, don't you think?'*

And what's a sentence like that, if not an invitation?

Noticing the front door open, Grant pulls himself upright. Gets out of the car to greet Angel, heading towards him in her pink dressing gown and slippers, like a walking candyfloss.

'Mum said to tell you to go away.'

'It's been a whole week now. She's had her space. Christ.' Grant frowns and shrugs, like a helpless old dad might. 'I miss my family. I haven't even done anything.'

'You knew about Ill Lothario, though.' Angel checks out their neighbours, to see if anyone's watching them. 'All that enabling ... But Grant shakes his head, smooths his beard as if he doesn't understand.

Ironic. How, after all the decades of constant philandering Lacey never liked, it's somebody else's misdeeds that's become the thing to fuck their marriage for good.

'Why are you not ready for school?'

'School's dead, Dad. I'm free till uni.' University. How fast time flies. 'Free for a nice holiday as well ...'

'I can't see it happening. Perhaps your mum—' Grant tries, but Angel rolls her eyes, still very much his youngest kid, the baby of the bunch. Grant's never let Angel meet anybody he works with. None of his children in fact. Which is telling.

Trust, he'd do a life stretch if Angel got caught up ...

With a man like him? The question has Grant making his goodbyes, keen to put distance between him and his baby, who at fucking eighteen is still four years older than Goldie had been on the night Miri took him back to hers.

What had he even been thinking, getting mixed up with Miri Burden in the first place? Her neediness as unattractive as her maternal neglect. Surface level, though, she was an incredible looker. Michelle Pfeiffer foxy. Plus there was her folklore connection to one of his musical heroes – rest in power, Amos Fliss, Master-Fly the Great.

There was also the fact that she put herself on a plate. So he kept on coming back.

Coming back for who, though – in the end?

Honey hair, skin, eyes, made to magnetize.

Goldie's lyrics. From day one ...

He's only a man.

Yet the awkwardness did brew in his gut, which had so little to do with being unfaithful, and more about Goldie's eyes, trying to weigh up what just happened between them after the first time.

Grant thinks of that calendar again, all his five-to and five-past analogies. It's the strangest of afflictions, feeling both lucky and loathing himself, to have been the first person to love her. But it mustn't be overlooked, how he then made her a star. And really, when thinking about it that way, Goldie owes him.

This tiny favour now, at least.

He'd been captivated. By her ambition; that streak of star quality which beamed out from her whenever she climbed into the recording booth, or onto a stage. And even Grant wasn't quite sure how it happened, when friend became lover became driver, became minder, that all rolled into being her manager. And then she was old enough anyway.

We've known each other since forever, Goldie liked to say in interviews, Grant paranoid by the brows she'd raise. And even when she was out of contract and of no interest to anybody, he'd stayed wary.

Just as selfish back then as he is now.

Twenty-Seven

VEE

Gossip Folks

Why isn't he on holiday? is the first thing Vee thinks when Jamie knocks on the door of her bedroom.

'Can we talk?'

'Now?' With a sigh, Vee stretches, feeling aches in her joints and in all the lovely places. It's almost lunchtime. Tucking her curls behind her ears, she opens the door.

'Have you seen this?' Jamie asks, turning his phone to show Vee a post from a girl group called The Canticles.

> We've always believed that our near-miss when signing the contract of our first album was a blessing in disguise. If not for the guts of another teenage artist, the only person with the front to protect us from the misogynistic machine that is Vine Recordings we might not have gone on to achieve all we have. But all

> the same we've never forgotten the bravery of Goldie
> Fliss-Burden
> X

Vee rubs her eyes. Asks Jamie to give her a minute, knowing it'll be much longer as she heads for the shower, her very awake mind trying to recall everything she knows about The Canticles.

The bravery of Goldie Fliss-Burden? What on earth happened?

And how extraordinarily random. The last musicians Vee would ever have thought to be connected to Vine Recordings would be the Canticle sisters, their music being folksy, ethereal and not at all in sync with the catalogue at Vine, which even back in the day had been dominated by house, dance, hip-hop and R & B music from mostly black musicians. Goldie easily mouldable between all their genres.

Apart from being about the same age at the same time, sixteen-year-old identical twins Melody and Allegra with their waist-length blonde hair was pretty much all they had in common with Goldie. And even back then, even as teenage girls, they'd looked worlds apart. Where Goldie could do little but exude hotness, the Canticles were fragile-looking waifs, channelling what soon became the classic nineties 'look', all haunted and hollow-eyed. They dressed in antique lace and long nightie-type dresses, played a multitude of instruments, favouring the flute and acoustic guitar, and wrote all their own songs.

And perhaps because there was two of them, how they

arrived on the cusp of a shift within the industry, or perhaps just their smart and timely decision not to sign with Vine after all, was what catapulted them into global superstardom. And kept them there.

Almost thirty years of The Canticles. Countless multi-platinum albums. A residency in Vegas. An Ivor Novello. The Pyramid Stage at Glasto.

Twice.

Them chipping in to the growing circus surrounding Vine will surely knock the whole thing into a blizzard storm, Vee's certain. And the moment she's out of the shower, Vee checks on the alerts she's set up on her hashtags, because she'd felt, hadn't she, in all her best spidey senses, how this story would be massive:

#IllLothario #GrantLove #IndustryExploitationMachine #MeToo #PowerAtTheTop #MusicCorruption #ArtCorruption

Again, they form a repeating pattern, a murky trail. Always leading back to Vine.

Vee clicks on a resurfaced clip she's not seen before. Of Grant Love as a talking head on some panel music show like *Never Mind the Buzzcocks*; grainy old footage. Probed by the host if the rumours were true – whether he and Goldie were a couple – with a quick lick of his lips Grant cast his eyes offstage, the side-eye telling them everything they needed to know as he'd lapped up the roars of male approval from the other panellists: who wouldn't though, right? Who wouldn't stick it?

It. A teenage girl.

Live, laugh, leer culture. Perverts – and every one of them

over thirty. The same sorts who were counting down the days to Charlotte Church's sixteenth birthday.

But times were different then.

Knocking on her door again, Jamie hovers on the landing with a cup of tea.

'It's been shared 650,000 times,' Vee says to him, dismayed.

'Made the lunchtime news, too. It's all coming out.' Jamie has all the latest. 'Silencing, NDAs, physical threats. All to protect that Lothario singer. Apparently, it's like Sav all over again, the number of women coming forward. Some of the stories ...'

For the first time it occurs to Vee whether Goldie knows she's in the headlines. There's a strong chance she doesn't, living without a smartphone. And if she's still in France without a TV, even less so, which makes Vee feel a bit sick as she remembers her promise never to mention Vine again. How Goldie had looked so vulnerable just from their mention.

Terrified, too.

And though she tries, constantly, to call her sister, all Vee's calls go straight to her voicemail.

'Please, G,' Vee begs, leaving another message. 'Just call me when you get this.' Jamie wafts his phone under her nose, her irritation rising as he knew it would, thanks to the *Daily Mail* gossip piece entitled, 'What Was Goldilocs' Act of Bravery?' Using a picture of Anita Doth from 2 Unlimited instead of a picture of Goldie herself. 'Yeah, yeah; we all look the same. Easy mistake,' she says, as she tries Goldie again. 'Please pick up ...' Vee swallows, suddenly wanting to cry. 'I'm so sorry.'

★

Twenty-Eight

GOLDIE

Brown Girl In The Ring

Goldie wakes to seven missed calls from Ben. Each message increasingly livid, which in the end Goldie stops listening to and deletes them all.

None of Ben's upcoming events made it into her diary. Not that she packed it, and not that she's bothered even replying to him since their last conversation. Really, she could've been dead for the past five weeks for all he'd have given a shit, but when he needs her ...

The phone rings again, and without checking who it is, Goldie switches it off. Better to keep her head in the sand and her body on the beach, so deeply bronze now, so wholesomely freckly, the sun making her hair lighter, and her eyes, too. Good weather has always suited her best. Goldie's been happy here with her weak entry-level French which thus far is faring her well. She can get herself fed and watered. Not that she's been particularly hungry; the nagging remnants of that horror show illness when the Valeria shit was going on has left her delicate. For someone perpetually thinking about her next meal, Goldie's suddenly all juices and olives, living on fruit.

Lolling in the pool, Goldie turns onto her back, squints up at the sun.

Knows it's time to go home.

Even though that means she'll have to fly, it's only an hour and a half, and she can suffer it. Probably sleep right through it, the way she's been going for it lately, must need the rest. Must finally feel like she can rest. What do they say, after a shock you sleep. The shock of dipping her toe into new romantic waters, then having it torn clean off.

Then, while walking wounded, to be stabbed in the back by Valeria.

The gate's intercom buzzes, like an alarm clock confirmation and just as persistent, which Goldie ignores though it cements her decision as she books an afternoon flight and a car to the airport.

Later, outside the gates to Villa Fleurie, are paparazzi. Two separate media outlets, that reanimate in Goldie's direction as she rolls out her suitcases, locking the doors. Surely they're not here for her? Glad she's wearing her sunglasses, Goldie hurries to her cab, which sets their cameras off as they shout something about The Canticles that she can't work out. Once on the A-road, Goldie switches on her phone, which takes forever to load and even longer to reveal her notifications. More infuriated calls from sulky-tits Ben which Goldie skips again, and two from Rufus, with no message.

Three from Valeria.

With an inwards growl, Goldie calls up the mailbox to listen.

'I'm sorry, G, but please ... You really, really need to ring me. Call me before you speak to anyone else. Goldie?' Sighing, Valeria gives up.

Once dropped at the airport, and with yards of time before departure, the next time Valeria rings, Goldie answers.

Waits for Valeria to speak first. 'H ... How are you?'

'Everyone's hounding me. Is somebody dead?' Yet Goldie's glad it's not Valeria who's curled her toes up; the anger that's been on perpetual simmer, suddenly boiled dry.

'Nobody's dead. Have, have you spoken to anyone? Here at home, I mean.'

'Just you. Your message was weird. Look, I can't talk for long, my flight leaves at four.'

'You're coming home?' Valeria sounds so relieved Goldie almost forgives her. 'To the Coach House?'

'For a bit.'

'I ... really don't think that's a good idea.' Valeria drifts off, as if she's conversing with somebody in the background. 'You're flying back into Stansted I take it? G, go to Gran's.'

Goldie's body runs cold. 'What's going on?'

'You made me promise not to mention it again. And I don't want to break the promise.'

'Can you stop being stupid and just bloody tell me?' But even as Goldie says it, something in her gut already knows.

'It ... it's not a terrible thing. You've just been mentioned – in a very, very good light – by The Canticles. You know, the—'

"Course I bloody know,' Goldie snaps, finds herself starting to shake.

'It's not really that, though. It's more what I think's coming. Have, have you noticed anything, like press?' Valeria asks, but Goldie stays silent. 'Look. Just call me when you're home. In fact, when are you landing? I can come and pick you up. I can—'

Goldie hangs up, a swamping anxiety claiming her as she takes a seat in the lounge. Thinks she might even throw up as she watches the television on mute in the corner, the rolling news, every so often punctuated with mentions of The Canticles.

> Canticles sisters get their mic drop moment on Vine Recordings, thirty years later.

Then afternoon fluff pieces. Speculation.

> What was Goldie Fliss-Burden aka Goldilocs' act of bravery, and where is she now?
> Rumour has it Goldie leads a reclusive life as a society wife.
> By choice – or was she silenced?
> As more accusations, now in their hundreds, paint an even darker picture, it's making the world question – is Goldie Fliss-Burden the key to the truth of Vine Recordings and Ill Lothario?

The case of the decade, both NBC and Sky News say. The Canticles' admission the final nail in Vine Recordings' coffin.

Few artists ever come close to reaching their level of stardom, The Canticles' fanbase almost like a version of church for their legions of worshippers. Thinking of Valeria's advice, Goldie quickly remembers the ropes. She won't talk until she's back, and for the tiniest moment thinks that she might find all this briefly thrilling, if she didn't know what was waiting, home like a big sharp set of jaws she's flying straight into.

Goldie feels hot, overheating and sticky. Dirty.

Coated by the awful sense that she'll never be rid of the skin she's in.

She's likely paranoid, yet Goldie feels the eyes of the other travellers nonetheless, which keeps her panicked and over-thinking, wishing she'd arranged a car to collect her from Stansted, too, or at least told Valeria where to pick her up from when she'd offered.

God. Valeria had been trying to warn her.

Goldie thinks of the letters from Vine Recordings lingering on in the bottom of one of her suitcases. Carrying the negs around like a ball and chain, unable to face ever opening them, unsure why she'd even bloody packed them.

When the drinks trolley passes, Goldie orders two whiskies and two Cokes, pocketing the tiny bottles for later. All the little crutches that come flooding back in a crisis.

Is it a crisis? It certainly feels like it, her foundations critically unsteady. Goldie feeling small, and worse than small. Powerless.

Powerless against it all.

*

It is 16:48 when Goldie lands, 17:25 when she wheels her cases through arrivals. Wearing her sunglasses, she holds her chin upwards, unsure of what to expect, and equally unwilling to give any tabloid ghoul an inch of vulnerability or weakness. If there's one thing crucial now, it's her practiced aloof mystique. No matter how different the truth.

It is crowded, stressful, but not the storm she'd imagined, whipping herself up on the plane and over-imagining scenes of camera flashes in her personal space, hounded like Princess Di, her name chanted over and over—

But this. This is all rather anticlimactic. People there for other people. And just like that, it's—

'Goldilocs!'

Goldie turns as a camera goes off in her face. Just as someone's hand grips her wrist, which she flings off, marching ahead and startled, as the same hand catches her jacket.

'It's her,' someone says, as another person tries commandeering her suitcase. 'Goldilocs, can we ask you some questions?'

Don't cry, she tells herself, keeping her head down as she hurries away. Don't bloody cry. 'Excuse me, please,' Goldie says on repeat, feels her panic rising as she comes to a stop, unable to weave her suitcases around the legs of someone who just won't move.

As she realizes.

It's Wolfie.

★

Twenty-Nine

Ru

My One Temptation

The Uber to work costing Ru the earth this morning came as absolutely no hardship. The night before worth even the giant bollocking from being late in, too.

Vee Hughes. Running his hands through his hair, Ru smiles to himself – the sexy bubble popping only when he remembers the missed calls from his father also from this morning. Ru had liked how Vee hadn't asked questions about his dad, which would've given her the first proper insight into his background. But she's not a person to pry – not much of a surprise either when you think about it, considering how hard she works to conceal herself.

She's a gift. In more ways than Ru can explain, which has only amped the impossibly exciting game of trying to figure her out as she leaves him clues and hints, like a slow undress, keeping him captivated. Ru's unsure what's doing it for him the most; the undercurrent of language which exists in her writing, so visceral and compelling – or the fact she's just fit as fuck. The way she sort of knows it, but hasn't made it her entire personality, which is another rare quality.

As is finding someone completely on the level. Who you might not mind letting in. Because there are not many people who truly know Ru. Mum, who loved him enough to not be a completely pushy parent, nor force him down the path of the family business – or what's left of it – which would've crushed his soul. Ru thanks God that his father wasn't on the scene when he was smaller, knows he would've become a vastly different person had he been packed off to boarding school aged four, just as his dad had been. Glad he wasn't another cookie-cutter replica in the chain of naturally successful men with the good family name.

A name Ru's never been able to claim as his.

When you teach classrooms full of teenagers in a regular everyday comprehensive in a regular everyday city, there are no special allowances for anybody. His kids are savage, hilarious, call him Ru and have no idea of his background, because they'd ruin him if they ever discovered his grandfather was a baron, let alone a former Tory MP. How Ru, their regular, everyday normal enough social sciences teacher is in fact a secret posho.

Which is conflicting. Because at twenty-eight years old, Ru is still a dirty secret. The largest part of him deeply relieved – there is truth in the disease of association. The only other person who understands that is the only other person who truly knows him.

Goldie.

He can't pretend otherwise, popping into the Coach House has become just like popping into any other house now she's gone. It feels too big, suddenly. Too soulless. And makes him hurt a little, that she's been there for so long, mostly alone. It must've taken an awful lot of her to fill it, to bring a place like that to life and for it to feel like home. And Ru misses her.

By mid-morning, he's seen the Canticles tweet, and by late afternoon, the photo of Goldie and Wolfie that's circulating on the news, of them at Stansted Airport, that brings real emotion to Ru's heart. Doesn't think a more perfectly loving moment could even be put into words.

As it begins to dawn why his father's been so persistent today.

Benedict doesn't say hello when Ru at last calls back. 'Did you know anything about this – about him?' *Thieving bastard,* Ru thinks he hears as his father's signal dips in and out.

'Hello to you, too,' Ru says, ignoring how he keeps on bleating over him. 'You're not even a real couple, anyway – why should it matter?'

'Of course it fucking matters, when the fat whore's splashed all over the news!'

'No wonder she wants a divorce.' Only just realizing he's dropped Goldie in it, Ru adds, 'Well, that's what I would've wanted, and long before now. You disgust me. You always have.'

'I disgust you?' Dad snarls, ready to explode. 'And who is it that you are, Rufus Fry?' How he loves to topple people with his skills of belittling. Ru's witnessed, probably every time they've ever been together, how his father's manners only ever last while someone's of use to him. 'This is all so fucking humiliating. She's supposed to be—'

'What, what is it she's supposed to be? You know, this could be your chance, your redemption. You could fuck off the money, sprout some decency and marry my mum.'

Because who'd really give a shit about the ancient family beef outside of his own unscrupulous circles anyway? It would be a good thing to lose the inheritance, to shake off the stigma of peripheral aristocracy, the old money cushion of never-ending wealth. Hoarding money, and the obsession with hoarding more, has left his father mean and close-chested. 'I am disgusted. And I don't blame Goldie for wanting out. I blame you.'

'It's *me* who wants her out. Both of you in fact. Tomorrow, first thing, I'm sending men. And vans.'

Men? And vans? He sounds like some ancient military brigadier, dictating from afar. It's almost funny.

Amazing, as a writer, an observer looking in, how his dad's entitled ego has taken such a gargantuan battering. Slighted in his loveless marriage, which was all his own creation, anyway. How it was always one rule for him but not for Goldie.

But it would work like that, wouldn't it?

Ru remembers his first visit to the Coach House; how it had been Goldie and not his estranged father who'd hugged him on arrival, his first time meeting her, aged around thirteen. Goldie, who'd said from the off to pay his father no mind, that he didn't know how to be, then did a dance, right there in the kitchen to a radio jingle, and made him some toast.

And suddenly it wasn't so bad.

It's all Ru can do to stop the words coming, the things he's longed to say since he'd been surprised with a surprise father who even on their first meeting couldn't take his hands out of his pockets to greet him. Just talked at Ru, instead of talking to, which was a step up from talking down, at least – schooling him on how old the Coach House was, and how many generations of Bickhams had played cricket on the lawns.

In all the talking at Ru, Benedict never once mentioned the story his mother Therese had shared. How the Bickhams tricked and embezzled her grandfather into parting with his shares to their literal fortune, which led to a loan, which led to asset stripping and such reputational damage the Fry name was forever muddied. Salacious talk, which made them such a bad smell in their circles, the Frys never recovered. Every so often one of the privileged few will come unstuck; get ejected from the nest, so to not pollute the rest – which is how it looks from the outside.

But when you are part of it, a big ugly crucial cog who keeps the old shit ticking, you really just can't see it.

Dad. Such a pointless word. Ru nothing but a threat from the off. A breathing jeopardy every time he got sent to the Coach House, where his father was rarely ever seen anyway; the only presence of Ru the picture of him in his pretend bedroom, put there by his pretend wife.

'How old am I?' Ru asks.

'What sort of a question's that?' his father huffs.

'You don't even know. Haven't congratulated me on my book. Haven't asked me what it's about. Then again, I don't think you've ever asked me anything about my life.'

'Oh, grow up. You never liked me. And I never ... took to you. What does it matter?'

'It matters because you're a terrible person who deserves to be lonely.' Charmless, pompous, non-human. Because frankly, who'd want to be associated, or be anything like him anyway? Cold, cutting and walking dead. 'I hope Goldie lives happily ever after. And I'm sure she will. Now she's away from—'

But he's hung up.

Thirty

WOLFIE

How Will I Know

'How are you here?' Goldie asks him, her face against Wolfie's chest as he holds her.

'The longest story,' he says, leaning his own face against the top of her head. 'Is this all your stuff? I'll fill you in on the way.'

'On the way where?'

'Saunders Road.' He smiles, strokes her face. 'Don't fret, G. Honestly, everything's all right.' Stopping short of clicking her into the passenger seat, a very delicate Goldie tries not to cry as Wolfie drives out of the short-stay car park. Legs apart, frowning at the sun from behind his shades, he gives her arm a squeeze.

'I don't understand. What's changed? All that's happening ... they're not exactly selling points.'

'I went to see my mum.' Wolfie shrugs, as if that more than explains it.

Goldie's quiet.

'She was right, as usual. Made me realize that it's better to have feelings than miss out by having none.' He glances over at Goldie. 'I find it hard ... showing myself, you know. It was wrong of me to expect so much from you. Connecting always feels like over revealing,' Wolfie admits. "Cos, despite what I said, I've not been able to stop thinking about you. Not gonna lie, even more so since we ...' He smiles, saucily. 'All that stuff, my reaction when you tried explaining about Vine ... And your past. It wasn't very grown-up of me. Then today ...'

Sitting up straight, Goldie interrupts him. 'I appreciate the lift, really I do, but ...'

'But what?'

'I can't be doing with another male saviour. Becoming somebody else's pet,' she says, confused by his instant amusement.

'Did you see the car you climbed into?' Wolfie laughs, shaking his head. 'I'm a forty-five-year-old failed footballer, living mostly with my mother, because until Benedict's buyout hits my account ...' Reaching across, he takes her hand. 'So, as saviours go ...'

'Why did you sell Ben your business?'

'Truthfully, I held my nose. Principles are one thing, but I'm three months behind on my mortgage. I can't continue the renovations without money. Another three months and ...'

'I could've helped you.'

'But wouldn't that make you my female saviour?' Wolfie catches her eye, and for a moment it's as though the kids in them are back, casting a lightness which feels almost healing, right at the centre of the madness.

*

Goldie's too fragile for her own good, looking lost and far smaller than the last time they'd sat together in her nan's front room. 'I'm not sure what I did to deserve you both,' she says to him and Rufus, 'but thanks ever so much.' Wolfie watches her eyes fill with another wave of almost crying she's just about keeping control of.

'We're keeping receipts,' Rufus says for a bit of kind deflection having noticed her upset, too, as he sets Goldie's tassel lamp down, the room such a cacophony of mismatched hell it's hurting eyes.

Goldie hugs him. And as they move out of the way for Wolfie to drag in another enormous holdall of clothing, she gives Rufus a key. 'Because I'll feel better knowing you have one for here,' she says. '*Mi casa, tu casa*. Just like always.'

Taking the key without question, Rufus hugs Goldie again.

Though Wolfie admires how Rufus is so unquestionably on Goldie's side, he can't help feeling sorry for him – caught in the web of family, of loyalties and disloyalties. With such a good heart, it's baffling he's the offspring of such an atrocious cunt.

What's also baffling, is how, at record speed, Rufus has somehow managed to rescue Goldie's belongings. Rallied the cleaner and gardener into helping him clear out the Coach House, apparently, after giving them the low-down on Benedict going ballistic on the phone, and then a heads-up about how 'men and vans' would soon be coming to gut out her stuff and take it to landfill. Rufus, along with Goldie's worldly goods, had arrived at Saunders Road not much after him and Goldie had reached their destination, making Wolfie think of Goldie's gran's old saying, about how when people say it's a small world, point them to Essex. She'd been spot on – in more ways than one.

'You all right, Rufus?' Goldie asks him suddenly, her face full of concern as she follows his eyes to the sideboard as he stares and stares at the framed pictures on display, mostly of Goldie and who Wolfie thinks must be her sister Valeria.

'I ... Yeah, of course,' Rufus says, though he does sound strange. And suddenly pale. Perhaps it's only just dawning on him what making an enemy of his father could mean.

Wolfie's already learning. How two Mondays back, almost £800k was supposed to arrive in his bank account. Paperwork signed. The sale of his business complete. But for Benedict's games. The manufacturing outlet in Basildon has been left in limbo, the same as the orders now backlogging along with distributions, contracts at risk and six really bloody worried employees, now questioning Wolfie's promises of smooth transitions. What Wolfie's struggling with most, though, is why Benedict seems set on running his business into the ground, considering how keen he'd been to buy it in the first place. But hadn't his gut – and Goldie for that matter – told him not to sell? It wasn't exactly long ago that his gut had pointed out how Benedict was a prick, too. Likely why Wolfie's enjoyed today so much, Rufus's rebellious two fingers up at the Bickham establishment – and Wolfie's own dash to the airport; Valeria tracking him down, thanks to the contact deets on his business website he's yet to cancel.

And then seeing Goldie again.

They're early judgements, but Wolfie likes the people who love her – though he'd clocked her face when he mentioned his mother, unable to remember if her own was still about, and knowing the same as the rest of planet what happened to her dad. There is so much unasked, unmentioned, that he'd like to know, to fill in the gaps of. Knowing also he's likely not the only one of them who feels like that.

A bit later, when Wolfie heads out for pizzas, he gives his own mum a ring.

'It's bloody well called getting to know each other,' she laughs once he's explained, before turning serious. 'She let you in, didn't she? Isn't it time you did the same?'

'Saying it, though,' Wolfie says, with a sigh because it hurts. 'Up it all comes again.'

'Perhaps it must. Just for a bit. Have you thought of it like that? A bit like Goldie, having her past splashed all over the papers. Disgusting how they get to do that.' His mum huffs. 'How is she?'

'Jumpy, a bit delicate, too, but I think she'll be all right. You'd like her.' Wolfie's phone beeps. 'I best go, Mum – pizzas to collect.'

Wolfie says his goodbyes, as a little further up the street a woman comes towards him; a stiffer, more purposeful, slightly taller, narrower Goldie, all in black but for fuchsia sandals. Making eye contact as they cross paths, Wolfie notes how her frown transforms from its worried look to one of curiosity as she raises a brow, vanishing into the house Wolfie's only just left.

★

Thirty-One

VEE

Foolish

'I came as fast as I could,' Vee shouts from the front door, slipping off her coat and throwing it over the banister. She heads into the kitchen. 'G?'

But no.

Holy fucking shit.

'I didn't know,' Ru says. 'I really, really, really didn't know.'

Vee's eyes dart about the room, as if expecting Goldie lying in wait.

'She's in the bathroom. Wolfie's just gone for pizzas.' Running his hands through his hair, it's clear Ru's just as rattled as she is.

'This . . .' Vee's voice drops to a whisper. 'This is very, very fucked up.' And not how Vee's life goes. She's truly had her fill of jump scares lately. And now Writing Ru is suddenly . . . Goldie's stepson. Jesus Christ. 'Tell me this isn't fucked up?'

'Exactly what I thought when I spotted that.' Ru points to

the sideboard, to the Montauk picture from Vee's fortieth of her and Goldie on an empty beach, the wind having sent their hair across their faces, Vee's hat pulled low over her eyes, but still obviously her. Ru looks awkward, conflicted.

But he would look like that, wouldn't he? Sleeping with his stepmother's sister ...

Aunt!

'For context, though,' Ru says at last, 'we're not blood, and I am almost thirty—'

'Almost?' Vee hides her face with her hands. 'I can't do this. Not now.' Yet even as she's saying it, she remembers Goldie's similar moment with Wolfie not so long ago, in almost the same spot as where she and Ru are now. And though Vee doesn't understand why, it puts a rising sensation inside her, which feels oddly pleasing. 'I need to be with my sister.'

'Of course.' For a moment Ru looks entirely lost. 'I'm so sorry.'

'Don't say sorry—' Sensing Goldie, Vee swoops round and unable to meet her eye, hugs her instead, strange and stiff but of course with love, thinking all the same how it's flipping typical that just as she's beginning to feel validated as a writer, emerging herself at last, it would be Goldie and all her peripheral baggage who smothers it.

Only Wolfie eats as the conversation remains fractured, Vee torn between wanting to know the ins and outs of the Canticles story and wishing it could be kept swept under the carpet for a little longer, or at least until Vee can get her own shit straight.

Ru. He sits there, slightly to her right on the sofa, breathing their own form of communication, as he tries, just as she's doing, to make it all make sense. How they've had this massive thing in common, yet Goldie's never even once been mentioned.

And now here they are. What the actual...

Goldie gets to the point. As best as she can recall it. 'I had a year left on my contract; I know that much.' She sips her rum, an old bottle with a dust crust which was lurking at the back of the larder, and smiles. 'Everything was going well, you know – I'd spent most of that summer out of the country,' she says, trying not to look at Vee. 'I don't remember much about it, except the travel. Never got past that mystery of flying from one country to another, without returning to check in here first. Everything before that had always been school then home, shops then home, Walton-on-the-Naze and then home. Just never got over it,' she adds, as Wolfie smiles into his lap. 'Anyway, there'd been this big anniversary showcase event for Vine; their offices had been turned over to the party, all the giants were there; it felt like a family effort, a very, very, fucking cool family it must be said. And there was this pair of singers, sweet and folksy, and just brand-new, trying so hard to not draw attention to themselves...' Goldie looks down into her own lap.

'The Canticles?' Vee checks, sensing Ru's eyes on her again as she tries focusing on her sister. Because even mere glancing is igniting pure hot sex flashbacks.

Which simply aren't stopping. Not even for Goldie's revelations. Oh, the shame of it.

The terrible, delicious shame.

'Ill Lothario and his entourage were being so ...' Goldie tries thinking of the right word. 'Lewd. Super fucking lewd. No one, as usual, brave enough to pull him in line.' She said she'd felt it most profoundly, their longing for someone to step in. 'I don't know why but watching them in that struggle just enraged me.' She sighs. 'Then he told them to kiss. Sixteen-year-old sisters.' She clicks her tongue, just as revolted now. 'Before I knew I'd even done it, I'd shoved him.' Goldie downs her drink in one. 'Little twat.'

Vee makes a spontaneous grab for her. 'Well done, G. I feel all proud.'

'Yeah, yeah – so did I. For about a second. Because he shoved me back, far worse than I'd shoved him. Grabbed my arm and twisted it up behind my back like it was second nature. Said old meat jealousy was ugly.' Goldie exhales, looks to her hands, to the shaking fingers ferociously picking off her nail polish. 'And to this day I can't tell you what hurt more; his violence or his words. Old meat. I was seventeen. Barely.'

Goldie had watched as their faces registered the seriousness of the assault, the pain excruciating; her vocals almost ripping the roof off. A real whopper of a problem, because they knew that the second the paps snapped a pic of her weirdly angled arm, or they risked Vine's rising star being snapped arriving at a hospital, then the questions would start. So much harder to smother someone with a public profile than to quiet the hordes of disposable unknown girls they hushed on the regular. And so, like the many times before that were so commonplace, especially at parties, everything went into 'hush-down' mode. Goldie ensconced in some private clinic, which was more like a five-star hotel, '... where Grant wore me down into accepting compensation.' Which was better than having Ill Lothario's lawyers, who he called his destroyers, trashing her life.

All because a girl dared ask him to be nice.

Goldie had a spiral fracture, swelling and bruising. With her good hand she'd signed an NDA, and Vine Recordings paid her £75,000. She took the family to Cancun for an all-inclusive fortnight, plus all the excursions they could stomach. And the remainder paid off the last of Granny Saunders' mortgage. Goldie bringing home the gold. And the bacon.

But back from her holidays, she'd found career-wise things were a lot quieter; Goldie very much on the outside of the cool circuit. Smothered out by fresh talent, before she got the chance to become the Goldie she'd imagined.

'I was scared. I didn't want my life pulled apart. Dad, Grant. You – how could I put you through that?' Goldie says looking at Vee. 'We'd been through enough.' She sniffs, with a nod as if to confirm it again. 'And that's the story. Amazing The Canticles even remembered me. What I did.' Goldie pulls a handful of envelopes from her dressing gown pocket. Putting them on the table, she points to the Vine Recordings logo. 'Makes me wonder if they remembered, too.'

Unable to resist, Vee swipes up the envelopes to study them, finding four in total, all unopened. 'You've just sat on this?' Vee double-checks the ones with postmarks. 'For over two bloody years?'

'You don't understand. They're scary people. Them shutting me up back then became the start of every door closing on me. When my contract ran out, I thought thank Christ, time for a fresh start, new management, a whole new era – but no. Vine ran my career into the ground. Ensured I could never recover. Mr Maybe aside, they've kept it that way.' Goldie can't resist either. 'Look at you, longing for X-ray vision. I'd let you open them, but I'm really enjoying your agony. My sister's the nosiest person you'll ever meet,' she informs Ru and Wolfie, making Vee wince.

'But you need to know what they say.' Embarrassment aside, Vee's full of wild thoughts; contracts, NDAs, and other such legal dramatics. This is all becoming rather exciting.

'You open them then.'

'Are you serious?' Vee winces again at the sound of herself, like she's been allowed a Christmas present early.

'I am. But would you make tea first?'

'I'll help.' Ru's on his feet before Vee's even decided to get up.

'Stop looking at me,' she tells him, once they're safely in the kitchen.

'Stop looking at me then.' Ru leans against her body, pressing them against the closed door.

Some people are born with a sixth sense. Clairvoyants obviously, and those people who suffer migraines before thunderstorms.

And Goldie.

'She'll suss what's going on in about five seconds.'

'So, there is still something then?' Ru's eye contact is bold as fuck, without any hint of regret. 'Between us?' Hesitating, Vee nods. Which sends them back to lingering pecks, and it's all she can do to contain herself as she finds they're full-on kissing anyway, with more ferocity than even last night.

Goldie's spilt her guts, and she's ... This is not Vee behaviour. Rarely has she ever put her fanny first. She is not reckless, prides her good moral compass.

'Just wait,' Ru says against her mouth, running his fingers around the waistband of her trousers. 'Wait till we're alone again.' And when the smoke alarm blares out performatively, it's almost as if it's giving them a run for their money.

But Goldie's the one responsible, setting fire to those letters in Gran's standing ashtray; it's clearly got a bit out of hand as she and Wolfie stamp out the last smoulders of paper before they damage the laminate flooring.

'Gone,' she declares, like it's true. 'Vine has no power here. And it's time to push the fuck on.'

Thirty-Two

JULIA

Waterfalls

'A weekend at home, Julia?' Mother says over Friday night dinner. 'That makes a change. I thought you and this new chap were getting serious.'

'You know, I always wondered if it were just my parents who asked such direct and ...' Julia leans into her mother's face, 'rude bloody questions.' She stands, stacking plates, bringing their meal for two to an abrupt close. Luxury Kyivs, asparagus and new potatoes, as if she's seventy-odd, too. Is this what her life's truly come to?

'Was I rude? Darling, I was just wondering, when we get to meet him ...'

'What for? So you can ask him his intentions and his salary? What his sperm count is?'

'Julia!' Mother places her bony little fingers to her overly blushed cheeks, looking like a rosy doll, like that woman from that old kid's programme, about the scarecrows – Aunt Sally. 'What on earth has got into you?'

Frustration. Being trapped in this magnolia hell with Mother and her imaginary ailments. The worrying email from work about redundancies, which short-term would be magic, but longer term ... What would Julia do next career-wise; to focus on the wellness the only logical forward step, and though she's outwardly winning at it, her socials are coasting. She needs something big. Something new.

'Daddy was wondering ... if there'd been any progress on the flat?'

Julia rolls her eyes. 'They've got to change the combustible cladding on seventy-two apartments. Things take time,' she adds, as if Mother were stupid.

'But ... but surely seventy-two sets of residents can't all be living elsewhere while the work's carried out?'

'Ah, you want me gone. So Mr Ocado can pop in and slip you his cucumber while Dad's visiting friends, I suppose?'

'You are a wicked, wicked girl, Julia. Sometimes ...' Mother's all hurt bewilderment as she sits there, staring at her daughter.

As confused as Julia, too; how they're even related.

It's 7:37 p.m. on a Friday night. Fifty-two pounds in her account to last until payday next week. Julia's brimming with numbers. At least the holiday got refunded, Jamie's insistence over the all-singing travel insurance, which had seemed an extravagance at the time, paying off.

Covid indeed. Perhaps he never wanted to go to Tuscany.

Just wanted to stay home to fuss around that mangy old mutt – which one, take your pick.

Stupid dog. Stupid, problematic Vee. Knew the second they'd found Onion frothing all over the tiles, that it would bode her return. And it had been so lovely without her. Glimmers of a happy future making themselves visible. Julia even cooked; the house easily becoming home …

Until Jamie began his lingering on Vee's Instagram, that Julia can't even access to dissect.

In her room, back at her dressing table desk, Julia returns to her MacBook. Vee's LinkedIn now a permanently open tab as she clicks across to Jamie's ancient Facebook account, last updated in 2019, when he'd reposted something sport-related. Whenever Jamie had mentioned his ex on their first dates – which had been an unnatural amount, thinking back – Julia would imagine the old wife as some dreary unlovable Trog, never in her wildests imagining Vee. Scrolling back through their Facebook years, they did look in love. Very happy. Doing the usual; lavishing their disposable income on holidays and quality kitchen fittings, including the dog in all their plans whenever they could – a baby substitute unquestionably.

Stupid fucking dog.

Stupid fucking problematic Vee.

But just as Julia tastes defeat, she has an idea.

It's so unlike her to alpha navigate like this. Never been the pushy one in relationships – but then, she never had to be. Obviously.

But something needs pushing on.

After a little bit of staging prep, Julia's ready to go; decides, for impact, to create an Instagram Live stream.

Taking a deep breath, tremblingly she lets it out. 'Hello everyone ...' she begins, in a sad girly voice which grows more impactful when the tears come, her bare face and childlike room perfect additions to the mood she's cast for her followers.

'Haven't we all made mistakes?' Julia continues. 'Had moments we're not proud of? God ...' She sniffs, eyes sparkling with emotion. 'I have.'

Hearts begin streaming upwards in response to her words, the go-ahead to settle into performance, which does feel like a game. A monologue of a bitch reformed, repaired, who's now the most wholesome person.

At the end, Julia adds a list of charities. As the comments flood in, so does support in the hugest of numbers. Because confronting your mistakes is such a brave thing to do.

And in a world where we can be anything ...

Thirty-Three

GOLDIE

U.N.I.T.Y.

The cold-sweat stress of a frozen bank account brings back the old fears never far from Goldie's memory; of having less than nothing and mattering about the same. Though none of the Coach House comforts had ever been taken for granted, they all unquestionably came at a cost.

But how much is true freedom worth?

When the rich talk about being skint, from struggling to pay their school fees to heating their stables, Goldie wouldn't be remotely embarrassed to call them out by saying how she knows true poverty, how the front door is never a truly secure barrier and can be ignored, just like any other boundary, once you've realized it's imaginary, that there are people in the world who will neither respect nor honour it as they push through into your personal space, your home or your body, claiming the things you're certain were yours, until they're taking it all away.

Be it your telly, your console, or the dining set you swore you'd pay off somehow.

Or your heart and your self-respect, which can't be so easily replaced.

When Wolfie left with the others, at Goldie's insistence that she'd be more than okay, she'd stayed on the sofa, not wanting to go upstairs to bed, as though she doesn't quite belong at Saunders Road. For a blue moon visit perhaps, but not overnight. And certainly not permanently. But better an unwelcoming roof over her head than no roof at all.

Goldie sits quietly, consumed with thoughts; how behind their current queue of grievances, it is Goldie's own period of absence from Valeria's life, like a blackout on their timelines, that's the true root of their problems.

Because Goldie chose escape. Knew Valeria was crumbling, and still left her in this house to have a breakdown all by herself.

Her eyes drift to the pictures that had so caught Rufus's interest earlier, arranged with love. But love is easier trapped in a photo. Kept distant. Because where is Gran now, while her two grown granddaughters could do with a bit of her stern affection? On a ferry as far away from them, here, this, as she can get. And Goldie totally understands.

It is burdensome to be so astronomically responsible for others. To always be depended upon makes her feel as if she's in sinky mud. And as Goldie tries to sleep, she wonders not for the first time if she's made of the same abandoning selfishness as her mother.

*

At ten past nine the next morning, Valeria lets herself in, opening the curtains and the windows in the living room as Onion bounds towards Goldie, pushing her head into the bedding for a fuss. 'I'll do tea,' Valeria says, 'then we've plans to make. Starting with a massive food shop; time to get you set up here properly.' She bustles about a bleary, puffy Goldie, who had only dropped off for the last hour or two thanks to fidgeting her way through most of the night.

Thank God for the money under the mattress.

'Now, don't get mad, G,' Valeria pre-empts, coming in with her cracked crateful of old books, and as Goldie groans, she rushes off again, reappearing with fresh armfuls of shit. 'As you know, I kept everything,' she says proudly. 'But now you need to go through these scrapbooks, the photos especially; anything remotely off-key put to one side. We need decent legal advice, too. I get why you did it, but you shouldn't have burnt those letters. We need all the evidence ...'

'I'll tell you what you need. A pinboard. A big one like they use on *Line Of Duty*, to plot up your evidence and tie string around key info.' Goldie can tell from the delight in Valeria's expression that she'd love nothing more.

'First things first, though,' Valeria says, as if she's checking off some internal list. 'Practicalities. Food shopping, then we can sort out mail redirection ...'

'A new phone, too, please.'

'A smartphone?'

'Just a new phone number would do. I've lost count of all the calls. Makes me feel sick.'

'I can help. I'll help you sort it all,' Valeria says, so together and formidable. Funnily enough, exactly the person Goldie's forever longed to see. Slipping on her glasses, she opens her notepad. 'First things first,' she repeats. 'Have you heard from Benedict?'

'No. Not since all the messages yesterday.'

'Good. Because from the outside looking in, France couldn't have been better timing. A month apart, distanced from him and all his crony connections. Imagine winning the internet one day, then getting cancelled for being married to a Tory the next.' She grins a big, smug I told you so, and though it's not as if Valeria's never made the point before, it creates a lighter energy between them. She is good at all this. Naturally dynamic.

Why couldn't Goldie be more like Valeria; organized, with a knack for pre-empting trouble, someone who knows so clearly and correctly how to do things – reading and researching people like books. Like a pig in shit.

And with a top-quality glow about her.

'What's going on?'

'What do you mean?' Valeria frowns.

'You . . .' With her hands, Goldie makes sweeping motions in Valeria's direction. 'The glow. You look fantastic. There's something you're not telling me.'

'Aren't we meant to be sorting you out?' Valeria says, a little too quickly. But Goldie doesn't answer; just observes her discomfort in the silence Valeria herself ends up filling. 'Jamie's having regrets. Like, wants to try again-sized regrets. I think.' She sighs. 'Why does this feel like we're bargaining?'

'Because I'm still not sure that I can trust you.'

'But I'm your sister.'

'Hmph,' Goldie snorts. 'Exactly.'

'I got it wrong. I said I was sorry – and I am. I get it. I took your experiences and ... and I didn't really think about you. It won't happen again. Please, G, I'm totally here to help.'

Goldie's mobile rings. Showing Valeria first that it's Ben calling, she smothers the phone with a cushion. 'He's put a hold on my accounts. Starving me out's the only language he bloody understands.'

'He can't do that – have you spoken to your solicitor?'

'Solicitor?'

'The person you've instructed to begin divorce proceedings?' Valeria stares at her in disbelief. 'Why am I not surprised?'

'I thought once Ben knew he'd get the ball rolling ...'

'Is it any wonder he's furious? Dumped in pretty much every way a person can be, apart from dumped directly. His son. National television—'

'You've met him what, five or six times? Yet you always take his side.'

'That's not true.' It is. Yet why is that so? How Valeria's so quick to take the side of the stable male and not her unpredictable sister. Who she loves.

But doesn't trust either.

'Look, what if I spoke to some solicitors for you – perhaps, perhaps I could even talk to Ben, too? I could, I don't know, be the buffer between you?' Valeria suggests with a shrug as Goldie feels her face lifting, despite herself, relief from the prospect of handing all this impossible stress over to somebody else. 'I know it's been a lot simpler going through it with Jamie, but it's all fresh in my mind.'

'Would you do that?' From under the cushion, Goldie's phone refuses to be quiet.

'Finally!' Ben roars, when his call is finally answered.

'This is Goldie's sister, speaking on her behalf. V ... Valeria ...'

'Fuck off,' he barks, hanging up.

The phone rings again. Chewing her nails, Goldie gestures for Valeria to answer it.

'Goldie Fliss-Burden?'

'Who's calling, please?'

'Kalista Yates, BBC researcher.' Eyes wide, Valeria stands and heads to the kitchen for a better signal, taking her notebook with her.

'For crying out loud,' Goldie says, because Valeria's far too pleased with herself. 'What did they want?'

'To book you for a fifteen-minute segment, in light of yesterday.' Valeria bites her lip, loving this. 'And in light of Ill Lothario being taken into custody early this morning.'

Crikey. The monster gets bigger and bigger.

'I've been thinking; you could really turn this Vine shite into an opportunity.'

'I am absolutely not that desperate.'

'Which is sort of my point. There is nothing desperate about you. I mean, look at your aesthetic – reclusive, not social media hungry but still totally juicy, recently choosing yourself instead of an unhappy marriage. Are you not exactly the role model women our age need?'

'You sound like my pimp.'

'In a sense, maybe. I could be your manager, PR person, whatever you like. Because I'm good at all this. You know I am. And let's be honest. You're not.' Valeria smiles. 'Plus, I'd never exploit ...' She tails off. 'I only want you to be seen as you deserve to be. Even while I was writing that stupid proposal, that's all I ever wanted.'

'But I don't. And I don't want to entertain gossips. The answer's no.'

'What about if you could do it from here – on Zoom or something?'

'What do they even want to ask me? Things I'm likely not allowed to answer. It's too risky. And it's not who I am. Jumping on a mention like I've just been waiting with my tongue hanging out for another round in the limelight. No.'

'You're so bloody stubborn.' Valeria is exasperated, hesitates like there's one final trick in her pocket. 'Answer me this then, at least; who's your favourite breakfast television person?'

Thanks to Valeria's meticulous record keeping, there's strong evidence of first love. A picture at a party where a very glamourous Goldie's sat on Grant's lap, his hands resting on parts of her that he's far too familiar with. Such intimate ease. Hands are one thing, but his tongue's also in her ear, her face set in pleasure, shoulders back, collarbones defined. Thinking she's in charge of it all.

She'd thought wrong. Grant had been humouring her.

Likely knew, even then, that she was just some foolish little hopeful, ripe for the taking.

Ripe for everything.

The glamour Goldie knows she's still providing in bucketloads, though it takes so, so much more work, rest and respectfulness than ever before to keep herself so. But even before the fame, even before she'd even come of age, there had always been the male, unwanted sort of attention, and truthfully their interest never held anything special. Looking back holds nothing special either. Valeria's box of old shit is the last thing she wants to root through, but because Goldie wouldn't even know where to begin looking for a solicitor, she carries on. Gran's Argos catalogue from Autumn/Winter 2007 captures her interest far more. Putting it aside for reward later, she sticks to her task and gets back to the box.

Cross-legged, Goldie marches a pair of their She-Ra dolls across the carpet, and rather than look through the scrapbooks, unearths a carrier bag of old cassette tapes. 'Goldie's songs March '95' says a label on the first tape she pulls from the bag, written in faded pink bubble writing. Gran's stereo is from about 1995 too, with a CD carousel and double cassette player she still thinks is cutting edge. Goldie pops it on.

The tape crackles for a bit, and then:

'Can you introduce yourself please?' Valeria, sounding so girly and sweet Goldie chokes, rather pained, which only worsens when she hears her own, very young, very cocky reply.

'I'm Goldie Burden. The golden voice of our generation.'

Throwing her head back, Goldie smiles up at the ceiling.

With a professional cough to set the tone, Goldie begins to sing Dina Carroll's 'Don't Be a Stranger' – which chimes strangely with Wolfie's words. It's all a bit warbly and over the top, with a lot of Whitney and Mariah-inspired harmonizing going on, but it's clear the voice has natural power.

Goldie can't remember the last time she sang anything, beyond along with the radio.

'Did I sound any good?' little Goldie asks little Valeria, like an excited bird might. 'Like Dina Carroll good?'

'Yeah, yeah, loads, sis,' comes the reply, making grown Goldie go from wanting to cry to wanting to laugh; she'd sounded nothing bloody like Dina Carroll.

But Valeria was cheerleading her anyway.

'Consider that a warm-up. Let's go again. I think I can do better.'

'Na. They're back.'

Valeria and Goldie's voices fall silent, replaced with sounds of movement, as if they've forgotten they're still recording.

Nothing ever stays the same, Goldie must remind herself of that. Whatever happens, she is grown, and she has this house. It's becoming a mantra, one she's thankful for. How she bought this house, which sits untouchable from everything else, like a protection for her and Valeria. All over again.

Goldie jumps at her own young voice. 'Don't start, Valeria.' Between scuffling noises, an actual growl comes from her. 'You're too immature, you can't possibly get it.'

'I might be a virgin, but I'm not stupid. Probably scarred for life, actually – because seriously, what about his wife?'

'Look, none of this will matter for much longer. When I go pro, we go legit.' Little Goldie sounds so convinced. 'The second I'm sixteen ...'

'And what about Mum? Downstairs now, thinking everything's normal.'

Goldie kisses her teeth. 'Come on, who d'you think he's really here to see?'

'Girls! Get yourselves down here.' Mum. That hard, can't-be-fucked-with-all-this-and-your-existence-I-merely-tolerate tone to her voice. 'Grant's brought takeaway.'

'How romantic.' Fourteen, and Valeria's quick, bone-dry sarcasm is unchanged. 'Someone call Mills & Boon ...'

'Turning your nose up at Kung Pao shrimp, then?' Goldie cuts in. 'I didn't think so ...' Her voice fades out, along with their descending footsteps. Downstairs to Grant.

And Mum.

Resentment is an ugly, immovable feeling. Going nowhere, even now.

She'd been a truly shit mother; rarely there, and them never not the afterthought. Missing all the signs of Valeria's hurt – though never missing any of the signs between Grant and Goldie, a fact which never gets any less disturbing; how in all the years of turning this over then trying to bury it, jealousy was the first real emotion Goldie had ever felt from her mother. Which was also likely why Wolfie had so surprised her, when he'd mentioned his own mum the other day. Proof that supportive parents do exist. How people have mums they love and treasure. And who love and treasure them back. Which must be nice. Goldie's glad Wolfie has that.

Wolfie. Smitten is the simplest, perhaps safest way to contextualize her feelings. The beautiful, strangely innocent thing happening between them.

How Goldie should've learnt. Which really fucking hurts.

Suddenly, overriding all else, is how Goldie longs to hold the girl version of herself on this tape. That it's dawning, after all this time, how they were just kids.

And it was never solely her fault.

Amazing how this old tape might somehow be worthy of interest.

Yet it would've been worthless forty-eight hours ago. Before Ill Lothario's arrest as he tried to flee, livestreamed on the news. Helplines specifically created to deal with the volume of women joining their voice to a collective which can't be ignored any longer. Another wave of people rising in the face of being exploited, abused and scared into silence.

Goldie's saddened by how long some have waited for this. Thirty years for one person, but as little as three weeks ago for one retail assistant subjected to a violent attack in a changing room, Ill Lothario breaking her nose because the trousers he'd tried on were too long.

Male fragility; as ugly as it is terrifying. Even Grant had excused Ill Lothario's behaviour, too. *'How does it reflect, image-wise, for him to be taking shit from a girl? Think of the fans. Plus, he's not had it easy . . .'*

'Not had it easy,' said Grant, the Black man born and raised in Tower Hamlets, the poorest borough of London, about the white male, Ill Lothario, aka Nathan Layton, spitting lyrics about 'pleading poverty to partying in penthouse suites . . .'

which he penned from his parent's cul-de-sac chalet bungalow in Berkshire. *'Image is everything, you know that. Think of the fans.'* Grant's words, delivered with such slick precision it felt scripted, like he had smoothed over similar situations thousands of times before. And clearly, he had.

But those other women hadn't been Goldie. It remains as distressing as when it happened, how instead of kicking the shit out of Ill Lothario, Grant had protected him. A spiral fracture. She'd needed surgery. Grant had thumped some men for simply looking at her.

The tape comes to an end, clicking itself off.

The second I'm sixteen . . .

Thirty-Four

VEE

Love Child

Imagining Ru on his way over lifts Vee from her running list of mostly Goldie-related tasks, and into hot mental abandon. Finds herself shaking as she slows to park outside the house, at the sight of him draped across her front steps, not killing time on his phone, but lost in a book with actual pages. Vee's neatly taking her driving glasses off when Ru clocks her.

Kneading her hips, Ru kisses her neck while she tries summoning the coordination to unlock the front door, which is all so deliciously distracting that Vee even forgets to check what it was that he'd been reading.

The moment they're in, Ru slides off Vee's sundress, nibbling across her bare shoulders until his mouth is on hers. Giving what she hopes is a staggeringly wanton look through her lashes, Vee takes Ru's hand, urging his fingers inside her knickers, and before anything's even been said, they're writhing all over the parquet.

When she's sure her knees can take it, Vee staggers to her feet and to the fridge for water, with lots of ice and lemon. She passes a glass to Ru, back in his pants and on the sofa. Observing, as is his way.

'What?'

'Ah, I don't know,' he says, with a smile Vee hopes she'll remember forever. 'What a fucking fortuitous day it was when you came to Write Pub.' But then he adds, 'Do you think she'll mind?'

'Does she really need to know? I mean, what even is this . . .' Yet even as Vee says it, he's kissing her again, making her body arc towards his like they're made from highly charged crotch magnets. What this is, is theirs. Private. New. And fun. 'Twenty-four hours ago, and this had nothing to do with Goldie. It still doesn't. Not really.'

'You want us to be a secret?'

'Not a secret. Just not common knowledge.' Vee winces. She's doing a lot of that lately. Checks herself. 'Though Jamie knows.'

'Whoa,' Ru says. 'Now that's pretty major.'

'Pretty final.'

Ru stands, crossing the room for a fluffy throw that he tucks around Vee before slipping in himself, snuggling into her back.

Easy to spot the truth of a person when they're unguarded. The Goldie connection, which Vee believed would translate into an instant turn-off, simply hasn't. Quite the opposite, in fact, as she'd watched the dynamic at Gran's; Ru's easy affability, how naturally people seem drawn to him. Ru's relationship with Goldie had surprised Vee; deeper than she ever would've thought.

And once the shock had settled, far from feeling over-exposed, Vee's instead found the strange yet complicated confirmation that Ru's a safe person. Somebody she can trust. They've shared words and bodies more than once now. Is it really that surprising to find themselves giving a little more conversationally, too? Hardly, in the light of things.

'We wanted other, different things,' Vee says. 'No one's in the wrong – and I still don't know if that's made separating easier or harder.' Would it be easier if there'd been raging hate between them? There'd be less blurred lines, that's for sure. 'Jamie wanted a family. I just never saw myself with kids, you know?'

Because really, was it so hard a reach for Vee to just self-parent, try lavishing a little self-love and make up for lost time instead? Why should she care about motherhood when she'd had a mother who made it so blatant that she didn't want to care for her? And why should she give up her inner selfishness, that wasn't selfishness at all when all she really bloody wanted was her own bloody company. Vee liking being just Vee should need no explanation. It's her body, her choice, after all.

Wasn't she doing the planet a massive favour, too? People always forget that, roll their eyes as if one more child in the world won't make a difference. But poor kid, too. Because wouldn't it be shit to subconsciously rub off all yours on some innocent little bubs? It's not even that Vee doesn't like babies.

'I totally get the someone to love part,' Vee says after a bit. 'But it's hard enough looking after, liking myself ... which, which I've never found easy.'

'Which is sheer madness.' Ru strokes her hair, soothing so much Vee's glad she can't see his face.

'And that's still who I am. Though I'm trying, so hard, to paint it differently.'

Vee always thought there was a special club of knowing, a uniform etiquette of how to be a proper adult, and if she could've had lessons, she would've.

Instead, she's mirrored; leaping on laughter, though keeping it low-key unremarkable. Nodding along when other people do, trying to focus on what's being said instead of jumping ahead and imagining what she might say next, that might make her seem worthy of talking to. Worth. It is all about value, how other people weigh you up, then decide on your price.

But what price would Vee put on herself now? She makes her brain challenge the concept. 'Jamie made all my writing feel like a phase I was going through. Like some whimsy pursuit of a bored housewife. It doesn't even matter now, yet it still infuriates me. Deeply.'

'You're a writer. It'll matter forever.'

'Also, I like it best when it's just me. I sit there at my desk, let my mind drift. Then the words come, and it's like heaven on earth. And I just want more of it.'

More. Of everything. To be the girl with the most cake. For the rest of her life.

'Writing's a lot easier than relationships. Which are fine until they begin feeling like a preamble to ... maybe not so much commitment, but family.' Ru pauses. 'Family always makes me feel like something I want to escape from.'

'Break the chains?' Vee asks.

'Absolutely, yes,' Ru says. 'You must already know plenty about my dad.'

But when Vee thinks about it, she doesn't. Has simply cast Benedict as a besotted monied lucky find, using her own labels and assumptions from the handful of times they've ever met.

'From the moment him and my mum got together, it was as if she adapted her whole world to accommodate him,' Ru says, shaking his head. 'It had just been us till then, which I know sounds rather like a boy who couldn't share his mum, and there might've been something in that – if it hadn't been for everything else. Like Goldie, for example.' Vee shifts, intrigued, as he smiles. 'Trust me, going to the Coach House every other weekend I'd fully expected to despise her too. The way he so brazenly split himself between the two of them, which even at thirteen or so made me feel a bit sick, though it wasn't a shock. There's only my grandfather left on Mum's side of the family – bafflingly old and hostile to everyone, which meant I knew every Bickham horror story before I even knew I was part of them. His hate for them all, particularly Tony, was pathological. Apparently, it had only been a fling, between him and my grandma – not that my grandfather ever fully saw it that way ...'

Even Vee knows of Tony Bickham's reputation. The East of

England's very own Casanova. Yet still quite the revelation – how the Fry assets weren't the only thing Tony Bickham had been stripping.

'Mum met Dad at uni, then it was on-off between them for years. I think he does love her, but nothing close to how she loves him – and certainly not as much as he loves himself. Marriage isn't up everyone's street, but in their case ...' Ru sighs, '... it would show my mum that she matters.'

'I don't understand. If they're together ...'

'Dad gets disinherited if he marries her. So can you imagine if they knew about me?'

'Ru, what the fuck?' Vee sits up, shifting to the opposite end of the sofa so they can face each other. 'You're a love child?'

'Not in your glamorous sense, but yeah. And if Dad's parents knew, then he won't get the three mil he's expecting. And that's just the tip of the iceberg when you consider the whole Bickham Estate. Anyway, the story goes that it's all written into a codicil.'

'Sounds like an atrociously posh period drama to me,' Vee says with a sniff, though it offers a strange, interesting parallel nonetheless, how they've both been denied who their father is.

How they are both secrets.

'Just the sort of shit I'd avoid, if I'm honest,' Ru says, and so would Vee, in regular circumstances. 'I used to think I was the threat, because it was all about the money, but as the years have gone on, I think it's more about him. Greed. Having to have it all. He doesn't have to marry Mum, and can look like a stud at parties with Goldie giving him a personality, so why should he choose?'

'Hold on,' Vee checks, just realizing what this means. 'You're telling me that for almost as long as Ben's been married to my sister, he's been romantically involved with your mum?'

'Well ... yes.' It's Ru's turn to look confused. 'But it's not like him and G are married-married, is it?'

'Married-married?'

'Yeah,' he says. 'Meaning love. The true meaning. Not for show. Easy hiding Mum behind Goldie's star quality. And so his inheritance stays safe.'

Vee's at a loss. Can't quite take this new influx of info in.

'I'm sure, even if there was no inheritance at risk, he'd carry on the same. I've spent too long trying to figure out why he didn't like me – honestly, it's true. He avoids me at all costs, can barely tolerate my presence. It's all right. It would hurt more if I loved him. There's a lot of comfort in the fact that I'm absolutely nothing like him.'

'I understand that – know, actually.' Saying this out loud is rare. 'My mum was much the same. From the second our dad died, Me and G became like, I don't know, living stones round her neck. She couldn't move on with us being so little, so she just lived her life as if we weren't there.'

'Sounds like a very lucky thing that you had each other. I always thought it must be nice having a sibling. Someone else who knows, y'know what I mean? Who's on your side, because they've lived it, too. I just channelled everything into proving that I was something standalone. That I'm enough in my own right. Despite him.'

'Everything you've achieved has nothing to do with him.

It's all about who you are. Your gifts.' It comes out far more impassioned than Vee anticipates, making him blush, and making Vee think again just how incredibly beautiful he is.

'Anybody who hasn't had a leg-up rattles him witless; you only need think of his reaction over Wolfie,' Ru adds with a look of pure devilry. 'Only a few months ago, he was describing him as an enigma – I mean, that's going to be living rent free for all eternity, isn't it?' Chuckling, Ru rubs his nose. 'He's not once asked me about the book, can you believe that?

'Isn't that common?' Vee says distractedly, her thoughts still on marriage-marriage. 'Writers in the family make things dreadfully awkward.'

And though she's talking about herself, Vee wonders again what it is that compels her to defend Benedict. Or is she playing a wee devil's advocate, to coax more, because is there anything as revealing as a person in defence mode?

'No, it's because he's a pig. That first never-ending lockdown, the weird one, when it was sunny every day and nothing felt real? He'd bubbled with mum. And while they were living their best life, he never checked in with Goldie once. Nothing social was going on, so G along with his best suits got completely forgotten about.'

Vee pulls the blanket up around her shoulders, suddenly cold.

'I popped by once we were allowed to. She looked the same, but she totally wasn't. She was sad. So bloody sad. She's always been amazing to me. Consistent. And I was worried. Worried enough to mention whether she should see a doctor. You know what his solution was?'

Vee stares at Ru, unblinking. Holds her hands tight and invisible beneath the blanket.

Was Goldie suicidal? Vee can't stand it, can't bring herself to ask it.

'The cleaner.' Ru answers his own question. 'Dad upped her hours.'

'I'm sorry, what?' Vee can't quite grip it. 'He paid the cleaner to keep G company?' Vee shakes her head. 'You can't be serious.'

'Then fast-forward to Wolfie at the Coach House, for some weird business dinner. The way he and G were around each other – the hope on his face when I made sure to say how it was all pretend.' Ru grins, making his own explosions of balled fists into jazz hands, like he'd masterminded the lot. 'I read that shit a mile off.'

'It's not exactly hard to read.' Vee feels a little bit better. 'It's like they can't quite believe the other likes them.'

There's something hesitant in their pairing; mistrustful yet at the same time optimistic. Of becoming true. Watching them the other evening reminded Vee of her favourite programme, *In the Doghouse*; all the guarded, nervous strays who you think might never recover from whatever cruelties their past owners bestowed, only to see them bound around the corner of a new home at the end of the show, all happy and healed with their new people.

Vee hopes with everything that it's a similar story for Goldie and Wolfie.

'The chemistry that captured a nation,' Ru says, alluding to the picture of Goldie and Wolfie's airport embrace – caught rather ironically by a fellow passenger and not the press; their joy, just from clapping eyes on each other. Seen on every media outlet in the country, shared in its millions online. Even declared by one internationally bestselling novelist who Vee's fangirled over all her life as one of the most romantic pictures ever taken. 'Do you think our connection's as obvious?'

'If anyone were to notice the state of my knees, most definitely.' There will be no more floor antics. Especially when she's a mattress upstairs that's barely had a moment's action since she bought it.

'Are you expecting someone?' Ru asks, craning his neck towards the window as a person in a suit comes up Vee's steps, ringing the bell.

Vee's confused, but only for a moment. 'It's the fucking estate agent.' Springing to life, she speaks through the doorbell to answer it. Dashing into the hall for Ru's clothes she throws them at him, slipping into her dress and pulling her hair in a top knot. 'When you're dressed, would you mind letting Onion out for a wee? Let me sort this quick.'

Twenty minutes later, Vee brings outside two cups of tea, squinting in the sun to watch Ru playing a very gentle game of fetch with Onion.

'She's lovely,' Ru says, sending Onion swooning as he nuzzles her ears.

'She is.' Vee can't say any more for wanting to cry.

'Reminds me of Mum's dogs, Bernie and Seb. The most beautiful black labs you've ever seen. Dad walks them every morning over at Greenlet Common, which might be the only nice thing—'

'Do you think Goldie was suicidal? When you said...' Vee pauses. 'How lonely—'

'I shouldn't have said it like that. Like I'd been keeping tabs.'

'But I should've been looking after her. She could've been here, I could've—' Vee shrugs, balls her own fists. 'I'm so angry. With myself. With fucking Benedict. Exploitative prick.'

'Only him. The rest of us love her to pieces.'

'I want to kick his teeth in.'

'Join the queue.' Ru chucks a tennis ball, but Onion's lost interest, settling across his feet instead. 'This is the fall-out. But she'll be fine. Especially now.' He bends to stroke her, charmed that she's chosen his feet to sleep on. 'So, what did the estate agent say?'

Vee sips her tea, not quite ready to process the good news valuation. 'We're back in profit. Just.' The thought of telling Jamie that they're now free to put the house on the market fills her with more sad guilt – though she shouldn't really feel guilty on either count. Selling up was always coming. And neither should it be forgotten how Jamie had leapt very happily into singledom; it's not Vee's fault that he's had a change of heart. Not that he's outright said so, but Vee senses it, the weight of which feels unfair. And Vee's no business feeling guilty over Goldie either, considering she'd literally no idea of the scale of separation between her and Benedict. Distant from the start.

That they don't share a bed has left Vee even more gobsmacked than the fact that Benedict lives with Ru's mother.

How had she missed all the signs? Even on their wedding day – which made *Hello!* magazine – Vee hadn't noticed any whiff of the facade. Which only pushes home that niggling sense of never seeing Goldie truly; never beyond some sex object starlet, who's now built for comfort, a kept pet with benefits for Benedict.

The same as everybody else thinks.

It's time Vee put that right. If Benedict won't speak to her on the phone, she'll confront him face to face.

Perhaps on one of his mornings turns around Greenlet Common.

Thirty-Five

BENEDICT

Manchild

Benedict used to pride himself on how he'd always been an excellent sleeper.

Things must be bad.

Waiting for his parents to die is taking too fucking long. Both being boozers and smokers and well into their eighties should've put them on borrowed time, yet on they go, sociable, sprightly, puppeteering every purse string, judging their only son from the lofty heights of perpetual disapproval. Even after he and Goldie divorce, the Coach House still won't be Benedict's to sell.

Dad's expression when he told him Goldie had gone. Benedict involuntarily shudders. As if it had always only been a matter of time before she saw sense. And though his father hadn't said so, Benedict knew he was enjoying the lot. Dining out on his failures.

And all the failures seem to be coming at once.

Benedict had often thought how it would likely be his father who'd end up having the affair with Goldie, given his reputation – softened with time, of course, but by no means forgotten – and his Hollywood looks, which skipped Benedict, who could only ever be described as nearly tall, mousey-to-dark, and, from certain kinder angles, almost handsome.

A rush of heat swamps him, making him push off the covers and notice Therese, tiny and snoring in a white vest and knickers set beside him. The only woman he's ever managed to keep hold of.

So beautifully pure, right from the start. Like she'd been made from a bar of soap. As it had come upon him like a curse to be the person to change that.

How could Benedict ever deny Rufus was his, when Therese always had been? Even at Trinity she'd never noticed anybody else – not even him, until he changed that, too. Until his father had baulked over their connection, suddenly ashen and never so serious. *Stay away from that girl!* Spelling out the financial consequences.

But 'no' simply doesn't feature in Benedict's vocabulary.

Benedict's raging hard-on acts in total dissonance with Therese, still peacefully sleeping, her red-brown hair sleep-scruffy, catching the early sun through the curtains, that briefly puts the image of their turncoat little twat of a son back in his thoughts. Benedict drags her close, sliding his cock between her thighs, as delicately proportioned as when they'd met, pushing into her without warning.

There is sometimes sex, but it's threadbare, for necessity

rather than true desire. A slightly more pleasurable trip than a visit to the gym. Benedict penetrates Therese in his usual claiming, selfish fashion, which speaks nothing of love and everything of need. Like an itch to scratch, a sweet tooth craving. And brief. Cupping her throat and in less than a minute he's snorting into the back of her neck with staggered, almost seething farmyard noises as he releases himself.

Like a true king of the world, Ben leaves their pheromones to linger and walks the dogs unwashed, imagining attraction hormones emanating like Jesus beams out of him as he heads along the street.

Who's Ben Bickham? Who is it? Big man. Best man. Be-ne-dict.

Keeping the dogs on a tight lead, at the zebra crossing Benedict waits by the small parade of shops with the bakery on the corner, café tables and pastel bunting outside, where all the yummiest will later gather after the school run. Queen blasts in his ears, as behind his shades Benedict smiles at two gym-attired women as he crosses over to the green, and when he and the dogs are safely beyond the boundary, he lets them off, watching them race across the grass as if in competition, before getting completely distracted by scent.

Breathing deep, too, and for the first time this morning Benedict stomachs a look at his phone. The auditors are due in any day, those flagged diversity issues still pending, even more humiliating considering his brown wife's now done a runner.

In the end, usually, Benedict gets what he wants. But never Goldie. Not truly. She does something to his usual dominance. Without even consciously knowing, she is magnetic, and if he could syphon and consume whatever it is she possesses, he would. Hot by proxy hasn't been such a bad position, though. And how often have people, given him a little wink, as if to say you lucky fucking so and so. Which makes it even more galling, losing to someone like Wolfie Meyer. The scum from the slums.

It had cost the earth to put on that fundraiser, just the latest in a long line of business decisions to backfire; his rescue plan to purchase then exploit those small start-ups leaving a deficit of such enormous numbers Benedict can't even look at them. All the time wasted. All that effort! And Goldie sabotaging every attempt at doing business – because they were fucking.

Scruffy, mullet-haired, junkie-looking loner – who's likely never owned a proper pair of trousers in his life. Benedict's amazed how people like Wolfie really exist. But clearly that's what does it for Goldie. Grubby commoners, spiked with colour. Just. Like. Her.

Twenty-six emails and it's only seven-forty – accompanied by a dizziness which puts a thick angry pulse in his neck, a pressure as if in premonition, that this might be how he dies. One big angry heart attack before he's even sixty, which would be typical.

The dogs head towards a woman in bright pink sandals, who's keen to fuss them, though she doesn't seem to have a dog of her own. Benedict's about to shout that they're harmless when he's hit by familiarity, to the point he blinks to be sure it isn't Goldie carrying a book of some sort, heading most purposefully towards him only lacking her bouncy charisma, because this one's slighter, on the offensive, likely a wildly different beast between the sheets, as his honeymoon night briefly flits through his thoughts, which had felt no conquest either. Just an experiment in his hands that he'd read wrong. He'd never had a problem performing before, the moment remarkably intimidating considering how removed and robotic she seemed anyway. As all Benedict could think about was Therese. How he could be so rough, and her so grateful.

Sucking in his stomach, Benedict keeps his shades on, forgetting his five shaving cuts from yesterday or the day before, beaded dark now with a small silver crust. And the red flare of eczema around his nostrils, that just a very basic Nivea cream could sort. Basics overlooked, because he's above them.

Ah. Of course. It's the effing, jeffing sister. Valerie. Or something.

'Benedict Bickham,' she states, far too directly for Benedict's liking. 'You can't just go ejecting wives from their homes and cutting off their money.'

'I didn't eject. She left. Now look, you ought to piss off, or I'll call the police.'

'With respect, you wouldn't speak to me on the telephone. I'd like to know if you've instructed a solicitor. Goldie's received no paperwork, email—'

'Trevor's dealing with this as we speak,' Benedict says smugly. 'Best you also remind her how there's also the pre-nup—'

'Well, there'll be no contesting that. Goldie just wants out. But that doesn't mean she shouldn't have access to whatever until now was at her disposal as your wife. Her personal accounts shouldn't even have any authority from you. I suggest you unfreeze—'

Benedict folds his arms. Leaning forward he notices her flinch. 'Or what?'

'Or ... our solicitor will.' Her shoulders curl inwards, perhaps not quite as confident as she'd have him believe.

'Like I told you on the phone ...' He leans further into her face. 'Fuck off.' Turning on his heel, Ben calls for the dogs and sets off across the grass.

'Honestly, how very dare you please?' She shouts into his back, making him stop. 'Did it make you feel good, letting her lose herself to loneliness in that big old house? What sort of man, because ... fifteen years, isn't it? How on earth did my sister manage that?' The bitch is alive with animosity, feral in her defence of Goldie. She really might be frightening if she wasn't so pretty. 'You've just locked her up like some prize in a cabinet. She's a human being.'

'I did her a favour. Which benefited both of us.'

'Until it didn't. All she wants to do is move on.' She looks him up and down slowly, like it's him who's the loser. 'Have some self-respect.'

Her eyes shine as though she knows she's struck a nerve, making him more furious.

'There are ... certain arrangements in place. Agreements which mustn't be broken.'

'Agreements I think you'll agree you've now jeopardized, since you cut off her money.'

From the moment his parents met Goldie, it was obvious how they liked her more than him. It would never have surprised Benedict if they swapped him out of the will and put Goldie in his place. They'd certainly dangled doing it before to his sister Camille, lost to the marching powder, and litres and litres of vodka.

'I had no choice. Besides, it serves her right. She's a public embarrassment.'

'Your delicious wife stands up for women's rights and it's an embarrassment?'

'You know very well it's not about that part. Look. I admit we need to bring this to a conclusion. Things are moving, so if she can just stop flaunting—'

From nowhere, she produces a letter. 'This is a copy of notice from Goldie's solicitor, that's currently on its way to you, too. There's no need to contact her by telephone any longer. In fact, she insists that you stop doing so.'

'How dare she be so, so ...' But Benedict's flummoxed. Fuming. 'Just who does she think she is? I swear to God, if she says anything remotely ...' He huffs, shaking his head. 'I'll make them both wish they'd never been born.'

'You don't love her. I don't understand why you're so angry.'

But Benedict's never going to say the words reputational damage, any more than he's going to admit to being skint. Divorce. The whole thing's become unrecoverably humiliating – because the world will look and know that it's her choice.

'Love's the last thing that matters when you're surrounded by bastards.' He spits, noticing how they're circling each other, the air between them loaded and nasty.

'Oh well.' She smiles sweetly, making sure to look him in the eye as she says it. 'I guess we can't all be enigmas, can we?' And though Benedict's never really had the urge for true violence, the desire to smack this bitch right in the face is strong. He'd likely not stop, if he imagined Goldie, too. Benedict grows even hotter, moving to run a finger around his collar for air before remembering he's in a loose tee without any restrictions.

He feels tight – tight is a good word; constricted and thick-breathed.

But again, the feeling passes.

Thirty-Six

GOLDIE

Lose Control

Curiosity has Goldie returning a missed call from Jamie.

'I hoped Vee might be with you.' He sounds so hurt that Goldie immediately begins hurting right along with him. Jamie catches his breath before speaking again. 'Onion's gone. Our girl ...'

'I'll be right over.'

For speed, Goldie decides on taking a cab, lifting Gran's mattress first, grateful for her cash stash, because what would she do without it? All the journey there, Goldie feels strangely needy as she checks her phone on repeat. Too tender for her own good. Where's Valeria? Without warning Goldie's eyes fill, her emotions these days changing at the click of her fingers, as she keeps her largest, darkest sunglasses on, high alert ever since the airport, in case of any further grabby intrusions.

Jamie's so lost and terribly boyish that Goldie doesn't

hesitate to hold him, as he clings back, like he really needs comforting. What can be done; Goldie doesn't ever like to see anyone hurting. A kindness smotherer.

There are worse things to be.

'It's gutting. She was lovely. I'm very, very sorry.'

'She's on Vee's bed. Like she's just gone to sleep,' Jamie says, his hand spanned on his chest. 'We just popped in from visiting Jules's mum and dad—'

In her peripheral vision, before he's even finished his sentence, in the corner of the living room Julia stands, beginning to distance herself, as in a stalking synchronized formation Goldie moves towards her. So many years between then and here, yet Goldie traps Julia at the foot of the stairs just like an animal would, reminiscent of their original fight, the claw of her nails perforating Julia's scalp as she'd flung her to the floor, her face flat against the tarmac as Goldie kicked her and kicked her.

Kicked her into an ambulance.

'Whoa!' Jamie exclaims, as it takes a few seconds for Goldie to register that she's got Julia against the bannisters. Jamie watches aghast, like they're the bad bit in a wildlife documentary, as perhaps the gravity of him bringing Julia into this house begins to truly register. What he's allowed.

'My sister's got far more self-control than I do. 'Cos the first fucking thing I would've asked you. *Julia*,' – releasing her, Goldie keeps one perfect fingernail aimed at her throat – 'is what exactly is your game?'

'I don't know what you mean.' Baby-voiced; Julia's eyes fill with tears.

'Bitches like you are always playing games.'

'Well, I'm not!' Julia turns her eyes towards Jamie. 'Are you just going to let her—'

'I'm right here,' Goldie interrupts her. 'Don't ask him. Ask me.' Goldie turns an ear towards Julia as she slowly takes off her sunglasses. Locks eyes. 'Nicely.'

'Please,' Julia begs, cradling herself in protection. 'Back off, please.'

Satisfied, making sure it's Julia who looks away first, Goldie's victory leaves her feeling hard as fuck, teenage again even, from the handling of a situation she understands like instinct. 'Why don't you run along back to that nice daddy of yours?' Done now, she takes up position next to Jamie, enjoying how Julia would really like to say something about that, too, but can't.

'I . . . think I'll go,' she says, only to Jamie.

'Good.' Goldie replies for him. 'But don't forget; I know what you are. And I'm watching you.'

Shielding her body with her bag, Julia casts a look of hurt disappointment over her shoulder for Jamie's benefit as she slams the front door.

'Probs the only thing we'll ever agree on.' Goldie shoots her eyes up and down Jamie, as disapprovingly as she can muster. 'I'm disappointed in you, too.'

Her words stain, like oil on cotton, not to be removed or forgotten.

As he bursts into tears.

Over tea and snot rags, Jamie's quick to proclaim his innocence.

But Goldie's having none of it. 'You're sweet, Jamie, I always did think so. But in this instance, you're a true bloody idiot. Why didn't you listen?'

'It was the first time I'd ever bloody heard about it. I thought she was ...' Jamie looks embarrassed. 'She was—'

'Jealous? Do me a favour.' With a *pfft*, Goldie can't help smiling.

'Yes, jealous. Which would be normal ...'

'You're a first-class, head in the sand, ostrich prick.'

'Ostrich prick?'

'Head so far up your own anus that you couldn't separate ego for truth,' Goldie says. 'Did you ever actually look at your wife?'

But Jamie stays silent.

'Julia crushed her soul. Made her hide all she is ever since. Terrified to stand out; to shine. Bullies do that. And you know what else?' Goldie adds another level of authority to the mix by putting her hands on her hips. 'Bullies never learn.' She huffs, feeling rather alive. 'And then here you are, humping it.'

Yep, she fucking said it.

He still doesn't answer.

'She's a monster, just like her monster family.' Goldie gives him the sly eyes, raising her brows. 'And it looks to me like you know it. How was your weekend, anyway?'

Jamie swallows. 'I admit, there are ... things about Julia which are unsettling. Her mum's sick, as well. Plus, I don't know how to ...' Jamie rakes his hands through his hair. 'I thought after I'd got cold feet about going on holiday ... I lied;

said I'd got Covid: that the insurance paid and refunded us but it was me...' he explains, rolling his eyes, awkward. 'But she won't take the hint. Just gets more and more involved, like she's moved in under my skin.' He looks shocked at his own words. 'I want you to know that I didn't let her see Onion. I made her stay downstairs.'

'That's your gut, Jamie. Telling you she's a demon.'

'I don't even know how we're here half the time,' he says wearily. 'Wish I could just click my fingers, and everything would go back to before, instead of all this.' Arms out, Jamie looks around, kicking his frustrations into a cardboard box, labelled FOR DUMP. 'There, see? All this, all dumped. While Vee's just ... permanently busy. How could I know all the writing was so important to her if she barely ever mentioned it? Doesn't seem to have any trouble communicating with her new bloke, though,' he adds with more than a dollop of his own jealousy, as Goldie's brows raise, antenna-like.

'You told her she was wasting her time trying to get published. Yes, she did tell me.'

'I never said it like that.'

'Well, it's what she heard. All those years together; surely you must know what she does, misinterpreting everything into a negative. Can't take a compliment, only understands concrete praise.'

'Concrete praise?'

'Promotions, certificates, visible achievements – which if you think about it, probably has a lot to do with why she resisted being creative. It's too subjective.' What's glorious for some will always be ghastly for others – the same rules applying to Goldie's own music. Which suddenly is everywhere, all over again.

It seems that the more Goldie rejects the limelight; turning down interviews – paid interviews – refusing so much as to even comment on the Vine furore, the more the noise builds around her.

Reinterest. Which is ghastly and glorious, too; but the feeling that's most all-consuming, is that it's come unwanted. Because who in their right mind wants to be linked with Ill Lothario, who's now been refused bail, his nineteen-year-old girlfriend on hunger strike in protest? Those who protected him turning tumbleweed silent, but all of them toppling, like a satisfying domino effect, that's catching on in unimaginable scale.

But it's the sudden speculation over her own suffering at the hands of Vine Recordings, which confuses Goldie more than anything else. Why should her story suddenly matter, just because of people and their current nosiness? But she knows how fads come in waves. The eye of the mainstream storm not a place she liked to be even back then. Mean folk picking over the bones of her private life.

'You're good; rushing over like you did.'

'It's Onion, though. Love her.'

'Love her.' Jamie sighs. 'For a moment I almost forgot, thinking she's just up there like normal.'

'She is. She's up there asleep, just like normal. In her favourite place.'

'Like she should be.' He really has the most astonishing eyes. Full of heart.

'Yes. Like she should be,' Goldie says. Thinks how this is the likely the longest she's ever spent with Jamie one on one.

As Valeria comes in, and her happy face crumples because she knows.

Thirty-Seven

VEE

Unfinished Sympathy

All those years of loving Onion does something to the pair of them, Vee and Jamie needing each other in a way they never have before, grief reuniting them. People can say all they like about how it's just a dog. Open your heart to a four-legged friend and it's guaranteed your heart will be broken.

But the love. It is worth every agony.

Subdued and sad, a dangerous game of remember when, which pulls them close again, and has Jamie's parents ringing to check in, also rather devastated by the news of Onion's passing.

Holding his phone towards Vee, Jamie pushes far too many fucking boundaries when he encourages her to speak, and they invite her to their anniversary party, which he knew they would. And as Vee tries making excuses, because she can't outright say no, they mention Julia. 'We're struggling to take to her, Vee dear,' says Jamie's mother, Billie.

'But we've only met her once,' finishes Edward, Jamie's gentle, eternally patient father, turning the subject back to Onion. 'She had good innings. How old is fourteen in dog years? She went in her sleep. All at peace. Focus on that, my lovely.'

Comforting words. But Vee can't forgive herself that she wasn't there. She'd been too busy moving on. Too busy involved in Goldie's world. Which is typical. Reminds herself that she did volunteer. Perhaps too enthusiastically. It is only the fact that Vee was also too busy to remember to lock her bedroom door that brings comfort. The memory of Onion in her best place ever. Because Vee doesn't know how she will ever get over this terrible hurt.

Her own phone rumbles. A message from Judith at Write Pub, wondering how the writing's going. Some motivational words, too, that Vee would've chewed over endlessly.

Usually.

Later, after a bit too much wine, Vee falls asleep leaning against Jamie. Needs him.

Vee's washing up from the takeaway they barely touched when Jamie puts his arms around her, kissing the top of her head as he used to, her shoulder blades skimming his chest as the glass Vee's soaping, hidden by the water, breaks in her hands.

'Jamie...'

Taking the hint, he returns to the dining table, pouring himself another enormous red, but only after he tops Vee up first, as she wraps the broken glass in kitchen roll, shocked not to find herself cut to pieces.

'I got a lot out of talking to Goldie,' he says. 'Christ, what a person to have in your corner. Her reaction to ... to Julia.' Jamie's head flops back as he says to the ceiling, 'Oh, Vee, I wish I'd never met her.'

What does it mean, when the first thing out of his mouth when Vee came home to a dead Onion, was how Julia had only been in the house for ten minutes. Ten tiny minutes while he picked up some things. Professing the point – twice – how hadn't let her upstairs.

But that's what learning the hard truth brings. Acid burns, alopecia, acute psychosis. And a shame how it took Goldie to make him realize.

'What are you hoping I do with this information, Jamie?'

'Why did you keep yourself so ... contained,' he asks her, shifting deeper. 'So full of secrets? I loved you so much. You could've told me anything.'

'I wouldn't have known where to start.' Vee's never been able to explain how Julia left a shadow over her life, like a haunting. Not even to herself.

'You could tell me now,' he offers, so hopeful it makes her sad, remembering the good news valuation which she hasn't yet mentioned.

'Haven't I eaten up enough of your life already?'

'How could you possibly ever think that?'

'We were never going to move on, were we – living like this? You've not even given Julia a proper chance.'

'And I won't, not now. Not knowing what I know.'

Even though Vee told him, months ago.

But she doesn't answer. Already knows how this certain subject shows up.

It was really fucking insulting to be called jealous.

Because it hit a spot of shame, Vee admits now; the oozy place within us, which we tell no motherfucker about, that we'd rather die than have exposed, because then ... then the world would know who we truly are, and spit us so far out of orbit, there'd be no return.

Yet it wasn't only shame which came misdiagnosed as jealousy for Vee. It was despair, too; reaching into her darkest, most hidden, most protected of cavities, like ET's glowing finger, sending all her insecurities raging back to life. Despair from her own self-loathing, that lurks, waiting, eating off all the negative messages Vee's ever fed herself. Since Julia.

And maybe, if Vee's even more honest, before Julia, too.

'It's not love between us. I can't lie that it's not been fun.' Jamie's eyes grow wide as he exhales, the act repulsing Vee. 'Exciting, even.'

Not from jealousy. Nor despair; but pure fucking rage.

The audacity. To conduct *and now discuss* his sex life in Vee's same breathing space, brings all Jamie's magnetism to an end. Though did Jamie ever, truly have any? Or has he always just been such an outwardly great catch that Vee fell into believing the same, her head in charge, as always.

Until recently.

Vee could predict every one of Jamie's moves; how long he'd spend doing each thing, her mind never becoming free enough to let her body go, to give in to sensation. Everything predictable – yet she, too, had made it that way, feeling safe that way, normal, in all its neatness. Vee doesn't know why or even when she started faking, just that pretending became a habit, a weird internal lie which every time she did it, she felt as if she was dying inside. He'd be so offended. And really, there are so, so many things.

But none of them matter anymore.

Vee takes no pleasure in how that's only true for her.

'I do – did – want a family, but here we are, and if you're not part of that, well then, it's not what I want either. Because I love you.' He stands, taking her hands. 'So much more than I knew, and for that, well, I'll never be sorrier. Because I think we could ... In fact, I know we—'

'Just for once think, Jamie. I know it's hard,' Vee says, because they can joke this way; are still familiar, and friends, and good people. 'Say we got back together. Back to all we know. What about a year of that? Five years of that. Then we're in our fifties.' She tells the truth. 'I don't ever want to be a mum.'

Pushing a baby out wasn't the only way to have a family. They could've adopted, fostered, explored the vast plethora of alternative routes to parenthood. Yet they barely ever touched on the topic. Because perhaps, deep down, Jamie knew how Vee truly felt, too.

And couldn't bear to hear it.

'I told you; I don't give a shit. I just want you.'

But they know already how this plays out; how, when Vee tells him he's plenty of time still to fill a car full of children, because he would be an excellent father, and could be happily fulfilled with someone else, Jamie reacts as if the thought's never occurred to him. Which is rubbish. Because Vee knows him, having comforted him through every disappointment when they couldn't conceive, Jamie's devastation always so much more than her own.

The family life he'll miss out on and resent Vee because of. When it's too late.

And Vee would resent him, too. Returning full circle to the same nagging worry; that her time, her life, could've been better spent doing something else. Incredible how she ever convinced herself that this, here, even him, was everything she ever dreamt of.

'The world's fucking horrible, Vee. I trust you.'

'It's not all horrible.' Neither is it a reason for them to cling together.

But then Vee thinks of Onion. And wants to cry again.

Thirty-Eight

GOLDIE

Fame

'Let's check if all this works.' Valeria plugs an enormous ring light into her laptop. It beams to life as Goldie sits in front of it at the kitchen table, her hands as sweaty as her armpits, unable to believe Valeria's talked her into an interview – on *BBC Breakfast*.

It's amazing what you'll do to cheer somebody up.

Valeria does look happier. A little bit lighter, too, Goldie thinks, as Onion's death sinks in, even making plans to move in here with Goldie at Saunders Road permanently and properly. With Gran due home in the New Year, it'll be officially Girl's Club all over again. Which brings the memory back.

'Do you remember Girl's Club?' Goldie asks for distraction. Girls Club was a running list of all their favourite women of the world. It would keep them occupied, debating who deserved membership, long into the nights way back when.

'Of course.' Untangling some wires, she plugs something

else in. 'I've still got my members lists upstairs. Yours too, probs.'

Of course she has. Is there nothing Valeria's not chronologically stashed? For someone so intent on distancing from her younger self, she's a proper conundrum.

There's fifty minutes before she clicks the link to connect them with Charlie and Naga. 'How do you feel?' she asks.

'Need you ask?' Goldie's distracted by her phone. 'Wolfie.' Will she ever be able to say his name without smiling? 'Wishing me luck – er, what are you doing?'

'Taking pics for your new Insta. Off guard and loved-up's clearly a look,' Valeria says, turning her phone to show Goldie.

'I still don't see the point.' But the pictures are amazing, even if Goldie says so herself. And after months of not feeling quite herself, Goldie seems to have turned a corner, has finally got her usual fullness back, both in her face and body, too.

Tonight, she will raise a glass with Wolfie in celebration of getting through this interview. And because it's three months since their reunion. Three months of astronomical change. Which brings a rise of panic.

'Let's hold off on the social media,' Goldie says, feeling sickly and hot again. 'I'm not feeling it.'

'But it's the easiest way for people to get in contact with you. Trust me. You need to be visible. Why are you so intent on hiding?'

'Excuse me, can you hear yourself?' Goldie tuts. 'How is Jamie anyway?' Straight away she's sorry she asked, as Valeria visibly folds.

'Sorting an open day with the estate agent. Taking it all very seriously.'

'And Julia?'

'No mention,' she says. 'I really fucking hate that I've hurt him.'

'It's because he matters.' Goldie smiles, wrinkles her nose. 'And he is deeply cute. Are you sure it's—'

'You sound like his mother. Treble-checking it's the right decision. It is.' She catches Goldie's eye in the mirror, as if to cement it. 'Talking of mothers ... I read this fascinating article the other day, about the mother wound.' Valeria goes a bit quiet. 'Do you ever think of her? Wonder what she did with her life.'

'With her freedom, you mean. Probs ballsed it up by getting pregnant by another almost-famous musician. We could have loads of other hard done by siblings – just like us, but with northern accents.' Goldie's glad Valeria's smiling again. Until she brings out the thinking face. 'Oh no. Dare I ask?'

'Just what you said then. About other siblings.' Her sparkling eyes flick to the corner of the room as if she'll find her answers there. 'Like, what if – and it's a massive what if – but what if we did have siblings? Not necessarily Mum's ...' she waves a hand dismissively, as if she's given her enough energy. 'But Dad.'

It's not the strangest notion Goldie's ever heard. 'Others like us?' Illegitimate. Denied. 'But he's dead. So how would we know even? And anyway, what difference will it make now?'

But Goldie already knows how much it would make a difference. For her to be undeniably Amos Fliss's daughter.

And for him to belong to them again, instead of shadowed by lies that've worked as a boundary.

'Perhaps through someone else's DNA, I don't know; we could prove he's ours.'

Prove. Despicable and wrong that they should have to, and probably explains why Goldie tries not to linger on it. Her fear when Grant pushed her into telling the press she was Master-Fly's daughter – highlighting her specialness, which reads now as exploitation. But there was never any comeback.

Dad's next of kin was his father. A man they never met, living in some far-off American state Goldie can't remember, but who she imagined as Mr Mean from the Mr Men books, sat in an empty room with an angry face, counting out the gold made off his son's talent because he was all about the money, instead of them. Denying his own grandkids' existence by sending those two men with their suits and paperwork, and because Mum was Mum, and mean and greedy too, she took the pay-off.

But that was then.

Goldie's baffled how this is the first time that having other relatives has occurred to either of them – but especially to Valeria. The possibility that they could somehow challenge whatever paid silence their mother signed away, by finding a living connection to Dad.

How could she have done that to her own babies? Claiming their paternity was a mystery. How much did it cost for her to do such a thing? To sell away her principles.

Goldie hates their similarity, the signing of things for money, choosing silence while knowing it's wrong. Apples and trees and mother-daughter ties, Goldie rejects from top to toe. And she always will.

Perhaps this interview is another means of breaking away from the past. Separating herself from her mother's shape. Dismantling their similarities, one obstacle at a time. Because Goldie is nothing like Miri Burden.

And she'll prove it.

'Half an hour to go,' Valeria says, cracking on though Goldie knows she'll turn the DNA idea over until her thoughts become a plan, which will be far superior to anything Goldie's current brain fog could ever come up with.

While it dawns exactly what's been wrong with her.

Menopause. Or perimenopause – must be. Best to sort out a blood test. Funny how in all the years of living at the Coach House, Goldie never did change doctor's surgeries, still belongs to the red brick building two streets away.

But she'll book it another day.

The overwhelming nerves and scrambled brain Goldie thinks will last forever vanish as soon as Charlie and Naga appear on the screen, welcoming her to the show, and thanking her for giving them her time. Goldie chats away easily as Valeria gives her a big thumbs up from the opposite side of the table, notepad and Sharpie in hand, ready to prompt should she falter.

Which she does, the moment she realizes it is not just her being interviewed, but some toxic spindle offering an alternative perspective, which has become a common thing. 'For balance.' Goldie can tell, just from her on-screen energy, how the woman, introduced as Katie Jones, journalist and author, doesn't like her. Which puts a flutter in her chest, a self-doubt, and Goldie takes a minute to check herself, looking at the camera to remind herself exactly who she is.

The ring light slays. Knows she couldn't look more incredible. Best she makes sure what comes out of her mouth is just as amazing.

Goldie's charming start has Charlie and Naga on her side.

'I was sixteen when I signed to Vine Recordings. Everything happened very quickly. I went from singing in my bedroom to making music videos before I could say top ten hit.'

'A platinum-selling number one single,' Naga interjects, and with a little half smile adds, 'Then two more international hits.' And as she rolls off Goldie's other accolades, it's as if she's proud to be doing it, which has Goldie wondering if perhaps she might've had her records back in the day.

'Which is exactly the trouble, wouldn't you say?' Katie twitches to life behind her statement glasses. 'So many of these alleged victims, some of them pop princesses from the past like yourself, only just now deciding to step out with their grievances – not only against Vine Recordings, but the music industry in general,' she adds, for factuality. 'Why keep it to yourself for so long? Or is this all more a convenient avenue to return to the spotlight you've so desperately missed?'

Goldie opens her mouth but Naga speaks over her. 'To be fair to Goldie Fliss-Burden, it was *BBC Breakfast*, and I do believe other numerous media outlets who requested interviews about her time at Vine Recordings in relation to the upcoming Ill Lothario trial.'

'Thank you, Naga.' Goldie makes sure to answer Katie directly, wishing she could see the eyes behind the glasses, but the glare of Katie's lighting system has turned her into an unfortunate pair of headlights. 'I would never consider myself a victim any more than I would hunger for any press attention. In fact, if it wasn't for my sister's lovely dog dying and me wanting to cheer her up, I wouldn't have agreed to this interview today.'

Feeling the warmth from their studio sofa, Goldie continues.

'When I was with Vine, I said yes to everything; they were a powerful business who I believed knew what was best for me. I was a kid. My first song – the best one, in my humble opinion ...' Goldie smiles, dazzles, knows it. '... was completely mine. My lyrics, my arrangements – being new I'd been a risk, on a budget production, so the more I did myself, the more it saved them money. But then came their input – some top-end DJ or another MC, and soon none of it was mine, but I kept on smiling and being grateful for the opportunity. Because girls like me don't usually get chances like that.'

Chances which dwindled into guest vocals on dance tracks. Remixes; nothing that Goldie wanted or was right for, and so grew the idea that she'd had her moment. So clever how they did it.

And horrendously sad.

'Gorgeous talented girls with limited life chances?' Katie sniffs. 'That's a new one on me.'

'There are gorgeous talented girls everywhere, and no one knows they exist,' Goldie claps back unthinkingly. 'Because they come from poverty or rubbish families or just don't mix in the circles where there's any opportunity. That's not their fault. It's circumstance.'

'Which seems a very good moment to mention The Canticles,' Charlie says, steering things well, as someone with such well-organized hair should be able to do. 'Two girls, sisters, and the same age as you, from a small low-income neighbourhood in the American Midwest who were also about to sign to Vine. How did you feel about that?'

'I didn't feel much of anything, really,' Goldie admits truthfully. 'It's always good when talent breaks through, especially when you're not from much. Their success, longevity, has been amazing. To be honest, the fact that there were a few more girls in the room was as deep as it went for me back then.'

'Must've been tough to navigate at times, being a young woman in such a male-dominated environment,' Charlie says probingly, but Goldie does as Valeria's written in her notebook and shuts up. He tries another way. 'So here we are, almost thirty years later, music and the spotlight the furthest things from your mind, and then you read their statement.'

'My sister read it, then told me. I'm not on social media. Shocking that they even remembered me. That was my first thought, how these megastars still even knew my name.'

'Clearly you left quite the impression,' adds Naga. 'Which leaves us with the question that's been on the world's lips. What on earth was it that you did when you stood up for them?' She leans forwards on the sofa, as if she's looking right at Goldie. Even through a screen, her eyes are beautiful. And human. None of that out-to-get-you toxicity like Katie in the headlights.

'I did nothing more than what every single person should do when they see somebody struggling in a situation they're not comfortable with.' Goldie shrugs. 'I called out bad behaviour when I saw it. It's nothing more exciting than that.' Goldie puts a hand on her chest. 'I'm glad it's nothing more exciting than that. I treasure my peace.' She smiles as Valeria watches on proudly.

She's done enough. The next flurry of questions is simpler, and Goldie relaxes enough to find herself unguarded, when Katie Jones speaks again.

'You must agree that it's rather interesting – especially when considering this new self-appointed positioning as an advocate for women.' Katie licks her lips. 'How you were once romantically linked to Vine Recordings producer Grant Love, now on their board of directors, accused of the systematic cover-up—'

For the briefest moment Goldie's eyelashes flicker in panic, hopes it doesn't show as she glances beyond the ring light for Valeria. Valeria – who's fucking disappeared!

'I . . .' Goldie pauses, swallows. Oh, God.

Valeria's back. Waving a handful of letters, she mouths. 'Doorbell. Sorry.'

'I'll rephrase,' Katie says, enjoying this. 'Considering your romance with the man at the helm of Vine Recordings, are you really the best person to be advocating for women's rights at all?'

'And what does that old rumour have to do with me

standing up for them girls, exactly?' Goldie frowns, but it doesn't show as Valeria nods along encouragingly. 'Because I really must educate you, that your question isn't women supporting women either. It's misogynistic. And toxic,' she adds, and because her face can't lie, Goldie gives cut eyes to the box on the laptop containing Katie Jones.

Goldie could give lectures on the damage of journalists like Katie, the savage gossip columns, which not only thrive on pulling apart what you look like but also ram home every myriad impossible piece of advice on how to be/behave/eat/dress/consume in order to be perceived as a certain type of woman – exactly the stuff Valeria gobbles up as if there's some mysterious formula for the correct way to live a correct life. But nobody has the answers. Nobody is ever truly grown enough, mature enough, informed enough. More just flawed. Trying. And normal. 'It's so very easy to judge, when you've walked your way through a textbook life doing as society says,' Goldie says, knowing Katie's nothing more than an exploiter. Just another wealthy, joyless pseudo-journalist, and very much another closet Julia. 'I'd choose my colourful, complicated life over all that conformity any day of the week. My life – which always has been private.'

'But what if I were to mention the name Wolfgang Meyer?' Naga knows she's on sure footing when Goldie's irritation turns into a smile which could power a small country. 'The most viewed picture this year, according to—'

'How even does anyone know that?'

'Likes, shares, click volume.' The airport snap of her and Wolfie appears on the studio wall behind the sofa. Naga leans across, gesturing to the picture. 'I think we can all see for ourselves how romance is certainly not dead for Goldie Fliss-Burden.'

Opening her mouth, she reads Valeria's SHUT UP sign. Closes it.

'So, final question,' Charlie says, like a swift safety net. 'How does it feel going from the peace you value, to being thrust back into the public interest? In other words, has all this attention made you want to pick up a microphone again?'

'New material?' Goldie checks. 'From me? I really couldn't see that happening.'

'Or maybe your golden oldies,' snips Katie Jones, as Goldie rolls her eyes.

Takes the reins.

'Naga, Charlie, it's been a pleasure.'

'I fucked it, didn't I?'

'Not at all,' assures Valeria, looking like she means it, too. 'You were brilliant. Especially the end part. Savage.'

'I know Naga liked it.'

'That's it. Focus on what's most important.'

'Katie Jones reminded me of Julia.'

'The researchers didn't mention anybody else being part of the interview, cheeky fucks.' Valeria tuts. 'And Katie's nothing bloody like Julia.'

'You know what I mean. Poisonous.'

'She's wildly popular online.'

'And there's my point. Who on earth wants to live inside their phones with her for company?' Goldie shudders. 'No.

Thank. You.' She shakes herself, as if shaking off the whole experience, which she would like to. Thinks it might be nice to have a shower. 'Could've died when you vanished. Who was it anyway?' Goldie asks, imagining a parcel, perhaps something she's forgotten ordering, arriving like a timely reward for getting through that interview, as Valeria looks a little bit shifty.

She's saved by the bell. Distracted, Goldie answers it, sniffing her armpits.

'How did it go?' Rufus. Armed with flowers, just like he'd been at fourteen and fifteen and forever. Goldie doesn't care if she's sticky as she hugs him tight.

'Better this side of things.' She puts her face in the bunch of gerberas and bright orange roses, and with a big smile says thank you.

Grinning back, he steps inside. 'Knew it.'

'If you ask nicely, I'm sure Valeria will make you a cuppa. I'm going to hop in the shower.' Pointing towards the kitchen Goldie bolts upstairs, hears him call up after her that he's not staying long as she shuts herself in the bathroom. Not entirely sure how she's feeling, other than she needs a room for a moment with nobody else in it.

Did she like being on TV? Would Goldie like that attention permanently? Because somewhere strange and forgotten, Goldie had been very good at being famous. Looking back really is the most bittersweet bullshit; like a golden ball covered in it, forever played down as if then was somebody else's heyday, some other young person's dream, because it was the only way she could ever bear it.

*

Though Goldie didn't hear Wolfie's knock, she can sense him. And there he is, waiting all handsome in the hall, and God the way she feels when his eyes meet hers ...

'You were amazing.'

'You think?'

'And now look.' He greets her at the foot of the stairs. Taking her hand, Wolfie gives her a twirl. 'Aren't you just the most incredible human?'

How can you get to forty-five and never have been kissed like this? Lost to the point where thinking isn't real.

Or doesn't matter.

'Where's Valeria?' Goldie asks when the world falls back in, though hopefully not for long.

'Left pretty much when Rufus did; something about estate agents.' Wolfie cups her face most gently. 'Reckon we're much better off here, wouldn't you say?'

Lord, this is Goldie. Being kissed properly. Kissed with ferocity and longing. Which makes her stomach drop and thoughts take flight, like her heart. Because there's never been anything like this.

The peace she found. From the moment she was no longer pretending.

Thirty-Nine

GRANT

Smooth Operator

Another emergency summit with the legal team, gathered to discuss the latest round of attacks on Vine, leaking from so many cracks now, this shit's become back-to-back meetings, fact-checking, corroborating information and the labour-intensive covering of tracks. Of some truly atrocious acts, if Grant's honest, which have kept him up at night, thinking how very likely he'd been on another floor or in a different room, though very much in the same vicinity as Ill and his misdemeanours.

Real crimes. Reported by real victims.

Yet Goldie on breakfast news is number one on their agenda.

It is their story under scrutiny this afternoon. Not the story itself, exactly, which though sleazy, he can fully admit to. It is the timeline. That little fucking year.

'So, the media frenzy will say look at her; she knew exactly what she was doing. Teenage or not – did Goldie Fliss-Burden look like a kid to you?' Trey Eastgate, legal advisor already to so many questionable types, says to the board, who look so fucking weary they're ready to go along with anything. A few of them grunt in confirmation. 'So, that's it,' Trey decides. 'That's what we're going for.'

'You know it's not her who's on trial here.' Because Grant sniffed out her crumple on the telly. Thinks if he could just somehow get to her ...

Because this latest strategy, of painting her as some teenage temptress, feels dated. The oldest trick in the book. No father figure; the type of tearaway delinquent who binge-drinks and sleeps around from early, setting her sights on her own mother's man – and well, doesn't that tell you everything you need to know about a girl like that? And though the legal team, the PR team, in fact all the teams with their slippery words want to push the narrative that way – which really might work if the world ignored the sweeping influx of all the other #MeToo stuck records – isn't the point that Grant was always the grown one?

But he says nothing more; just lets them make their plans.

Too long's been spent thinking what it would be like to see her again. That eyelash flicker during her interview, which had shown oh-so transparently that he's still in her head, has him mystified. For years he's turned over what happened between them. How it started. How he'd been trusted with someone so lovely. And ruined her.

Yet she looked far from ruined putting that moose bitch in place this morning. As tempting as the day they first ...

And surely if that's the case, that he'd be as sexually enthusiastic with the forty-something-year-old Goldie as he'd been with the—

Grant still won't allow his mind to fully compute what all the glaring pervy arrows point to. Had never been with anyone as young, before or since. Because it was never about her age at all, he'd swear it on the Bible, which he might just have to do.

Just simply because it was her.

Forty

Ru

Sweetest Taboo

If the Coach House had seemed like the land of the landed made-its, the official Bickham Estate shits all over it. The house even has a moat. A drive, that's a quarter of a mile long, wide enough for two cars and lined with cedar trees, managing to look both menacing and deeply impressive as their branches span horizontally across a remarkably beautiful sky.

'Very *Saltburn*,' Ru says, his white Ford Fiesta looking rather out of place, as he parks next to an enormous stone sundial. 'Unadulterated fuckery and privilege. I've been thinking it for weeks.'

Vee offers him a Polo mint. 'You've completely got this.'

'Have I? What even are we doing here? Actually, don't answer that.' Shaking his head, he exhales. 'One man playing all the people isn't right in any set-up. Dad needs exposing.' Said as if to remind himself, unable still to process the fury of him freezing Goldie's money and now playing massively damaging games with Wolfie's finances, too. 'G's enough on her plate as it is.'

Not risking Goldie setting fire to another letter, Vee had opened the latest, at Ru's encouragement – because post with an official court stamp which requires a signature can't be ignored. An inquiry into Vine Recordings begins in November. Four months' time. Goldie Fliss-Burden's presence will be required for her to make a formal statement, answering any questions they have. This is separate from the Ill Lothario stuff; he seems more and more just the poster boy for all which was festering inside the machine. He'll have his own day in court.

And so, now she's summoned, will Goldie.

She needs lawyers. Money. Dad's games of withholding funds needs to stop. Plus there's Vee, juggling far too many plates, some spinning in territories they're all clueless about now. It's time the lot of it got handed over to people who know what they're doing. Then she can get back to writing, and Judith can get off Ru's back permanently – so very keen to discuss Vee's new pages and concerned she's losing heart.

It's more than time for everybody to move on.

Minus Dad.

'It doesn't need to be you who does this,' Vee says, offering him a get-out, too, because she's kind like that. But she also knows what comes from ignoring your own demons.

Ru's done his homework and had a good nosey online, wanting fact instead of old family folklore – though the Bickham stories match up well. Tony had been the Conservative MP for Glasswood Village, a market town on the Essex-Suffolk border, until about a decade ago. Loved by his constituents – and not just Grandma Fry, apparently, Tony appears with frequency in the local news, pictured with ladies in garish florals competing in bake sales he's judged, where he looks eternally dashing. Ru's rather taken aback by his own astonishing resemblance to the scoundrel, who according to an article in the *Glasswood Chronicle*, had been illicitly involved in a suspected dalliance with the village rector's wife in the late 1980s, the affair gaining local notoriety when Tony was caught romantically with the rector's visiting niece one fireworks night in the back of his Bentley. Handsome. Charismatic; a man who cared about his constituency, all rare characteristics, for a—

'But it does. I want to be the one to blow all their shit to pieces.' Chucking his head back, Ru huffs out as hard as he can. Expands and retracts his fingers, as if testing his own freedom. 'I'm not in anybody's pocket. Not anybody's secret now,' he says, before looking straight at Vee. 'Except yours.'

She smiles, squeezing his thigh as she nudges him, so fluid in her gestures these days. Tactile and languid and existing on some next-level foxiness. 'The sooner we do this, the sooner—' He stops again, just to gaze at her. 'You've got me losing my words, Vee Hughes.' Very soon to be losing the Hughes, her divorce now imminent.

Valeria Fliss-Burden. It's a great writing name. He's already told her so.

'Best you find them again,' Vee says, nodding toward the double doors which wouldn't look out of place on a castle, that are now opening as a woman, looking positively miniature by scale, shields her eyes from the sun with the back of her hand and spots them.

Exiting the car, Ru and Vee make their ways towards her.

It's the grandmother, Barbara, living in Ru's imagination as some austere lady of the manor, someone old and dusty who smiles from time to time as if for proof she's still alive. Lots of hairspray and two-piece knitwear.

Ru got her about right.

'Gracious!' she says in a voice which booms, not remotely elderly sounding, as Ru stands in front of her. 'You could be Tony when we met.' Taking Ru's arm, she pulls him into the house and directly to the sitting room, where she points to a picture of Tony Bickham at thirty-something, with a babe in arms, who Ru presumes is his father.

Making Ru feels things he didn't expect to.

'Who are you, young chap?' Barbara eyes him curiously, charmed.

He'd imagined her just like Dad; mean and monied, highly rude, never bothering to colour her in further. Barbara drags him along again, only this time through the back of the house and outside across the lawns the size of playing fields.

Tony's pruning his rose garden, in mauve Crocs and tailored shorts; remarkably toned for a fellow of his age.

'Company!' Barbara calls, as Tony slips on a shirt, leaving it undone, his wisps of white chest hair showing along with the tiniest nipples Ru's ever seen, which he hopes Vee's noticed too. 'Tony. I think we have a long-lost relative, don't you?' She claps her hands. 'What fun!'

Dare Ru burst the bubble yet – tell them who his mother is?

Perhaps one step at a time.

Or maybe leave Dad to do his own explaining.

Their house is museum-like, yet comfortable. No strange posh rules or unrelatable etiquette to try guessing at. They seem – and Ru's entirely unrecovered from the fact – welcoming; incredibly pleasant people, too. People who surprisingly adore Goldie. Where Ru had expected to find himself defending her honour, imagining how they'd been fed the tale of how she's broken their beloved Benedict's heart, no.

No with bells on.

'Tosspot!' pronounces Barbara. 'That's what I called him as he left, didn't I, Tony?'

'It's a long story,' Tony says, rather clipped as he heads for his drinks trolley. 'Can I top anybody up? How are those Martinis?'

'Perfect,' says Ru, 'but I best not have another. I'm driving.'

'Oh, a little one for the road won't hurt.' Barbara winks as Ru puts a hand over his glass.

Vee gets poured one anyway. 'You're very kind. Thank you.'

'Anything for Goldie's sister,' says Barbara. 'Would you like a cigarette?'

'Ah, no – but thanks.' Knowing he'll be cross with himself later if he doesn't ask, Ru adds. 'You mentioned that my dad had left?'

'All the time he was here, he was interrupted by phone calls,' Barbara reveals, without drama. 'I'LL GET YOUR FUCKING MONEY!' she barks, not a bad impersonation of her son. Returning to her normal voice, she looks across at Tony. 'Which is when you reached for your chequebook – again.'

'I wouldn't mind so much if he hadn't so vastly benefitted from my politics. Sad little boy, stuffing his face with good cake, claiming all the while it's not to his taste. Makes you wonder where the fuck we went wrong.' Pull the thread and Dad's fraying in vaster sections. But how can somebody like him, from this, be struggling for money? It doesn't make sense.

Ru tries working it out, watching Tony reach for Barbara's hand, the epitome of a united front. His unbuttoned shirt gapes as he does so, revealing those miniscule nipples, as Ru notices something else. On Tony's bare midriff, prominent through his chest hair, is a mole. Dark red and central, like a second belly button, and about the same size, which is quite a coincidence.

'Do visit us again.' Tony holds Vee's hands for a little too long. 'And send my love to your angel of a sister.'

'Oh yes, do,' Barbara chips in. 'She's welcome any time she likes. We always so loved having her here, didn't we, Tony? I know it's out of touch to say so, but ...' Pausing, she looks a little awkwardly at Vee. 'We don't know many POCs. And she was such a breath of fresh air.'

'POC; never bloody meant anything to me,' Tony says, as Ru braces himself, feeling the urge to dive in front of Vee to shield her from whatever off-key bullshit's coming next, but Tony starts to laugh. 'It would just be nice to see in any colour at all.'

'One of his little jokes from his MP days.' Barbara chuckles along too, before Ru asks – because he just can't not – 'You're colour-blind?'

'Are you, too?' Clasping her hands together in expectation, Barbara's almost disappointed when Ru says no. 'It never passed on to your father either. I suppose if you hear from him before we do—'

'Tell him I want my bloody boat back.'

'And good luck with your teaching.' Barbara's all smiley eyes. 'I was always excellent at humanities.'

Ru's tempted to tell them about his book. Much of its content stems from this giant secret; of his invisibility, feeling unloved and unlovable because of it. Trusts his gut and leaves without over-revealing. There's a lot to process, and welcoming as they've been, it's far too soon to be shoehorning them into his book world.

Book world.

For the first time in a long time, the nervous, mind-blowing reality of publication takes his breath away. His words in the world, and his feelings. It'll be quite something, letting strangers inside your head, for is that not what a book is, leaving yourself open?

Ru hopes it'll be a good thing. Freeing, from every entanglement that's never been his.

The fantasy is for all his people to fill the pub, where the launch naturally will be hosted, from his students and colleagues to the writers at Write Pub, his mates, flatmates and, of course, Mum, who can't wait and always knew the moment would come for him, pre-ordering it from every bookshop in London and the Home Counties. Goldie, too, who's always promised to be there.

To Vee. Who he's imagined by his side, them some sizzling,

slinky literary couple, who both might prove groundbreaking one day, as the critics put them together and think, of course. Vee and her gifts. How he could watch her taking on and off those glasses all day long ...

'Aunt, isn't she, son?' Tony winks. 'They never made them like that in my day.'

Son.

And though Ru doesn't show it, the use of the word significantly moves him. Compares it to Dad's pernicious overuse of the word 'boy'. Absent, numb, mechanical twat.

Now vanished. With the few pence he could ponce off his parents. Gone the same way as his sister, who's hiding in Switzerland, too, with a rich man she apparently once hated. What a family.

But he must stop mattering now. Ru will never be at peace otherwise, and there are real, clear glimmers that he could be. It's time the tiny role Dad played is set aside, made defunct like an unnecessary chess piece, like the silly staged game in the study he never used. And though Mum will doubtlessly lose her shit when she finds out Dad's gone, Ru swears that when she hears what he's got to say, she'll be glad to be free of him, too.

Forty-One

GOLDIE

Losing You

'I know what you've been doing.' Wolfie leaves his wine to reach across the table for Goldie's hand. 'But you don't have to. You can talk to me. About Vine. About Grant. All of it.'

But Goldie doesn't think she wants to. Today's been an exhausting, boundary-breaking day. Would rather sit here looking into Wolfie's eyes, all soft and earnest, as they decide on their tapas.

'Well done, G.' He clinks her glass. 'Must've been nice; having Vee there today, then Rufus turning up. Okay …' Wolfie reads her, as he's learning to. 'What's that face for? Vee and Rufus? What've they done?'

'All the things, Wolfie. All over the kitchen. Even when I was showering, I could hear them at it. And I never felt more like his mother,' she adds as Wolfie laughs, can't help himself. 'They don't know I know. Yet. I don't know what I'm waiting for – Valeria, I guess. To tell me herself. I don't know, maybe it's a test. Trusting her again, after all the holiday stuff,' Goldie explains, still unsure how she truly feels – other than it being fucking weird. 'You think you know someone ...'

But Goldie knows how people only ever give what they're prepared to show you.

After an evening where nothing remotely current, stressful nor too probing gets a mention, Goldie and Wolfie walk back to Saunders Road hand in hand.

With happiness seeming like a very real choice.

'Do you ... want to stay?' Goldie asks him, never not amazed by her own sheer bashfulness.

'Yeah, please.' Tilting her chin to look in her eyes, he adds, 'If that's all right.'

Heading towards the house, Goldie's struck with premonition, as every instinct she possesses roars to attention.

Feels Grant in her very bones, before he even says her name.

'G.' One tiny letter has Goldie sucking her guts in. A strange forgotten reflex. 'I'm not here for trouble ... I just thought, after the court summons today ...' Grant says. What court summons? Goldie must look as confused as she feels, unwilling to meet his eyes which feel too searching – oddly violating, somehow. 'I ... I just want to know what you're planning to say ...'

Reading the situation, Wolfie steps in front of Goldie, as from a monster of a black car, out jump two burly men in Grant's defence.

'Look,' Grant says, with his palms up at Wolfie, 'you don't know me, and I've no beef with you.'

'Trust me, old man, I do know you.' Wolfie does not budge. And he doesn't look away first. Without turning, he reaches behind him, offering his hand for Goldie to take.

From the top of the road, someone calls her name, as another person spots them, too, turning their cameras on the scene, closing in, multiplying in their numbers, which puts something so primal in Goldie that she flees, running through the growing onslaught of press and into the road, where for one brilliant moment she pictures most vividly those glasses old Katie Headlights had on in their interview earlier, as a car rushes towards her.

Forty-Two

VEE

My Life

From this morning's BBC interview to the court summons she'd signed for – which Vee's yet to tell Goldie about – to the very knee-jerk decision to accompany Ru to his grandparents', Vee had thought she'd be in bed by now, not at Write Pub, feeling more awake than ever. But there is no group tonight. She is here to meet Judith, just the two of them, to discuss her progress.

There's power to Vee these days, she knows it. Power in her pen, from writing the wrongs of her entire existence, casting delicious karma against not only Julia, but all the people who've hurt her most. Yet also so much more than that.

It is Vee's story. Her life story.

And it is truth telling. Vee knows she is growing, producing the best work she's ever written. Writing about the past has given her structure, a distraction from the very missed, very yearned-for Onion, and against the upside-down tumultuousness of now. Words are needed more than ever. As an escape. A way to block out the chaos of situations she's no concept of how to resolve. Better, to self-protect in her own head.

If only there was more time to do it. Putting everyone else first was the habit she'd been so keen to break after Jamie. Life's busier than she's ever known it, and though Vee can't say she's suffering, she's certainly out of her depth. Ru was right, encouraging her into meeting Judith; the mystery, both around her interest in Vee's new pages and her influence on Ru, has not passed Vee unnoticed.

The interest, which stepped up from emails to a physical invitation, before making perfect sense.

'Vee,' Judith says, as Vee drops down from her bar stool to greet her. 'Not kept you waiting, I hope?'

'You haven't. I'm just early for everything.' Said without apology. Simply Vee being Vee. Her meticulous, dedicated way of doing things.

And look what comes from daring to be herself.

Because, as it turns out, Judith's a secret agent.

'Most thoughtful!' she says, spotting the glass of red Vee ordered for her, when she'd got her own drink in. Along with some emergency chips.

'Now, as you know, I'm a writer through and through, which is why I'm here in the trenches, forever trying. Fortunately, I am much, much better at my day job,' Judith explains, with a little twinkle about her. 'Which brings us to you, Vee.'

Vee tries to focus on remembering all the things being said

to her, and not just the standout words thrilling her socks off, like miniature electric shocks.

A timely book. Such precise attention to character. Sharp, impeccable prose.

Unquestionably, a breakthrough novel.

'I've always resisted approaching writers here for my own gain – which feels all a bit cross-contaminating to me. Ru was different, I don't represent poetic prose anyway, and his work was so . . .' She smiles, positively celestial. 'Agents bit his hand off. Have you read it yet?'

'I'm waiting till I buy it. He's invited me to his launch,' Vee says, as Judith beams approvingly.

'I helped with his submissions. All he needed was a push. I hope the book lands well. He deserves it.'

Vee thinks of Ru, rather in shock after leaving his grandparents, offering for her to stay over at his place in Forest Gate – not far from the pub. It's very Ru, how he lived so close, without ever any early pressure to lure her back to his.

He does, absolutely, deserve to fly.

'How are you finding it, returning to your subject?' Judith wants to know and is further pleased when Vee tells her that it's coming out with far less hurt than she anticipated.

'But is there time in your life now,' she asks, not without concern, 'to write a whole book?'

Perhaps Judith's clocked the bags under Vee's eyes. It had always been the problem, prioritizing the time to write. How she'd begin things with such passion, but never finished the stories because of life and time and just because it felt a totally pointless pursuit. Perhaps if she'd have had some encouragement—

But it's time to stop all that. Because here she is.

Here the fuck she is.

'I absolutely do.' When she separates herself from everybody else's chaos, it's true.

Because when else will be the perfect time to make writing Vee's priority, taking full advantage of the – currently rather fortunate – lull in her freelance work, and how she'll soon be free of the cyclic worry of finding funds for the money-pit mortgage? The house sold on its first open day, as it should, being beautiful. Time for somebody else to make it a home.

'I'm not sold on the title. *Bad Adults*, though catchy, spotlights the worst characters, when this is your story.'

Vee's not offended nor attached to the title. The content so much more important to her anyway.

'And how would you feel, Vee; about having me as your agent?'

Unable to do much else, Vee laughs, nods, all enthusiasm. Thinks she'd love it.

At the bottom of their celebratory Proseccos, Vee and Judith say their goodbyes; Vee making a promise to have a full manuscript with her by the end of September.

Six weeks' time.

But Vee knows, even if she's dead, that she'll deliver.

It is so bafflingly late. Vee and Ru having given up on the notion of sleep, settling for bed and further dissection of the day, after scrambled eggs on toast, with the best bottle of red Vee could find on her way over to celebrate.

But it's not long before their conversation works its way back to the Bickhams.

Ru's matching moles story Vee really felt was reaching, until he googled colour-blindness, the 100 per cent fact that fathers pass it to their daughters, who either share the condition, or carry it. Then he showed her pictures of his mum – mostly dressed in white; the only colour she can safely wear without the risk of any clashing. A female version of Ru; same hair shade, identical eye colour, even down to the same posture. All the same components as Tony Bickham. And the photograph, which could literally have been Ru, too.

Is this why Tony Bickham lost his shit when Therese and Benedict fell for each other at uni? Because they were both his children? Therese the result of his affair with Grandma Fry? Fact he was a chronic philanderer, but it seems all too suffocatingly debauched to be real.

Half-siblings. Surely not.

Though the whole Bickham secret makes a lot more sense.

'What the fuck though, Vee? What if Mum's a Bickham, too?' Going quiet, Ru doesn't say it, but Vee knows what he's thinking, because she'd be thinking the same.

What does this mean for him?

'I do know one thing,' Vee says after a bit. 'Your dad will be livid. Having to split that precious fortune another way.'

If Benedict now even qualifies for his inheritance at all.

★

Forty-Three

GOLDIE

Slave To The Rhythm

No matter the decade you arrived in, NHS hospitals are all the same. It's amazing how they even function, such are the mazes of dated corridors, peeling window frames, rickety lifts and confusion.

And then there's A & E.

Early evening in the Accident and Emergency finds a waiting room packed with kid accidents; a button lost up a toddler's nostril, a fractured collarbone from cartwheeling, remembering herself falling to a similar injury in primary school as Goldie's confirmed as high, but not critical priority, once a brief essential once-over's given on arrival. Later, the nightlife and alcohol-related accidents begin; a beer glass in somebody's chest rushed through without suffering the waiting room. Two slurry men who've come off on the bad end of a fight – likely because they like the sound of their own voices a bit too much. As Wolfie and

Goldie upgrade from the main waiting room to a cubicle made from curtains.

For three and a half hours.

Grant. Right in front of her. Outside Gran's, because of course he'd know where to find her. Saving his skin, which was always his number one priority. But face to face.

Every part of Goldie's body aches, yet none more than her heart. Which feels shameful, with Wolfie here holding her hand. So fucking kind, and nice ...

It must've been Grant who hand delivered that letter to the Coach House, then. So close, too close to home.

He's aged, massively. Late sixties now, at least. Which only brings more discomfort.

'Can you stay?' Goldie asks Wolfie when it's finally her turn.

'I got run over,' she blurts, almost embarrassed, to the doctor, because it sounds like a kid accident. She'd felt like a child when she fled. And she feels like a child now.

'You were unconscious?' the doctor asks, with such kind concern that Goldie bites her lip as she nods.

'For about twenty to thirty seconds,' Wolfie chips in. 'The car came from nowhere, caught her hip.' He bunches his face up as if it hurts to recall it, completely rattled.

'And you say you're bleeding?'

'I wouldn't say bleeding. More like the start of a period. It's my back that hurts most,' Goldie says, explaining the pain coming in waves, radiating around her hip that's bruising nastily already, and is tender when she's examined on the small bed, lying awkwardly as the doctor presses across her tummy.

'And when was the date of your last period?' the doctor asks, looking over her glasses at Goldie as she continues her prodding.

Goldie's blank. 'I've never had the most regular cycles,' she says. Her last period was before France. 'A few weeks ago. Maybe.'

'And is there any possibility you might be pregnant?'

Sent to the loo, Goldie pees mostly on her hand as she holds the cardboard bowl between her legs, aiming the best she can. Barely filling the sample pot, she trembles as she screws the lid on. There is no more blood, just a series of dots, not one any bigger than a five pence piece in her knickers, and no longer bright red.

Unable to meet Wolfie's eye as she hands her sample over, the doctor dips a stick into Goldie's pee pot.

Instead of an X-ray, an ultrasound is organized.

Upgraded to a side room, Goldie and Wolfie wait without speaking as Goldie stares into the corner, thinking what an astronomical idiot she is. What a naive teenager she still is. And the sheer irony of how she's thought of their passion possibly every hour since it happened, yet never once had the thought that the consequences of their unprotected moment has been at work without her knowing, that she's dismissed as:

Food poisoning. Norovirus. Something life-threateningly terminal. Menopause. Peri . . .

How embarrassing. The most obvious, logical reason staring her straight in the face.

Just like when she'd been pregnant before.

Teenage Goldie and her chronic denial, until the need to know for sure roared upon her like a ticking bomb that had reached detonation. In the big anonymous supermarket on the edge of town, Goldie had bought a test; remembers having the thought that at least she could afford to buy a pregnancy kit now she was a popstar, but made her wonder why they were so prohibitive, considering how they're just fucking litmus paper and plastic.

In the Asda lavs, because she couldn't wait, and because she hadn't wanted to be carrying the paraphernalia evidence home with her, Goldie had taken her test. Two blue positive lines.

That day in the toilet cubicle, Goldie's most locked away thoughts had unleashed themselves, aligning parallel with the same baffled emotions of now; how she's unable to quite believe it. How she'd sat on the loo seat for goodness knows how long, knees trembling, then jolting; in the throes of shock. Goldie can't remember putting herself back together back then, though she must've.

And when she tried to phone Grant on both of his mobiles, he ignored her calls.

Eventually, he answered. And when Goldie told him, Grant had asked with a detachment as if he barely even knew her,

How do I know it's mine?

Those words. How they'd reverberated through Goldie as if he'd assaulted her. Because there never had been anyone else. Denying their love, stomaching his deflections of her having a silly teen crush, when it was Grant. Grant who'd been the one. The only one.

Prove it, he'd said.

To Goldie. At sixteen.

Sixteen. With the world's most terrible secret. Every private moment spent wondering if she could feel any symptoms, when all she felt was fear. And absolute sadness. The terror and the self-loathing over how she could be so bloody stupid – and again isn't this just so typical, when the sex is honest, when her feelings are so real that lovemaking's become baby-making. A terrifying loneliness wraps itself around Goldie, pronouncing her isolated.

And vulnerable.

People do, regularly, destroy themselves trying to distance from fact, but we are always us. Goldie at forty-five – WTF fuck WTF – is no different to the Goldie at sixteen, which feels frightening as it dawns on her how very little she's changed deep down, how the same sense of fear remains, a flight instinct away from whatever's scared and scarred her the most, because to sit in it ...

To face the truth. The pain of all Goldie's abandonments. Dad. To acknowledge how very much Goldie had once loved her mum. Wants to be loved. Which is all she's ever really wanted.

And how this will likely come to nothing, the same as her first pregnancy.

All over again.

'When do you think we can speak, G?' Wolfie asks, breaking Goldie from her spell.

'What can I say? I'm stupid.'

'We're stupid.' He smiles, as if unable to help himself. '*Were* stupid. Once.'

'You think those odds are impressive; that 'once' was the only time in fifteen years.' And that's only if she counts the non-event on her wedding night. Goldie watches his surprise. 'For me, anyway,' she adds, not much liking the ripple of envy when she thinks of Wolfie with somebody else. 'God, we hardly know each other; I don't even know when your birthday is.'

'I'll be forty-six. Next Tuesday,' he says, making her smile, just for a moment.

'Good job you told me. Unless. Unless, of course . . .' Unable to think let alone say it, she avoids his face, blinking her eyes dry.

'Unless of course what?' Mirroring Goldie, he lowers his head to look at her. 'I'm going to run off into the night never to be seen again? I had a dad like that. No thanks.'

'So did I,' Goldie says. 'Not that I wasn't loved – could feel I was, every time I was ever in front of him. But he did take off one night, and we never saw him again.' She sighs. 'And few years after that, we were told never to speak about him again. Sorry—' She checks herself. 'Me and Valeria were only talking about this earlier. I really don't think you need to be thinking along the parenting lines, anyway.' Goldie shifts in her seat, lifting her jumper and wishing she hadn't as she traces the purple speckle of deep bruising, cruel on her skin. Making her so tearful, there's no hope this time of blinking them back.

'I'll fucking kill him.'

'You can't.' Goldie sighs, tries. 'You won't win.'

'I keep going over it. Must've been a panic after today's interview?'

'Do you think I'm in danger?' Goldie asks the question she's been considering even before Naga and Charlie; the Vine-related consequences for having a voice. From pointing a finger.

But she hadn't said anything untoward. If anything, she'd sanitized the truth. Which suddenly makes her feel deeply shitty. But there's little else she can do until the meeting Valeria's arranged with their newly appointed legal team, Stanley Sisters at Law – who scouted Goldie, if you please, on a conditional fee agreement, or CFA, which meant nothing until Valeria explained they were willing to represent her on a no-win no-fee, just for the hell of it. Seems women supporting women is a way of life.

'My gut says your gran's is off limits,' Wolfie admits. 'Too many people know where you are there. How about staying somewhere else for a bit? What do you think? My place? Valeria's?'

'I might end up staying in here. Which would be typical. I've never seen your place.'

'It's a bit of a work in progress. I wouldn't get excited.'

'Everything you do excites me.' Far too much, she knows. Wants to take it back the moment she says it.

'That's very lucky then.' Picking up the arms of his chair, Wolfie sit-walks over, parking up as close as he can to Goldie. ''Cos, I feel the same. Now, I'm not gonna lie, I'm shocked, truly. And though I'd never want to influence any decision you come to ... I'm not disappointed ... about any of this.' He makes sure she knows he means it. 'Not in the slightest.'

'At our age, though.'

'And what age is that?' Wolfie asks gently, humouring her.

'Top end pregnancy risk age. Seriously liking and needing my sleep age. Being in my fucking sixties when they turn twenty-one age ...' And the biggest, most important reason of all. 'Not wanting a baby age.' Goldie exhales. 'Maybe ... I don't know. I never had any massive desire for kids. I just couldn't picture it.' There's never been one definite reason. 'And ... and what if I was just shit at it. Like my mum.'

Wolfie shakes his head.

'It's genetics, you know. Cruelty. Passing on all the bad shit.' Goldie clicks her fingers. 'Generational trauma. Have you heard of the mother wound?' But though she tries, Goldie can't call to mind a single fact from her conversation with Valeria earlier. How that now seems like somebody else's morning, only increasing her feelings of instability. 'My mum left us when I was fifteen. And ...' Goldie gulps, her biggest regret in the world. 'And six months later, I left Valeria, too. No ...' Because he mustn't comfort her, must know the worst of her. 'She needed me so much she was fucking sectioned, and I was touring. Escaping, for all the same reasons Mum had. Because I was tired. Because I was sick of being the one carrying all the feelings. All the responsibility.' She sobs. 'I just wanted to be free!'

'Of course you did. Because you were a child, too.'

A child with a pop career, who escaped the family dysfunction by getting pregnant by her forty-odd-year-old boss and lover.

'And you're not Vee's mum either. I do know who you are, though.' Wolfie rubs her leg. 'You're kind, Goldie. You always have been. And I know, because I remember.' He swipes her tears away, this nice, ordinary man she doesn't deserve. 'So please don't cry.'

But Goldie can't stop. She hurts. Everywhere, but most of all her brain. Emotionally driven, and unreliable. People have babies in far shittier circumstances every second. They do. But regardless of circumstance, the obvious remains. Whether Goldie wants a baby at all.

It could be so lovely. Unexpectedly expecting. And him.

A proper family.

They've taken things so slowly. Ever since coming home, Goldie's been so cautious not to rely on him nor need too much; remaining open while also in protective mode, where Wolfie seems to operate himself. Their romantic steps, though very surface, have been gentle, strangely committed, in no rush because there's all the time in the world. To become a couple.

Goldie mustn't let this influence her. And besides, there's still so much she doesn't know about him. Her own overexposure hasn't led to any of his own deep revelations. And he must have quite the romantic back catalogue; because ... well, just flipping look at him.

But his earnestness has vanished. Looking very much like crying himself, Wolfie stands. 'I need a bit of air ... do you mind?'

'Of course not.'

He squeezes Goldie's shoulder, and by the time her hand moves to squeeze back ...

He's gone.

See?

Circumstance cannot make this decision. Just because she's pregnant doesn't mean she has to be. Isn't it enough in the world to simply get by looking after yourself?

All women do, have ever done, is care and get roached off. When does it stop? When will it become a neutral option, okay to opt out of the lot of it, and not be frowned upon, questioned, or misunderstood? How motherhood's a choice. As personal as they come.

Forty-Four

WOLFIE

Unbreak My Heart

It feels the most childish thing on earth to admit, how much Wolfie needs his mother.

He resists ringing. Worrying her. Instead, he sits on the exact same spot of brick wall outside the same fucking hospital where he'd spent that terrible, terrible night.

But now is not then. Not the same.

Wolfie hopes.

Forty-Five

GOLDIE

Golden

The silence is heavy and intolerable as the sonographer sits cagily turned towards their equipment, behaving as if Goldie's trying to copy their homework. This cold person, who'll be first to know the info, which seems a baffling order of things.

They are taking too long.

The wand begins its journey over her stomach, grayscale on the screen, with a black centre, which makes Goldie think of space, the massiveness of the universe, as an emptiness rushes in. Doesn't think she can suffer the sudden enormity of feeling.

How there is suddenly no doubt that no baby would be a very terrible thing.

'Must just quickly confer with my colleague.' Rising, the sonographer opens the door, gesturing to another hospital person who's most conveniently passing. 'Do you have a mo to look over my shoulder?'

It's hard for Goldie to eavesdrop on their low-level mumbling, as her head thumps along with her own heartbeat, pumping in her hand too, wrapped tight around Wolfie's as if they're delivering already. Flying off the bed and out of the room, Goldie just makes it into the corridor before she's sick.

And when she's cleaned herself up, they try again. More gel, and the wand's back, pushing peculiarly into Goldie's abdomen, making her desperate for the loo.

'No visible signs of trauma, which is excellent.' The sonographer mumbles to his colleague, who, with a nod, stands back. With the tiniest smile he folds his arms, as if to help him keep a secret.

The sonographer turns the monitor towards Goldie and Wolfie, circling the screen with a finger. 'See this dark sac?' he asks, as they nod in confirmation. 'See the tiny kidney bean, with the flickering light? There's your heartbeat.'

A flickering light.

'So everything's okay?' Wolfie squeezes his eyes shut.

'Everything's okay. Times two.' Enlarging the screen, the sonographer makes a V-shape with his finger, indicating two matching images. 'Measuring eleven weeks six days gestation,' he confirms, as the other doctor with his arms folded smiles so widely that it takes over his whole face, staying put to watch the moment. 'Two beating hearts in two separate sacs. Non-identical multiples.'

'Two that are okay?' Wolfie checks, as nausea rises in Goldie again.

'Everything's good,' he confirms. 'And going by the numbers, Christmas deliveries.'

Just like Goldie herself had been, once upon a time. Back in 1979.

Only she'll be nothing like her mum. If everything stays okay, Goldie will love her Christmas babies with all her heart. For always.

And by the look of Wolfie, weeping as he kisses her, so will he.

Forty-Six

BENEDICT

Sinnerman

'Cruelty has a long tail.' What the fuck does it even mean? But Benedict does know.

And it has him scared.

He's never been in true, life-threatening danger before. The reality of that serrated beast of a knife at his throat. That close to danger.

Jesus Christ. That close.

Benedict peeks through the curtains of the boat and into endless night. He couldn't see anyone coming to get him anyway, until they were—

'Fuck!' For a moment, Benedict's soul exits his body as he smashes his head into the panelled ceiling.

But it's only Trevor. Trevor, who's been delivering him food parcels. Trevor, who'll now think he's even more of a pussy.

Because pussies run. Pussies hide when the bigger boys

come. And it was only a matter of time before somebody Benedict pushed decided to push back.

Pussies fail when playing games with other people's money, too. Though lately Benedict's not been playing games. It's the terrifying truth that he can't afford to exchange monies from the purchase of those start-ups – which includes Wolfie's, and which, yes, had been rather enjoyable at first, when it was only affecting him. Goldie's golden ISA got snatched back quick, just as he was sinking, literally drowning – which feels a wrong and ominous turn of phrase considering his current location. And then came the threat on his life.

He'd never seen a knife like it. Everything for a moment just like a horror film.

Covid forced Benedict to make several redundancies, of mostly unfortunate but on the whole forgettable bottom-rung employees. Forgettable, that was, until a fortnight ago, when the maniac son of one of those employees tracked Benedict down to avenge their parent's recent suicide.

How is that even Benedict's fault?

'Have you signed the forms?' Trevor asks.

'All of them. Even the divorce bollocks.' Benedict nods to the small stack of signed paperwork, a self-addressed envelope on top destined for Goldie's solicitors. 'Though she's by far the cheapest thing to cut loose.' He shakes his head wistfully, downs his Scotch, feeling a bit of a prick. 'How the hell did it come to this?'

Strange, coming from a family like his, how marrying Goldie was the cowardly choice.

'Cruelty has a long tail,' Trevor says, not knowing even half of it – and not without a hint of enjoyment either. Handing over Benedict's cold Pret supper, by phone light he heads home to his family. And a bed which doesn't feel like a fucking bench.

Alone in the dark, because turning on a light would draw attention, Benedict can't face switching on his own tech either, and as he eats his BLT, he considers what the hell's next. Whether to really flee the country instead of simply mooring Dad's boat along another part of the Thames. More pussy behaviours. But he's desperate. He really is.

Truly not having a pot to piss in seems bizarre. Being poor. Worse than death. Maybe.

Forty-Seven

GOLDIE

Dirty Cash

Valeria's waiting next to Goldie's bed when she wakes up. Kept in for observation and given her own side room – thanks to the clearly unchanged intrusiveness of the British press. Seeing Goldie's awake, she whips out her phone. 'I said I'd text Wolfie the second you opened your eyes,' Valeria says, doing so before hugging her, Goldie finding her pain still atrocious when she moves to hold her sister back. 'I don't blame him for being worried. I couldn't sleep a wink once I knew what'd happened.' Valeria strokes her face, which feels deeply nurturing, and needed. 'I'm so glad you're all right, G. Don't know what I'd do …' Valeria sniffs. Pulling herself together, she changes the subject. 'After today I hope we get some answers.'

'We look a right fucking pair,' Goldie says a bit later, because even with her clean teeth and neater hair, she still looks about a hundred, and as for Valeria.

Frazzled. Still terrified.

Suddenly Goldie's glad Valeria has Rufus in her life. That they have each other.

But looks, as Goldie knows, can be deceitful. Valeria might be exhausted, but her brain is working wonders. She is dynamic, and clearly a force, having rearranged their meeting with Stanley Sisters at Law to be held here, around Goldie's sickbed, rather than in their own shiny offices in Stratford.

The Stanley sisters. Three siblings, from East London themselves, dismantling the system one case at a time. All of them at her bedside today, who came of age to her music just as she'd done herself.

They say representing her will be an honour – and Goldie just can't quite believe it.

Benedict is the smallest part of business on their agenda. Undone in one signature. Amazing what happens when the right sort of pressure's applied in the right areas. Annulled. As if their unconsummated marriage had never happened. The contents of Goldie's current account back in her control. Minus her ISA, but she can live with that. Thinks it might be best anyway – a fresh uncontaminated start.

So that's that.

But surely it can't be.

The Stanley sisters start gentle; their aim to investigate the reasons behind the alteration of Goldie's original contract not once but nineteen times in the twenty-two months she was signed to Vine Recordings. Add on six NDAs, the contents of which they are still chasing.

Then there's the question of royalties. And unanimous

disgust when they're all amazed to learn how Goldie's never received a penny from her original songs. Which provokes the further question of whether she'd really signed away those rights of her own volition, because on what planet would she have done that?

And then they hit her; Trina Stanley, with her gorgeous side-plaited braids, sets it out plainly. 'Look, Goldie. I think we're beyond massaging egos and mediocre plonkers ...'

With her permission, the Stanley sisters would like to continue building a case around her conflict-of-interest relationship with Grant. Just quietly, alongside the inquiry that's going on. So that it's just there and ready – along with all Valeria's flawlessly curated evidence.

'We've managed, don't ask how, to get hold of some paperwork already. Your first contract, signed on 23 April 1996, which would've made you sixteen and four months old,' Kiley Stanley, the eldest sister at Stanley Law, says. 'And this photo.' She places a copy, in a plastic pocket, on Goldie's lap.

Proof of how it never gets any easier, looking at what Goldie thought was love.

Is glad she's learning the difference.

The photograph is pure nostalgia; a dancing shot of gorgeous celebrity people. Grant in the background, wearing a tight tee, and all bulging muscles, with Goldie's hair bunched in his fist as he's kissing her.

Grant then. Five feet nine of perfection. Straight shoulders and hips of sheer fucking glory. His close haze of a beard tracing his jawline, and leisurewear in monied colours. Not the Sports Direct plastic logo tat Nan would palm them off with on birthdays. Air Jordan 2s on his feet in brilliant white; trainers forever the first thing Goldie notices, and conflicting looking back, when she checks out her own feet, those limited-edition retro Nikes that she'd loved more than anything. Her love affair with Lycra too, clearly already begun. Though, hadn't it been Grant in the first place who encouraged her bodysuits, the leotards and unitards? Harder access to her tempting flesh. Too much effort for opportunists and their wandering hands. Never, however, too much effort for him.

Goldie remembers well the clothes, the trainers; his many, many gifts. Remembers being held, just like that.

How much she'd enjoyed it.

But all the feels and gifts in the world could never match how short she sold herself. The times she'd let him back between her legs, forgiving though never really knowing why – but thinking back, perhaps it had a massive lot to do with him being a grown, powerful forty-something year-old man whereas she was an ordinary girl, with no real power, nor autonomy, and quite frankly—

What's new?

'That was after a concert we'd been to watch.' Goldie can't take her eyes off the picture, holding it with her hand full of tubes, the image thick with the same vibe Goldie's worn forever; how Grant was a hungry consumer, and she was a snack. 'Our first time together out in public, because we were in the States,' Goldie says. 'But this isn't useful – I wasn't even signed to Vine then. Grant's likely no idea this exists.'

'Can you remember the date of the concert, Goldie?' Kiley

asks gently, making Goldie feel babied, and useless, because of course she can't fucking remember.

She shrugs. 'There were loads of different acts – Wu Tang, Queen Latifah; I remember meeting Nas. I told Valeria once, I'm sure, how he was a very polite man.' Goldie tries, but that's truly all she's got.

'Your first time in public, but not your first time being intimate?'

'Intimate? I look like his dinner.' Goldie studies the picture again. Their kiss. How fucking small she was. 'Not the first time by any means, no.'

The covert glances going on around the room are really beginning to grate.

And upset her.

'The concert you attended was in Brooklyn,' says Alice Stanley, the youngest, tallest, with a high bun to make her even taller. 'June 1995. Five months before your sixteenth birthday. Which puts you five months under the age of consent, Goldie.'

But really, what does that matter if she wanted to be there?

'It seems the right time to inform you that there's been a whistleblower at Vine,' Alice continues. 'He mentioned you a lot, and though it's confidential, because you know him by a different name, I just thought it might be a good thing.' She smiles. 'For you to know that there's someone in your corner.'

Good old Mr Maybe.

'I just thought he was a lover. Like the one who got away,' Valeria says, not quite able to lift her eyes from the floor, over judging Goldie based on her look, just like the rest of them.

If you're ever to love me well, discover the truth beneath my shell.

The birth of a new lyric. Sun streams through the window, bathing Goldie in light, warm as a kiss. Glances for a second to her tummy full of secrets. Knows she's not done yet.

Goldie's accrued quite the army. All chomping to fight.

For her.

'We really believe this to be the final blow that topples the lot of them,' Kiley says. 'Which will turn all this into so much more than a slap on the wrist. We foresee prison sentences. Perhaps even changes in legislation.'

'Abuses, personal harm against recording artists by their companies, is one of the oldest stories there is. Which gets worse when you add in other factors, like ethnicity, gender, your socio-economic background – and in your case, your age. At no time was there an official adult looking out for any of your needs. Which puts Vine in astronomical breaches.'

News Goldie's quite unprepared for. Because never before has a corporate, legal situation like this left her feeling even remotely human. Or supported.

Apparently Trevor the lickspittle had been most uncomfortable in their offices earlier.

And for Vine Recordings, Stanley Sisters at Law are a proper coven of kryptonite. Weak in the face of a role reversal – where it's their fit for once that's up for question.

'So, what do you want out of all this?' Because she's sure Goldie can pretty much name her price for her silence. And wouldn't that be something? She could think of any ridiculous number then treble it. A number so life-changing, she'd never need worry about numbers again, or need to panic hoard skincare from Amazon. 'The court summons doesn't stand if you're still unwell, so we do have ways out of it. Though it's worth remembering that it is only testimony of your time there. But this . . .' Catching Goldie's eye, Kiley taps the picture.

And though Goldie has her babies and their hopeful future to think about, they are exactly why she cannot be bought off. There has been enough of that.

'I must warn you that it's highly unlikely you'll receive any compensation as generous from an inquiry.'

'But it's the principle,' Goldie says.

And it is.

Alongside the whistleblower, the paperwork and the photograph Goldie never wants to see again, there's Valeria's paraphernalia at home, the tapes and scrapbooks – plus both their eyewitness testimonies. There's also her meticulous record-keeping of Goldie's life, and her more recent digging, too, from when she'd been sniffing round with her documentary plans.

And it is only in the standing back that Goldie sees how very loved she is.

But Valeria's still imperfect. Much as she's tried, Goldie can't forget the kitchen antics between her and Rufus. But isn't everything a fuckery anyway? Especially family.

'Goldie, can I say something?' Vee clears her throat nervously, as if she's about to confess to a crime. 'On my heart, I'm sorry. How blamed you always were when we were kids.

Because of what you looked like – judged by adult measures. It wasn't fair.' But a fact; how girls like Goldie have a reputation by default, even through the eyes of their baby sisters. 'I allowed my own preconceptions to cloud my own view of you, too,' Valeria admits. 'I also know that for you to ever trust me again you need the truth.' Nervously, she glances to the ceiling. 'God, there's a lot to say ... Rufus – your Rufus? Well ... he's also ...' She stops again, stalling. 'We met a few months ago, through a writing group. And for a while we really, really, didn't know.' Vee looks at Goldie. 'How we had you in common.'

'And when you did?'

'I think we expected that'd kill it off,' Vee says truthfully. 'But the thing is, we really get a lot out of being together.'

With a huff, Goldie adjusts herself. Tired now of being in bed.

'I'm being honest. And I know it seems weird and all super unethical, but, but ... when you think about it, Ru's almost thirty.'

'Twenty-eight,' Goldie corrects. 'He's twenty-eight.'

'Which doesn't make me Jeffrey fucking Epstein, Goldie! We were adults who met in a pub. He liked my writing, which I got a massive fucking kick out of, actually. And you know what else? We've got a lot in common. And I'm not even done yet with the shit I need to get off my chest – are you listening to me?' Whipped up to the point of no return, just as she'd get as a kid with no sleep, Valeria bursts into tears. 'I've got an agent, too. The thing I wrote about Julia? About growing up and coming face to face all over again? Well, it's almost a book. And from the sounds of things, really fucking hopeful. That this might be it.'

'That's your dream, Valeria.' Goldie's moved as well. After all the years of smothering herself, the universe is rewarding her sister, now she's recognized at last what she is truly made from. 'Amazing how one day your mass of hoarded shite might end up in the British Library, in a collection just for you. Proof of the writer you always were.' Growing emotional, she feels her nostrils tightening. 'You've always deserved the world.' She squeezes Valeria's hands between hers. 'I always wanted to give you the world.'

'That was never for you to do.'

'I'm going to be a mum, Valeria.' Goldie's tears spill uncontrollably onto her chest, which heaves in step with all her emotions. 'Me. This old state.'

'What?' Vee can't seem quite to take it in.

'Wolfie and his super sperm hit a golden egg. Eggs plural, actually. Two babies, if you can believe it.' She searches and searches Valeria's face for signs of upset, or pretending, or masking of the truth.

'I think you're going to be the most brilliant mother.'

'Valeria, if it hurts you, then I'm—'

'It doesn't. Don't even for a second think it.' Kicking her shoes off quite spontaneously, Valeria climbs into bed with her, snuggling up close, which brings back so many similar moments of them – so very much like this, feeling lost and scrappy, with only each other – that Goldie's heart feels too big for her body.

'I was never completely sure about a baby anyway; just

went along with trying because of Jamie,' she says, so matter of fact, that Goldie knows it's true.

'And you think you didn't love him.'

Forty-Eight

Ru

Finest Dreams

With a fortnight until publication day, Ru's still unsure. It could all be a wild coincidence.

Is he the only person to question it? So much time spent doubting that old codicil rumour in the will; whether it was just an elaborate threat, dangled to wager some kind of control over a super-spending, entitled and very pompous son ...

Or a real, very serious warning.

It seems almost comical how Ru thought he'd be setting himself free by meeting his grandparents and exposing his father. Yet if it's true, that Mum is Tony's child, too, then there'll never be any escaping the Bickhams. With Dad missing and Mum clueless anyway, and after thinking of so little else, Ru's decided that he doesn't want to know. Already so caught in the family bullshit he never wanted, what's needed most is distance.

One person who's absolutely flown free of the Bickham

web – though it must be said still banging on, even as she was discharged from the hospital, how the only reason she's off to cosy down with Wolfie is because of safety instead of being crazy in love – is Goldie. Who shows, proves, how good things do happen.

And Christ, Ru's only to look at his own facts of life to see he's lucky, too.

Mum's unchanged; still his kind, loving, unfalteringly supportive mum – innocent, in the whole mucky lot of it, just like him. Life is much the same, too; full, mostly happy, and improving all the time – but for family fuckery which could be left undisturbed. And why not.

Because hadn't he always wanted Dad to disappear?

Forty-Nine

WOLFIE

Whatta Man

On leaving the hospital, Wolfie knows just where to take Goldie.

Entrusting her with the other person he loves most feels apt. So, it's back to the little street where he comes from. Just off Wellsend seafront. Peeling paint and windy as fuck.

For days, Goldie's barely left Mum's sofa, recovering and comfy on the chintz print covered in fluffy alpaca cushions. Wearing one of his mum's velour blingy Y2K tracksuits, she's currently half a packet of dark chocolate digestives down, watching *Dangerous Minds*.

'I've got the soundtrack upstairs.' He gets under the blanket that she's sharing with Muffintop, Mum's scrappy mutt with ungodly wind, and Goldie snuggles into him in a way that makes Wolfie feel purposeful, and needed, which is a warm, forgotten feeling.

He is learning how to look after her; to be gentle, but always straightforward.

'How are you feeling?' Wolfie checks. 'No more blood?'

'No more blood,' Goldie says, a whole range of emotions at play on her face, like a time-lapse video. 'How are you feeling?'

'I'm good if you're good.'

'And is your mum all right still, with me being here?'

She'd been horrified when Wolfie had said how much Goldie reminded him of his mum – until they met, and Trisha welcomed them in at silly o'clock wearing her zebra print dressing gown and UGG slippers and animal print eye mask, worn like an Alice band, holding back her masses of dyed black hair. Same Essex-ness, glamour, kindness and energy. 'I know, it's hard to believe,' Trish had said, hugging Goldie like she knew what she was thinking. 'I had him at fourteen. Best mistake I ever made.' Which had pricked something in Wolfie, watching Goldie so unsure, so unused to female nurturing. Wary, like a little stray cat, that Wolfie knew his mum could see, too, as she'd looked at him over Goldie's shoulder, with her own look of relief that he was finally moving forwards.

'I think she likes you being here even more than me,' Wolfie says.

'Good.' Goldie's posture relaxes. 'That's good.'

Lots of other things continue to bubble away; likely that those burnt letters from Vine were early attempts to woo Goldie into an out-of-court settlement. Had she opened them, she might've been too terrified to do anything other than accept and stay silent. And though Wolfie understands how she's glad to have avoided any more blood money, it is also true when his mother says that Goldie deserves her dues. Because it is not dirty cash but compensation. A settled debt for all her troubles, paid in full. Goldie's reparations.

But she needs things clean; he gets that. No more compromising herself. It's time, and it's only fair that Vine, Benedict and all Goldie's troubles were over for good.

Rejecting any notion of a payout without a second thought has Wolfie adoring her even more. Not that he has any money either. At all. The situation stays the same; his business dying in limbo, Wolfie unwilling to put any more in, while the sale money hangs on in a mystery, with Benedict still missing.

But there's a far bigger unfinished energy aggravating Wolfie's peace right now.

He thinks of the pictures in rotation on the news. Another dark facet of Vine's story; the sheer amount of unagented, unaccompanied young talent left in the care of Vine Recordings – Goldie included in the latest montage of images, sat on that greasy motherfucker's lap, looking not much different than when he'd gone to school with her. Grant Love, named as if his mother wanted him to grow into a fucking pervert. Wolfie blinks the image away.

Leaning into him, Goldie makes butterfly kisses on his neck. 'You know what, I feel up for a little walk. I think it'd do us good. We can take Muffintop.'

'There aren't enough poo bags on the planet to risk me taking that dog out,' he says, making Goldie laugh, and his heart warm, and full from Goldie's use of 'us'. 'Besides, where we're off to he's not welcome. It's time to show you my work in progress.'

A fifteen-minute stroll puts them outside an empty shop at the end of the promenade, curving from the seafront into a side road, its door opening out on the corner.

'Now,' Wolfie says, as he guides Goldie inside, 'you need to have some vision. According to the deets, the place was on its last legs even in its last use. But it's a big old drum, and it's bloody massive upstairs. Commercial space and three bedrooms in an area that's defo on the up and coming, yet rough around the edges.' He wiggles his brows. 'Needless to say, we had an affinity.'

After showing Goldie around the grubby shell of a ground floor, stuck in 1986, it is gratifying when she gasps at the top of the stairs, an honest reaction at the sight of the open-plan kitchen made from white oak, tying together restfully and perfectly the seascape view from the floor-to-ceiling windows, as if you're living in a picture.

'My mate's a chippie,' Wolfie explains. 'I've been his apprentice whenever he's had a bit of spare time. Did a bit of rubbing down here and there, got the sandwiches in. Do you like it?'

'Like? I love it.' Goldie sweeps her hand across the enormous dining table, made from the same wood. 'It's beautiful.'

'There's a story behind choosing that,' Wolfie says, watching her blush.

'A story that's just had a massive plot twist. I still can't believe I didn't know.'

'Well, it's been a tumultuous time.'

'But a lot of that time I spent in the sun, hun, eating olives. I don't even like olives.' Goldie goes quiet, and back to looking out of the window. At odds with the person who loves a proper natter, her long moments of silence feel heavy. Heavy with the sorts of thoughts Wolfie himself recognizes.

The thoughts he's scared to share.

'When will you move in properly?' she asks at last.

'It once depended on what I decided to do with the downstairs. Now it's all in the hands of Ben Bickham. I can't believe I'm saying it, but I wish he'd crawl out of the woodwork to tie my loose ends, too.' Wolfie sighs, wishing that it had come out better, but Goldie knows. Understands. 'Do you think he came out of the womb wearing that smug face?'

'I'm pretty sure our ancestors were living much like this. The Bens all lording it, with us merely surviving. But he hasn't really won anything, has he?'

It's true. Wolfie wouldn't swap places with Ben for all the money in the world.

Which doesn't mean he's happy being broke.

Apart from the bathroom, awaiting tiling, and new cupboard doors for the bedroom wardrobes, the homely part of Wolfie's renovation is complete. The whole place decorated in such natural neutrals, it feels like a whole fresh start – one, if he's truthful, he never fully could imagine.

Until Goldie.

'Mum used to run a video shop,' he says, watching her interest, so keen to know the smallest things about him. 'We rented upstairs, and I slept in the front room on the sofa bed. No true privacy, but honestly, I think that was the best time of my life. I'd help after school – till I stopped bothering with school. Just films and music all day long. Not a single worry, and I didn't even know it.' The bliss era. A period Wolfie thinks he might like to recreate should he keep this shop.

Is it really such a bad thing, though, to try pot-matching a period of happiness?

'A video shop might be a bit niche, but I thought it might work you know, if it was a bit trash-luxe, a bit retro – deeply cool, of course. And it'd only be a side hustle ...'

Goldie looks doubtful. 'I don't know anyone besides Valeria who has a VHS player. What with streaming and shit, it could be an expensive mistake. Unless you went down the music route. Vinyl never dies.'

'Now there's an idea. You could help; lend your expertise.' For a moment, Wolfie imagines his sudden family most clearly; their forever home above their own shop. A true possibility of happiness. Because despite his better nature, that's tried tirelessly to protect his heart, Wolfie's certain that this unexpected chaos is how life works. Happy accidents, and tragedies. The unpredictability of living.

'Look at you, so together. All these ideas and self-sufficiency – a business you invented. You've got family, God, a mum who bloody adores you. You know yourself, Wolfie.' Goldie exhales. 'And it still feels like you're saving me.'

She stays put, looking out of the window at the never-ending sea. 'Weird innit, I feel so bloody vulnerable suddenly, but it's also made me realize how ... how I've never felt entirely safe. Or at peace. Like truly.' Goldie puts her hand on her chest. 'In here. And I know you are good and that this is different, but I feel ... I'll feel,' she corrects, 'like I've failed myself, if I can't exist on my own.'

'I've not been exactly thriving in life myself.' But it's so hard, too hard, to know the words to start explaining. In one movement, Wolfie pulls his hoodie and tee over his head. 'G,' he says softly. 'Remember when I said this was for my mum?' He points out the tattoo of the giant tree between his shoulder blades.

'Yeah, which must've hurt for years,' Goldie says through bared teeth, having no tattoos, and no piercings other than her ears, and only once.

'There's also this pair. Who are ... deeply, deeply significant.' He puts a hand over the two tiny birds inked on his heart. 'This one's for Alex, who was my wife. And the slightly littler one,' Wolfie pauses, struggles, 'is for Pip. My son.'

The best human Wolfie ever knew. Almost three when he died, along with Alex, in an accident in 2017, and that was all Wolfie had to hold on to – how they'd gone together. That neither of them had been left with the immeasurable hurt, like his, alone in their house which felt torturous and silent without them.

'Every time there was a noise, I half expected them to come in. It was like being punched in the guts over and over again,' Wolfie explains. 'So yeah, 'cos I had nothing else, I threw myself into work, where things quickly – and I guess looking back now, luckily – became successful. I sold the house so I could buy and just work on this, floating between living at Mum's and my sister Carmen's, when she's not got her own shit going on.' It occurs to Wolfie how this is the most he's given of himself to Goldie, other than his DNA. 'So mostly I'm just here, where I can sort of go back to pretending that I'm twenty again. Not because I want to be youthful and beautiful, but because nothing then is linked to all the hurt that came. When they died and I didn't.' He stops as Goldie holds him, comforting without a single word.

'I know it's a lie,' Wolfie says into her hair, into the warmth of her. 'But it helped. And then I met you all over again, and it made me feel a bit sick. Much as I trust this ... all I'm feeling.' He stops, won't let her play herself short. 'Don't roll them eyes at me, beautiful girl. You made me remember a time when I was happy. Made me think I could be happy again. Which is right here. Now. With you.' He smiles, wipes her tears, sniffing his own away, too. 'So believe me when I tell you I ain't fucking about, G. None of this I'm taking lightly. 'Cos I really do think that we get to save each other.'

A little later, as he locks the door behind them, Wolfie's phone begins to ring.

'Answer it,' Goldie says. 'I'll get us some chips. Meet me over on that bench when you're done.'

'Don't hang up. Please,' Benedict says, so breathless he sounds as if he's in gale force winds. 'We must talk. Man to man.'

'Where's my money?'

'Where's all our money?' Benedict says, as though his world's coming to an end, though he's not fooling anyone, would say anything to get out of a sticky spot. The fact he's also almost apologizing, too, smells more suspect than a meat truck in channel-crossing traffic. 'I've dropped all the hold-up, and as of now Starling-Meyer is back in your full control. Your business is yours again, no strings attached.' Sycophantic and toady, he adds, 'The best man won.'

'Are you unwell?' Not waiting for an answer, Wolfie hangs up. Checks his email, and indeed there are two new messages from his solicitor, regarding the falling through of the sale of Starling-Meyer. Wolfie's almost disappointed. Feeling like a deadweight's returned to him. Hates how he thought to use that word.

Wolfie had gone along to Benedict's fundraiser doubtful of selling. It had all felt a bit like when his childhood dog had pups; how, when it came to parting with the litter, Mum caught a vibe with a potential buyer and said that the last puppy had sold, and Wolfie ended up keeping him. Marlon. Best friends forever.

For the very same reason, Wolfie shouldn't have done business with an arsehole; he'd clocked Ben's shadiness and still chose to ignore it. Because he understood when Goldie said about needing to be free of the past.

'Defo an area on the up and coming,' Goldie says when Wolfie joins her on the bench. 'Where's the arcades, the dead rat by the bins?' She grins, offering chips drenched in so much vinegar they're turning to mush. 'I like it here.'

Wolfie thinks that if happy ever afters were to fall from the sky, they'd be this.

'But I've got to go back. I've got to go to court.' Goldie's happiness vanishes, as back comes the hunted, wary expression. Wolfie swears when she is past this, she'll never, ever look that way again. 'And I keep thinking of Valeria. Her and Jamie; they had rounds and rounds of infertility treatment. Took a loan against the house to pay for IVF at one point,' Goldie says. 'I know I've told her, but I keep having visions, that she's hurt—'

'Er, rewind a bit. Just remind me again how hurt she sounded in that kitchen with Rufus, please?' With a smile, he raises his brows. 'Exactly. Now stop your worrying. And just be my queen.' On this stretch of British beachfront, spitting rain on the cusp of thunder, the frenzy in the sky suits his rush of feeling. 'From the moment we met again ...' Wolfie strokes her face. 'I just adored you, Goldie. I love you.'

'I'm scared.' It's as if she's admitting a secret, which hurts his heart. 'And I know you are, too.' She closes her eyes. 'But hiding from happiness will only keep me scared. And sad. Hey.' Goldie nudges him into opening his own eyes, squeezed shut as if in anticipation of the worst. 'I've never been more myself with anyone.'

Which is true. Right from the off they have both been completely themselves.

And so blessed to have met each other twice.

Cupping his face, her fingers stinking of vinegar, Goldie gazes at him. 'And I love you, too, Wolfgang Meyer. So much.'

Fifty

GOLDIE

This Time I Know It's For Real

'You think what you did for that stepson of yours wasn't mum shit? When did his father think to feed him on your weekends? Or check he'd rung his own mum? You're a good girl, G. And you'll do it all with your eyes shut.'

Mums don't normally like Goldie was what she told Wolfie when he said they were coming here. Yet his reply of 'remember, she made me' had settled her. Trisha, just like her son, is instinctively decent. Wanting to nurture and look after Goldie, which leaves her uncomfortable, so unfamiliar with motherliness, having fought against all forms of domesticity. Down to learning to cook.

Yet here she is, peeling potatoes for Sunday lunch, feeling like part of the family.

Which frightens her more than anything else.

How Goldie wants to offer Wolfie her heart, that vulnerable thing, and trust him to take care of it. How secure she feels in his presence. His directness. Kindness. So uncomplicated. But love's become a thing to be afraid of.

'But if your heart says no, and means it,' Trisha says, 'well then, it's totally your choice, love. I'd even come to the clinic if you like. There will be no judgements here. You'll know what's right for you, anyway.' Goldie's as appreciative of Trisha's plain speaking as she is of her hospitality. Knows she can trust her.

And though trust, as it always does, comes with the same flip feeling, as if she should run, Goldie's tired. And as much as Goldie doesn't think she could take another love disappointment, she doesn't think she could stand another moment as she had been. Living lonely. 'I worry I'm not brave enough, young enough, to do this.'

'Young's in here.' Trisha points to her head. 'That's the secret. You keep learning, growing, keep that tender heart open. Otherwise, it's that turn in the road, the fast track to the wooden box. Fuck that for a laugh, I can tell you.'

'How do I know, though? If I'll be any good at it?' Goldie asks. 'Being a mum.'

She thinks of the faded portrait on their old upstairs landing of her, Valeria and Mum, taken one Christmas in Woolworths, sometime deep in the 1980s. The colour bleached from years on the window ledge into bare silhouette and then a pale nothing, like their connection, over time. Mother's hold. Less.

And less.

So if Goldie's scared to love Wolfie, then she's truly fucking petrified to love these miniature uninvited prawn people. Because what if she doesn't? What if she can't? What if she wants to escape, head somewhere up north, never to be seen again?

'You'll just know. It's what mums do.'

What mums do.

But what if they don't?

Plus, relying on not only another man but also his mother is no way to start parenthood. Yet the idea of raising these babies at Saunders Road leaves Goldie feeling constricted, the thought working its way in, the entirely plausible fear that she'll be absorbed back into everything she tried to escape. Staying on, the old bird down Saunders Road, reluctantly raising the next gen, a fresh pair of Burdens who'll know all over again how Mummy's heart is just not in it.

'This isn't the first time. That I've been pregnant,' Goldie admits, for the first time ever. 'I'd presumed Wolfie would distance, which was what happened before. I was sixteen. He was forty-something. Knocking about with my mum, too, already had kids. I know,' Goldie says, because she does. 'Some with his wife, and others he didn't see.'

'Girl, I know this story,' Trisha says with a shake of her head.

'Yeah? It's a common one. Though mine's got a different sort of ending. When I went to the doctor to talk about an abortion, right in the waiting room, I started bleeding. And when I took another test, it was only a faint positive, nowhere near as clear as before. The doctor said to go home, see what happened. And you know what, by the next appointment, the test was negative.' Facing the ceiling, Goldie says it plainly, with just the same relief as then. 'And I felt I'd been massively let off the hook.'

Goldie's wondered, often, if Grant stayed with his wife,

whether they had any more kids. Likely, by now, grandkids, too.

And if he truly ever loved Goldie, even though she kept on loving him. Even after their almost baby.

Tremors of rage come, because she's always known the truth. That she was a fool, and men are unhealthy.

And Wolfie?

Well. There are always exceptions.

Goldie also knows, though, that no matter how people may profess to love her, their feelings are only ever temporary. The same as she knows like a life lesson how she's always been powerless too. Her pride the sole thing that's kept her shoulders back and chin up and her image going all this time. Front. So never will they see the truth of her. How very, very lost she is at her centre. How emotionally homeless she's been. All her life.

'Well, I think you can safely call that story your lucky escape. Tied to him, and there'd have been trouble forever.' Shoving the potatoes aside, they move on to peeling the carrots. 'I dated enough wrong-uns to see the succession of fucking idiots were forming a pattern. So I thought bollocks, you know what I mean? Me, him and Car were totally better off here on our tod.' Trisha glances to the ceiling, acknowledging the noise coming from Wolfie upstairs. 'Though what he's doing up there now I don't know. Which reminds me; what did you make of his project?'

'I thought it was incredible.' Goldie tells Trish the way the door opened on the diagonal off the street, put her in mind of the corner shop when she was a kid, how it gave her the edge when she decided which way to bolt after pinching magazines, or her and Valeria's dinner.

Behaviour she won't be able to recreate as a geriatric mother.

One thing Goldie's certain of is how she doesn't want her babies to start their lives in the same cycle as then. An entirely fresh start is beyond overdue.

'Weird shit happens every day,' Trisha says, and it sounds profound. 'Good shit, bad shit. And terrible shit.' She sighs, so sadly. 'He's told you about Alex and little Pip?'

'A bit. How very terrible. I'm so sorry.' Goldie thinks of yesterday. How they died is the question Goldie wanted to ask, yet it had felt too intrusive. Too impolite.

'Went beyond my capabilities of how to put him back together.' Trisha stops peeling, putting her knife down. 'He's been here on and off for the past seven years, but he's not really been himself. Caught up in the hurt, and guilt.'

'Guilt?'

'Guilt he'd not been with them. They were only going to Sainsbury's. Drunk driver. You know how it goes. Just a sad fucking tragedy.' Trisha takes a deep breath, keeping her grief at a distance. 'But you. I see it; like the sun's shining through all the cracks of his hurt. And I don't think I'll ever have to worry about him again.' Trisha stands, as if she's remembered something. 'Which reminds me.'

From a dusty plastic storage container, not dissimilar to Valeria's, Trisha pulls out a very dated album. From its enormous cushioned cover, strips of negatives escape which have Trisha's excellent reflexes catching them before they hit the floor. 'Never could bear the thought of all Wolfie's proofs and negatives being set fire to if I didn't buy his school pictures.'

Setting the album on the table, she opens it next to Goldie. 'There he is. Year 8. Autumn term, 1992.' Trisha points to her own handwriting as Goldie studies the picture; a class photograph she's never seen before, of thirty or so classmates, every one of them caught in that godawful gawkiness of being about twelve or thirteen, when you're so flipping far from being an adult, yet have lost all shape of the kid you'd been only seconds before.

'My mum never kept anything like this,' Goldie says, resentful and sad and longing all at once. Loves her, fucking hates her, but mostly would just like to forget how she ever briefly had a mother. Miri Burden's never coming back.

And hand on heart, Goldie wouldn't want her to.

She'd held her at knifepoint. Valeria, witnessing the lot.

The reckoning, when Mum learnt about Goldie and Grant, was traumatic as much as it was educational. Because for Valeria and Goldie, everything they'd ever questioned about their mother, whether she truly wanted them, whether she loved them, became clear. Uncertainty had been a cruel tormentor, and damaging as it was to know for certain, it became peculiar closure for them both. Mum with that vicious little veg knife, eyeing her first-born girl as if she were a rival, competition and nothing else, can never be forgotten.

'Wait till it happens to you.' Goldie can hear her mother saying it now.

Yet Goldie's still waiting. Never will make peace with how

any mother on earth could turn on her own child like that, like Miri did to Goldie, while the grown man got to slip off and perfectly vanish back to his amazing life.

'Well, it's a good job I did,' Trisha says, pointing out Goldie on the end of the front row, because she was one of the shorter kids. That awful bottle green uniform. And obviously her; the frizzy blondeness in a long scruffy plait over one shoulder. Her round face made from one big happy smile. A hand on her hip. Classic. 'Weren't you cute?'

In the second row back, just behind her, is Wolfie. The longest boy on earth; his dark eyes full of fun, looking positively up to no good, his hair not quite as dark then, but still with a curl to it. Wishing she had the fundraiser picture to match them up, compare then and now, she hears Wolfie shout from the stairs.

'Found it!' On the table, between the photo album and their saucepan of peeled spuds, he places a CD with a scuffed cover, the entirety of which is an extreme close-up of Goldie's arse in sequinned animal print shorts. 'Free Me, Be Me' Goldilocs. Our Price £1.99.

'Reduced?' But she's wildly proud, regardless.

The sun makes a fleeting appearance, and dazzles in from outside, showing off through Trisha's sparkling windows, enhancing all Wolfie's ruddy loveliness, the skin that'd almost certainly catch a good deep tan and bring out the freckles if they were sat out in it, just like Goldie. Obvious even more so since meeting Trisha, dual heritage too, that he's a mix of many ethnicities. Which does, like it always does, being made the same way herself, bring another connection, something else they share.

Wolfie gives her the loveliest kiss. 'Fancy a walk?'

Christ, Goldie fancies his socks off. Adores his mouth, his moustache, his lankiness, his effortless elegance, right down to the thrilling hint of suggestion as he squats in those lush joggers – all the things that can't be bought because they are priceless, precious when they come together in a man like him.

In a man who loves her, too.

It's a bit too blowy along the seafront, the biting wind leaving Goldie's ears red and achy, so Wolfie suggests warming up in a café, choosing the first one they come to, which on first impression doesn't feel like somewhere you'd want to eat eggs in. Goldie follows Wolfie to the table by a window as the waft of old cooking fat knocks her socks off.

'No pain?' Wolfie checks. 'Good.'

Watching him work his way through his secret all-day breakfast – which he's promised won't ruin his roast – Goldie's as mesmerized as she is revolted as she sips a bottle of Sprite. And though it's all she can manage, as he uses the toast to mop up his beans, finds herself longing to be that mouthful. Catching her watching him, Wolfie winks, all cheeky and lopsided, and has her wanting to crawl onto his lap.

Oh God, she has it bad, in a way that's caught her off-guard, rather like her uterus, truly believing she'd become immune to feelings like this.

Goldie touches her stomach through her sweatshirt, though there's nothing to feel other than her usual rounded belly. By magic this has happened, and though she would never have chosen this, she is so very glad to be living it.

On his empty plate, Wolfie sets his knife and fork together. 'That was proper smashing. Thank you,' he says to the server, who seems rather taken with him, too.

'More tea?' she offers, 'Can I do you a bit more toast?'

'No ta, just the bill please.' How Wolfie talks to people remains refreshing. Like now, his back and forth with the server, a fluffy-haired lady of indeterminate middle-age, absolutely someone Ben would consider beneath his effort.

'I don't understand why he's just rolled over.' Goldie thinks aloud, though Wolfie knows what she's talking about. 'It gives me the creeps a bit.'

'I should've listened to you. Once I'd made up my mind about wanting out, I just wanted it sold. I still do.'

'But there's no panic now,' Goldie assures him.

Giving Wolfie the £16k from under the mattress to keep his project going is the only way Goldie can balance the nagging worry of him as her knight in shining armour. Both Valeria and Trisha said it was nonsense; a strong, independent woman doesn't have to mean a lonely woman. But to Goldie it had all still felt a bit man to the fucking rescue – and hasn't there been enough of that?

Keeping the dream alive of the family home above a family business means (please God) that Goldie's saving all four of them. The record shop plans are growing, too.

There's also the budding rumour that Mr Maybe is setting up an independent label. And though Goldie's a little nervous to think what that might mean for her, she's open to suggestion. A career again. Out in the open. Not singing – will she ever – but producing. Hands-on creative. All those years of watching, hanging about in the studio; Goldie knows she could do Grant's job with her eyes shut.

Paying for them, Goldie leaves the server a five pound tip, securing it beneath the edge of Wolfie's teacup, and as she puts her mac on, the lady tidying their table smiles when she clocks it.

'I must ask, love; were you in that band Five Star?'

A compliment is a compliment. And though they're a bit before Goldie's time, she'd still consider them influential – not only to her music, but to her spirit. 'Chance would be a fine thing. I'm Goldilocs.'

'"Free Me, Be Me",' the woman says with a wistful twinkle, as if she might've burned up the dancefloor to it once upon a time. 'Thought you looked familiar.'

Later, after roast beef and second portions, Wolfie falls asleep in front of the telly. With his head on Goldie's lap, he looks smooth and at peace, like a man with no worries at all.

'It's you who's done that,' Trisha says as she gets off to the fridge to top up her wine, making Goldie's throat swell.

Kissing her fingers, Goldie rests them gently against Wolfie's chest, over the birds beneath his tee. Catches herself making a silent prayer; a promise, to Alex, and Pip. Goldie will look after him. Will treasure his precious heart, so reassuring and strong against her touch, as she hopes – God, she hopes with everything she's got – that it never stops beating before hers.

★

Fifty-One

JULIA

The Boy Is Mine

It's not like Jamie's parents will have bouncers on the door of their party, but Julia's bought a gift to blend in with, just in case. They've hired out a section of their favourite restaurant, the Blue Strawberry, a high-end yet cosy eatery in a tiny village near Chelmsford. There's a train station a ten-minute walk away, but it was better to drive. Julia won't be drinking, and so has parked, early and inconspicuously, around the back of the building.

She'd tried visiting the house, but Jamie hadn't answered, same as she tried just after the dog popped its clogs – which does sound terribly desperate, but when they're face to face, when she tells Jamie their news, everything will fall into place again, just like when they met.

He can't pretend not to have known what Julia was implying when she'd suggested he leave his very sensible Durex off, to 'see what happened'.

Seven to eight weeks. Perilously early days, but absolutely worth the party crash. Julia takes her bag from the passenger seat to stare once more at the positive test. Considering how her own mother spent half her life in bed, it can't be that hard. A baby to cement them is the perfect solution – the neatest fix. Jamie gets his dream come true and she'll become one of those demanding ice cream and gherkins at three in the morning types of mums-to-be ... before perhaps a spell of high stress will have her confessing to him how she's now edging – because interest is a total bastard – £116,000 in debt.

She'll move in. Problems solved. Nothing fundamental will change, and babies are only small things at first – plus, grandparents love all that looking after. And you know what else?

It might be nice.

She looks at the app on her phone; this week the embryo is the size of a grain of rice.

A notification follows. Julia swipes to Instagram, then across the rest of her socials, collecting compliments, mostly still in response to the 'people change' video she posted, that night she pushed Mother too far.

They want her gone. Julia has three months to find somewhere else. The atmosphere she creates upsetting mother's senses. She'd even admitted that it had been a joke, about Mr. Ocado. Knows Mum's as detached from her private parts as a plastic doll with none at all.

Dad on the other hand.

Putting away the test, Julia checks to see if any new guests have arrived, before closing her eyes. Cross that instead of playing the moment when Jamie's face breaks into pure joy, it's her game-playing, sex addict father she's thinking about. Which brings her back to thinking about Goldie. Fat black bitch.

Exactly Dad's type.

Julia already had her suspicions – yonks ago, when Dad insisted on giving Goldie a lift home after netball; Julia resenting her riding up front with him, which was naturally her seat. A twenty-minute drive to the shit end of town, with her dad almost purple, breathing noisily, as in the rear-view mirror Julia watched his concentration stray from the road to Goldie's body as if his eyeballs were rolling downhill, before they'd realign, with a quick glance at Julia, who would avert her own gaze to focus out of the window, pretending she hadn't noticed.

Until the leg grab. Impossible to pretend any longer. Julia had been transfixed by what was happening as he'd leant across Goldie, one hand around her enormous thigh, as his other found the door handle. 'Rude little girl,' he'd said quietly, close enough to kiss her, when Goldie had started to fidget. 'Just letting you out.' Swinging the door open, he had then taken his sweet lecherous time retracting back into his own seat.

As he'd watched Goldie flee towards her front door, with that frizzy plait bouncing along with the rest of her, Julia had instead stared at the back of his headrest, thinking of the stacks of pornography in the hidden drawer of his desk at home, and under the divan in the spare bedroom; close-up pictures of the spread fannies of big black women, and a collection of tiny slides Julia never quite had the front to put into his projector. In time, the internet kept his habits tidier, spending longer and longer paying for the company of his fat friends of colour than with her. Dad, with a next-level fascination Julia could never compete with. And how in one car journey, Julia knew she'd not only lost his attention, but her respect, too, when once they'd been each other's worlds.

Imagine, losing to a girl like Goldie?

Worse, to Vee.

At the sound of tyres on the gravel, Julia opens her eyes to watch a car pull up, a good distance from the restaurant; another person clearly wanting a bit of camouflage from the guests, beginning to arrive in number now.

All the hair gives it away. What the fuck is she doing here? Vee sweeps her curls over her shoulder as she climbs from the car, along with a man Julia narrows her eyes to get a better look at.

From the way he helps her into her mac, it's obvious they're fucking. Julia can't put a number on his age from this distance, other than he's clearly younger than Vee.

What is it with these women? Always having everyone so entranced.

Just like Dad that day. Julia detests the pervading sense of unravelling, how she's gone from winning in the dynamic, poking at Vee's vulnerabilities, like a worm on the end of a garden fork. But without her interest the game just doesn't work.

Older now, though no less irritating, really. And rather like Mother, in that she's so very easy to toy with. Julia could've dined out for decades on those first delicious moments when Vee saw her again. The silliness of her terror; all Bambi-eyed and just as rewarding, giving Julia far more power than she has.

Had.

Their conversation seems serious, before her man claps his hands as if to lighten things, getting a gift bag from the boot, playing the game of pretending to pass it to Vee only to pull it out of her reach, and just as she gives up, he lets her have it. Pulling her close, he kisses her, saying something into her ear that makes her smile, turning Vee soft and tender before he gets back into the car and drives away. Wild, how into her he seems to be.

But she couldn't get pregnant, Julia self-comforts, stroking her stomach.

Fifty-Two

Vee

Dy-Na-Mi-Tee

It's 6.45 p.m. Vee will stay at the anniversary party for an hour, then hotfoot it to the station for the 7.56 p.m. train, so she'll hopefully catch the last dregs of Write Pub. To meet with Judith and discuss her latest pages before returning to Saunders Road to continue her edits, the house slowly beginning to feel lived in, but not home. It is a temporary stop. A helping hand. Because Vee's got plans.

Pushing her way through the circular doors and into the conservatory bar, Jamie's the first person Vee sees. Picking two Bellinis off a tray, he offers her a glass.

'Cheers,' Vee says, keeping the I-can't-stay-for-long part in her head.

'Thanks for coming.'

'Well, it's Billie and Edward.' Vee lifts a gift bag. 'Celebratory champers – where shall I put it?'

The delight on Billie's face, as it registers that it's Vee with her son, is most telling. And though there is something triumphant about it, the feeling leaves Vee empty. She has evolved. Which is better than any petty one-upmanship.

Pressing her hands to Vee's face, Billie kisses her. 'Hello, darling, how we miss you.' She hugs Vee, swaying her from side to side, which feels rather nourishing.

'Mum,' Jamie says, a bit embarrassed.

'It's lovely to see you, too.' Vee gives Billie her gift bag. 'Happy anniversary.'

'Naughty!' Billie's cheeks colour at the sight of the bottle of Bollinger. 'Thank you, dear,' she says, just as a silver tray of canapés is encouraged into their eyeline. 'Mini spring roll?'

'No, thank you.' Vee declines politely, then gets it out quick. 'I can't stay for long.'

Billie's disappointment hits Vee in a weak spot, which she knows is guilt, and she would be cross at Jamie for pushing her into a corner over coming tonight if it wasn't for his face. Set resolvedly; rather as if he knows this is it.

'You know, I'll never understand why you two couldn't—' begins Billie, her eyelids fluttering in confusion, because she'll never fully fathom their separation.

'Mum, didn't we talk about this? Vee and I, well ...' Jamie makes sure to hold Vee's eye. 'We're over.'

'We still like each other, though,' Vee says, more to Jamie than anyone else.

'And I don't think many divorcees can say that – or dee-vorce-ay, which is how I'll be pronouncing it when I'm off on my travels. It adds a little something, don't you think?' Lately, there's been a sliver of the old Jamie emerging, the easy, laid-back confidence that had so appealed to Vee back then. That's just as good to see back now.

He'll be all right.

'It does.' Vee's strange guilt grows a smidge lighter. 'So, where are you off to?'

Jamie seems happy that she's asked, takes a deep breath. 'Sydney. Mid-life spontaneity after dropping off in front of that show *Wanted Down Under*. So I put my name forward at work on the off-chance, and they bit. Three months' time, and I'll be off. Conveyancers are in demand. Which feels pretty great.'

'Good,' Vee says, rather emotional. 'That's really good.'

'Well. Things move on.'

'They do.' Without the worry of any further blurred lines, it feels as if they've crossed a significant one. Both know it.

Vee holds Jamie close, wanting to feel his heart on hers so he knows she means it when she says, 'Be my friend, always. Do you promise?'

'Ah, shit Vee.' He smiles down at her. 'Of course—'

'Well, this is nice. Memory lane or big reunion? Unkind to steal your parents' thunder, though,' Julia says, with such easy finesse it's as if she's played this part before. Flawless in her delivery as Vee wonders, as she's always wondered, what she gets from such drama. Wonders if Julia herself knows.

It's not just Vee who's troubled by Julia's presence which manages to freeze the room like the Snow Queen from Narnia's rocked up. Billie stiffens with awkwardness as Julia kisses her on both cheeks.

'Why are you here?' Jamie's arm around Vee again has her

feeling victorious. A deviant pleasure against her better self. Gratifying – but Vee remembers being on the reverse end all those years ago, making any enjoyment from the moment vanish as if Vee's blown out a candle. They are not the same. Not built from the same heartless motivations. Because Julia is hard, even now as she begins to cry, as frozen on the inside as poor Billie is on the out, visibly changed just from standing next to her.

A reminder that it is not only Vee who feels it.

'To think I came in the hope of building bridges, Jamie.' Julia sniffs, tears misting her gorgeous blue eyes as her shoulders give, feigning delicacy in a way which Vee would never in a million years be able to pull off. 'The emotional strain of this.' She turns up her palms, as if in offering.

The curious nature of Vee would love to unravel Julia, peel her right down to the truth, yet something in her gut says it would be the worst mistake in the world. To bear witness to all what makes Julia Julia. All the hateful little cogs and absence of heart, that even as a teenager made her terrifying.

'I don't want to build bridges,' Jamie says, stern and final. 'This isn't normal . . .'

'Why are you being like this? Everything was wonderful until she got in your head. With her lies.' Julia twists with such sophistication it's as if she's been the one terrorized for a lifetime. 'You witnessed her sister attack me. They're . . . like animals. Jealous of our happiness. I'm a good person. I am!' Julia stamps a foot, breaking the spell she's cast on the room as everybody returns to their own business.

'We need to talk.' Jamie puts his hands in his pockets, as

avoiding Julia, Vee excuses herself, heading for the loos. 'Let's have a drink outside.'

'I don't want a drink!' And before you can think Veruca Salt, Jamie's father bellows out an enormous:

'Enough of this!'

Vee doesn't catch the end of what he says, when the toilet door swings shut behind her.

Finds herself shaking.

Vee washes her hands, takes her time drying and moisturizing them. And then, absolutely not ready to rejoin the party, she video calls Goldie.

'How's Wellsend treating you?' she asks, relieved Goldie's smiling, how much better just a few days' rest and privacy has her looking.

'Wolfie's looking after me.'

'I bet he is. So, what's his mum like? And how are them bubs?'

The more Goldie talks, the more Vee settles, trying not to think of what's going on outside. 'I've been thinking, Valeria. About your documentary – all those notes I lost my shit over.'

Vee's heart kicks up again, ferocious in her chest, at Goldie's mention of the latest development from Stanley Sisters at Law. Entertainment law, to be specific, though that hadn't deterred Vee from calling up Kiley Stanley a few days back to pick her brains about her and Jamie's final order that's now imminent. Which was when Kiley mentioned the interest from *Dispatches*, keen to cover the downfall of Vine Recordings.

'And as a documentarian,' Kiley had said, 'I just imagined

that you'd naturally be interested.' Vee's genius gut had been spot fucking on. Sadly, that also means everyone will be wanting in – same as *Dispatches*. And though she'd talked Kiley enthusiastically through her own independent project, it came as a surprise when she suggested broaching the idea again with Goldie.

'Might sound different coming from someone else. Eldests communicate on another level, I can tell you. Leave it to me,' Kiley had said. And so Vee had. Obviously, its release would need to be sensitively timed and after the inquiry, but Vee wouldn't have the time just now anyway; her book remains top priority, the thought dawning on her how so much of her subject matter exists on the other side of the toilet door. Currently breaking up with Jamie. Which he should've done, and properly, by now.

Straight after Julia's throwaway comment, actually; how Onion was 'just a dog' when he'd found her dead.

But none of it is any longer her problem.

'I just keep thinking; if a documentary's coming anyway, and some stranger makes it, and it all feels wrong ... At least if it's you—' Goldie sighs. 'If you'd still want to do it, then I trust you to tell my truth. All our truth.'

G has her own plans. Wants in. To help find the lost voices of Vine Recordings.

And with that, their documentary has a title.

First-hand accounts of staff and talent who worked for Vine between 1982 and 2001. Lifting the mask of surface success to expose the toxic power structure responsible for the mistreatments and abuses of so many.

'This time, I'll go about things differently, I promise. You tell me what's right, and I'll just be the conduit, only with better technical skills.' Valeria smiles. 'And if you don't like anything—'

'I do want something, though.' Goldie swallows. 'I want my lyrics to feature. It's time to reclaim everything that's rightfully mine. My words, my songs, hopefully some fucking royalties at some point. My own story.' Goldie's return is a brilliant thing to see.

'How's Rufus?' she asks, with a little less strangeness than before. 'I've not heard from him, do worry—'

Vee's surprised. 'Ru's fine. Was away for most of last week, on a break with his mum. But ... they've found Tony's boat, G. All Ben's stuff was on there, so he'd definitely been hiding, but no sign of him. It's like he vanished into thin air.' Like a Netflix true crime docudrama; Vee's empathy too easily detached in her hunger to know a story. 'Ru's okay. Verging on indifferent, actually. And it's good he's got his book to focus on. You are still coming for that?' she checks, which she supposes is wholesome confirmation that's she's not quite as detached from her feelings as she thinks.

Is Ru a love relationship? It seems an odd notion to dive from marriage straight into another committed partnership. But Vee reminds herself how it was not love that she decided against. She simply didn't want those things with Jamie. Vee won't ever compromise her own company for just anybody, but a fit-as-fuck boyfriend is an exceptionally pleasant addition to her new happy independent life – like a flake in a decent Mr Whippy; delicious, with or without it.

'I am, but I'll speak to him before then.' Goldie smiles. 'And shall we video call again? This is the nicest part of modern tech. I like it, how we're closer. I want to get better at keeping it that way.'

'So do I. Very much.' Hearing footsteps, Vee glances towards the door. 'Look, I've got to go. Love to them bubs.'

She slips into a cubicle, locking herself in just as the main door bursts open. Through a crack, Vee watches Julia stalk up and down in front of the row of sinks. She stops in front of the last one, opening and closing her handbag as if checking something's there, with a restless unpredictability about her that makes Vee wary to unlock the door.

Vee exhales, worries she's made a noise, but she's been holding her breath ever since Julia walked in. Unsure what to do, she looks at her phone, trembling as it lights up, her index finger hovering over the camera button.

Flushing, Vee opens the door, leaving it wide as she heads for the sink directly in front of it, where, keeping her shoulders back, she begins slowly washing her hands.

'Why,' Julia sniffs, wiping her nose, 'it's the turd you just can't flush.' In one gross flashback, Vee sees all her moments; in the loos, lunchtimes, break times, her rounds of UTIs due to holding her bladder, to avoid risking this.

Nowhere to hide. No one to help. As Julia dead-eyes Vee in the mirror behind her.

But what's she going to do here; bite her again?

Vee keeps her shoulders back.

'Does it not bother you,' Julia asks, 'how I've practically taken your life?' In the mirror's reflection, she makes sure to meet Vee's eye. 'Jamie filled me in very early, about your infertility battle.'

'Yep, I'm sure he did. Most mornings I was up, polishing my sword and planning my strategy.' Vee's surprised by her own flip ease. Which surely must come from how Julia seems so much less threatening, now she's almost transparent.

It's her inner protection, too, that Vee's been nurturing, forgiving; peace that's come from feeling she's at last on a road made just for her, which has built her this fortress. A new self-respect made from her own strong bricks and fine vision, that's come from creating her very own world. A place where Julia and all those like her simply don't feature.

'Whatever you have is nothing I want.' Fluffing her hair, Vee glances at Julia, still on her shoulder. 'You're just a mean, jealous, beautiful girl who thinks everything should be hers. But Jamie doesn't want to be.' Readying herself, Vee turns to face her. 'And I'm not scared of you.'

Julia sneers, with the little half smile which smacks of the teen she'd been. 'You're not fooling anyone.'

By rights, this last hurdle drama, like the final boss in a computer game, like the crux of a play where the hero must confront their tormentor, is the part of the story where Vee should finally, at long last, feel capable of succeeding.

In the old days, Vee would've chosen to run by now. Anticipating this same fear that she now remembers, but also conflictingly how Julia was often the only person who ever noticed her. The hunt which at least proved Vee was real, visible and existing.

As Julia keeps her pinned, Vee's hair grazes the mirror,

moving her just a fraction back into direct line with the toilet cubicle, her phone set up just above the cistern, recording the lot.

Because Vee these days is a Teflon goddess, and Julia's power games are over.

'Still the same.' Seething her S's through her tiny vampire teeth, Julia examines Vee as though she's riddled with defects. 'Just as pointless. Should've been drowned at birth, along with your fat bitch of a sister.'

Since the BBC Breakfast interview, Vee's watched Goldie's followers grow before her eyes, the response to her new Instagram supportive – mostly old fans having their curiosity quenched; which is refreshing against the mean streak of negativity which pervades the other platforms. Because Vee's read the poison beneath articles about Goldie; comments that've kept Vee grateful she's no interest in social media.

Many comments are generalized trolling; ageist, sizeist, insulting Goldie's looks, while others are more frightening, full of sexualized threat, mysogynoir and hate speech:

> Take your fat black arse and shit music back to the nineties and drown yourself.

> Once a slag always a slag.

And they're the mild ones. No profile pictures. No proper names. There never, ever are. Just anonymous avatars, Templar Knights and flag shaggers.

Which is a bit unfair to the flag shaggers, most of whom

Vee bets would love nothing more than pressing pause on their bigotries in exchange for a moment with Goldie's incredible backside. What's most unsettling is how many of the truly dark comments about Goldie land with the same energy as the witches who already like to demonize a certain demographic. Posts from other women ...

They smell of racism. Feministic poison. And a big waft of jealousy, impossible to logicize, because this hatred comes from the women who've been raised and brainwashed to believe they come first, destined to forever be the most beautiful, desired and sought-after prizes. And it must be the worst kind of shock for all the grown Julias of the world to realize they're only the centre of their own tiny orbits. Taking to their keyboards and comments boxes, a disturbia of online haters, masking their meanness behind pseudo lifestyles and acres of bullshit.

But Vee also knows how to use social media. There's no way the cowering girl of long ago is making a comeback. With a twinge up her spine, Vee knows just what to do with this recording.

'I saw you outside, with your toyboy. So why are you here, what are you still in the way for?' Julia's energy seems to reignite as she finds her posture, and though she looks unhinged, Vee needs more.

'I was invited.' It is Vee's turn to lean in close as she whispers, 'Because everybody out there loves me.' Vee's words seize Julia, like she's possessed, and she can't stop herself from grabbing Vee's head in both her hands.

And smashing her into the mirror. 'Bitch. You fucking ugly

bitch.' Smash. 'Ugly then.' Smash. 'Ugly now. A total, utter waste of space.' Again. Vee feels the mirror crack against her shoulders. Terrified by the thought of perforation, her fear seems to energize Julia even more. 'You should've done us all a favour and killed yourself then!' Every one of Julia's fingers dents Vee's skull as she puts her whole weight into flinging Vee into the mirror before she lets go.

Catching her breath, standing just above Vee, now woozy, double-visioned and slumped at her feet, Julia looks in the broken glass to neaten her hair. Remembering her bag, checking its contents again, she makes to go before turning back.

'On my unborn baby, I wish you were dead,' she says, with a smile that's truly beautiful. The gratification from managing to squeeze out a few fresh drops of pain, which has so little to do with Vee's split skull.

As Vee, bleeding yet triumphant, is left hurting all over again.

In forty-eight hours, Vee's out of hospital. What she lost in blood she's made up for in hardcore evidence that Julia's a first-class bitch.

A bitch with a restraining order – who's also cancelled.

Vee's vengeance took an epic twist, one she couldn't even have thought to write. Hadn't even watched Julia's video post entitled 'people change' where she'd angelically cried through another whitewashed version of her bullying days. *What happens when an empath looks back on themselves, and isn't proud of what they see?* The response to which was incredible, and Vee still can't understand it. So many people keen to excuse their own shittiness.

It had seemed almost too perfect; replying to the video with Julia's own vicious bathroom antics that Vee successfully recorded, posting it from her hospital bed following thirty cranial stitches, across all Julia's social media platforms, tagging her workplace, and all the brands and businesses she's ever worked with. And like magic, it's as if Julia's vanished with the same alarming suddenness as she appeared.

The story goes that Julia had been dangling some news over Jamie. People will say anything to save themselves. But unless she chooses to share it, Julia's news will remain Julia's news. There's a flicker of a thought for the baby – if there even is a baby, because isn't it exactly the kind of trick Julia would pull, especially in last-ditch desperation?

And if there really is ... well it's simply not Vee's circus. Thank fuck.

Vee knows all this, because today their divorce papers came through, and they scattered Onion's ashes in the park, toasting her life with a bottle of Cava like they'd drunk back in the old days when it all first started; when bottles were £2.50 from Tesco and they'd smash them unreservedly, and without pretention. The fizz not quite a celebration, but a quiet acknowledgement. For Vee and Jamie to share a moment before the final knot's untied. The last remaining bond.

Property. A completion date confirmed. At last.

Done with the heart, it's down to bare bricks.

★

NOVEMBER 2025

Fifty-Three

GOLDIE

Free Your Mind

Outside court, behind her Gucci shades, Goldie spots Grant, and wraps her cape around her bump like a protective instinct, discomfort she'd not anticipated from the sight of him being accompanied by a young woman of about twenty. With occasional upbeat little smiles of encouragement at one another, they hold hands. Perhaps a new girlfriend.

'Suits you, G.' Bafflingly, Grant's eyes mist as he swallows, taking her in, pregnancy and all, because there's really no disguising it now. 'You look good.'

'Good?' The girl pulls a face. 'Isn't she part of this mess, Dad?'

Dad. Goldie works it out. Thinks Grant looks defeated already. More so when the Stanley Sisters flank her, their sudden grouping giving girl band energy, and having Goldie feeling like she's in En Vogue.

'It was never my intention to hurt you,' he says, which would be nice if it's true, but it doesn't change anything.

First kiss, first date, first love, first everything. Grant left no stone unturned of what he taught her.

What he took.

'I lost my mum because of you,' Goldie tells him, because Grant should carry it all.

Yet he shrugs. 'You never had a mum.'

But Goldie won't give him her upset. He is so 1996.

And she is tired as fuck.

In a bronze-coloured maxi dress, swapping her shades for thick gold-framed reading glasses, her bouffant hair blow-dried into a whole power move, Goldie's ready to take the stage.

The stand.

Eyes are on her as they've always been, Goldie eternally caught between it being the best thing and the very worst. Her unhideability. Not that she's come understated today. A court usher rushes forwards to assist her into the witness box and a seat, which she gracefully perches on, cradling her stomach, almost due, meaning she could've swerved all this drama. But Goldie's hiding no longer.

Glancing towards the gallery, Goldie spots her family in the front row. Trisha, Wolfie, Valeria – with her new Toni Braxton nineties-inspired haircut, a killer move after all her stitches, elfin cropped and foxy as hell; dear Rufus. And Therese. Who wanted to come. The world is full of surprises.

And strange what happens when one bad seed drops out of the picture.

'Do you swear ...?' The legalities begin, the hushed seriousness, Goldie's manicured hand on the Bible, which feels like she's on the telly. She ain't even nervous. Has played far bigger crowds. Only today is not playing.

This is Goldie. Very much being herself.

Eyes on Grant, so steady, Goldie swears she can see his eyelid a-twitching, even from their distance. 'I do.'

The longer Goldie's on the stand, the more secure she becomes in her subject. When the Stanley Sisters said during all their hours of coaching how this was Goldie's story, that no one could tell it better than Goldie herself, they were right.

And once their questions regarding her evening with The Canticles is over, where for the first time Goldie sees the X-ray of her broken arm, her medical records discovered in the thousands of seized documents, and the Chair thanks her for her co-operation, she could totally leave shit there.

'If you don't mind, I've prepared a personal account of my time at Vine Recordings.' They have settled on this. Instead of any ongoing court battle, Goldie's decision, with the full backing of the Stanley Sisters, is to end everything Vine-related at this inquiry. Money comes and money goes – but too much of it is ruinous.

And besides all that, Goldie is far too pregnant.

'You'll know of my connection to Grant Love from your investigations,' Goldie begins. 'You'll know the rags to riches media-friendly version, of how he'd been my manager, an A & R exec at Vine; how I badgered him to give me a chance, and he was so impressed he signed me on the spot.' *The finest thing to ever sign with Vine.* Goldie remembers the press release. The giddy disbelief that it was real.

'But the truth is that Grant discovered me when he was in a relationship with my mother. I was coming up for fifteen when he said I had star quality.' Goldie pauses to sip her water. 'It's only a recent thing for me, certainly since I became pregnant and started imagining the futures of these babies, my own girls, that I've considered how I'd react should a man like Grant enter their worlds, with ill intentions.

'Singing was all I did as a kid. I'd perform for my sister non-stop; we spent our lives glued to the *Chart Show* and MTV – reckon I'd been planning my future look in my head, too, dreaming of the day my dreams would come true. I'd never had a boyfriend, and despite what everyone seemed to think about me, I'd never even been kissed before, either. Before Grant.' Goldie nods over to where he's sat with his silly mouth-breathing daughter, watching Goldie down her nose, just as she had outside. A princess with no clue of real life, because she's been raised by a man who's revelled in its underbelly, won, and knows how to shield her from it.

It is Grant's discomfort which steadies her voice as she begins speaking with more surety. 'He was forty-four. Had a wife, little kids. A very adult life. Couldn't resist me, he said, which I understood of course.' Goldie flips her hair, and with uncontainable assurance, sits up straight. 'And in all that time together, and pretty much forever since, I believed that we were equals. What I didn't realize was his control. I didn't have the vocabulary for what was happening in our relationship; how he'd done it all before. I believed the things we did together were my own choices. Choices which made me grown in the world. A mature woman in an adult consensual relationship. Music was just the crossover. Signing with Vine meant escaping a life I'd never have thrived in, so I gave them everything. And I also gave myself to him.'

Goldie's engagement with the courtroom is incredible. Perfect silence, all eyes on her as she tells it from the heart. Which is interesting also, because the more she explains, the more Goldie seems to understand herself, in real time, her brain finally accepting the truth.

A hand settles on the edge of Goldie's witness box, along with a whispered reminder to avoid addressing Mr Love in person. Taking another sip of water, she clasps her hands across her bump, adjusting her posture back to excellent. 'Even the sight of him this morning had me longing to bolt, for having all this in my head again, because there are so many better things in my life than this current can of worms that I am so very done with.

'And that's exactly who Vine Recordings are. Not snakes really, nothing as enigmatic, just greedy bloodsucking worms. Vine was built on the manipulative exploitation of their talent. They gave with one hand, and silenced with the other, while grinding their way through every personal boundary. I wrote a song the whole world knows, and as much as they might think their lying paperwork proves differently, I know from the bottom of my heart that song belongs to me. Do I regret my career there? No. How else was a girl like me going to get herself anywhere near anything so brilliant? Do I regret letting that lizard-looking—' A tired sound fizzes out of her as Goldie keeps the rest in her head. 'In my bed? My God, of course I do. And do I regret defending The Canticles, which effectively ended my career? Hell, yes, I do. But still, I'm glad I did it.'

Because it's important to be on the right side.

'Women supporting women. For some of us, that code is all we'll ever have, even when no one's looking.' Goldie feels Valeria watching from the gallery, knows she's been with her through every breath, every doubt and every sentence in this courtroom today. 'For standing up, they stole my voice. So many layers of scared, I isolated myself into a life, a world, I barely recognized. I almost lost my soul.

'When all this old history came back, I'd wanted to hide even more, but there was nowhere left to vanish. I thought it was the worst thing that could ever happen to me, but it's been enlightening. I had no business carrying such shame. And neither did the many others in situations that I couldn't imagine. But we talk, and we bond, and we see we are no different, and that the true monster always lies with the power.'

Goldie hopes she never understands why those with such incredible influence try cramming in as many bad things as they can. How it becomes a way of life to step on people, instead of picking them up.

'I was fifteen. I wanted to be famous. But just as much, I wanted Grant to love me.'

'Ms Fliss-Burden, can you state for the court, that you were involved in a sexual relationship with Mr Grant Love when you were underage – fifteen years old – and before any contract association with Vine Recordings?'

'Which, for the record,' Kiley Stanley adds pointedly, 'is statutory rape.'

Plain as. And true.

Grant drops his head. Won't meet his daughter's eyes as the pedestal she's put him on crashes beneath him, as she sees what he truly is. What's taken Goldie a lifetime to understand, his own girl grasps in seconds, when very visibly she withdraws, turning herself away, her body language exactly the reaction necessary.

When in the company of a predator.

'Yes,' she confirms. 'Including my duration under signing at Vine Recordings.'

So what if it took a lifetime? Goldie's got her voice back.

And she is free.

In the bath at Saunders Road, Goldie tops up the water by keeping her toe on the hot tap, as she finishes reading Valeria's manuscript.

Strange how her sister had known that here was where Goldie would want to be after the inquiry. A sentimental full circle, rather like today. Clearly hovering, Valeria knocks on the door, slipping into the bathroom and putting down the loo seat to sit on it.

'So, tell me.' She's straight to the point. 'What did you think?'

'It's so real.'

'Honestly?' Valeria's face lights up like she's ten again, glowing from praise. Further proof, how we are always us.

'It's alive,' Goldie says. 'Vivid. Like I'm inside your head.' Which keeps Valeria smiling.

'Do you want a hand getting out?' Cracking a window,

steam slowly slips away through the gap. 'You remind me of a gorgeous mermaid.'

'Not yet. The girls like it.' Touching eight months pregnant, she barely fits in the tub. Though their arrival's in sight, after such a risky, risky start, Goldie's no less terrified by how much she wants an untroubled future. 'I might've been in here even longer, but I skim-read the rude bits,' she says in a typically snippy, older sister way, thinking of Valeria and Rufus earlier, holding hands outside court, no sign of turning inwards for either of them. And literally flying, because tomorrow, they're off to Toronto, for the Canadian publication of his book. Their relationship might always be strange to Goldie, but it's very clearly working for them.

It's also none of her business.

Still, Goldie can't help feeling a bit smug over how the powers of hypnotherapy have managed to get her sister on a plane. Perhaps not so foolish after all.

'You know what I loved most about your book, though?' She gives a little smile, now rather overwhelmed. 'How you've written it as if Gran's still alive. I wish she was.' Crying into her own bathwater, Goldie fully gives herself over to being emotionally delicate probably forever. 'Rest in peace, Gran,' Goldie says softly, doing what she's done for the past few weeks since Gran died, and thanks her for her three-way potatoes. For her arms-length care. For giving them a home.

And for keeping them girls together.

In the little back bedroom on Saunders Road, Goldie and Valeria hold hands between the gap of their old twin beds for the last time. And with the same thought in her head as when she left the courtroom earlier, Goldie knows the outcome of today makes no bloody difference. Because of tomorrow.

Tomorrow. When Wolfie takes them home, to their family house by the sea.

For good.

EPILOGUE

Musician Goldie Fliss-Burden and partner Wolfgang Meyer welcome daughters Mel and Kim on Christmas Eve. Fliss-Burden rumored to be hosting Eurovision 2026.

Two-book pre-empt deal with Imprint Aquarius for Valeria Fliss-Burden's 'raw and insightful' debut novel *Them Girls*.

Independent Film Award nomination for Fliss-Burden's groundbreaking film-length documentary on the dark side of the music industry, *The Lost Voices of Vine Recordings*.

Amos 'Master-Fly' Fliss's daughters inherit family estate, estimated to be worth sixty-two million dollars, in landmark case thanks to the stellar work of Stanley Sisters at Law

★

because sometimes dreams do come true

Acknowledgements

I'm taking my thanks right back to the '80s:

For captivating my child heart in all the best of ways; Diana Ross in her unforgettable 'Chain Reaction' red fishtail dress, the entire cast of the Kids from 'Fame' TV series – note also to the eternally inspiring Irene Cara – and closer to home, cementing my London-Essex foundations, Five Star (God bless forever the *Silk and Steel* LP) and, of course, Mel and Kim.

Enormous love and thanks to Abi Fellows, agent of dreams and enabler of this bookish life, and Clare Hey, my brilliant editor, who let me crack out this story while cleverly prompting the best from me, our amazingly supportive team, SJV, Sabah, Judith and everyone at Simon & Schuster who I'm lucky enough to have in my corner, thank you forever.

To my readers: it's a joy to share this incredible writing journey with you, and all the wonderful people who really don't have be supportive, but because you are kind, decent and believe in me and my books are, therefore a special mention to Mr Andrew Marsh of Dial Lane Books, your love and community means so very much to me. Thank you immensely.

And to my heart, which is my family: Matt, I love you so

much, ditto them girls of our own – Zoe, Joanie and Eliza – and, of course, our shining best boy Steve.

My thanks too, for all the moments which felt profound and internal in my life, and put this gut, incredible need in me to express myself. Until I learnt to channel my emotional energies, I often ignored this compulsive urge to create, which would then curdle into frustration. Because why write? Why waste my time? Best get on with something proper. Creativity is often dismissed as frivolity. Not for the likes of you.

And so bloody terrible, when you begin believing it, too.

I was a happy little kid from not much, leaping from chair to chair in my front room, watching *Fame*, believing I was part of the show, dancing and cartwheeling wherever I went – grubby palms from the grubby pavements of Forest Gate, a hazard I risked daily, convincing my mum to take me to a tap class, begging for the hair piece that dangled in the window of the chemist on the way to school, that cost three quid and one day became mine, a dangly ponytail on a comb, that I'd just randomly stick into my 'fro, but no matter, so swishy, and all part of the sweet dream built from innocent imagination.

Then slowly, sadly, insidiously as we grow, dreaming becomes foolish. I can't tell you the times I was told to 'get in the real world.' But just look at the state of it. Why would anyone ever discourage imagination, to try stamping out the hope that everything's possible? Because is there anything more exciting than dozens of high energy performing arts students pirouetting into New York City traffic? Picturing myself as part of it all, catching the moon in my little hands, feeling all those feels?

Yet the world says 'not you' in a million tiny ways, which at first land insignificantly before becoming lived reality. And suddenly the child with dreams becomes a child who feels lacking and less. From the age of ten until almost forty, I would've done anything to step out of the shell of who I was, to disappear into some unremarkable version of a person who 'fits'. Mostly masking to avoid standing out. Conforming to everything life tells you you're supposed to want, while smothering my own calling.

Split me in half and I'm neatly Vee and – music aside – messy G; their dreams and backstories all my own components. Storytelling's a brilliant thing, because not only do I get to live out so many variations of life, but I also get to look back on my own, see my experiences from different angles. It's amazing what happens when you take away your own critical version of events – viewing situations from a grown perspective too. And if that isn't slightly genius and a lot cathartic, I don't know what is.

Writing *Them Girls*, as with my other books, has proved enormously healing. So perhaps I should also thank myself. All the versions who got me here, sat at my desk in my Lycra and legwarmers. For realizing all that I am. And all that I've always been.

Forever enough.

Eva Verde is a writer from East London. Identity, class and female rage are recurring themes throughout her work. She has published two novels with Simon & Schuster: *Lives Like Mine* and *In Bloom*.

Eva's love song to libraries, *I Am Not Your Tituba* forms part of Kit De Waal's *Common People: An Anthology of Working-Class Writers*. Her words have featured in *Marie Claire*, *Grazia*, *Elle* and *The Big Issue*, also penning the new foreword for the international bestselling author Jackie Collins *Goddess of Vengeance*.

Eva lives in Essex with her husband, children and dogs.

Twitter @Evakinder
Instagram @evakinderwrites

Praise for Eva Verde

'Visceral, authentic and funny, Eva's prose reads like something between a conversation and a confession. An exciting new voice and a joy to read' **Kit de Waal**

'A confident and original voice, with a sharp eye for detail, wonderful characterisation and some seriously badass humour' **Yvvette Edwards**

'Bittersweet, funny, very real. I couldn't put it down' **Louise Hare**

'Sensitively explores the lives of three generations of women as they search for freedom from guilt and regret ... [and] shows that there is always the potential for a second chance' **Sarah Armstrong**

'Tender, true, wise and warm but utterly unflinching ... will stay with me always and haunt my thoughts in the most welcome way' **Rose Ruane**

'Raw and insightful' *Good Housekeeping*

'A beautiful tale of resilience' *Heat*

'Breathtaking' *New!*

'A really powerful, beautifully written story about three generations of working class women, with each character so vividly drawn that they leap off the page' *Red*

Also by Eva Verde

Lives Like Mine
In Bloom